Echoes On The Fens

ALSO BY JOY ELLIS

DETECTIVE MATT BALLARD

Book 1: Heaven...
Book 2: The Bloody...
Book 3: The Dying Light
Book 4: Watershight
Book 5: ...OF The Night
Track... The Boy Out There...

NOVELLA

A Candle For What You Lost

ECHOES ON THE FENS

Joy Ellis

Detective Nikki Galena Book 15

Joffe Books, London
www.joffebooks.com

First published in Great Britain in 2024

Cover art by Nick Castle

ISBN: 978-1-83526-828-5

This book is dedicated to all the staff working in the ICU department at The Pilgrim Hospital in Boston, Lincolnshire. A big thank you for all your incredible care and kindness in pulling me through the aftermath of my surgery. What a brilliant unit, and such dedicated workers, right across the board. Couldn't have had better care anywhere. Five gold stars!

PROLOGUE

DI Nikki Galena stared at the letter lying before her on the office desk. Shocked, she picked it up and read it yet again.

Skipping the official jargon, she went straight to the part that read, '. . . *on the recommendation of DCI Morgan Flint, we are pleased to offer you the opportunity to interview for the position of Detective Chief Inspector in charge of a new Serious Crimes Unit operating out of the Fenland Constabulary HQ.*'

There was another letter that had arrived at the same time, from her friend, DCI Morgan Flint. Morgan had said that she'd decided to write, rather than sending a text, in case Nikki wanted to consider the offer in private. She explained that Nikki was the first person she had thought of the moment the new position had been discussed. Morgan was one of the few people who knew of Nikki's involvement with her detective sergeant, Joseph Easter, and she believed it might prove to be a way forward for the couple. HQ was not that far away, and as no doubt Joseph would apply for her old job, they could be together openly while still doing the work they loved. She added that, with her recommendation, the job was Nikki's if she wanted it.

It sounded so easy, didn't it? A win-win situation.

Nikki sighed. It was far from easy. How many times had she weighed up their options? How many times had she sat down and listed the pros and cons? How many times had she and Joseph discussed their situation far into the small hours of the morning Separation was out of the question, so they remained as they were, a couple who loved each other, and who, because of the dictates of their jobs in the police, had to be together in secret.

Maybe it was that easy? Could Morgan be right? Nikki put the official letter back in its envelope and slipped it into her drawer, along with the one from Morgan. Joseph had been distracted for weeks now. Since their last big case, which had affected them both deeply, he had seemed uncharacteristically introspective. She had tried to draw him out over what was worrying him, but so far had failed. Maybe this double life was taking its toll on him?

Nikki stared at the closed drawer. Was it time to move on, away from Greenborough? She would certainly need to show Joseph the letter . . . but not right now. She needed to think.

* * *

'Right. Got everything?'

The woman gave the man she was obliged to work with a disdainful sneer. 'Of course I'm ready. Who do you think planned this?'

He shrugged. 'You did.'

'Then I'm hardly likely to forget something, am I?' she snapped.

They made a good team, she and Terence, and she trusted her former partner completely — unlike this moron. She had little faith that today's job would go well. If it had been something she could have done alone, she'd gladly have ditched her new partner and gone solo. Sadly, it was a two-hander, and it needed to be sorted quickly, so she had been forced to take what was on offer. Unfortunately, what was on offer was Neville.

'Okay, let's get this over with.' Haydn looked at her watch. 'You drive, I'll navigate. When we get there, we follow my plan to the letter. No improvising. Understood?'

Neville rolled his eyes. 'We've been over it so many times I could do it in my sleep. It's simple, and I've got it. Okay?' His tone was belligerent.

Telling herself she'd get this sewn up and make some new arrangements regarding Neville, she placed her holdall in the back of the four by four and exhaled. She needed to push aside her dislike of her temporary working partner and concentrate. They had to do the job properly. If anything went wrong, the buck would stop with her, so she needed to make quite sure it went smoothly. Neville had been correct when he said it was an easy hit — at least it should be. They knew their mark's routine as well as they knew their own. A neat job would mean a lot of money coming her way, but . . . Haydn gave an involuntary shiver. A hitch in the operation was not an option.

'Head for Greenborough. I'll give you directions when we get closer.' She clicked her seat belt into place, turned and gave him a steely glare. 'I want no mistakes, Neville.'

He dredged up a smile. 'Relax, Haydn, I've got it. Like I said, it's simple.'

CHAPTER ONE

Nikki's mother, Eve Anderson, considered Joseph's family as her own, so when she had a call from his daughter Tamsin, asking her if she fancied a morning coffee, a walk with the dog, and to inspect what she and her husband, Niall, had done with their old fen cottage, she jumped at the chance.

Now they were ambling along the lane outside Herondene, and Eve was gazing across the flat fields of Jacobs Mere to an old, deserted mill. 'You'd think someone would do something with that, wouldn't you?' she commented to Tamsin. 'People make such lovely homes from those old places. Nikki was telling me that one of her colleagues, another DI, has a beautifully converted mill.'

'And you live in a beautifully converted chapel,' smiled Tamsin. 'I think Monks Lantern is a dream of a home.'

Eve laughed. 'Oh, it is, and believe me, I give thanks for it every single day, but I didn't have the upheaval of the conversion. That was down to my dear friend who saw its potential.'

They walked together along the fen lane, with Tamsin and Niall's dog, Skipper, racing ahead, then running back to dance around their legs before rushing off again. It was early spring, but even so, the weather had been windy and far from warm. Today, however, it was beautiful, a perfect day for a walk across the fields.

'I think you guys have worked wonders on your cottage,' said Eve. 'You've managed to make it modern, yet you've lost none of the character.'

Tamsin sighed. 'It's very much a work in progress. Because we both work, it's taking a lot longer than we'd hoped, but we've got plenty of time, I guess, and it is coming together.'

'It certainly is, and it's a credit to you both.' Niall Farrow was a uniformed police sergeant, and Tamsin worked part time for a company that provided ecological advice for farmers and landowners. Working on the house and the garden was likely to be a long haul. 'If you want a hand with the garden, you do know that Wendy and I would be happy to come and help out, don't you?'

Tamsin's face lit up. 'Really? Oh, that would be perfect! I've got so many ideas, but we need to tackle the groundwork first. It's a bit of a jungle. But Niall's right, we must make the house liveable before we hit the outside.'

Eve laughed. 'I've seen worse. And gardening is a good way to relax, no matter how strenuous. How about we come over this Friday morning? I know we have nothing on, and Wendy has just bought a new battery-powered strimmer that she's dying to try out. She can let it loose on your jungle! It would be good to make some headway before summer's here.'

'And I've got a few days off, so I'll get lunch! Deal?' said Tamsin.

'Deal. But don't go to too much trouble, we'll enjoy ourselves — unless it's pouring with rain, then maybe we'll reschedule. I love gardening, but not in a downpour!' She stopped for a moment. 'Um . . . would you mind if we brought our metal detectors? We could give the areas being cleared a quick sweep, to make sure there's nothing buried beneath the top soil. An old friend of mine told me he decided to clear part of his lawn and make it into a vegetable patch. As he began to dig, he hit something hard, and discovered his grandfather had buried a piano in the back garden!'

Tamsin burst out laughing, but before she could comment, they saw a man striding down the lane towards them, a very large dog at his side.

Skipper was a friendly animal, but he did a double take when he saw the size of the dog loping towards him. Deciding to hedge his bets he retreated behind Tamsin.

'You great wuss!' she murmured, fondling his head, then she whispered, 'Hey, Eve! I think that's the new owner of Jacobs Mere House — that big property on the right as you turn into our lane.'

'The one with a beautiful old red-brick wall surrounding it?' asked Eve. 'That looks very grand.'

'It is, it's massive,' replied Tamsin. 'I've been dying to see this man; I'm told he's some kind of celebrity.'

'I say! Sounds exciting,' Eve said softly.

As they drew closer, Eve found herself looking at the dog, not the man. It was like a great thick-coated black, brown and white bear, but it had the most adorable face. 'Oh, it's a Bernese Mountain dog! How gorgeous.'

'You're right,' said the owner, in a soft, cultured voice. 'This is Bernie, and he's a gentle giant, so you can tell that shivering wreck behind you that he can come out now — the new neighbour is friendly.'

Eve's gaze travelled from dog to man. 'Justin?'

Equally as shocked, the man said, 'Eve?'

'Good Lord! What on earth are you doing here?' gasped Eve.

'I could say the same to you. The last time I saw you,' the man puffed out his cheeks, 'must have been in London. *Years* ago.'

'Oh, do you two . . . ?' Tamsin looked from one to the other of them in surprise.

'I'm so sorry!' the man held out his hand. 'Shock got the better of my manners! I'm Justin Connaught, I've just moved into Jacobs Mere House.'

'Tamsin Farrow. My husband and I live just over there, in the cottage called Herondene.' Tamsin shook his hand. 'I gather you know Eve?'

The man's smile broadened. 'Oh, I know Eve, all right. Come here, you wily old bird!'

Before she knew it, Eve was enveloped in a delighted hug. 'It's *so* good to see you again.'

'Have you got time for a coffee, Mr Connaught?' asked Tamsin. 'It's clear you two have a lot to talk about, and we are only a few minutes from my house.'

'First off, it's Justin, and yes, that would be lovely. As long as I can bring Bernie?'

Eve looked down to see Skipper sitting happily next to the fur-mountain, so that was settled.

A few minutes later, they were seated around the kitchen table, drinking coffee and munching on chocolate digestive biscuits.

Eve explained to a bemused Tamsin how she knew this rugged and extremely good-looking man. 'I worked with Justin's father, Lionel, at the MOD for many years. At one point we used his home as a sort of unofficial headquarters. That was when I met Justin and his sister, Heather. We kept in touch for years, but, well, life gets in the way sometimes. I haven't seen Lionel since I retired. Unforgivable really. We were such good friends.'

'He still talks about you, Eve. I don't think he ever forgave you for turning him down, though.' Justin laughed. 'Neither did I! You'd have been such a cool stepmother.'

Eve felt herself blushing. 'Rubbish! I'd have been appalling. I'm sure I did you all a big favour by refusing.'

'He never re-married, you know.' Justin looked at her thoughtfully. 'And you, Eve?'

She shrugged. 'I told him I wasn't the marrying kind, and I meant it. Now, tell me about you. I hear you're a bit of a celebrity, and if you've purchased that great pile up the road, you must be doing quite well.'

It was Justin's turn to look embarrassed. 'It's all a bit weird, to be honest. The TV show has been a far greater success than we ever dreamed. As for the house, well, it belonged to a distant relative on my mother's side of the family. The old boy died intestate, and it remained empty for years while the legal ins and outs were sorted. It wasn't in the best condition, and trying to sell it was a bit of a nightmare. Then father stepped in, and between us, we got it for a song. Turns out it's not as bad as we thought; the damage is mostly cosmetic, mainly down to lack of maintenance. Oh, and a proper heating system has given it a new lease of life. I'm really pleased with it.'

Tamsin was looking at him with interest. 'Please forgive me, Justin, but though I recognise your face, I don't really watch much television. What is your TV programme called?'

'It's called *Digging History*. I'm an archaeologist. We take groups of young people to digs in different parts of the country and teach them the rudiments of archaeological excavation.'

'Of course! I've seen the trailers. It's very popular, isn't it?' Tamsin said.

'We've been ridiculously lucky in making some significant finds. So many of these programmes are of little interest to the average viewer, but we've hit some real corkers. One of the kids found an extremely rare coin. They call me the "Treasure Magnet".'

Tamsin laughed. 'A bit like Eve. She and her friend Wendy have metal detectors, and they recently made some very, er, interesting finds in a neighbouring farmer's field.'

'Really?' exclaimed Justin. 'You are detectorists? Well, I'm blowed! Not that I should be surprised. You always did have a talent for uncovering hidden mysteries. And would that be Wendy Avery, who you used to work with in London? I remember her well.'

Yes, Eve said, it was indeed the same Wendy, and he must visit them as soon as possible, she'd be thrilled to see him again.

'Why don't you all come and see my "Great Pile", as you so aptly named it?' said Justin. 'How about tomorrow

8

evening? Come for supper and I'll give you the guided tour.' He turned to Tamsin. 'And, please do bring your husband. I'd like to meet him.'

Tamsin nodded enthusiastically. 'He's a police sergeant, and he's on early shift right now, so I'm sure that will be fine — if you can cope with my vegetarian diet? Oh, and if it's good for you and Wendy, Eve?'

'We'll be there,' Eve said, knowing that Wendy would be delighted to meet Justin again.

Justin stood up. 'That's settled then. Sorry, but I'm afraid I have to go. I just remembered I have a man calling to see about cleaning the chimneys. Seven o'clock tomorrow okay with you?'

'We'll look forward to it,' replied Eve.

After he and Bernie had left, Eve turned to Tamsin, her eyes sparkling. 'I can't believe he's your new neighbour! Talk about coincidence.'

'And we get to see inside the Great Pile as well.' Tamsin grinned broadly. 'That old place has fascinated me since we first moved in. It's supposed to have a rather creepy history.' She leaned forward. 'Now, I want to know all about you and Lionel. You turned him down, eh?'

Awash with memories, Eve didn't quite know where to start. 'There's very little to tell really,' she lied. 'He wanted to get married and I didn't, so that was that.'

Tamsin raised a disbelieving eyebrow.

'Oh, all right. Well, to be honest, I never got over Frank, Nikki's father. And I knew that somewhere in the world there was a daughter I hadn't seen since I gave birth to her. The thought of marrying another man, well, it was out of the question.'

Tamsin put her hand over Eve's. 'I'm so sorry, Eve. I can't imagine how hard it must have been for you — giving up Frank, and your child.'

'It was the right thing to do, for him and his wife. For Nikki too. And what with the job I did, my life was far from secure. Being in the military was dangerous back then, but I loved my work, and losing myself in it helped ease the pain.' She smiled, a little sadly. 'And I did, and Frank and his wife and Nikki had a good life, so . . . I know I did the right thing — for everybody concerned.'

'Except you,' whispered Tamsin, and squeezed Eve's hand. They sat in silence for a few moments. 'Anyway, tell me about Justin. Are his family well off? What does his father do now? Is he retired?'

Relieved, Eve returned to the here and now. 'Oh yes, they were well off all right. They had a lovely house in Richmond, down in Surrey. Family money, along with a successful business, something to do with animal feeds and equestrian equipment, I think. When he came out of the MOD, Lionel took over the running of the family business. I heard they recently moved into organic pet foods too, and their factories are supposed to be about as eco-friendly as it's possible to get. As to Lionel, I doubt he ever relinquished the reins. Knowing him, I bet he's working as hard as ever.'

Tamsin, who would very likely have become an eco-warrior had she not fallen for her policeman, nodded approvingly. She still held to her high ideals, and was passionate about the countryside. 'And from what he said, Justin's a real archaeologist, not just a TV presenter made to look like one.'

'Oh, he's the real deal all right,' Eve said, smiling. 'According to his father, he's totally obsessed with it. He's travelled all over the world, not just visiting but working in some of the most difficult places you could find. His father said it all started when he was a little boy and dug up a hunk of what looked like glassy rock. He was so fascinated that he pestered his dad to get it analysed. It turned out to be a very old piece of slag rock, a clinker which is a byproduct of smelting ore into metal, usually found near old foundries. What it was doing under a Richmond garden, he had no idea. It was a simple thing, but it sparked a lifetime's curiosity in what lies beneath the ground.'

'And now he's our neighbour, and famous to boot. Even if he is a quarter of a mile away.'

Eve often worried about Tamsin being so isolated, especially when Niall worked nights or late shifts. Tamsin herself seemed to thrive in her rural home, and she did have Skipper. Even if their rescue dog had been in awe of the giant Bernie, he would most certainly protect Tamsin if the need arose. He was no lapdog, and Eve had seen him react when he felt concerned for Tamsin's safety. She was quite sure that he would do his best to protect her from danger.

They wandered around the garden, deciding how best she and Wendy might help, and what tools they should bring. After half an hour or so, Eve said she should get back, as Wendy would have their lunch ready. 'I can't wait to tell her who we met.'

'And that we'll be going on a guided tour of the Great Pile,' added Tamsin with a grin. 'Oh dear, I'm afraid that name is going to stick.'

'It is, isn't it? Justin won't mind, though, he's got a good sense of humour. Unlike his sister. Heather wasn't a bit like Justin. I hate to say it but I never really warmed to her. Still, we can't like everyone, can we?'

Just as Eve was about to get into her car, Tamsin said, 'Eve, have you seen Dad recently?'

'Not for a week or two, why?'

'I'm worried about him. He's not his usual positive self.' Tamsin frowned. 'I think something's wrong, but I'm afraid to ask what.'

'Come to think of it, the last time I saw him he did seem a little under the weather.' Eve looked at Tamsin's worried expression. 'Leave it with me. I'll grill my daughter. And if that fails, I'll interrogate Joseph. I'll let you know the upshot tomorrow evening. I'm sure it's just work overload, or "man flu". You know what they're like. The smallest thing and they're at death's door.'

Eve drove home, wondering. She had made light of it to Tamsin, but now she was starting to feel rather concerned. Joseph was a definite 'glass-half-full' kind of person, able to bring a calm, even-tempered attitude to even the most serious of issues. For his daughter to notice something wrong, it could only mean a personal problem. She just hoped it had nothing to do with his relationship with Nikki. No, impossible, they adored each other. What, then? Now she really was worried.

* * *

Back from her lunch break, Joanne Andrews raced up the steps to the old building that was now an antiques and crafts centre. She waved a greeting to Mac, who manned the till by the exit, and went up the old oak staircase to the second floor. It had been a grand old house in years gone by, thankfully saved from the wrecker's ball by an investor who turned it into a venue for small businesses and outlets to sell their goods from. Now the ground floor heaved with antiques, collectibles, books, and all manner of crafts and memorabilia, while the floor above was dedicated to more 'spiritual' objects. Here you could purchase healing crystals, incense sticks, divination and angel cards, and a host of other related items. It was also home to various practitioners, from aromatherapists to clairvoyants.

Joanne's boss, Claire, rented two units. From one, she sold rocks, crystals, and minerals, while from the other she ran a bereavement and grief counselling service. Claire Hereward was a life coach, who had found her special niche in helping people through times of great personal loss so they might move on and find meaningful lives.

Joanne was in awe of her. Claire was her guide star, one of those totally self-assured people who exude an aura of peace and imperturbability. If ever there was a woman who was comfortable in her own skin, it was Claire. She was a good boss too, and Joanne loved working for her.

In the sales room, Joanne went directly to the computer and checked for any incoming online orders. They had a website that generated a good income, especially with crystal healers, although most of her best sales had been customers who simply fell in love with the specimens on display. In the three years that she had been working here, Jo had learned a lot about crystals. Now there were few that she couldn't identify immediately, along with their country of origin and their specific healing properties. She secretly suspected that she probably knew considerably more than Claire, who had simply seen a market that would complement her counselling practice.

She checked the orders, printed them off, along with sticky address labels, and was about to select the specific pieces ready for packing, when an email flashed up. As it was for Claire, Jo printed it off, and went to see if Claire was in her consulting room. She knew from her appointments diary that her next client was not due for another half an hour.

Jo knocked and went in, to find Claire looking anything but serene.

'Claire? Is something wrong?' Jo asked anxiously.

Claire sat back, rubbed her eyes, then handed Jo a handwritten letter. 'From a relative of one of my old clients. Take a look.'

Jo stared at it and saw the words, 'My father is dead, and I hold you accountable! Call yourself a counsellor? I don't think so! Your insidious words poisoned an old man's mind.' It continued in that vein, and Jo could hardly bear to read it. Jo shook it. 'But this is rubbish. It's vitriolic! I remember this gentleman. He was so grateful for your help he even came back with a box of chocolates! I don't understand this at all.'

'And as if that wasn't bad enough, I've had another cancellation. All very apologetic and conciliatory, but a cancellation nevertheless.' Claire glanced at the email printout Jo had given her, and gave a dry, humourless laugh. 'And another! This one's from Andrea Johnson, and we were progressing brilliantly! I was so proud of how she was dealing with her loss.' She looked up. 'What's happening, Jo?'

Jo didn't have an answer for her. Claire was very good at what she did — Jo could personally attest to that. She had a drawer full of letters of thanks and recommendations. Now, suddenly, her clients were leaving after a few visits, before finishing their course.

This wasn't fair. 'Is anyone else setting up in competition around here? This sounds to me like someone is blackening your name in order to steal your clients.'

'Not that I know of.' Claire sighed. 'But I did wonder if someone had a grudge against me. That horrible letter does point in that direction. I thought I was being paranoid at first, but it's getting worse, isn't it?'

It was true, although Jo had not been aware of how serious it had become. Claire had kept that to herself. 'Perhaps you could ask one of them? I thought that Andrea Johnson was such a nice woman, maybe she'd open up if you told her what's happening.'

'I don't think I can do that, Jo. What if it's me? What if I'm going wrong somewhere? I'd hate to put someone in the position of having to tell me the truth — that I'm not helping them.'

'What rot!' said Jo. 'Sorry, Claire, that was rude, but you are an excellent life coach, the best, and I should know! You're not doing anything wrong. I'd stake my life on it. It's someone else.'

Claire smiled wanly. 'Thank you for your loyalty, Jo, but it's not just this . . .'

'There's something else?' asked Jo softly. 'Can I help?'

Claire shook her head. 'No, it's just me being neurotic. All these cancellations must have got to me. Anyway, I'd better get ready for my next client.'

Jo left the room, her head buzzing. Someone was out to ruin her boss, she was certain. Well then, if Claire didn't want to talk about it, she'd just have to take it up herself. No way was she going to see a caring professional like Claire Hereward put out of business. Not if she could help it.

* * *

14

Though it pained her to say so, Haydn couldn't fault Neville's work. Contrary to her original suspicions, once he was actually out on a job, he dropped the attitude and acted with consummate professionalism. They achieved what they set out to do, speedily and efficiently. Careful preparation had been vital to the outcome of today's mission, and she had feared the worst. As it turned out, she ended the day a hundred per cent confident that they would complete the next part of their assignment without a hitch. In two nights' time, they would be returning to their mark's home to bring the thing to a close. Permanently.

CHAPTER TWO

Nikki had lain awake most of the night, thinking about that letter. She had to tell Joseph, but for some reason she hadn't yet found the right moment to bring the subject up. For one thing, given his present frame of mind, she had no idea how to approach it. She had always been forthright, but her no-nonsense attitude just wasn't appropriate in this case. For one thing, she was dealing with the man she loved, and this promotion had arisen just when Joseph was not his normal self. Nikki had pinpointed the change in him to the time of their last case, but for the life of her she couldn't fathom what there was about it that had affected him so badly. It had been grim, but so were all their serious cases. On numerous occasions over the last weeks, she had tried to bring it up, but he had brushed it off or made light of it, and she was no nearer understanding the root cause of his apparent depression.

Now their bedroom was filled with dawn's early light. Joseph still slept, it was not yet six, and their alarm was set for half past. Nikki lay, her arm draped across him, but without the usual feeling of strength and peace that she drew from his sleeping form.

After lying like this for a few moments, she made her decision. She couldn't put this off any longer. The time was never going to be right, so she would wake him now, gently, and get him to talk. Hopefully, he would still be sleepy and defenceless, and would tell her what was worrying him before he could put up his guard. Then, depending on his answer, she would either tell him of the offer that she had received, and they could weigh up its possibilities, or she would refuse the offer without even mentioning it, and burn the letter.

Nikki took a deep breath . . . and the phone rang.

She cursed under her breath and raised herself up. 'Yes?'

'Sorry to ring so early, ma'am. It's Danny — sorry, Sergeant Danny Cryer. We've attended a sudden death, and the officers have drawn my attention to a couple of anomalies. In short, it was an apparent suicide, but they aren't happy about it. We'd like a CID presence, and DI Mercer is unavailable. Would you be able to take this one, ma'am?'

'Where is this?' she asked, grabbing the pen and notepad she kept by the bed.

'Four, Tennyson Court. You might know it, ma'am, it's that old place that used to be a TB sanatorium back in the forties. It's now apartments, mainly for retired people. The entrance is off the Marshdyke Road, about a hundred yards past the Applegreen service station as you enter Greenborough from your direction. The deceased's name is Angela Sandford. PCs Carole Greengrass and Adrian Lomax are on scene.'

'Okay, I'll alert Sergeant Easter and we'll attend. Tell them we'll be there as soon as we can.' She hung up, both angry at having her plans ruined, and relieved that she could legitimately postpone the inevitable for a bit longer.

'What's occurring?' Joseph was awake and already getting out of bed.

'Sudden death, query suicide,' she replied, grabbing clean clothes from the wardrobe. 'But Carole and Adrian aren't happy bunnies. As it's them, their concerns are most likely valid, so, grab a swift shower. We'll check it out and then have breakfast in the office.'

Twenty minutes later, they were in the car and driving towards the address they had been given. Nikki knew the place but hadn't actually been inside. It had had a chequered history, reinventing itself a number of times following the closure of the TB sanatoriums in the fifties. It had been a cottage hospital for a while, and then an art college, after which the rooms had been let to small businesses. All had failed and it had remained empty for years. Now it was a retirement village, a very expensive one at that. The new owners had gambled a whole lot of money on marketing it as a very exclusive place to live, and for once, their bet had paid off.

Number four was immediately obvious from the police vehicles and other cars drawn up outside. It was not in the main building, but one of several single storey dwellings that provided their residents independent living while still enjoying all the amenities of the big house if they so wished.

As Nikki locked the car door, she saw PC Adrian Lomax hurrying towards her. He was a likable and enthusiastic young officer, who had found the perfect partner in his crewmate, PC Carole Greengrass, another young constable who already showed abilities beyond her years.

'I hope this isn't a wild goose chase, ma'am,' he said apologetically, 'but both Carole and I think this one is hinky.'

'Hinky?' asked Nikki. She hadn't heard that one before.

'You know, right suspicious, though there's nothing obvious as far as we can see.' Adrian frowned. 'It struck us as soon as we walked in, and after talking to the night manager and a few of the staff, we feel it even more. We didn't want to miss something, so we had the sarge request your presence.'

'Fair enough,' said Nikki. 'Then we'd better take a look, hadn't we?'

They followed Adrian inside, through an immaculate and tastefully decorated lounge. It wasn't overloaded with ornaments or photographs like many older people's rooms. Angela Sandford seemed not to have felt the need for the clutter of memorabilia. The carpet was plush, the furniture leather and very expensive. The decorations were minimal; Nikki noted a few framed photographs, a couple of well-cared-for houseplants, two exquisite vases and a single watercolour painting on the wall.

'Comfortable, and very classy,' breathed Joseph, as he looked around. 'Those Moorcroft vases are worth a fair bit, and I'm pretty sure that watercolour is an original, it could even be one of the twentieth century romantics. Whatever, this lady had taste *and* money.'

Nikki agreed, although good taste didn't prevent Mrs Sandford from suffering with depression, or from taking her own life.

'Is the lady still here, Adrian?' she asked.

'Yes, ma'am. The doctor that looks after this complex was called as soon as she was discovered. He pronounced life extinct, but he said he was grateful that we were in attendance. He'd given the lady her regular health check-up only the week before, and was shocked to be called out to an apparent suicide. He said she'd been in good health and good spirits. He can't understand it. And after checking a few things for ourselves, we decided to call you. The funeral directors are on their way, but we wanted you to see her first.'

'Thanks, Adrian,' said Nikki. 'We'll take a look, then you can fill us in on your concerns. Where is Carole?'

'Talking to the night manager again, trying to build up a picture of this poor lady's life, and also getting a list of Mrs Sandford's closest friends here.'

They walked down a hallway to the largest of two bedrooms, situated at the back of the bungalow. Once again, the room was clean, tidy, and the furniture was of high quality. Nikki took in a French-style sleigh bed, with a matching solid oak chest of drawers and wardrobe. The only thing out of place was the dead body of Angela Sandford.

She appeared to be a woman in her late sixties, possibly early seventies. She was still fully clothed, and was lying on top of the bedspread on her side, in a tight foetal position. Nikki had to force herself to look closely. Angela's passing had not been a peaceful one. Overdoses rarely were.

On the bedside cabinet there was a bottle of water, an empty glass, and a whole lot of empty foil sheets that had contained medication of some kind.

'Is the doctor still here?' Nikki asked Adrian.

'Yes, ma'am, he's outside waiting for the funeral director.'

'I think I'd like a word with him when we're done here, Adrian. Can you ask him if he'd mind hanging on a bit longer?'

The constable left the room. Meanwhile, Nikki was beginning to understand the meaning of hinky. She had no idea why this death had made the others suspect possible foul play, but she was feeling it too. There was no hard and fast rule governing the behaviour of suicides. People often acted in unusual ways, or did things that seemed completely illogical and out of character, and Nikki knew nothing about Angela Sandford. But something just didn't feel right. She glanced at Joseph, who was staring thoughtfully at the empty tablet foils.

He must have sensed her gaze on him, because he looked up, his forehead creased in a frown. 'Why do I get the feeling that Adrian and Carole were right to call us?'

She threw him a small smile. 'I've no idea, but I think we'd better try to find out. Let's start with the GP, shall we?'

Dr Bill French looked more like a retired rugby player than a doctor. He was fairly short and heavily built, and despite the grey hair, gave the impression of being as strong as an ox. This did not gel with the pale face and anguished expression.

'I don't get it, Officers, I really don't. Angie was planning a holiday for next month. Trip of a lifetime, she said, which is why she came to see me, she wanted to make sure she was fit enough.'

'And was she?' asked Joseph.

'She was a damned sight fitter than me!' exclaimed the doctor. 'She was an avid walker, did long distances and fell walking. This trip she was planning was a trekking holiday in

Bulgaria, and she wasn't taking the easy options either. She said it was pure fairy-tale country, and it's long been a dream of hers to walk the Rodopi Mountains and see the ancient woodlands where wolves still roam.' He shook his head. 'Not the kind of thing you hear from someone contemplating taking their own life, is it?'

Nikki nodded. At the same time she knew that some sudden change in circumstance could easily throw a human mind into turmoil. 'Dr French, you told our colleagues you were glad they had come. Was that because of what you've just told us, or was it something else?'

Bill French bit his lip. 'This might sound stupid. We all know that someone intent on killing themselves can do things that would normally be impossible for them to do, but,' he looked from Nikki to Joseph, 'those tablets, whatever they are, were not prescribed by me. Yes, I know you can get most things online, but Angie . . . well, it's my belief that if she really had wanted to die, it wouldn't have been that way.'

'Why do you say that?' enquired Nikki.

'She couldn't swallow tablets, Detective Inspector. Plain and simple. The act of trying to swallow a tablet made her heave. She would be physically sick. Even a painkiller. If I couldn't supply something in liquid form, she had to either crush them and hide them in a fruit squash or jam, or chew them, and she hated that. Angela Sandford did everything possible *not* to take medication at all. I cannot believe in a month of Sundays that she would have swallowed a great handful of drugs.' He shook his head vigorously. 'I've been her GP for over ten years, she'd become a friend, and I'm telling you, she just couldn't have done it.'

Joseph flashed her a look. So they were right to be concerned about this lady's death. The doctor's words weren't nearly enough to base an inquiry on, but those warning bells were ringing louder with every minute.

'And another thing,' added the doctor, almost belligerently, 'Angie showed me over this place when she first moved in. The moment I set eyes on that bedroom today, I knew something wasn't right.'

Nikki narrowed her eyes. 'And what was that?'

'That lovely double sleigh bed? It has two bedside cabinets, one each side, doesn't it?'

Nikki nodded. 'Yeees.'

'Well, when she showed me the room, her reading lamp, an alarm clock, and a book were all on the cabinet on the left side of the bed. She was left-handed, so that was natural for her. So, why are all those tablets and the water on the right-hand side?'

There could, of course, be a dozen reasons, so again, not enough to make a case, but it was adding up. 'I think we need to come and talk to you in depth about Angela Sandford, Dr French. Would you be able to see us later today?'

'I can free myself up at lunchtime, if that helps. Say, one p.m. at my surgery?' He handed Nikki a card. 'The address is on that. It's a small practice and most of my patients live here in Tennyson Court. Ring me if you get held up and we'll sort out another time.' He looked up as a dark-windowed vehicle pulled up. 'Forgive me, I need to have a word with the funeral director.'

She thanked the doctor and watched him leave. 'I think that funeral director is going to have to wait, don't you, Joseph?'

'I think you are right. Because you are about to make a phone call and get a SOCO in.'

'I certainly am. I think we are looking at a suspicious death here.'

Joseph nodded. 'My thoughts precisely. I'll go and tell Carole and Adrian to ring their sergeant. They'll need help out here. This could be a crime scene.'

CHAPTER THREE

Joanne Andrews had hardly slept. All night she been turning over in her mind the question of who could possibly want to destroy Claire Hereward's reputation. Claire wasn't someone people thought badly of. She was known to be kind, a woman with a genuine desire to help those in distress, especially people struggling to deal with the pain of bereavement.

Having come to no conclusion, Joanne was up at six, tired and still angry. She hated injustice, and to her mind, a lovely and talented woman was being targeted by someone with a serious axe to grind. There was also that mention of something else being wrong. Claire had brushed it aside, but it was clearly bothering her. What was that all about?

Pouring milk onto her cereal, she admitted to herself that Claire herself seemed to be in no hurry to fathom out who might be behind this vendetta. She didn't even know if it was an individual or another business. And why try to ruin her?

Joanne added more sugar than she knew was good for her and decided that given Claire's reluctance to act on the situation it would be down to her, Joanne, to turn detective. As soon as she got into work, she would check the files. During her sleepless night, she had come up with the names of two clients who had had successful outcomes, and had registered their gratitude and respect for Claire and her work. Both had recommended her to others. She would start with them. She wasn't too sure of the best approach to take, but concluded that the truth was the best way to go. She would simply tell them what was happening. They might have discussed Claire with other clients of hers, in the course of which someone might have bad-mouthed her.

That decided, Joanne got ready for work. She had a lot to do today besides selling crystals.

* * *

Wendy was delighted to hear that Justin was to be Niall and Tamsin's new neighbour. This had led them, over breakfast, to reminisce about their days in the MOD.

'Do you ever wonder what your life would have been like if you had married Lionel?' Wendy asked. 'He was mad about you, wasn't he?'

Slightly embarrassed by the question, Eve shrugged it off. 'No, I can't say that I do. And anyway, if I'd married him, I would probably never have found my daughter, and that is unthinkable. Pass the marmalade, Wendy.'

Wendy handed Eve the jar. 'You did think about it at the time, though, I know you did. Come on, you must have been tempted; Lionel was a very good-looking man, wealthy too.'

Wendy was obviously not going to drop the subject. 'Of course I thought about it,' Eve said. 'What woman in her right mind wouldn't consider such an option? I just . . . well, you know very well why I turned him down.'

'Yes, I do.' With a glance at her friend, Wendy sipped her tea. 'Even though you knew there was no chance of you ever making a life with Nikki's father. I must admit, old girl, that at the time I thought you were stark staring mad. It took me a while to really understand.'

'Understand?' Eve said, surprised. 'What do you mean?'

24

'Well, you know. How deeply in love you were with Frank.' Wendy gave her an affectionate smile, which turned into a mischievous grin. 'I wonder if Lionel has aged as well as you have? Do you think he'll be at Justin's tonight?'

'Oh, I doubt it,' Eve said. 'He doesn't live around here. I think Justin mentioned somewhere up north.'

'Well, as long as that god-awful sister of his doesn't turn up, it should be a lovely evening. Is it a big house? I can't say I've ever really noticed it, what with that high wall all around it.'

'Oh, it's big all right!' said Eve. 'Vast. Justin is going to be rattling around in it.'

Eve hadn't thought about it before, now she began to wonder why he needed such a rambling old property when he spent such a lot of time away on his various archaeological digs. He'd mentioned that it had belonged to an uncle, so perhaps he felt it should stay in the family. She'd have to remember to ask him.

'We haven't been out to dinner for ages,' said Wendy, as she collected up the breakfast things. 'I'm really looking forward to this evening.'

Eve said that she was too. She was also looking forward to catching up with Justin. He had been a delightful boy, who had obviously grown into an equally delightful man. And she was keen to get an inside look at the 'Great Pile'. At the back of her mind was the thought that she'd be taking a step into the past, and a part of her wondered if that was a wise thing to do.

* * *

When Nikki and Joseph arrived back from Tennyson Court, the CID investigation room was its usual hive of activity. Crime never let up, and although there were few actual cases of homicide, Nikki's team were always busy.

Nikki noticed several enquiring glances as she made her way between the desks, but she decided to let them wait. She wanted a proper talk with Angela Sandford's doctor before she told them of their suspicions about her supposed suicide.

A few minutes later, Joseph came into her office carrying two cups of coffee. He set them down on her desk, closed the door and sat down opposite her. The old Joseph had resurfaced while they were at the scene of the death, but back in the office he had little to say, and a slightly strained silence fell between them.

After several seconds of this, Nikki unlocked her top drawer and took out the letter. Before she realised what she was doing, she had taken it from the envelope and thrust it at him, without saying a word.

He took it, briefly glancing up at her when he saw the official letterhead. There was no expression on his face as he read it. He folded it in two and handed it back.

'What am I supposed to say to that?'

'I have no idea, but anything would be good.' She returned his gaze. 'I don't know what's wrong with you right now, Joseph, but something is. It's eating away at you, and you are keeping it to yourself. This letter arrived yesterday, and I'm beginning to wonder if it might be an answer to whatever is causing you to withdraw like this. Talk to me, Joseph! Tell me what's wrong.'

She caught a brief flash of anger, and then he looked down, avoiding her gaze. 'Are you considering that offer, Nikki?'

'I don't know what to decide right now, not while you're being so . . . uncommunicative.' She sighed. 'What's bothering you, my darling? Is it me? Something I've done?'

He looked up, momentarily meeting her gaze. 'No! No, it's not you. It's me.'

What, then? Nikki began to worry even more. She loved Joseph more than she'd ever dreamed she could love anyone, other than her beloved Hannah. But Hannah was dead. Joseph was very much alive, and she couldn't conceive of what her life would be without him.

When it seemed he might be about to speak, her phone rang. She groaned. After struggling with herself for a moment, she snatched it up with a brusque, 'Yes.'

It was Dr French. 'He says his last morning patient didn't show,' she told Joseph, 'and could we go to the surgery straightaway.'

Joseph stood up. 'Then we'd better go, I suppose. But, Nikki, I promise I'll tell you tonight, and I'm sorry for the way I've been. You're right. We do need to talk. Now more than ever.' He nodded at the letter, lying on the desk between them.

She gave him a weak smile, locked the letter back in her drawer and got to her feet. They had a job to do, they couldn't shirk that, but it didn't stop her worrying about what Joseph would have to say.

* * *

Joseph tried desperately to get on with his job, while every part of him wanted to flee. Now the arrival of that letter had brought it all to a head. He had been dreading having to talk to Nikki, but he couldn't put it off any longer. He simply had no idea what her reaction would be. Meanwhile, all he could do was concentrate on work. It wasn't going to be easy.

Dr French was there to meet them at the surgery door. He led them through to a meeting room, used, he said, by the Patient Participation Group for their monthly gatherings, or for reps from the drug companies to show their wares.

'I'm still trying to get my head around her death,' he began. 'It's been such a shock. Anyway, Officers, what would you like to know about Angie?'

'Given that Mrs Sandford's death is possibly suspicious, we need to know everything we can about her and her life. You are the starting point, Doctor,' Nikki said.

Joseph had a pretty good idea that Bill French had been very fond of Angela Sandford, possibly more than just fond. His constant referral to her as 'Angie', and his reaction to her death seemed to hint at something deeper than the usual doctor/patient relationship.

'I gather you were quite close to her,' he asked gently.

The doctor stared down at the table for a moment, and then gave a shrug. 'Yes, I was. She felt the same way, but I was also her doctor. I couldn't possibly have approached her in anything other than a professional capacity . . . unless . . .' he tailed off, looking miserable.

Poor man. It sounded rather like him and Nikki. An impossible position.

'Angie was quite a bit older than me,' Bill French was saying, 'and, bless her, she'd been through the mill, what with one thing and another. I wasn't sure whether she needed anything — well, anything further in her life, other than a friendship. And now it's too late.' He managed a faint smile. 'Younger people always consider it strange that older people can be deeply in love, that it's possible to have a romance.'

Nikki said how sorry she was for his loss. Did he think he was able to tell them a little more about Angela Sandford?

It didn't take long to comprehend why the doctor was so convinced that Angie had not taken her own life. Meanwhile, Joseph played devil's advocate, suggesting that perhaps she had received some piece of devastating news that might have prompted an extreme reaction.

'Not that I know of. Oh, I'm well aware of what shock can do to the mind,' agreed Bill French. 'I've read about what used to be termed "shell shock", and I've personally witnessed a number of quite extraordinary cases. In the course of my training I spent quite some time in a psychiatric hospital. I even thought of going down that route myself at one point. I've thought of nothing else since I saw her this morning, and I remain utterly convinced that something about her death is terribly wrong.' He sighed. 'The thing is, I was going with her on that walking holiday in Bulgaria. We hadn't mentioned it to anyone, naturally . . . Anyway, when I found I couldn't get a locum for those dates, we were forced to abandon the trip. Even so, we were making arrangements to go walking in the Lake District later in the year. It . . . I believed it would have provided us with an opportunity to discuss a possible future together.' He fell silent.

'And you are certain that nothing occurred in the last few days that might have been too much for her to handle?' Nikki asked.

'Nothing at all. We spoke only two nights ago, and she was on top form. She told me she planned to go shopping in Lincoln with an old friend this coming weekend. If anything had been the matter, I would have picked it up at once, but she was just . . . Angie.'

'And you've already confirmed that there were no underlying health issues that might have prompted her to, er, take such a drastic step,' Nikki mused.

'As I said, she was very fit for her age,' he said. 'There is one thing. She mentioned that she was becoming forgetful — you know, mislaying things. But, hell, I do the same thing myself. I'm always getting to the top of the stairs and wondering what I went up for. It's a natural part of aging, happens to all of us. And it didn't actually worry her, it was more of a joke really, you know, "senior moments".'

Joseph wondered. A lot of people were terrified of succumbing to dementia. It was something to bear in mind, especially if they found no plausible answers to the other questions surrounding her death.

The doctor went on to tell them all he knew about Angela's life and background. When he had finished, they thanked him and returned to their vehicle.

'I'm going to be very interested to hear what Carole and Adrian have to report after they've spoken to her friends at Tennyson Court,' said Nikki.

'And I'm anxious to know about those tablets she took, both what they were and where they came from. I think it might be time for a chat with our friend Rory.'

Professor Rory Wilkinson was the Home Office pathologist for the Fenland Constabulary. Over the years he had become one of Nikki and Joseph's closest friends, and they relished his quirky sense of humour. Camp witticisms aside, Rory was a stellar forensic pathologist who had often been key to resolving any number of their most challenging cases.

'Why don't you ring him now, Joseph? Tell him of our concerns about Angela Sandford and ask him if he could make her a priority.'

A few moments later, Rory's dulcet tones resounded through the car. 'This had better be good, dear cherubs! Yours truly is knee deep in viscera as we speak — that's internal organs to you, dear hearts. Entrails and innards everywhere, and all before lunch.'

Despite his mood, Joseph was forced to smile. 'Too much information, Rory. You do realise you've probably scarred me for life, don't you?'

'Nonsense, dear boy! You love it, the more visceral the better. Now, what can I do for you?'

Joseph told him about their case. 'There's a lot of niggling indications of foul play, but we badly need solid evidence.'

'Then you've come to the right man. I assure you that Mrs Sandford will receive my fullest attention. I will attend to her just as soon as I can extricate myself from the job in hand. Which, I might add, will be something of a relief. Fear not, I'll be in touch the moment I have some of that solid evidence you so desperately crave. Now, back to my entrails — well, not mine, of course. Ciao, bambinos!'

'Never changes, does he?' Joseph murmured.

'And let's hope he never does,' added Nikki. 'So now we wait, because if anyone can tell us what really happened, it'll be Rory.'

'And in the meantime?'

'We get back to the station and find Carole and Adrian. So far, we have only Bill French's word for Angela's state of mind. Sure, he's a doctor, with some knowledge of psychiatry, but he loved her, so he's biased, he might well have seen her through rose-tinted specs. On the other hand, he could be absolutely right. Who knows? I want to hear what the others have to say about that lady. He mentioned that she'd had a rough time in recent years, and I'd like to hear another woman's take on that, preferably someone close. And I'm betting it will be nothing like what we just heard.'

Joseph knew all that. The problem was, for the first time since he joined the force, his heart wasn't in it. Yes, he'd do his job, and he'd do it to the best of his ability, but . . . But he was deeply troubled, and finding it well-nigh impossible to concentrate fully on his work. He gazed through the car window, out across the fields. Maybe tonight's conversation would make things at least a bit clearer. Maybe.

* * *

For once, there were no cancellations, and all Claire's morning clients had been positive about the help she was providing them. While Claire was busy in a consultation, Joanne called two of the people on her list of former clients. The first, a man named Richard Duckworth, lived a ten-minute walk from the centre, and on hearing her concerns, immediately suggested that she call round to his house in her lunch break. He sounded eager to help, and outraged that such a thing should happen. The second client, Mrs Lizzie Harper, lived in one of the Greenborough villages, about six miles away. She, too, had been upset by what Joanne told her, and said that if Jo wished, she could call in after work.

It seemed an age till lunchtime. Asking Cally from the unit next door to keep an eye on the shop for her, Joanne made her way to Richard Duckworth's house.

It turned out to be a large terraced house in an upmarket area of Greenborough. Joanne had often wondered what these grand old houses were like inside, so if nothing else came of it, at least this visit would give her an opportunity to see for herself.

He welcomed her with an offer of tea or coffee, which she gratefully accepted.

It was comfortable, but very much a man's home, with none of the softer touches a woman might have brought to it. Now she was sitting in a small conservatory at the rear of the property, looking out over an immaculate garden.

'It's a bit of a passion of mine,' admitted Richard, following her gaze over the neatly trimmed lawn and the pots of brightly coloured flowers. 'Claire suggested I might treat it as therapy, and it's certainly helped me.'

Joanne wasn't too sure about gardening's therapeutic value. It seemed to her like a battle you never won. As for nurturing, you were constantly hacking things back and pulling things up.

He looked steadily at her over the rim of his cup. 'Okay, Miss Andrews, tell me what's been going on. And don't worry, I'm the soul of discretion. I'm a retired police officer, and what you've told me so far intrigues me.'

Joanne tried not to look too excited. Having someone like this man on her side could be just what she needed. Despite his age, he was still rather good-looking, a sort of gentle giant with greying hair and a neatly trimmed beard. She noticed his strong, capable hands. She trusted him at once.

She placed her mug on a glass-topped table and explained what was being done to Claire and her reputation.

'Damned bloody shame!' he said fiercely. 'Claire's an angel. She certainly doesn't deserve this. You'll be aware that Claire put me back on track after I lost my son, and my wife couldn't cope and left me, but she probably didn't say exactly how bad I was. I was at rock bottom. There is no doubt in my mind that she saved my life.' He nodded, as if to emphasise his words. 'So, if there's anything I can do to help, please, just say.'

Joanne gave him a grateful smile. 'Just being able to talk it through with you is a great help. I'm out of my depth with this, and I don't quite know how to proceed. There's certainly not enough to take to the police, not that they'd be interested anyway. I can't bear seeing Claire so low and unsure of herself. It's just not like her. She's one of the most "together" people I've ever met. And she's such a thoughtful and caring counsellor. It's wicked that someone should want to hurt her like this.'

'I agree with every word you say, Joanne.' He sighed. 'There are some bad people out there. Being an ex-copper, I should know. To me, it stinks of some kind of scam. I need a bit of time to think it over, get a handle on what kind of person would do this and what they could possibly get out of it. Maybe someone stands to gain from her business collapsing?'

Joanne admitted she'd considered that, too, but it didn't seem to add up. There were several empty units in the centre, so it couldn't be someone needing her space, and as far as she knew, Claire was the only person in the area offering that specific form of counselling, so with no competitors, that line of enquiry seemed a dead end.

'So it must be someone with a personal grudge,' said Richard thoughtfully.

Joanne nodded. 'And as most of her clients are of the same opinion as you about her competence, I'm completely at a loss.'

'It might have nothing to do with her clients, Joanne. From my experience of things like this, it'll be someone closer to her. What do you know about her private life?'

'Not much, really. She's my boss, so I tend not to pry — I don't want to appear too nosy. I know she lives alone, and she has occasionally mentioned an ex, but there doesn't seem to be anyone in her life right now. I do know she has siblings — a brother and a sister — but come to think of it, she's never mentioned her parents. I have no idea if they're still alive, or whether there was a split, and she doesn't like to talk about them.' Joanne frowned. 'I don't know. I get the feeling that her work is everything to her.'

'And someone wants to wreck it,' said Richard thoughtfully, 'or her. I wonder which they are targeting — the business, or the person?'

Joanne hadn't considered that. She had believed it was entirely the business that was under threat. She now felt even more worried. 'I wish I could tell you more, Richard, but it's only just dawned on me that after working with her for three years, I still know next to nothing about her.'

Richard smiled kindly. 'I can see how concerned you are, so would you like me to help you dig deeper? I have more experience than you with that sort of thing, and as I said, I owe Claire more than I can ever repay. I'm happy to see what I can find out — discreetly, of course.'

This was a lot better than Joanne had hoped for. She had come to see Richard expecting no more than a promise to listen out for any gossip about her boss. Now she found she had an ally.

'In that case we need a plan of action,' Richard said. 'Do you think you could print off one or two of those malicious emails? I don't need to know the senders' names — that would be a breach of privacy. I'd like to get a feel for the wording, it might give me a clue as to the intent. If you leave me your mobile number, I'll contact you as soon as I have anything to say. And keep me updated of any more, er, happenings.'

Joanne got up to leave. At the door, she paused and looked up at him. 'You don't think I'm overreacting do you, Richard?'

He gave her a fatherly pat on the shoulder. 'Far from it. From what you've told me, you have every right to be concerned, and I'm glad you've not tried to shoulder this alone.'

Joanne returned to the shop in much better spirits than when she set out.

CHAPTER FOUR

At three o'clock, Nikki decided to brief the team on her morning visit to Tennyson Court. If a new investigation was about to break, they needed to be prepared. She had invited PCs Greengrass and Lomax to join them in the CID room to report on what they had learned from Angela Sandford's fellow residents.

It had soon become apparent that not one of them was of the opinion that Angie had been contemplating taking her own life. 'Her closest friend was a woman called Maggie Snow,' said Carole. 'We spoke to her at length. She is devastated by the news. She went on to say she had been speaking to Angie last night, and she was her normal ebullient self. They had chatted about Angie's forthcoming walking holiday, which Angie was looking forward to with a great deal of enthusiasm. Only that morning, she said, she had ordered a pair of very expensive hiking boots. Hardly the action of someone planning to top themselves, is it?'

'So, added to what the doctor has told us,' said Nikki, 'it seems unlikely the death was a suicide. I think we need to find out all we can about Angela Sandford.' She looked at the attentive faces of her team. 'Cat, would you and Ben take that on, please? I want everything you can dig up on her life and background. Dr French mentioned that a while back she'd had what he described as a "terrible time", but didn't elucidate further. I want to know what that was. Okay?'

Cat nodded. 'We've just completed our current workload, so we can start immediately.'

'Good timing, boss,' added DC Ben Radly. 'We were just wondering what to do next.'

'Well, it might be nothing, Ben, but if something happened in Angie's life, either last night or in the recent past that might have a bearing on the case, I want to know what it was.'

'We'll give Maggie Snow a little while to come to terms with her loss, and pay her a visit,' said Cat, with a glance at Carole. 'She sounds like someone Angela might have confided in.'

'Absolutely,' Carole said. 'According to her, they were very close. We did warn her that we might need to talk to her again, and she said she was more than willing to help.'

'Okay, I'll leave that with you,' said Nikki. 'Joseph and I will keep you updated with the forensic reports as soon as they arrive. Now, Carole and Adrian. You said the staff at Tennyson Court all affirmed that Angela was not the suicidal type — if there is such a thing. Is that right?'

'They were adamant,' said Adrian. 'A member of the night staff described Angela as full of life. She was also a very sensible woman. He said he knew about Angela's problem with swallowing tablets, and he reckoned she couldn't have taken even one, let alone the number those empty packets indicated.'

'Which her GP confirmed,' added Joseph. 'So, if this does turn out to be murder, her killer obviously didn't know her very well.'

'Or he *did* know her, and forced them down, having chosen the cruellest method of killing her.'

The voice belonged to Yvonne Collins, their civilian interviewing officer. Everyone looked at her. It was unlike Vonnie to be so harsh.

'That's something forensics will be able to confirm or dispute, Vonnie.' Nikki grimaced. 'And let's hope that wasn't the case.'

Having allotted their tasks, Nikki returned to her office. With her forthcoming conversation with Joseph ever present in her mind, it was hard to concentrate on the task at hand. She slumped heavily onto her chair and stared into the distance. Like all couples, they had had their disagreements, but their barneys had all been pretty vocal and soon resolved. Joseph's present reticence was new, and it scared Nikki.

She was relieved when her phone buzzed with a message. It was Eve. A healthy dose of her mother's good cheer was just what she needed right now.

Can I call you, or are you busy, darling? the text read.

Nikki rang her immediately. 'Hi, Mum. I'm free right now, although who knows how long that might last. Are you okay?'

'You'll be pleased to know that this very evening your mother is going to dine with a TV celebrity. So she's very okay, thank you.'

'Really! Who? Where? Why?'

Eve laughed. 'Actually, he's someone I knew as a boy. His father and I were in the MOD together. Justin has grown into a lovely young man. You may have seen his programme on TV. And to top it all, he's Niall and Tamsin's next-door neighbour.'

Nikki racked her brains to think of a celebrity named Justin but nothing came up. Watching television wasn't high on her list of priorities when it came to entertainment.

'We bumped into him while we were out walking Skipper. Nikki, I have never been so gobsmacked in my whole life! There, along a remote fen lane, someone from the distant past appearing right in front of me. It was quite unreal.'

'Is he, what, a comedian? Tell me it's not reality TV,' said Nikki with a giggle.

'No, nothing like that. He's an archaeologist, Nikki. His programme is called—'

'Ah, I know. *Digging History*,' said Nikki. 'Joseph watches it. He takes kids on archaeological digs.'

'That's the one.'

'He's quite a looker, isn't he? And doesn't he always have this great big dog with him?'

'That's right, a Bernese Mountain dog, who, by the way, is now Skipper's best buddy.' Eve lowered her voice. 'Are you alone, Nikki?'

'Yeees.'

'Justin isn't the real reason I called. It's Joseph. Tamsin is worried about him, and to be honest, so am I.'

Nikki groaned. 'Oh, Mum, I'm worried sick. It's been going on for weeks now, and every time I broach the subject, he brushes it off. However, I finally confronted him this morning, and he's promised to explain what it's all about tonight. Mum, I'm terrified of what he's going to say.'

'And you've no idea what the cause of it is?'

'None whatsoever. All I do know is that he's not been the same since the Pelham case. I can pinpoint the change in him to the moment when David Pelham was arrested. It was a horrible case, we all suffered. What I don't understand is why it seems to have affected Joseph in particular. I mean, if anyone should be suffering, it's me, not Joseph. I was the one directly involved.'

'Then maybe that's it, sweetheart,' said Eve thoughtfully. 'Think about it. He loves you, and perhaps it brought home to him that you might be seriously harmed.'

That was always possible, of course, but somehow Nikki doubted that this was the case. Joseph was remarkable in that he was a deeply spiritual person, while at the same time possessing a cool, rational mind. Nikki had always envied that quality in him. 'He says it isn't anything to do with me. He says it's him. I'm dreading what he's going to tell me, Mum. I can't lose him, I can't!'

'Oh, Nikki darling! You won't lose Joseph. He adores you. Just take a deep breath, and listen to what he has to say without interrupting. Whatever it is, keep calm, and then discuss it.'

'It sounds so easy put like that.' Nikki sighed. 'But you're right. I mustn't lose my rag.'

'Well, if you need to, ring me, no matter what time it is. I'll be on tenterhooks waiting to hear. Promise?'

'I promise. As soon as I'm on my own and can talk.'

After ending the call, Nikki sat back with a frown. So, Tamsin and Eve had noticed the change in him too. Well, at least she wasn't being paranoid, Joseph's current behaviour was worrying everyone. And they needed to put it right.

* * *

Haydn sat in her small hotel room and, yet again, went over the plan for the following day. She'd do this a dozen times more by the evening. It was how she conducted an operation — she went through it in her head, each time adding some small glitch, some way it might go wrong. To each of these hypothetical scenarios she appended a Plan B, sometimes even a Plan C, until there was no contingency left. When that was done, she would brief Neville, and they would both agree on a strategy.

Neville was staying in a small hotel a few streets away from hers. Operatives were never booked into the same places. That way, should one fall into the hands of the law, the other had a better chance of escaping. Soon, she would ring him and they'd meet in some out of the way café, or a park somewhere, and go over the programme in detail.

Haydn threw herself down on the bed and stared up at the ceiling. She no longer worried about Neville failing in his part of the job. In fact, she was beginning to warm to the idea of working with a man she could regard with indifference. There was no bond between them, whereas she and Terence had been close. This could give them an edge. With both focusing solely on the job in hand, a successful outcome was more likely. Everything so far had gone smoothly, and she saw no reason why this hit wouldn't go the same way.

Haydn sighed. Then she could go home. The moment she reported to her client that the mark had been terminated, the promised money would drop into her account. A lot of money. Enough to allow her to relax, live a 'normal' life. Until her services were needed again.

She shook herself. She mustn't start thinking of the future. It was too soon for that. So, Haydn went back to the beginning and went through the whole thing again.

* * *

Now that she had Richard on her side, Joanne almost considered cancelling her appointment with Lizzie Harper. Then, as she was cashing up, she decided that besides being rude, she risked missing some vital piece of information. Anyway, the village where Lizzie lived wasn't far, and it wouldn't take too long. Joanne had no one waiting for her at home, so as soon as she had handed the daily takings to Claire, she would be off to Fenny Bridge Village.

Joanne was surprised not to find Claire in her office, or the consulting room. Then she saw a note with her name on it propped up against Claire's computer.

> *Sorry, Jo, you were with a customer and I didn't want to interrupt. Not feeling very well so have left early. Put the takings in the safe and lock up for me, would you? I'll see you tomorrow. Claire.*

Joanne's brow furrowed. This wasn't like Claire. She never left without having a word with her. She pushed the note into her pocket and bent down to open the little safe on the floor. She opened it up, put the cash inside and locked it again. As she stood up, she noticed Claire's diary lying open on the desk. There was a thick black line through the entry for the last patient of the day, with the word 'Cancelled' across it in large capital letters.

Joanne groaned. Claire wasn't ill. She was at the end of her tether.

This couldn't go on. She needed to work fast before her boss and friend broke down completely.

In twenty minutes, she was pulling up outside a large house overlooking a village green. Lizzie Harper was waiting for her at the door.

'Joanne, my dear! I've been thinking of nothing else since you rang me. Come on in and tell me everything. The kettle's on.'

Joanne followed her into an unexpectedly modern kitchen twice the size of Joanne's lounge and dining room combined. The stainless steel and marble counters didn't quite fit with the plump and homely Lizzie, who looked like she would have been more at home among copper pots and sprigs of drying herbs.

Lizzie indicated one of two high leather stools at the central island. 'Tea or coffee? I'm a tea person myself.' She nodded towards the integral oven, where a hi-tech coffee maker blended in with other glistening, black-fronted appliances. 'Which makes that little beauty something of a white elephant, doesn't it?'

Joanne shook her head in amazement. It was all like something from a magazine. 'I'm a tea woman, too, much as I'd like to see that machine in action.'

As Lizzie made the tea, she explained that her late husband had been a kitchen designer, and this had been his last project. 'I suppose it's beautiful in its way,' said Lizzie rather sadly. 'Easy to keep clean and all that, but it's not really me. And since he's been gone, I haven't had the heart to move away. We lived in an old farmhouse when we were first married, my kitchen was my cosy, happy place. I know what he'd say, he'd tell me I was being a silly old sod and should get this place on the market. Then I could move into a nice little country cottage where I'd be far more at home. Well . . . it's early days yet, too soon to make the break from all the things that remind me of him.'

Joanne didn't need to ask why she had been seeing Claire. Who would certainly have advised her not to do anything until it felt right for her.

Lizzie handed her a mug of tea and hoisted herself up onto the other stool. 'So, I gather someone has got it in for Claire. Why on earth would anyone want to do that? Claire is one of few people who've actually made a difference to my life. I cannot tell you how much she has helped me since I lost my Philip.'

Joanne told her that Richard Duckworth had said much the same, and had promised to help.

'Well, count me in, my dear. I hate injustice, it's the one thing that really gets me angry. I'm not sure what I can do, but just say the word, and I'll do whatever I can.' Lizzie sipped her tea. 'One thing that comes to mind is that I know a couple of Claire's other clients quite well. One is a close friend, so maybe I could have a quiet word and see what they think. They might even know something about who might be behind it.'

'Oh, please, Lizzie, if you would. There are more and more cancellations every day, and one or two of the emails Claire has received have been quite hateful.'

'Then I'll ring Andrea tonight and see if she's heard anything.'

'Andrea? You don't mean Andrea Johnson?' asked Joanne.

'Why yes, she's been a friend of mine for years.' Lizzie smiled. 'I recommended Claire to her after her husband passed away.'

'I'm afraid that she is one of the cancellations, Lizzie,' said Joanne soberly.

'Andrea? Surely not!' Lizzie looked aghast. 'Well, in that case I'll certainly be ringing her.'

'Please don't mention you heard about it from me,' said Joanne anxiously. 'I have no idea what's going on, and if whoever is behind it gets to hear of our suspicions, it might cause even more trouble for Claire.'

'Oh, don't worry, I won't mention you at all. I'll simply chat like we usually do. You never know, she might even bring up the subject herself. If not, I'll just ask her how she's getting on with the counselling.' She put her cup down, shaking her head. 'I can't think why Andrea would have cancelled. She's been doing so much better over the last couple of months. Far from complaining, she's always saying how good Claire is. It doesn't make sense. Did she give a reason?'

'She simply said she wouldn't be coming back, she gave no reason at all. It was quite a formal message, too, not like Andrea at all.' Andrea Johnson was a gentle and kind person, but the message was cool, to say the least.

'What puzzles me,' said Lizzie, 'is why Andrea hasn't said anything to me about it. We tell each other everything, yet she's never even mentioned it.'

'Perhaps she knows how fond you are of Claire, and doesn't want to worry you,' Joanne said.

'Yes, that's probably it,' Lizzie said doubtfully. 'Anyway, I'll talk to her and let you know the outcome immediately. Give me your contact details, and I'll ring you. Will you be at home this evening?'

'Yes, I'm on my way home now.' She scribbled her details on the notepad Lizzie handed her, and smiled. 'Thank you for listening, and for offering to help. I do appreciate it.'

'Heavens, it's no problem at all. I talk to Andrea most evenings at around half seven or eight o'clock, so I'll contact you after that.'

Joanne left her second ally, pleased she had made the effort to see her. If she hadn't visited Lizzie, she wouldn't have known how on earth to approach one of the actual people who had cancelled. With Richard and Lizzie's support, she'd have a much better chance of helping Claire.

Once she got home, Joanne realised that she had forgotten to shop, and there was precious little in the fridge. Feeling hungry but unenthusiastic about cobbling together something out of her paltry stock of food, she decided to treat herself to a fish supper. There was an excellent fish and chip shop on the outskirts of Greenborough, just a five-minute drive from home. So, she picked up her bag and car keys and went back out.

The place was busy when she got there, but it always was, so Jo parked in a side road and walked back to the shop. The queue moved fast, and soon she was on her way back to the car bearing a parcel of freshly cooked haddock and a large portion of chips like a prize.

With her mind on Claire and her troubles, she stepped off the pavement to unlock her car. She was blissfully unaware of the rumble of wheels, or the dazzling glare of the headlights as the big vehicle bore down on her.

* * *

The man strolling towards the main road stopped in his tracks and yelled out in horror. He ran toward the scene. What he found when he got there would stay with him for the rest of his life. A twisted, motionless body, and a road scattered with chips that were mingling with fresh red blood.

CHAPTER FIVE

Eve and Wendy arrived at Jacobs Mere House to find the gates wide open. Tamsin and Niall, hand in hand, were just ahead of them on the drive, Skipper trotting along beside them.

'It's not often your host insists you bring your dog when he invites you over for a meal, is it?' said Niall with a grin. 'I like this guy already.'

Wendy pulled up in the parking area and gazed up at the big old house. 'My! Our Justin has done well for himself, hasn't he? This is impressive!'

Eve nodded mutely. The normally calm and unflappable Eve was suffering from an unprecedented case of butterflies. She was terrified at the prospect of meeting Justin's father again. He didn't belong in her new Fenland life, he belonged to the past, and she thought she'd rather keep him as a memory of times gone by.

'Ladies! Welcome!' Justin appeared on the driveway, Bernie lumbering along behind. 'Wendy Avery! Hellfire, woman, you haven't changed a bit!' In seconds, he was by their side, and enveloping Wendy in a bear hug. 'This is *so* good! I can't believe we're all living close to each other again. It's just magic!'

At that point they were joined by Tamsin and Niall. Tamsin introduced her husband, who gazed admiringly at Bernie.

'Boy! He's a dog and a half!' exclaimed Niall, ruffling the dog's thick fur.

'Not the sharpest tool in the shed,' added Justin, smiling fondly. 'I think he could have a few brain cells missing, but he's the perfect companion. Frankly, the fact that he's a bit loopy makes me love him all the more.'

He ushered them all inside. Eve paused in the imposing hallway and looked around, taken aback by its elegant beauty. Justin had said how much work needed doing on it — including adding a modern heating system — and she had expected a work in progress, but it was immaculate, and bore every sign of an expert interior designer having been at work. Wendy had been right. Justin had done well for himself.

Justin beamed at them. 'I suggest we do the "Grand Tour" before we sit down to eat — but we'll do it with a glass in hand. This way, guys. There's champagne in the kitchen, all ready to toast my first proper visitors.'

They followed him to the kitchen, where Justin began to uncork the promised champagne. Eve did a quick surreptitious count of the glasses — five — and gave a sigh of relief. As she began to unwind, the delicious aroma of cooking wafted from the stove, and she smiled happily at their host. This was going to be a very pleasant evening.

'I drew the short straw, so I'm the driver tonight,' said Wendy, rather wistfully. 'Still, a single glass of champers will hardly push me over the edge.'

When they all had their drinks, Justin beckoned them forward with a sweep of his hand. 'If you'd care to follow me, folks . . . I've always wanted to be a tour guide.'

It took them about half an hour, Justin entertaining them with tales of the old country house, its history and some of the disasters that had occurred in the course of revamping it.

'There's an added bonus where I'm concerned,' Justin added. 'We are pretty certain that this area, and especially part of the grounds, could be the site of an old Roman settlement. In fact, we are going to film an episode of *Digging History* right here at the house.'

Tamsin's face lit up at the prospect of her next-door neighbour's property being on TV. Then the smile faded. Eve guessed she was worried about an invasion of rubber-neckers, along with hordes of journalists trampling all over their privacy.

Justin must have noticed it, too, because he immediately went on to say, 'But don't worry, it'll be low key. I don't want too many people knowing where I live. We'll be bringing in a couple of videographers rather than a film crew, and for this episode it'll be just me, no kids. I thought of doing a series of short cameos, possibly in black and white, or sepia, a bit of nostalgia interspersed with our regular shows. You're welcome to come and watch, although a shoot gets a bit boring when you're not actually taking part. Anyway, if you feel like watching Bernie and me digging up my garden, feel free.' His smile widened. 'Now, I think it's time to eat.'

Looking rather shame-faced, Justin admitted that he had brought in a catering company, and all he'd done was heat it up. 'Cooking isn't one of my better skills, to say the least. In fact, my culinary expertise is limited to scrambled eggs.'

His words made Eve think of her daughter. If it hadn't been for Joseph, the local takeaways would have done well out of Nikki. She wondered how Nikki and Joseph's 'heart to heart' was going. Her daughter had never before sounded so anxious about their relationship. Eve worried about her vola-tile daughter losing her cool, although Nikki had said she was aware of the danger of that happening, and was determined to be understanding.

Wendy elbowed her in the ribs. 'Hello! Where are you? Justin's asking if you'd like a top-up.'

'Oh, I'm sorry. Wool-gathering. Yes, please, I'd love some more. I'm making the most of having a chauffeur tonight.' Eve smiled.

While Justin was busy pouring the drinks, Wendy whispered, 'Are you okay? You look troubled.'

'I'll tell you on the way home,' Eve whispered back.

Niall was telling a funny story about the antics of a drunk they'd recently had in the custody suite. Justin followed it with a tale of how he himself had once been thrown in jail for embarking on an excavation too close to a temple.

Inevitably, the conversation got round Wendy and Eve's connection with him and his family. Tactfully, Wendy was able to steer it away from Eve's relationship with Justin's father.

'So, where's your sister Heather these days?' Wendy asked casually, secretly hoping, Eve knew, that Justin would tell her she'd gone abroad.

No chance. Justin's face fell. 'She lives in Grantham with her husband and two children.'

Dammit, thought Eve. Far too close. Grantham was less than an hour's drive away. 'And what does she think of your amazing new home?' she asked brightly.

'We've fallen out big-time over it. Not that we ever did agree on very much,' he muttered, playing with the stem of his glass. He looked up. 'The fact is, as soon as there was money to be put on the table, she didn't want to know. She wasn't about to waste her money on some crumbling wreck in a bloody cesspit of a fen — her words, not mine.'

Making light of it, Niall said, 'The Fens have always been something of a "Marmite" area. You know, you either love it or you hate it.'

'Well, I love it,' said Justin vehemently. 'Anyway, Heather only described it like that because she's tight as duck's backside, if you'll excuse the expression. She never even bothered to view it. Dad and I bought it between us, and funded all the work, then when it's almost completed, Heather turns up and accuses us of excluding her. Suddenly she was prepared to chip in. I put my foot down, even though Dad wasn't so sure, and now she's fighting tooth and nail to get her name on the deeds.'

Eve wasn't surprised. Even as a child, Heather had been a sly one. You never really knew what she was thinking — or scheming.

'She can't, surely,' said Tamsin. 'You and your father paid for it. It belongs to you. She hasn't any claim to it.'

Justin shrugged. 'True. Not in law she doesn't, but she's playing the family card. She's working on Dad, making him feel guilty. Poor Heather only has an ordinary house while her brother is living in a luxurious mansion.'

'Lionel isn't that gullible,' Eve said, 'or he wasn't when Wendy and I knew him.'

'I'm afraid he still sees my sister as "Daddy's Little Princess". She's always been able to twist him around her little finger — when it suits her to do so,' Justin said bitterly.

Eve was surprised Lionel still thought that way about his daughter. Surely, by now he would have seen her for what she really was.

'Anyway, enough about my sister,' Justin said. 'She's not living here, and she never will, so let's forget about her and enjoy the rest of our evening.'

And Justin launched into a series of anecdotes about exciting archaeological finds, and the difficulties of making the profession exciting enough for TV. Entranced, none of them wanted to leave, but Niall was on early shift the next day, so, reluctantly, they prised Skipper out of the big, comfy bed he was sharing with Bernie, and headed for the door.

After Niall and Tamsin had left, Justin and the faithful Bernie accompanied Eve and Wendy to their car. Wendy was about to start the engine when Justin said, 'Do you think you could you come back, just the two of you? Tomorrow afternoon if you can make it. There's something I'd like to talk to you about.'

He looked so serious, suddenly, that Eve asked him if there was something wrong.

'I'm not sure. Maybe, maybe not. I ask you because I know you from the old days, and if anyone can tell me if I'm being neurotic, it's you two.'

'We could stay and talk now, if you like,' offered Wendy.

'No, no, it's not that serious. I'm quite probably imagining things, plus I hate to think how many glasses of champers I've had tonight. Tomorrow afternoon will be fine. Say, around two thirty?'

Eve and Wendy drove off, picturing all sorts of scenarios. 'I bet it's something to do with that bloody sister of his,' muttered Wendy. 'I never liked that woman.'

'And you made that patently obvious!' Eve laughed. 'But don't you hate being left guessing? At least he said it wasn't that serious. I just hope it's something we can help him with.'

Wendy steered the car along the pitch black lane. 'I don't know about you, but I'm beginning to detect a whiff of another little mystery in the air.'

'Too right I am,' said Eve. 'I wonder what little puzzle our lovely Justin is going to entrust to his father's old friends.'

* * *

Knowing there was no way he could avoid talking to Nikki, Joseph took his time preparing supper. As he served it up, Nikki poured them each a large glass of wine. They were accustomed to sit, at the end of the day, at the old pine kitchen table, discussing their work, poring over puzzling cases, talking through complex police matters. Laughing together. There was none of this tonight.

After a few moments, Nikki lifted her glass. 'To us, Joseph. And no matter what passes between us tonight, remember that I love you, and I always will.'

As if he could forget. It was the very reason why he had been feeling so disturbed lately. He clinked glasses with her. 'Me too.'

It had been his intention to eat first, and then — in the lounge, in front of the fire — try to explain. Suddenly, he found himself speaking.

He stared down at his plate, pushing his food around with his fork. 'I'm afraid, Nikki. Afraid that we are making a terrible mistake . . .'

Seeing the look of apprehension on her face, he smiled gently at her, reached across and stroked her cheek. 'It's not what you think, my darling. The mistake I'm talking about is that we're wasting what we have by putting the job before ourselves, our happiness.'

She made to speak, but he raised his hand. 'I know. We've been here a hundred times before, and each time we've decided not to rock the boat, not to split the team up. I believe our priorities have become skewed. Surely, love should come first. Shouldn't it?'

She almost laughed aloud in her relief. 'God. I thought . . . I thought you were going to say . . .' She shook her head. 'I mean, you've been so distant. I really believed you wanted to leave me.'

'That's the *last* thing I want!' He took her hand and squeezed it. 'I'm sorry. I've put you through hell, haven't I? It was that last case. Something Pelham said that has never left me. It has haunted my thoughts until I've begun to doubt my ability to carry on working.' He looked away. 'I've, er . . . I never told you, but it affected me so badly that I've been seeing the force psychologist for counselling. She helped me to see that what he'd said was a simple truth, something anyone might say, but because it came from the lips of a deranged murderer, I couldn't accept it for what it was.' Joseph took a deep breath. 'I want to put love first. Nikki, I want to marry you.'

* * *

For a few moments, Nikki didn't know what to say. This was what she had always dreamed of, it was her dearest wish. 'I want it, too, Joseph, but — oh, I don't know. I suppose I'm scared that we'll fall back into the same old rut. We've been through it all before, the unwillingness to break up the dynamic among

51

a brilliant team of detectives that is so rarely found these days, and that we might be better off not working together anymore. Neither of us wants to be anything other than a police officer, but then I think that our job is preventing us doing all the things other couples do. Taking off on a holiday. Enjoying an evening out without having to constantly listen for a call summoning us to the next murder scene.' She gazed into his eyes. 'How do we make a decision we can live with?'

'That's what I've been so troubled about, Nikki. We can't go on this way indefinitely. Someday, something is going to happen and when it does, the choice will no longer be ours to make.'

What to say? They resumed eating, and the food tasted of nothing.

'I have one suggestion,' said Joseph, pushing his plate away. 'Suppose we talk it through with Cam again. Yes, he's our superintendent, but he and his lovely wife Kaye are also two of our closest friends. Ultimately, it's our decision to make, but meanwhile, it might help to talk about it with people who care about us while also understanding how we feel about the job we love so much. And this time we tell them we are not prepared to allow things to drag on. It's crunch-time, and we would appreciate their thoughts.'

It sounded reasonable to Nikki. At least it was something. 'Yes, that would be good. And if it's okay with you, I'd like to talk to my mother as well. She knows about our situation, and I'd value her opinion.'

'Of course,' Joseph said. 'After all, if anyone knows all about loving and losing, it's Eve. Let's give ourselves a week. We'll listen to our friends, and then make a decision. How's that sound?'

'Agreed. One week.' Nikki resolved to respond to the letter still locked in her drawer, asking for a week in which to consider their offer, then all bases would be covered.

They cleared the plates away, poured another glass of wine, and went into the lounge. After a while, Nikki realised she was exhausted. All that fearful anxiety had left her feeling drained. Drained, but closer to Joseph than ever.

CHAPTER SIX

When Nikki and Joseph arrived at work the following morning, their new-found optimism was subsumed by a fatal hit and run that had occurred overnight. A young woman had been deliberately run down while getting into her car. A witness had called the emergency services immediately, but the victim was pronounced dead on arrival at hospital.

Gill Mercer, who had been called to the scene, was livid. Raging at the appalling loss of a young life, she was currently moving heaven and earth to track the vehicle via CCTV, and any ANPR (automatic number plate recognition) cameras that happened to be in the area.

Nikki found her in the CID room.

'Bastard covered the sodding number plates!'

'There's no doubt about it being deliberate then.' Nikki sighed. 'Have you got an ID for the victim yet?'

'Yes,' said Gill, echoing the sigh. 'Joanne Andrews, twenty-five years old. Lived alone in a little two up, two down in Castle Street. Ran one of those new age shops in the Craft and Antique Centre, selling crystals and rocks. We haven't spoken to the employer yet, I'm just about to pay her a visit. The kid was clean as a whistle, so for the life of me I can't think why she was killed like that.'

'If it weren't for those number plates being obscured, I'd say it was a random act of violence perpetrated by some kid high on drugs,' said Nikki grimly. 'But—'

'Yes, but. What happened was anything but random. The witness is in bits, poor sod. Says he can't stop hearing the roar of the engine as it accelerated towards her.'

'Did he get the make of the car?' asked Nikki.

Gill shook her head. 'It's all a blur to him. All he can remember was that it was dark grey in colour and spattered with mud. There's a chance he might recall the make when the shock wears off, but he said it happened so quickly and was so violent that it didn't register.'

'And the camera that picked it up? Surely that would show what make the car was?'

'You'd think so, wouldn't you? But any insignia had been removed from both front and rear of the vehicle. We'll work it out of course, by the shape and design, but it wasn't obvious.' Gill rose wearily to her feet. 'Well, I'd better get over there and talk to the woman's employer. She'll be wondering why Joanne hasn't turned up for work.'

Nikki wished her luck and made her way into her office. There was a feeling of gloom and despondency about the station following this news. Joseph was waiting for her with coffee. 'I suggest we check the overnight reports, and then as soon as Cam gets in, we'll go and talk to him. That okay?'

He was right. They couldn't keep putting things off until the time was right, because that time would never arrive.

The notes from the previous night, apart from a few petty crimes, referred mainly to Gill's hit and run. Just as Nikki was draining her mug, there was a knock at the door.

The sight of Niall Farrow's pale face immediately set off alarm bells.

'Niall, whatever's the matter?' Nikki asked.

'Oh God. Not Tamsin?' whispered Joseph.

'No, nothing like that, Dad,' Niall said. 'We've just had a shout to an incoming 999 call. A cleaner let herself into her employer's house to start work this morning and she found him dead.'

Nikki was taken aback. Niall never called Joseph 'Dad' at work, never. He was clearly very distressed. 'Okay, so you want us to handle it?'

'Nikki, it's Justin Connaught. Our new neighbour.'

Joseph let out a low whistle.

'Oh hell,' Nikki said. 'You mean my mum's old friend?'

'Yes. The four of us — me, Tam, Eve and Wendy — had dinner with him last night at Jacobs Mere House. I just can't believe he's dead. He was on such good form, such an amazing personality. I really liked him, and now . . .' Niall fell silent.

Since Niall had become a sergeant, he had changed radically. The eager schoolboyish recruit had grown into a calm, level-headed officer. Nikki had never seen him so shocked by an incident.

Goodness. Eve. 'Niall, does my mother know about this?'

'No, the call only just came in. I've dispatched two cars and I'm waiting for a situation report. Then I ran straight up here. Will you take it?'

'Of course we will, son,' said Joseph. 'And I suggest you get yourself a very strong coffee. You look pole-axed.'

'I'm okay now,' Niall said. 'It's just having been with him last night. He was so vibrant, so full of life . . . I'm struggling to get my head around the fact that he's dead.'

Nikki was about to answer when Niall's radio crackled into life. The three of them listened as the officer at the scene gave his report of what they had discovered.

Glancing at Joseph, Nikki pushed her chair back. 'Grab your jacket, Sergeant. This is one for us.'

Justin Connaught had been shot. But was it murder, or suicide?

'Okay, Niall. Show us heading towards Jacobs Mere. We'll contact you asap.' She patted his shoulder. 'We've got this, son, okay?'

With Joseph driving as fast as he dared, they were at the house in less than twenty minutes.

Going inside, they were met by the familiar face of PC Ernie Bass. Nikki was glad to find him in attendance. He and his crewmate, PC Peter Marsh, were like the proverbial chalk and cheese. Whereas Peter was a slab of a man complete with shaven head, Ernie was thin almost to the point of emaciation with fine, wispy hair and sharp features. The differences extended beyond their appearances, too, Peter being soft as butter, especially regarding kids, the old, and all animals, while Ernie was as tough as old boots. They made a good team, each complementing the other, and what's more, they understood how she operated.

'Nothing's been touched, ma'am,' said Ernie. 'The cleaning lady never went near him; as soon as she saw the blood, she ran from the room and called 999. The paramedics pronounced life extinct, after which we cordoned the area off. There is a gun lying by the body, but we are making no assumptions about that.' He turned and they followed him across a wide hallway. 'I'll take you to the dining room. That's where he was found.'

'Hang on a minute,' Nikki said. 'What's that noise?'

'Ah, we have a bit of a problem there.' Ernie made a face. 'Pete's with him now.'

'With who?'

'Not exactly a who, ma'am, more an *it*.' He pointed to a slightly open door, through which Nikki caught a glimpse of the largest dog she'd ever seen.

'He wants to get to his master,' called Peter. 'Poor little devil's distraught. He'd been shut in this study, and by the time we got here, he'd nearly had the door off its hinges.'

'What on earth is it?' asked Nikki.

'A Bernese,' said Peter, stroking him fondly. 'As soon as we know what's occurring here, I'll trace the family and get one of them to collect him.'

'You'd better stay there with him, Peter,' said Nikki, staring at the massive animal. 'He probably senses what's happened, and he needs some reassurance. That's apart from the fact that if he gets into that dining room, he might well trash all the evidence. Our favourite pathologist would never forgive us!'

'I will, ma'am. I'd already thought of that.' He ruffled the whimpering Bernie's neck. 'Animals know things. And this guy went everywhere with that poor bloke. I've watched all his programmes, and I've never seen him without this dog by his side.' Peter's voice cracked.

Niall had sent the right crew to this shout. If anyone could calm that dog, it would be 'Marshmallow Pete', as the mess room liked to call him.

While she was talking to Peter, Joseph was standing at the entrance to the dining room, appraising the scene. She joined him in the doorway.

The table was still littered with plates, glasses and serving dishes from the dinner party of the night before. Nikki had a sudden vision of her mother and Wendy, Niall and Tamsin, all merrily enjoying themselves. Now their genial host lay dead, his lifeblood leaching into the brand-new carpet.

No forensic evidence was needed for them to know that this was a crime. The whole scenario reeked of it. For some reason, Justin Connaught had been murdered, and, apart from his killer, her mother was probably the last person to have seen him alive. Nikki closed her eyes for a moment. Not again! What was it about her mother that always seemed to draw death to her, like a moth to a flame?

'I know just what you're thinking,' Joseph whispered.

'And?'

'And nothing. It beggars belief, doesn't it?'

It did indeed. Nikki turned to the waiting Ernie. 'Have you called forensics?'

'On their way, ma'am. ETA, five minutes.'

Thanking him, she turned to Joseph. 'We'll let the SOCOs get in first, then we'll suit up and try to make sense of this.'

'I've a feeling that will be easier said than done,' muttered Joseph, then, 'Oh, shit! This man was a TV celebrity, wasn't he? I dread to think of the media fest that's going to descend as soon as the news breaks.'

Nikki groaned. Any murder brought the newshounds buzzing around like flies, but the death of a celebrity made an investigation hell on earth. It became public property, with every man and his dog having their own theory as to what lay behind it.

Back at the car, Joseph rang Niall. They would need him to organise a proper cordon. Until the forensic pathologist gave his opinion, Jacobs Mere House was off limits.

While Joseph discussed details with Niall, Nikki, realising it would be down to her to break the news, called her mother. She had sounded so pleased to be back in touch with her 'lovely young man' that Nikki feared she would take the news of his death badly.

Eve sounded stunned but did not fall apart. That wasn't her way. Thanks to her background in the military and the MOD, she took the news in her stride.

'Are you sure it was murder, Nikki?'

'It hasn't yet been confirmed, but it stinks of foul play. Plus, Niall described how cheerful Justin was last night. He said he showed no signs of being anxious or depressed, quite the opposite. I think we can rule out suicide. I won't know more until the SOCOs have been; they're on their way now. Listen, Mum, I'll get over to Monks Lantern as soon as we've finished here — we need to talk. I hate to tell you this, but you and Wendy were most likely the last people to have seen him alive.'

'Sure,' Eve said. 'Whenever you're ready.' There was a moment's silence. 'Does Justin's father know yet?'

'We'll be contacting the family as soon as we have all the details.'

There was another brief pause. 'Nikki, darling, do you think you can break the news to Lionel yourself? He adores his son, and I think he'd appreciate this terrible news coming directly from my daughter.'

'Me?'

'Just tell him you're Eve Anderson's daughter. I know it will help him.'

For a moment Eve sounded on the verge of tears. Then, with unaccustomed passion, she said, 'If it is murder, find the killer. Justin was a gentle, kind and funny young man who didn't deserve to die. Someone must pay for his death. Find the killer, Nikki. For me.'

Nikki was left feeling bewildered. There was a lot more going on here than she knew about, but now was not the time to ask. 'We'll see you a bit later, Mum, and I'm sorry I had to be the one to tell you.'

'Better you than anyone else, my love. We'll see you later, we'll be here. And now I must go and break it to Wendy.'

Nikki ended the call and looked up to see Joseph pointing to an ancient lime-green Citroën Dolly rattling its way up the drive.

She smiled in relief. Good. The man himself had turned out. Soon they would know just what had happened to Justin Connaught.

'Dear hearts and gentle people!' Rory cried, heaving himself out of the little car. 'Am I right in what the trusty grapevine tells me? That this particular, er, *demise* has a personal connection?'

'He was an old friend of my mum's, Rory.'

'And Tamsin and Niall's next-door neighbour,' added Joseph. 'They were here last night for dinner.'

'And I doubt the food was the cause of death,' added Rory. 'Never fear, all will be revealed; lead on, and let me take a look at this unfortunate gentleman.' As they turned, another car was heard on the drive. 'Ah,' said Rory, 'here comes my trusty photographer, the lovely Ella. Excellent. We'll just get suited up and then we can crack on.'

Inside the dining room, Rory surveyed the scene. 'Well, my oh my. If you'd told me the door had been locked from the inside, I'd have told you to call Monsieur Poirot! This bears all the hallmarks of the *doyenne* of crime herself.' With a sweep of his arm, he gestured towards the table. 'See what I mean? The table still set, the crystal sparkling, the flowers as yet unwilted. All looks as if the occupants have only just stepped from the room . . .' He glanced at the sideboard. 'And there. Three empty champagne bottles, one still half-full — Bollinger, no less. Dear me, what a waste. And speaking of waste,' his gaze came to rest on the body lying on the floor, 'here we have the greatest waste of all.'

Rory's eloquence was brought to a halt by the arrival of two scene of crime officers and Ella Jarvis, his senior forensic photographer.

'I want you to photograph absolutely everything, dear girl. Make sure you miss nothing. This is a curious case, to be sure.'

Nikki frowned. 'Curious in what way, Rory?'

'Well, to start with — and bear in mind that the maestro has yet to even approach our poor victim — he wasn't shot with that gun lying on the floor beside him. If it had been the weapon, our victim would have been splattered halfway across the room. Does it belong to our victim, I ask myself. Or someone else? And why should it be in a dining room? Hardly a conversation piece to be admired along with the stilton, is it?'

'I did wonder about that gun,' said Joseph. 'But the body is partially obscured by the table and his wound isn't visible, plus we didn't want to contaminate the crime scene, so I reserved judgement.'

'Good boy! I've clearly taught you well. But now, if you cherubs would give me a moment or two with your friend here, you may then approach, and we'll see what other anomalies we can uncover. So, run along now, children. Uncle Rory has work to do.'

Duly dismissed, Nikki and Joseph went to their car.

'So much for our chat with Cam,' said Nikki despondently. 'I was determined that nothing was going to get in the way of it today. And look at us now.'

'I know,' said Joseph. 'Still, it's a bit different this time, isn't it? Okay, you and I didn't know Justin personally, but everyone around us did — Eve and Wendy, Tamsin and Niall. We could hardly fob it off on Gill, could we, especially since she has that hit and run to deal with.'

'The trouble is, there's always something. Anyway, promise me that the moment we get back, we go and see Cam. All right?'

'Agreed. But right now, would you mind if I took a walk over to Tamsin's? She's not at work today, and we'll be talking to her anyway.'

'Of course. She might need her dad after receiving a shock like this. I'll hang on here and keep an eye on developments. I'll also see if I can get a chat with the cleaner who found him.'

'Ring me if you need me for anything. If not, I'll see you in half an hour or so.' Joseph opened the car door. 'And I definitely want to be here if Rory calls us back to the scene. That death is beginning to intrigue me.'

More than intrigued, Nikki was starting to grow anxious, and for some reason this feeling was connected with her mother. Nikki couldn't remember Eve ever having mentioned Justin Connaught, or his family. So what was the story?

CHAPTER SEVEN

When DI Gill Mercer gave Claire Hereward the news about Joanne, she broke down in tears.

Gill was somewhat surprised by her reaction. Claire evidently felt deeply for her employee. It appeared they had been closer than she realised.

'So, it was just the two of you here. Is that right?' asked Gill, handing her a tissue.

Claire dabbed at her eyes and nodded. 'Except for a parttime girl called Harriet, who covers— oh dear, I mean *covered* for Jo when she was off for some reason. Harriet sometimes helps with packing if we get a lot of orders for crystals coming in, but that's not often. The two of us worked so well together — Jo in the shop, and me in the consulting room . . . I just can't believe she's dead!' Claire put her head in her hands and wept.

This was hard going. Gill had expected shock, even a few tears, but not this outpouring of grief. 'It sounds like you were very fond of her.'

Claire swallowed, and pulled herself together. 'I'm sorry, Officer. It's just, well, you don't know Jo's history. She's been so brave, and she's done wonders getting her life together . . . it's just so unfair. She didn't deserve to have it end like this.'

Gill looked at the woman with interest. 'Do you think you'll be up to telling me more about Joanne? The smallest detail will help. You see, we are treating her death as murder. She was deliberately run down; we have a reliable witness who saw the whole thing. Now what's bothering me is why. Why would anyone want to harm a lovely woman like her?'

Claire Hereward looked stunned at this revelation. 'Murder! Of course, Detective. I'll tell you everything I know.'

An hour later, Gill was back in her car, her head spinning. Joanne Andrews was not the name she had been born with. She had originally been called Katy Hobbs, the sole survivor of one of the worst family tragedies that Gill had ever heard of.

Katy's younger brother had severe learning difficulties that, despite constant care and treatment, only grew worse as he got older. The only member of the family he had any kind of connection with was Katy. That was probably why he chose a night when she was away on a sleepover with her best friend to burn the house down. His mother, father, and little sister Emily were all inside. Only twelve at the time, Timothy locked all the doors from the inside and hid the keys, then lit fires in each of the downstairs rooms. None survived, except Katy.

Gill felt sick just thinking about it. Katy had been given whatever help was available. Her only remaining family, her grandparents, were in no state to care for her properly after the loss of their daughter and two grandchildren. Fortunately, her best friend's parents, rather than see her go into foster care, gave her a home. And over the course of the next couple of years, under their wing and with the constant companionship of her best friend, Katy managed to assimilate what had happened and move forward. At the age of twenty, she changed her name by deed poll, and using the money inherited from her parents, purchased a small house in Greenborough, and got a job. Young as she was, she recognised that in order to cope with her new circumstances after what she had experienced, she would need counselling. That was when she met Claire Hereward, and embarked on her new life.

Gill marvelled at her resilience. She wasn't sure that she would have survived such a thing at that age and come out of it comparatively unscathed. Now she understood why Claire had broken down when she heard the news. She would probably have done so herself.

Gill let out a long sigh. How unfair life was. The brave survivor, now a murder victim. It didn't get much shittier than that.

As she drove away, her pity turned to rage. Whoever was responsible for Joanne's death would not get away with it. And it was down to her, Gill, to make sure that didn't happen. She had never felt so passionate about a case in all her working career. God help the bastard who had done this!

* * *

Rory was uncharacteristically baffled. Usually he had merely to cast his eyes over the scene of a crime in order to make sense of the course of events. More often than not, it was simply a case of joining the dots. He was also a little miffed. He had been hoping to give Nikki something solid that would bring about a quick outcome to an investigation that had a personal aspect to it.

Ella had photographed the scene as a whole, along with dozens of salient details. The SOCOs, meanwhile, had been busy dusting and retrieving evidence, and Rory himself had completed his examination of Justin Connaught's mortal remains. All that remained was to tell Nikki and Joseph of his findings — or in this case, lack of.

Nikki arrived alone. Joseph, she said, had been to see Tamsin but was on his way back now. She grimaced. 'I've just had a gruelling half hour on the phone. I found a list of numbers stored on the house phone, one of which was his father's. It wasn't the easiest conversation I've ever had, but it turns out he's in Lincoln visiting a friend, so he'll be here within the hour. Justin's sister, Heather, will join him here later.'

'Well, I'm about to get this unfortunate young man back to the peace and quiet of my mortuary. I guess it'll be his father making the formal identification?'

'Yes, he said he'll do it, although given his celebrity status, half the country could ID Justin.'

Rory nodded. 'I'll make him look as presentable as possible, never fear. Just give me a couple of hours to get him back and sorted out.'

'Of course.' Nikki glanced over to the door, where Joseph was hurriedly pulling on a protective overall. 'So, Prof. What do you have to tell us?'

'Not much, I'm afraid, dear heart — galling as that may be. To be perfectly frank, nothing here makes sense, other than my surmise about the gun. It's a twelve bore, and it hasn't been fired for some considerable time, probably months, so that's one big red herring you can dismiss. Justin was certainly shot, but not with a twelve bore. And I'd say it was a lucky shot, too, hit the right axillary artery. I suspect it caused haemorrhagic shock, followed by death. He would have died very quickly, if that's a comfort to anyone.'

'It might be.' Nikki pulled a face. 'Maybe later, after the shock has worn off. It would be a relief to know he didn't suffer alone and in agony.'

Joseph stared down at the body. 'You said a lucky shot, Rory? Does that mean we can rule out a professional hit?'

'I would say so,' said Rory. 'In fact, I'm sure of it. It's a difficult area to target, and to take a direct hit in that specific place could mean that the victim had his arm raised in defence. No, it was a chance shot, possibly not even intended to be fatal. Or maybe the shooter was aiming for a different spot and missed. Until you catch the killer, my dears, that might remain a mystery.' He looked around. 'There is no mess, no sign of a struggle, and absolutely no forced entry.'

'The cleaning lady said the front door was locked, and she used her own key to get in. Uniform checked the other doors — the kitchen door was closed but unlocked,' said Nikki.

'I'd say he knew his killer,' said Joseph. 'And after the murder, the man, or woman, just walked out the back door and closed it behind them.'

'Even if Justin didn't know the killer, he certainly must have let him in,' added Nikki. 'Mary, the cleaner, said that Justin always locked all the outer doors, even in the daytime. You'd have to in a big house like this. You'd never hear someone come in if they were left unlocked.'

'And, sadly, Justin had ordered a CCTV system, but it's not due to be fitted until next week,' said Josph. 'Tamsin told me he mentioned it during dinner.'

'A tad late, I fear,' murmured Rory. 'For this poor soul anyway. Now, I'd better get him out of here and spruce him up for his father's visit. All I can really add, my cherubs, is that I think he died between the hours of midnight and one o'clock.'

Nikki raised an eyebrow. 'So, not long after his guests left?'

'Tamsin said they left at eleven o'clock,' said Joseph. 'Hardly any time at all. What the hell happened here?'

For once, Rory didn't have an answer. 'I wish I knew. However, I'll make this a priority, and the minute I discover something, I'll ring you. Rest assured, my preliminary report will be with you as soon as is humanly possible.'

Rory watched them leave and gazed around the room despondently. Why did nothing speak to him? No tiny piece of evidence that called out for attention. Everything was so damn . . . ordinary! Rory disliked being defeated. He disliked it intensely. 'You need to get a grip, old boy,' he muttered to himself. 'I'd have expected more from the redoubtable Professor Wilkinson.'

* * *

Just after midday, a sleek black BMW drew up outside Jacobs Mere House.

'Justin's father is here!' Nikki called out from the hallway. 'We'd better go and meet him. Can you come with me, Joseph?'

Outside, a tall, grey-haired, strikingly handsome man was just getting out.

'Eve's daughter?' he asked, looking at Nikki from deep brown eyes.

'I am, sir. DI Nikki Galena, and this is DS Joseph Easter. We're very sorry for your loss, sir.' She looked back at the house. 'My apologies for the mess, and all the personnel, but—'

He held up a hand. 'Please don't apologise. It has to be done. But my son. Is he still here?'

'No, sir, he's been taken to the chapel of rest. If we could just have a few words, and then when you are ready, we'll take you to him.' Nikki indicated the front door. 'Let's see if we can find somewhere quiet, shall we?'

'One thing before we go in,' Lionel said. 'This might sound odd, but where is Bernie? You know, Justin's dog. He'll be in bits, poor animal.'

'He's being looked after by one of our officers, sir. Peter is very good with animals, dogs in particular. We spoke to him a few minutes ago, and he said that Bernie's calmed down a lot. Don't worry, Peter won't leave him until we've discussed what is going to happen with him.'

Lionel shook his head sadly. 'Yes, we must make a decision. Unfortunately, I can't have him. My sister, who now lives with me, is allergic to dogs. I'm hoping that Heather might consider taking him on — her children would adore him. It's a big undertaking, in more ways than one, but the dog needs familiar faces around him, and as little change as possible. We'll certainly sort something out.'

Nikki guessed this man was dealing with his grief by taking charge. It was probably his way, something he always did in a crisis. Fair enough. Whatever works — until it doesn't, until some tiny little thing causes the floodgates to open. She understood what Lionel was going through, having suffered the loss of a child herself. It was always something small that tipped you over the edge, and always at a moment when you least expected it.

'Let's use the drawing room,' said Joseph, opening a door into a room filled with light, its ceiling decorated with beautiful Victorian cornice work and an elegant white scrollwork fireplace surround.

Nikki and Lionel took seats in the plush chairs, while Joseph offered to make tea or coffee.

When he had left the room, Lionel smiled at her. 'I would have recognised you anywhere. You have Eve's eyes. She was a very beautiful woman, you know.'

Nikki returned the smile. 'She still is, sir.'

'Please, do call me Lionel.'

'Okay, Lionel. I was, well, curious. I've been wondering why Mum hasn't ever mentioned you before.'

'It's a long story, and I think I'll leave it to Eve to tell it.' He gazed at the fireplace for a moment, and then back to Nikki. 'I hope you don't think I'm being callous in my reaction to my son's death. I've had a long career in the forces, and then the MOD, and in the course of that time I've seen far too much death. It hasn't made me a hard man, however. It's just that right now, I want to assist you in any way I can. I'll do my grieving later, in private, after we find out what happened here last night. Justin and my daughter are the most precious things in the world to me, but I am determined to remain strong until I know the truth. Does that make sense to you?'

She said that it did. That she probably understood what he meant better than most. Suddenly, she found herself telling him about Hannah.

Joseph came back, bearing three mugs of steaming coffee, and found them deep in conversation. Nikki looked up and smiled. 'Thanks, Joseph. Lionel and I were just talking about lost children.'

Joseph nodded understandingly. These occasions weren't easy for her. But now it was time to get back to the case in hand, so between them they told Lionel, as gently as possible, everything they knew so far.

'There are a number of unanswered questions about what happened,' Nikki said. 'The forensics will tell us quite a lot, but the bottom line is that Justin was shot and killed by someone, and we don't know if it was a terrible accident, and that "someone" was too frightened to come forward and admit to it, or a deliberate act. In light of that, do you know if Justin had any enemies? Can you think of anyone who might have held a grudge against him?'

Lionel shook his head. 'Absolutely no one that I can think of. You'd have to have known him to understand why I say that with such certainty. I know he was my son, but he really was a good man, Nikki. It's a bit of a cliché to say he didn't have an enemy in the world, but in his case, that was actually true.'

Nikki remembered her mother saying that Justin was a lovely, kind, and funny young man. Even Tamsin and Niall had warmed to him immediately. So why was this universally liked man now lying in a mortuary with a bullet in him?

'Did he seem anxious about anything — or anybody — of late?' asked Joseph. 'Something to do with his work, or someone connected to it?'

Lionel shook his head slowly. 'Justin loved what he did, and did well out of it, although he'd never been short of money. We are fortunate in being a fairly wealthy family, Sergeant. I don't know if you saw any of his TV programmes, but you could tell from those how passionate he was about his work. He told me it was his dream come true. He certainly never mentioned anyone he didn't get on with; in fact, he said he had a great crew.' Lionel chewed on his thumbnail, thinking. 'And not only that, he was over the moon about this house and his new life here. Only the day before yesterday he was telling me how he'd bumped into Eve. He was really pleased to have met her after all these years. His last words to me were, *"Life's good, Dad, really good."*'

Lionel's voice cracked. For the first time he appeared close to breaking down. He took a deep breath and carried on. 'He'd just signed a contract for a new season of *Digging*

History . . .' his voice tailed off. 'No. It must have been an accident. It must have been.'

Nikki didn't voice her doubts. She glanced at Joseph.

'Tell me, did your son own a twelve bore shotgun?' he asked.

'Ah, the twelve bore. It was a family heirloom. It had belonged to his grandfather, and I thought it only right that Justin should have it.' Then he looked at them, aghast. 'Oh my God! You mean that's what . . . what fired the shot?'

'No,' said Joseph, 'it's just that we found it lying by his body and it's been puzzling us. It wasn't loaded and it hadn't been fired, so we've been wondering what it was doing there.'

'It's been taken for forensic testing,' added Nikki, 'but you'll get it back, I promise.'

In order to build up a picture of their victim, they asked Lionel to tell them more about his son. When he had finished, Nikki asked him if he was ready to do the formal identification.

He got to his feet immediately. 'Yes. I want to see my boy . . . one last time.'

CHAPTER EIGHT

It was after four o'clock when they arrived at Monks Lantern.

Eve met them at the door. 'I bet you two skipped lunch. You did, didn't you?'

Nikki hadn't even realised it until Eve asked. 'Come to think of it, we probably did.'

'I thought so. Straight into the kitchen with you, you can eat while we talk. It's not much, but it'll keep you going until the evening.'

Eve had prepared sandwiches, along with crisps, some slices of salmon and asparagus quiche. Wendy made them tea, and they sat down at the kitchen table. For a few moments they were silent. Eve and Wendy were obviously badly shaken by the news of Justin's death.

In an attempt to lighten the heavy atmosphere, Nikki said, 'Well, it seems that once again, our two supposedly retired action heroes have found themselves in the thick of a mystery.'

'At least for once, it's not of our own making,' said Wendy glumly. 'And it's the last thing we wanted to happen.'

'Yes, I'm sure,' Nikki said. 'And I'm truly sorry. He was a close friend.' She pulled a scrap of paper from her pocket.

'Before I forget, Lionel asked me to give you his mobile number. He'd like you to call him as soon as you can.'

Eve hesitated for a second before taking the slip of paper.

Another silence descended while Nikki and Joseph ate. Finally, Joseph took out his notebook. 'Sorry, but it has to be done. Let's get the formal details over with, and then we can talk properly. Can you tell me what time you arrived last night, and when you left?'

In the course of their discussion, Nikki noted two disparities between their accounts and Lionel's. One, that there was one person — Justin's sister, Heather — who harboured ill-feeling towards him; in fact, they were openly hostile towards each other, Eve said. Two, that there *was* something bothering Justin, prompting him to ask Eve and Wendy to return the following day. Lionel had insisted that his son didn't have a care in the world, but that didn't seem to be the case. Nikki wondered what Justin had wanted to speak to Eve and Wendy about so urgently.

'Correct me if I'm wrong, Wendy,' Eve said. 'His precise words were, *"There's something I'd like to talk to you about."* I then asked him if there was anything wrong, to which he said, *"Maybe, maybe not, but because I recall you two from the old days, if anyone can tell me if I'm being neurotic, it's you two."*'

'His words exactly,' said Wendy, passing Joseph another sandwich. 'And if he hadn't had a fair bit to drink, I think he might have told us there and then. Sadly, it's too late now.'

'I almost forgot,' said Joseph. 'During the evening, did he by any chance show you a shotgun, a family heirloom that had belonged to his grandfather?'

Both women shook their heads. 'No,' said Wendy. 'Although I did see a locked gun cabinet in the boot room.'

'Oh yes, I remember. I saw it too when we were on our guided tour. And it was definitely locked.'

Nikki hadn't been in the small boot room, but she was sure that uniform would have looked in there. It was something to bring up at the following day's briefing.

72

'Mum?' Nikki asked tentatively. 'I know you said you knew Justin well as a boy, but how well did you know Lionel? He spoke of you very affectionately.'

The glance that passed between her mother and Wendy spoke volumes, but for once, her mother was reticent.

'Oh, it's a long story, sweetheart,' said Eve dismissively. 'To make it short, we worked together for a number of years. At one point, Lionel asked me to marry him. I refused.' She cleared her throat. 'He was a wonderful man, but it just wasn't the right time for me to make such a commitment. I'm sure he still is wonderful, and I'll certainly ring him this evening. It will take a bit of courage on my part, given the circumstances. Wendy and I really cared for young Justin, and were over the moon at finding him again, only for this to happen. Life is just so unfair.'

Like when Hannah died, thought Nikki. It was the unfairness of it that ate away at you. Willing herself not to dwell on it, Nikki returned to the events of the previous night. 'I can't help wondering about that very tight window of time — from when you left at around, what, eleven fifteen, to the death, as little as forty-five minutes later. That's weird.'

'Yeah,' said Joseph. 'It does limit possibilities, doesn't it?' He turned to Eve and Wendy. 'You're absolutely sure there was no one else in the house while you were there?'

Eve puffed out her cheeks. 'Well, we did go round the whole place, although it's a very big property, and we certainly didn't look in the wardrobes or anything, did we? I suppose someone could have been hiding somewhere.'

'I keep thinking that they arrived very shortly after we left, and Justin must have let them in.' Wendy looked pensive. 'I'd swear this is to do with whatever he wanted to talk to us about.'

'Now I'm cursing myself for not insisting he tell us there and then,' said Eve. 'But he looked so tired we didn't want to push him.'

'Be fair, Eve, we did offer to stay and talk last night, but he said it wasn't serious and anyway, he'd had too much to drink,' Wendy said.

'I wonder what will happen to the house?' asked Eve. 'Oh, Nikki, you should have heard the way he spoke about it. He really loved that place. He was so happy to have found somewhere so special.'

'He was even going to set part of his next TV series there,' added Wendy sadly.

'I have no idea what Lionel will do with it,' said Nikki, 'but he does seem like a sensible man. I suppose it could be marketed as a retreat, or a very exclusive hotel. It's too big for a family home, unless you've got pots of money.'

'Just so long as Heather doesn't get her claws into it,' said Wendy darkly. 'Justin would turn in his grave. He was adamant that she would never live in his home.'

'Well, she was all for staying there tonight, apparently,' said Joseph. 'She suggested it to her father, until we informed him that it was still a crime scene, so it wouldn't be possible. He's booked them both into the Travelodge in Greenborough.'

'Mark my words, that cow will be planning something devious,' muttered Wendy. 'I never liked that woman.'

Despite herself, Eve chuckled. 'And don't we know it! You weren't shy of hiding your opinion of her, were you?' She turned to Nikki. 'Heather was very wary of Wendy, and I'm sure it was because she knew Wendy had the measure of her right from the start.'

Nikki sipped her tea thoughtfully. 'Yet Lionel loved both his children. He said they were his life, and I'm sure he meant it.'

'Oh, I'm sure he did,' Eve said. 'He never could see the spiteful side of Heather, he always believed she was just misunderstood.'

Wendy grunted. 'Plus, she was crafty enough never to show that side of herself when he was around. She was all sweetness and light with Daddy.'

Joseph grinned at Nikki. 'I can't wait to meet her.'

'That'll be your treat for tomorrow,' Nikki said. 'Right now, we have to get back to Jacobs Mere House and make sure it's secured for the night. And thanks for the food, Mum. Heaven knows what time we'll get supper.'

'Oh!' Eve suddenly exclaimed. 'Bernie! What's happened to that dog?'

Nikki told them that Peter, who had a way with dogs, was taking care of Bernie.

'But your man can't stay there all night, can he? And Lionel and Heather are going to a hotel, so what's that poor dog going to do?'

Joseph patted her arm affectionately. 'Don't worry, Eve. We'll make sure he's not left alone. I'll ring you, okay? Lionel was very concerned about that furry monster, he'll sort something out.'

Eve still didn't look convinced.

By five fifteen they were heading back towards the crime scene. Nikki was wondering if they'd ever get to have their talk with Cam Walker. She had rung to apprise him of the situation regarding the death of Justin Connaught, and he had said he would hang on until they got back to base. By that time, it would be too late, and their talk would probably be postponed to the following day. Oh well, at least for once it hadn't been her fault.

* * *

Richard Duckworth stared at the television screen in horrified disbelief. He had seen the news about a hit and run that had occurred the night before. Now, they had just named the victim as twenty-five-year-old Miss Joanne Andrews, of Greenborough. An appeal followed for witnesses to the accident. Richard turned off the TV and closed his eyes, trying to make sense of what he'd just heard. They were treating the death as murder. Apparently, a car had driven straight for her, at speed, deliberately knocking her off her feet as she was unlocking her car.

Richard found himself looking at this incident through the eyes of the policeman he once had been; he went through each of the events leading up to her death. He had been approached by a young woman who suspected that her employer, Claire Hereward, was being targeted by someone for no apparent reason. In support of her suspicions, she had sent him a couple of emails from former clients. The tone of both had been vitriolic, one almost threatening. Now Joanne was dead. What was going on?

Before he could make up his mind what to do, his doorbell rang. He opened the door. The caller was a woman he'd never seen before. And she was looking very anxious.

'Mr Duckworth?'

'That's right. And you are?'

'Oh, thank heavens! Can I talk to you? It's important. It's about Joanne Andrews. She told me she'd been to see you yesterday . . . Oh, I'm sorry, you have no idea who I am. My name is Lizzie Harper, and I'm one of Claire Hereward's former clients.'

Richard held the door open. 'Come in, come in.'

He showed her to an armchair in the lounge, where Lizzie Harper promptly burst into tears. 'I've just heard the news that she's dead! That lovely girl, mown down like . . . like roadkill. I can't believe it's happened.'

Richard made her a cup of tea, telling her that he too had been shocked to the core by what had happened. After a while, Lizzie regained her composure.

'I'm so sorry. It must have been the shock,' apologised Lizzie. 'Really, I'm as tough as old boots. I can't imagine what poor Claire must be feeling.'

'I was wondering if I should go and see her. I expect she could do with some support right now,' said Richard. 'We could go together, if you like?'

Lizzie said she'd be happy to go with him. 'But before we go, and now I'm back to my normal self again, I should tell you why I came.'

Richard knew very well why, but let her explain.

'Joanne came to see me yesterday with some very disturbing news,' she began. 'She said she'd visited you, so you'll know what it was. Well, after she left I rang a friend of mine, Andrea Johnson. I'd recommended Claire to her after the death of her husband. She was very impressed with Claire, who she said was really helping her to move forward. However, last night, we had a very strange conversation . . .'

Richard sat forward in his chair. 'Oh?'

'When I asked her how the counselling was going, Andrea became very cagey. I found that odd, as usually she's full of it, I can hardly shut her up. Not last night.' Lizzie looked puzzled and a little hurt. 'She refused to talk about it, and finished up by telling me that perhaps Claire Hereward wasn't the person I'd thought she was. I asked her to explain what she meant, but she refused to say another word about it. I've known Andrea for ages, and she's never been so abrupt. I don't understand it.'

'I think I do,' murmured Richard. 'Your friend Andrea has been got at. What I'd like to know is why.' Looking at Lizzie Harper's candid expression, he decided that he rather liked her, and was sure he could trust her. He'd been good at that when he was a copper, he had the ability to sum a person up almost at once, and he was rarely wrong. 'Listen, Lizzie, I think we need to go into this more deeply. Are you in a hurry to get away?'

Lizzie shook her head. 'My time is my own, and, to be honest, I'm finding this situation a bit frightening. I'd be very glad of a talk, because I'm starting to wonder if I'm imagining things, or whether something very nasty is going on.'

'Oh, it's nasty all right. "Nasty" doesn't even come close. Someone saw fit to kill poor innocent Joanne. No, this is deadly serious.' Lizzie opened her mouth to speak, but he raised his hand. 'I'm a retired policeman, a detective sergeant, and before that I did over ten years in uniform on the streets of Nottingham, so I know what I'm talking about.'

'Oh my!' said Lizzie. 'I'm not sure if that makes me feel better, or worse.'

'Hopefully better. At least you don't have to agonise over it alone. You came here because you knew Joanne had spoken to me, and you're scared.'

Lizzie nodded. 'Yes, I'm scared. What on earth could be so important as to make someone kill a young woman who was simply being loyal and looking out for her employer? Joanne knew nothing! That's why she came to us, she wanted our help. What's going on, Richard? Or have we got this completely wrong? Maybe it's got nothing to do with why Joanne came to see us both? I hardly knew the girl, maybe it's something totally unrelated?'

'True, we didn't know her. She might have had a dark past that caught up with her, but, realistically, what are the chances of that? The fact is, she was very concerned about what was going on around Claire. Concerned enough to seek our help. There's a possibility that she was stopped before she could take it further, or,' he thought for a moment, 'perhaps she had found something out, but was unaware of its significance.'

As he spoke, the realisation hit him that if that really was the case, he and Lizzie Harper could also be in danger, given that Joanne had been to see them. One look at Lizzie's expression told him that she had come to the same conclusion.

After a moment's silence, she asked, 'So, what do we do now?'

His immediate reaction was to say that they should go to the police, but the first thing the police would have done would have been to talk to Claire, and she would have told them what was behind the threats and cancelled appointments. Or would she? 'I think we need to talk to Claire, as soon as possible. For a start, she will know more about Joanne than we certainly do, and she can also tell us if the police are aware of the threats being made against her. If she's told them nothing, then we go to the police. The only thing is, I don't know where she lives, she most certainly won't be at work after a shock like this.'

'Oh, I know where she lives,' said Lizzie. 'A while back, the craft centre had to close while the electrical system was being repaired, so Claire saw some of her clients in her own home. She lives in a house called Silvermere, in Lime Grove,

Greenborough.' She smiled. 'And if you're wondering how I found your address, Joanne told me where you lived, but not the number, so I called at three houses before someone could tell me.'

Richard smiled back. 'Yes, I was a bit puzzled about that.' He stood up. 'Okay, so if you are up for it, I'll get the car keys, shall I?'

'Anything is better than sitting around fretting.' Lizzie set her jaw. 'And I hate injustice. Even my best friend Andrea isn't going to convince me that Claire Hereward is anything other than a caring, thoughtful counsellor.'

CHAPTER NINE

Nikki put away her phone and stared at Joseph. 'That was Rory. He called to say that their preliminary findings from the examination of Angela Sandford show that she did not swallow those tablets willingly. He has discovered small but uncharacteristic abrasions and slight bruising on both wrists, her jaw, and also inside her mouth. He says that these marks indicate that her wrists were tied and someone forced the tablets down her throat. He doesn't have the results back yet to say what those drugs were, but he's certain the empty packets were intended as a decoy, and whatever she was given was not a normal prescription drug. I'm afraid that we have another murder on our hands, Joseph.'

'Great,' muttered Joseph. 'Though I suppose we did suspect it. It's the last thing we need along with the death of Justin Connaught.'

'And with Gill tearing the streets up looking for her hit and run driver, we can hardly hand it over to her.' Yet again, Nikki cursed the cutbacks that had seen Greenborough CID reduced to just two DIs. A murder victim deserved the investigating officers' full attention, and shouldn't have to be juggled between other cases. Luckily, her own team was still intact, so they'd manage. 'I'm thinking of handing Angela Sandford over to Cat and Ben, while we deal with Justin. Vonnie can float between both investigations depending on who needs her help the most. How does that sound?'

'Like the best option,' Joseph said. 'It's not perfect, but we'll cope. We usually do.'

They were back at Jacobs Mere House, about to go in and meet Heather Blake, Lionel's daughter. Nikki was very interested to see what she and Joseph would make of this woman whom nobody, apart from her father, seemed to like. Eve and Wendy in particular were both very perceptive, as might be expected from former security services operatives. Just because they were retired didn't mean they had lost their skills — as they had already proved on many an occasion.

'Okay, let's get this over with,' said Joseph. 'In any event, we're going to have a very late night. We still have to try to get back to Cam before he bails out.'

The house was still being searched by uniformed officers, with anything of significance being either removed, or dusted by the SOCOs. Lionel and Heather had been confined to the drawing room. Nikki and Joseph found them there.

Nikki began by offering Heather their condolences. She said she was sorry she and her father would be obliged to stay in a hotel tonight, but the forensic officers would be finished by the following day, and then they could come back.

Lionel was perfectly understanding. Heather, on the other hand, was anything but. She said she couldn't understand why the police had to be trampling all over the whole house, leaving a trail of disruption, when it was only one room that needed investigating.

Nikki felt her hackles begin to rise. Already she was beginning to see why her mother and Wendy disliked this woman so much.

'It's the shock, DI Galena,' Lionel interposed quickly. 'As you can imagine, Heather is terribly distressed and angry at the death of her beloved brother.' Then to Heather, 'Darling, if they want to catch whoever killed our Justin, I'm afraid they have no choice but to go over the house in detail.'

Joseph regarded the tight-lipped and silent Heather, and decided to turn on the charm.

'Believe me, Mrs Blake, the last thing we want to do is add to your distress at such a sad time. That said, I'm afraid we really do have to carry out a thorough inspection. If we don't, and miss some vital piece of evidence, we might fail to catch your brother's killer, and that would be unforgivable, as I'm sure you'll agree.'

Here we go again, thought Nikki, watching Heather's expression soften. It was a ploy that nearly always worked, and it never ceased to amaze her that he managed to sound so sincere.

They asked Heather much the same questions as they'd put to her father. 'There will be a police presence here all night, so you mustn't be concerned about security,' added Nikki. 'We'll be back in the morning to make sure everything is in good order. Meanwhile, here's my card, and if you think of anything at all that might help us, please ring, day or night.' She was about to leave when she remembered her mother's request. 'Oh, and Lionel, what will happen to Bernie while you're away at the hotel?'

'I'm afraid he'll be shut in the kitchen for tonight, poor fellow. We'll have to make some more satisfactory arrangements for him tomorrow,' Lionel said.

At the mention of the dog, Heather assumed an expression of distaste. She glanced at Lionel. 'Father had thought I might take him, but that's quite out of the question. I'm not a dog person, and anyway, I'm not sure I'd trust him with my children.'

Personally, Nikki thought, she wouldn't trust the children with the dog, especially if the kids were anything like their mother.

'Surely you have a dog pound or something, don't you?' asked Heather. 'For strays and the like?'

Seeing Nikki's reaction, Joseph threw her a warning glance. Abruptly, he stood up. 'Excuse me for a moment. I need to make a call.'

He was back in minutes, pushing his phone back into his pocket. 'My daughter is on her way here,' he said to Lionel. 'She lives in the next property, a little further down the lane. She will take Bernie. He can't be left here alone, not after what he's been through.'

He kept his eyes on Lionel, who looked grateful, but Nikki saw Heather's look of disdain. Clearly, she was *not* a dog person.

Outside the room, Nikki let out a long breath. 'What a cow! But Joseph, is Tam really okay to take the dog?'

'Dead right she is. And we'd better keep her well away from Heather. She isn't fond of people who say "dog pound". You know what Tam's like about animals. Luckily, she's got her work's Land Rover, and she's going to ferry Bernie home in that, along with anything he needs. She reckons it'll be kinder than trying to drag him away from his house on a lead.'

'In that case, we'd better find Peter and tell him what's occurring. He can give her a hand before he goes off duty.'

Minutes later, the Land Rover drew up and Tamsin strode into the house. 'It's okay,' she whispered to her dad, 'I won't kick off, I don't want to upset the dog. But really—'

Joseph put his hand on her arm. 'It's okay, kid, we feel the same. If we stay here much longer, I'll be needing a leash and a muzzle for Nikki!'

They found Peter out in the grounds, walking the giant creature in the walled garden, and Joseph explained what was going to happen.

'I've got Skipper in the Land Rover, so Bernie won't feel so alone,' Tamsin said. 'I'll be needing some of his usual food, I don't want him getting an upset stomach. His bed, too, and maybe some of his toys. I wonder where he sleeps. I need to keep everything as normal as possible for him.'

'I've found where Justin kept all his stuff,' said Peter. 'I'll come and help you collect what you need, and if you think it would help, I can go with you in the vehicle and help settle him in.'

Tamsin smiled at him gratefully. 'If you don't mind, that would be great. I know a bit about this breed; they are high maintenance, but once they get used to strangers, they are really affectionate.' As she bent to ruffle the dog's thick fur, she whispered, 'Can you imagine anyone wanting to leave the poor lad overnight? He's grieving! For heaven's sake, Justin was his world.'

'Ah, by the way,' Peter said, looking anxious, 'you said he's grieving, and he is. So I took the liberty of allowing him to see Justin before they took him away.'

Tam squeezed the big policeman's arm. 'That's good to know. Well done, Peter.' She turned to Nikki and Joseph. 'Animals understand about death. Now he's seen Justin, he can grieve. If he'd never seen his owner again, he'd have spent the rest of his days waiting for him to come back, so that's the best thing Peter could have done.'

'I see what you mean,' said Nikki. 'I hadn't thought about that. Nevertheless, I suspect you'll be having a disturbed night.'

'It's a bit of luck I've got three days off work, then. I was going to do some gardening, but I can see myself spending them catching up on sleep instead.' Tamsin looked fondly at the big dog. 'The garden can wait. This poor guy comes first.'

'Well then,' said Peter. 'Let's gather up his things and get him to your place. Hopefully, he'll be so exhausted after all the uproar that he'll crash out for a while.' He grinned at Tamsin. 'The sarge is going to have a bit of a shock when he gets home tonight.'

Tamsin smiled back. 'Niall already knows. It was him told me to get myself down here and pick him up.'

'Thank you, sweetheart,' said Joseph, kissing his daughter on the cheek. 'We owe you one.'

'No sweat, Dad. It's the least I can do. Come on, Peter, let's find him some dinner and gather up his bed.'

'And we can hand over to the officer on duty tonight,' said Nikki to Joseph, 'and get back to Greenborough.' *And have that talk with Cameron Walker. This time, it will happen.*

* * *

84

As Tamsin and her escort were coaxing the miserable, bewildered dog into her Land Rover, Claire Hereward was pouring herself a very large drink. Having seen what it did to her father, Claire almost never touched alcohol, but this evening, she needed something to get her through the coming hours. The news of Joanne's death had hit her like an express train. Racked with doubts and suspicions, uppermost in her mind was the thought that Joanne's death was her fault. She remembered how incensed Jo had been when she heard of the threats to her boss and friend. Had she possibly tried to find out what was going on and been killed for it? Surely not. Maybe the pain she had absorbed in her years as a counsellor had skewed her thinking. Some of the scenarios she was beginning to envision were like something out of a badly written novel.

She paced the room, her thoughts on the one person in the world she could trust. If only she could call him, beg him for his help. No, she couldn't do that to him. He had enough to worry about, and he needed her to be his rock, his tower of strength. She couldn't let him see that she was crumbling.

The doorbell rang. Gripped with sudden fear, she turned to the monitor from the security camera outside. On her doorstep stood two familiar figures, one holding a bunch of flowers. Richard Duckworth and Lizzie Harper. They must have heard the news about Joanne.

Relieved that it wasn't anyone more sinister, Claire nevertheless wasn't sure she was really ready to receive them. Funny that they should both turn up at the same time; she wasn't aware they knew each other.

Claire opened the door and, unable to speak, endeavoured to smile in greeting.

Richard proffered the flowers, while Lizzie said, 'Oh my dear, we are so very sorry.'

Fighting back tears, she found her voice and invited them in. Would they like tea? Or maybe something stronger. To her slight disappointment, they opted for tea. *Probably for the best*, she thought.

They took their cups into her lounge, where she told them to make themselves comfortable. She had expected to hear them express their shock at the death of Joanne, and how lovely she had been. So, when Richard set his cup on the coffee table and said he thought they should come straight to the point, Claire felt a stab of concern. What point? she wondered anxiously.

When it all came out, she was at first stunned, and then her heart began to race. The last person to have been involved in her problem was dead. So, what of these two? Claire the counsellor had to fight to stop herself succumbing to a panic attack.

'It's all right,' said Richard calmly. 'Don't be upset. We already realise that this is a dangerous situation, but we both agree that we can't just step away from it. We'd like to talk the whole thing through with you and get all the facts, and then we'll decide how to proceed. I hope that's all right with you? We really do want to help, you know.'

Richard, her former client, had a wonderfully sonorous voice, deep and reassuring, and Claire found herself responding to it. 'Okay. What can I tell you?'

Richard told her that Joanne had visited each of them and enlisted their help. He asked Claire how long she had been receiving these hateful messages.

'A couple of weeks, I suppose, and there has been an increasing number of cancellations in the past week.' She stared into her tea. 'I kept a lot of it from Joanne because I didn't want to worry her.'

'Have you been to the police about it?' Richard asked.

'They came to ask about Joanne, of course. I just told them the story of her sad past, but not about the emails and cancelled appointments.'

'Sad past?' said Lizzie. 'But she always seemed so happy.'

'I think that first, you should tell us everything you know about Jo, and then about the things you never told her,' Richard said.

'All that will take some time,' Claire said, 'so would either of you like something a bit stronger than tea? I know I would!'

* * *

True to his word, Cam had waited for them to get back. At last, Nikki and Joseph were seated in his office, the door firmly closed, nursing glasses of Cam's best malt whisky.

They gave him an account of their dilemma, their hopes, and their fears for their future, while Cam listened in silence. When they had finished, he said, 'I've been expecting this for quite some time, dear friends. Coincidentally, Kaye and I were talking about you only the other night, and we agreed that things had to come to a head, probably sooner than later. Now they have.'

'We know we have to make a decision,' said Nikki, 'but we've gone over it so often, and for so long, that we've lost perspective. We need your opinion — Kaye's too. It seems to us that we're damned if we do, and damned if we don't.'

'Let me talk to Kaye this evening. Then we'll meet again tomorrow, and I'll tell you what we think — and I promise we'll be truthful.' He smiled at each of them. 'And try not to worry. I've a feeling there might be a happy ending in sight.'

Nikki stared at him, puzzled. 'I wish we had your optimism. The trouble is, every solution seems to entail so much sacrifice.'

'We'll see,' said Cam enigmatically, 'But as I say, come back tomorrow, at the end of the day. My Kaye is very good with problems like yours. We'll have a chat tonight and see what we can come up with.' He took a drink of his whisky. 'Now, back to business. These murders. Is there anything I can do to help, now that you seem to have two on your plate? Oh, and incidentally, I've managed to hold off the media where our celebrity is concerned. We've kept them happy by feeding them a lot of sentimental hogwash about young Joanne Andrews' hit and run. It's given the public something to emote about, and so far, none of our hotshot newshounds are even aware of the tragedy at Jacobs Mere.'

'I expect its remote location has helped there,' suggested Joseph. 'And the nearest neighbours being Tamsin and Niall are hardly likely to be phoning the press.'

'I guess it will hit the headlines tomorrow,' Cam said. 'Someone is bound to notice the police presence and all the comings and goings, but at least you've got the unfortunate victim away from the murder scene, and the initial, most important forensic sweep has been completed.' He downed the rest of his whisky. 'And I can't think that your suspicious death will even be noticed, not with everything else that's going on.'

Cam got to his feet. 'Get off home now, and I'll try to get uniform to give you a couple of officers to help out. Will Carole and Adrian be all right — if I can wangle it?'

'That would be perfect, Cam,' said Nikki gratefully. 'It was they who first had suspicions about the death Angela Sandford, so it would only be fair to let them continue to work on it.'

'I'll do my best. Now, vamoose! And try not to worry, it will all work out for the best.'

He sounded so confident. Nikki only wished she could feel the same way.

CHAPTER TEN

'A death threat! Oh, Claire! Why in heaven's name didn't you show it to the police? Did you keep it? Throw it away? Did you believe it, or did you think it was just some cruel joke?' Richard brought himself up short. 'Sorry, Claire, it's just that I'm horrified that you've been living with something like that hanging over your head, and bearing it all alone.'

'It seems ridiculous, I know. I guess I couldn't decide what to do, so I did nothing. But, to answer your question, yes, I did keep it, and no, I didn't take it seriously. I thought someone was trying to scare me for some reason.' She laughed bitterly. 'And they did that all right. I haven't slept properly for weeks.'

'Can I see it, Claire?' asked Richard. Oh, where were the nitrile gloves he always kept in his pocket back in the days when he was in the police?

Claire got up and opened the drawer of a glass-fronted display cabinet. She took out a plain white envelope with her first name written on it, and held it out to Richard, who raised his hands.

'I don't want to touch it,' said Richard. 'You've already handled it, so just open it and lay it on the coffee table. I'll read it from here.'

You know what you've done, and you are going to pay . . .
with your life.

One sentence, chilling in its simplicity.

'Do you have any idea what you're supposed to have done, Claire?' Richard asked.

'I haven't a clue,' she said. 'I've been over and over it, and I can't come up with a thing. Until this started, I've always believed I was helping my clients. They've always told me they've found ways to move forward and even take pleasure in their lives once more. In the seven years I've been practising, I can't think of one real failure.'

'Then maybe it's not related to your work,' mused Richard. 'I'm beginning to think this is personal.'

'Whatever the reason for it, Claire, you have to tell the police,' Lizzie said. 'This can't go on.'

'Lizzie's right, Claire. I suggest that first, we make a detailed list of each one of these occurrences, with as many dates as you can recall. We'll print off all the messages, so we're armed with as much information as we can muster. That way, it will help them build up a picture of what might lie behind it.'

Claire looked at him hopefully. 'We? Does that mean you'll be coming with me?'

'We both will,' said Lizzie. 'You're not going anywhere alone after that.' Lizzie pointed at the note.

Smiling in relief, Claire said, 'I'll get that list done at once. Tomorrow, if that's okay with you, we'll go to my consulting room and print off the emails.'

'Then we'll go directly to Greenborough police station,' Richard said. 'By the way, what was the name of the officer who came to speak to you about Joanne's death?'

Claire went to the mantelpiece and took down a business card. 'Detective Inspector Gill Mercer, of Greenborough CID.'

'Okay. I know her by reputation, and she's a good detective, but I've never worked with her.'

They spent the next half hour going through all the various odd misfortunes, the cancellations and veiled threats. 'I guess all this must have made me absent-minded, because apart from all these more concrete events, there are stupid little things too. I keep losing things, and, well, don't laugh, but my things seem to move around. I've always been a very orderly person, you know, everything in its place, but I've been getting really forgetful lately.'

'How do you mean, Claire?' asked Lizzie.

'Oh, things aren't in their usual place. Take those two porcelain figurines on that shelf over there.' Claire pointed. 'They belonged to my grandmother. It's a shepherd and a shepherdess. Well, I always have him on the left and her on the right. Yesterday they were the other way around. Then there was this.' She went to the mantelpiece and picked up a glossy card. 'It's an invite to a wedding. I left it there to remind me to reply, and I could swear I had it propped up against the clock, but this morning it was in front of that framed photo. I suppose it must be the stress, but it's very annoying.'

Richard didn't like the sound of this at all. He had been seeing Claire in her consulting room, now he had seen her house, and both places were neat as a pin. And Claire had always been sharp and on the ball. He decided not to make too much of it in case he frightened her even more.

In his lifetime on the force Richard had dealt with one or two particularly nasty cases. As Claire spoke, he was beginning to make a connection between this and one of those crimes. It had upset him badly at the time.

'The more I think about this, the more I think it's someone from your past, and not a client at all,' Richard said. 'I reckon they are making use of your clients as a way to get at you, by destroying the thing you most care about — your work. And they're making it look as if it's another business trying to discredit you in order to muscle in on your patch.'

'I think you may be right,' said Lizzie. 'And what an insidious way to go about it!'

Richard thought 'insidious' was right on the nail.

'But why hurt Joanne?' Claire was asking. 'Okay, she'd just been to see the two of you, but she didn't know what was going on any more than I do. Why kill her? It's such a drastic step to take.'

'Like I said, it's to destroy the things you care about, that you love.' *Listen to me*, Richard thought. *I sound like the prophet of doom.* Nevertheless, he was certain he was on the right track. 'You cared for Jo, and you looked out for her. I don't know much about her, but I do know she lived alone, and she worked all hours, which indicates she had no ties. I have a feeling you were very important to her, because there wasn't much else in her life.'

'You are right, Richard.' Claire regarded him thoughtfully. 'I guess since it's too late to hurt anyone, I might as well tell you what I told that police officer about Jo.'

Claire told them the story of the terrible events of Jo's early life. Lizzie listened in shocked silence. As for himself, Richard was beginning to feel the first glimmerings of that intense excitement that always gripped him at the start of a major investigation. Someone needed to pay for what was being done to this woman. Oh, if only this was his case, and he had all the resources available to the police. Thinking of the police brought him to the realisation that they only knew about Joanne. They knew nothing of Claire's situation.

'Ladies,' he said, 'I think we need to go to Greenborough police station this evening, and not wait until tomorrow. Furthermore, neither of you should be on your own tonight. We have no idea what is going on, but someone is threatening you, Claire, and they could be deadly serious. Lizzie, these people were obviously watching Joanne, and as she was killed not long after leaving you, they know where you live, and most likely that you live alone. I'm going to suggest that each of you gathers what you need for a night away from home, we go to the police, and then you both come and stay with me. Okay, they have my address, too, but there's safety in numbers, and they'll get more than they bargained for if they try to get into my house. I have a nephew who's in the domestic security business. He persuaded me to shell out for a bloody fortune's worth of CCTV, and my home is like Fort Knox.'

It took a while to convince Claire, but after some coaxing she agreed to go with them. They then drove to Lizzie's home, and after she'd packed a bag, they were on their way to Greenborough police station.

* * *

Eve didn't feel like eating her evening meal but didn't want to disappoint Wendy, who had gone to the trouble of cooking it. Thoughts of Justin's death constrained their usual lively chat, it was all they could think of.

'At least Tamsin has taken that lovely dog,' said Eve, pushing salmon around her plate. 'I just hope he recovers. I've heard of dogs that are so attached to their owners that—'

'Don't even go there, Eve,' Wendy said firmly. 'Bernie will be fine. He's quite young, and as long as he goes to a really understanding new owner and is well loved, he'll have a good life.' She gave Eve a mocking glare. 'And if you've finished mutilating that poor fish that never did you any harm, perhaps I can clear the dishes?'

Eve smiled for the first time that evening, ate the fish, and apologised to her friend for being so down.

'Oh, for heaven's sake, Eve, after what's happened neither of us is going to be a bundle of laughs. Admit it, though. It's not just that, is it? You're dreading having to talk to Lionel. Am I right?'

'Ah, you know me so well.' Eve sighed heavily. 'I really don't feel like digging up the past again, and it's going to be doubly hard after the death of his lovely son.'

'I know,' Wendy said. 'What on earth can you say at such a time?' She sat forward. 'One thing . . . maybe this isn't the right time to say it, but I've been thinking . . .'

Eve looked at Wendy suspiciously. 'Thinking what? I'm not sure I like that steely glint in your eye.'

'Justin's murder. I don't know about you, but seeing as how we were the last ones to see him alive — other than whoever killed him, of course — gives us a kind of personal connection to the case. And, well, there's your connection to the family. So, given all that, don't you think we . . . ?'

'Wendy Avery! Can you imagine what my daughter would say? It doesn't bear thinking about. In case you'd forgotten, we've been grounded from being private investigators, we're now confined to gardening and playing with our metal detectors.'

Wendy assumed an air of innocence. 'Oh, but a little intelligence gathering couldn't do much harm, could it? Purely as an aid to the police investigation, of course.'

Eve shook her head. 'Absolutely not. On this occasion, my dear friend, I think we must leave it to Nikki and her very capable team. I admit I was curious to know what Justin wanted to talk to us about, but to be honest, his death has knocked the wind out of my sails, and I really don't know if I've got it in me to take on a case right now.'

She saw Wendy give her an odd look, but chose to disregard it. She knew full well that this was not how she would normally react, but there it was. This death had hit her hard, harder than she'd thought possible.

'Ring Lionel now, Eve. Get it over with, and then I'll pour you a stiff brandy.' Wendy grimaced. 'Because I really don't feel like spending the rest of the evening with you looking like some angst-ridden Lady Macbeth.'

Lionel answered almost immediately.

'Eve! Oh, I can't tell you how good it is to hear your voice again after all this time.'

Eve wasn't sure she could honestly say she felt the same way, but she made all the right noises. 'Wendy and I are devastated by what happened. We both want you to know that we are thinking of you at this awful time.'

'I don't think it's registered yet, Eve. There's so much going on at the house, what with the police and their forensics people all over the place. And now we're stuck in a hotel until tomorrow. Frankly, my head's in a whirl.'

'Maybe that's all for the best, Lionel,' said Eve. 'At such a critical time in an investigation keeping emotions at bay can be of enormous help.'

Listen to me, she thought, *trotting out all the old clichés*. Still, she had to say something. Finally, she opted for the truth. 'Oh, Lionel, he was so happy at dinner last night, he was over the moon about Jacobs Mere House. I can't believe that this terrible thing could have happened so soon after we'd left him. Justin was still the same boy I knew all those years ago — kind and caring, and funny too.' Then, without even meaning to, she said, 'Lionel, have you any idea what was going on in Justin's life that could have prompted someone to kill him?'

He said nothing for a while. 'During the process of buying and renovating that house, we became very close. Closer than we'd been for some considerable time. I suppose the house became a shared passion, and working on it together with my boy was one of the most enjoyable times of my life.'

Eve didn't know what to say.

'Anyway, to answer your question, there was nothing at all. His life was going well, he was doing work he loved, and he was proud of what we'd achieved with Jacobs Mere House. He wasn't in any relationship that I knew of; he had parted with his former girlfriend, perfectly amicably, months prior to buying the property. His health was good, he was more than comfortably off, and he had no family problems. You could say he had it all. I'm obviously biased, but I can in all honesty say that Justin was universally liked.'

'He always was popular, even when he was a boy. You said he had no family problems,' Eve said, 'but I got the feeling he and his sister had fallen out over the house. He even mentioned it at the dinner. And there's something else, too. Just as we were leaving last night, he told me he was concerned about something. In fact, he invited us back today in order to tell us about it. Oh dear, maybe I shouldn't have mentioned it . . .'

'Oh now, Eve, you remember what Heather and he were like as kids. They disagreed over everything, but it didn't stop them loving each other. Heather's in a desperate state right now.' He fell silent for a moment. 'But the fact that Justin felt the need to talk to you about something that was worrying him, that is more serious. It has to be something that arose after I returned home, which means it was fairly recent. Listen, would you and Wendy come over to Jacobs Mere tomorrow afternoon? I don't know anyone here, and I could do with a friendly face or two right now. More importantly, you know me and you knew Justin, and I'd really like to talk to you about what he said.'

She couldn't very well refuse, could she? 'Of course we will, Lionel. Two o'clock okay?'

'That's fine. The police should be finished by then. Thank you, Eve. I appreciate it, and I'm so looking forward to seeing you again. I just wish it could have been at a happier time.'

Eve put down the phone, sank into a chair and shook her head. 'Still with his head firmly stuck in the sand regarding dear Heather. I suppose he'll never change now.'

She told Wendy about the following day's visit. Wendy said it was a good idea. 'Just don't let me get within striking distance of Heather if she brings up the subject of Bernie. Dog pound indeed! I'd rather see *her* locked in a cage than that poor dog.'

Eve raised an eyebrow. 'Methinks age hath not mellowed you where that woman's concerned.'

'Fat chance,' muttered Wendy, and held out a balloon glass of cognac. 'Now, drink this, and let's talk about something else — anything at all, so long as it's not bloody Heather.'

* * *

Perplexed, Haydn and Neville stared from their car at the unlit windows of an obviously empty house. What was going on? Their mark never went out, you could set your watch by their comings and goings, so why, tonight of all nights, would they change their routine?

Haydn chewed on her lip. The previous hit had been textbook, so what had gone wrong with this one?

After they'd gazed at the blank windows in silence for a while longer, Haydn suddenly announced, 'I'm going in. I want to make sure it's really empty. There's a chance they've had an early night, or an accident. I don't want to abort if we can help it.' She took a set of keys from her pocket.

'Want me to come?' Neville asked.

'No. You stay in the car and keep a lookout.'

Haydn was soon back. 'Mission aborted. We'll reconvene tomorrow. Stand down, Neville.'

Thirty minutes later, Haydn was back in her hotel room, seething. So much for payday.

CHAPTER ELEVEN

Having finished their supper, Gill Mercer and her family were settling down to watch a box set. Gill, of course, would be asleep in minutes, but her husband and two kids were used to that. It was the only real rest she ever got, because as soon as she'd climbed into bed, her mind kicked in, and she began to go over whatever case she was currently involved in.

This evening her sleep was delayed. A mere five minutes into the TV drama, her phone rang, prompting a collective groan.

'I'm sorry to disturb you, ma'am, I wouldn't normally call at this time, but we have some people here, and I think you should hear what they have to say. One of them is a retired policeman, none other than the hero, Richard Duckworth.'

Gill sat up. She knew that 'Dickie Ducky' lived in the area, but she'd never actually met him. Dickie's face had been all over the media some ten years back, after he received a medal for saving the lives of two children at considerable risk to his own safety.

Twenty minutes later, she was opening the door to an interview room, where she found Duckworth, along with two women. One of them was Claire Hereward, the employer of the hit and run victim.

Richard stood up, extended a hand and apologised for dragging her back into work. He introduced himself and the second woman, whose name was Lizzie Harper.

Ever the policeman, Richard immediately proceeded with their story. Gill listened with growing concern. She had had no idea why Joanne Andrews had been targeted, but had assumed it to be connected to her tragic past, though it still didn't make sense. Now, it seemed, it went far deeper. Not only that, she had three more potential victims, all seated opposite her in Interview Room Three.

She wished Claire had told her about this when she'd visited her that morning, but said nothing. She didn't have the heart. Claire Hereward was at the centre of a vicious crusade, which had already led to the death of an innocent woman, and she obviously had no idea why. Gill felt for her.

'It was very sensible of you to suggest sticking together, Mr Duckworth. I'll get uniform to keep an eye on your house overnight.'

'Please skip the Duckworth, ma'am, it's Richard. And if I might make a suggestion?'

'Of course.'

'Well, it's a big house, and as I explained to the ladies here, I had an up-to-date alarm system installed. In addition to that, I have a trusted friend who lives on the opposite side of the road facing me. If you have the manpower, he'd certainly let you use an upstairs room as an observation point. Anyway, it's worth a thought.'

'It's certainly better than a car with a couple of bored coppers in it. I'll take the details and get it organised.'

'Fantastic. I'll ring my friend and tell him to expect a couple of "old mates" later this evening.' Richard glanced at his companions. 'I think Claire and Lizzie here will feel a great deal better now they know we have the support of the law behind us.'

Gill smiled at Richard. His positive attitude and calm manner were going to make matters a whole lot easier to deal with.

She turned to Claire. 'I'm afraid we're going to have to go through your personal life in some detail. If this does originate with someone from your past, we'll have to discover who that person is, and fast. He, or she, is clearly very dangerous.'

An exhausted-looking Claire said she completely understood and would give them all the help she could.

'In that case, how would it be if I came to your place tomorrow, Richard? Maybe nine, or half past, if that's okay? Then I can have a proper talk with Claire. And, Claire, it will give you tonight to think about anyone — friend or relative — from your past who might bear a grudge against you for some reason.' She glanced down at the white envelope, now sealed in an evidence bag, lying on the table in front of her. 'There's a lot of hate there, even though it's so short. This is not something to be taken lightly, either by you, or us.' Gill looked back to Richard. 'You were right to bring Claire and Lizzie here, and most certainly right not to let them spend the night alone. One of you is already dead, and we cannot undo that, but we can prevent anything further happening. I am treating this as a very serious crime. This means that in the event of a further threat being made, I'll approach my superintendent with a view to having you all spirited away to a safe house. Though I can't promise that that will happen — our budget has shrunk to the size of a kid's pocket money. Still, if I rattle enough cages, we might be able to manage it.'

Having taken their details, Gill suggested they go straight to Richard's house, while she organised two officers for observation duty at the neighbour's.

Richard hung back for a moment after Claire and Lizzie had left the room.

'Please don't think I'm telling you your job, DI Mercer, but this reminds me of an old case of mine, and it's bothering me. Do you recall the Cardew investigation? If not, do check it out. It was a campaign of pure, unmitigated vengeance, very similar to this one. It took us far too long to unravel all the strands and find the killer.'

The name rang a bell. 'I'll check it out, Richard, thank you. And thank you for all your help.'

After they left, and when she had sorted out two men to watch Richard's house, Gill went into her office and looked up the Cardew investigation.

The similarities between the two cases were all too clear. There was no guaranteeing that this case would follow the same pattern, but it was worth getting her sergeant to read it in more depth.

It had been a harrowing case that had upset many of the officers working it, Richard Duckworth being one of them. A woman had been targeted over a period of six months, by means of odd happenings that made her doubt her sanity. People she cared about began to disappear, and at one point, she herself became the prime suspect. When her youngest child was found dead and she had no alibi, she was arrested. Only a chance sighting of her, captured on a CCTV camera, showed that she had been nowhere near the scene at the time of his death.

Too tired to read it all, Gill left a note for DS Ryan Compton to read the whole thing thoroughly as soon as he got in, and then report to her. She left it propped up against his screen and pulled on her coat. She had better get home and grab whatever rest she could, because it looked like it would be yet another early start tomorrow.

* * *

Cat and Ben had opted for a takeaway supper, and were now at home tucking into grilled peri-peri chicken wraps. Earlier in the day, they had spent a long time with Angela Sandford's best friend, Maggie Snow, and were now going over what they had learned.

'The boss reckoned she'd give us a different story to the doctor, but basically, they were pretty similar, weren't they?' Cat said.

'Apart from one glaring difference,' added Ben, wiping his mouth thoughtfully.

'Ah, the disparity between what Angie felt about the good doctor, and what he thought were her feelings for him.' Cat took an olive from the bowl and popped it in her mouth.

'Yeah. I dunno what to make of that, if anything,' said Ben. 'Maybe she gave him the wrong impression. She sounds like a very nice person, so I wouldn't think she led him on deliberately. Perhaps she didn't want to hurt his feelings. After all, Maggie did say they were good friends.'

'That's not the impression I got,' said Cat. 'Maggie told us that Angie suggested that walking holiday in the Lake District specifically to make their situation clear. You know, she enjoyed his companionship but wasn't up for any form of serious commitment. And from what Maggie said, I don't think it was ever on the cards that he would accompany her on her Bulgarian trip. I reckon that was wishful thinking on his part.'

'Maybe you're right.' Ben helped himself to another spicy potato wedge. 'Everything else he told us concurred with what Maggie said. Plus she told us the story of what had happened to her friend. Maybe the doctor didn't know about that.'

Cat nodded. 'Poor woman. No one should have to cope with a thing like that.' According to Maggie, Angie, who had been widowed in her early forties, had been out shopping in the local supermarket with her only son. While she was waiting at the fish counter, he had gone off to get dog food for his girlfriend's Labrador. Still in the queue, she had heard shouting and seen people running but didn't like to go and gawk. When her son failed to come back and find her, she started to get concerned, and made her way over to the source of the commotion. She found her son lying dead in the pet food aisle. The post-mortem revealed that he had suffered sudden arrhythmic death syndrome. There had been no warning signs, and he had seemed perfectly fit and healthy. The shock had devastated Angie, but she had managed to get through it by taking long-distance hikes — literally walking herself to recovery. She sold her house, moved to St Nicholas Court and got on with her life, although it was very different to the one she'd known before.

'That took guts,' Ben said, and sighed. 'I wish I could have handled things as well as her.'

Cat's heart went out to him. Ben, too, had lost his child. 'You didn't do badly. Everyone deals with grief differently, don't they? You coped in the way that suited you. There's no rule book for something like that.'

He straightened up. 'Anyway. Fancy a beer?'

'Why not?' she said, realising that Ben wasn't keen to dwell on the subject. 'It might help me think straighter. Who's your money on for the murderer?'

'The doc?' suggested Ben, fishing two bottles of beer from the fridge.

'Nah. Can't see it, can you?' Cat finished off the last potato wedge. 'According to the boss and the sarge, he was proper cut up over her death. Unless it's all an act. We've seen a few Oscar winners in our time, haven't we?'

'That we have,' said Ben, handing her a beer. 'I think we should speak to some more of her friends, don't you?'

'Yes, first thing tomorrow. And top of my list is that vicar.' Maggie had given them the names of a number of people Angie used to see, including the Reverend Judy Cornwell. People confided in their spiritual advisors, and although she was unlikely to reveal the secrets of the confessional, the Reverend Judy could help build up a picture of the victim and her life. And, since Angie was dead, the Reverend might be more forthcoming.

'And I'm well interested in talking to that other woman Maggie mentioned,' Ben said. 'You know, the grief counsellor, life coach, or whatever she was called. Claire someone?'

Cat thought for a minute. 'Oh, yes. Erm . . . Oh, I know. Claire Hereward. Angie consulted her after her son died. Maggie said she was still going to her for six-monthly catch-ups.' She drank some of her beer. 'Wasn't it this Claire woman who suggested walking as a kind of therapy? Yeah, she's definitely on our list.'

They finished their beers in companionable silence. Cat yawned. 'I'm bushed! I'll clear up here, and then let's turn in. What with this case, and Nikki and Joseph's TV celebrity, I get the feeling we'll be having a good few late nights in the weeks to come.'

* * *

Fortunately for Richard, both his guest bedrooms were already made up with fresh linen. His nephew and a work colleague had been coming to stay for a couple of nights while they attended a conference in Greenborough, which had been cancelled at the last minute. Now, Claire and Lizzie were upstairs unpacking their few things and getting ready for bed.

Richard sat in his conservatory, nursing a malt whisky and staring out into the dark. While he was setting his alarm system, he had spotted his neighbour opposite welcoming a couple of 'visitors' into his house. By now they should be settled in a front bedroom, their eyes trained on the road. Seeing them made him think of Claire Hereward, and what the hell was going on around her.

He slowly swirled the scotch around in its glass, and turned his mind to the Cardew investigation. It involved a woman called Theresa Cardew, who had been hounded by someone who wished her ill. Theresa herself had been pushed to the limits, and the police had been frustrated at every turn. Theresa, whom everyone described as an 'earth angel', was arrested, accused of killing her own child, a little boy of six. Fortunately for her, she was caught on camera some ten miles away. The evidence that had led to her arrest was found to have been tampered with, and her angelic status was restored. Not only was it restored, it was elevated, while public opinion turned against the police, who were accused of letting her down when they should have been protecting her. While Theresa achieved apparent sainthood, Richard and his team were back to square one, only this time they had the press clamouring for a result.

Richard closed his eyes, picturing Theresa as clearly as if she was standing before him — a small, slender woman of thirty-five, her hair in a dark brown bob, reaching to just above her shoulders. Not by any means beautiful, Theresa's deep, chestnut brown eyes were nevertheless striking. She had an open, kind face that Richard found very attractive. He had never believed her capable of killing anyone, let alone her own child, but the evidence all pointed in her direction, so they had no choice but to bring her in. When he was finally able to let her go, his relief was almost overwhelming. He upped his game, determined that she should receive justice. He went days without sleep and a proper meal. It had become personal.

Richard sipped his drink. Looking back on it now, that case had been the worst of his long, distinguished career. He didn't relish becoming involved with a similar crime. He compared the two: Theresa had been a special needs teacher who had also been a volunteer at the local Samaritans. Her aim in life was to make use of her particular skills to help people who were in trouble. Similarly, Claire helped troubled souls to come to terms with a bereavement and used her skill as a counsellor to guide them towards achieving some peace of mind. Both were discredited — by email, phone calls, and word of mouth, to the point where they doubted their own professional abilities. Both received a death threat. Three of Theresa's close friends had disappeared, two of them were subsequently found murdered, and one was never found at all. To date, Claire had lost two clients and had been blamed for their deaths. Theresa's own child had been murdered, while in Claire's case, Joanne, a young woman she cared for deeply, had been brutally run down and killed. Finally, both women had had things going missing or rearranged in their respective homes, causing them to doubt their own sanity. Theresa's nightmare dragged on for over a year, leading her to consider taking her own life. Then, just as matters reached crisis point, Richard and his team finally discovered the killer and apprehended him.

He recalled that first interview with a shudder. Those eyes, returning his gaze with not a glimmer of remorse. That's what made it all so much worse; the killer had been so 'reasonable'. Calmly, one leg crossed over the other, he had described just what he'd done to his victims, as nonchalantly as someone explaining how to bake an apple crumble, or fix a frozen pipe.

It wasn't the same person; he was securely locked up with no chance of remission. But there must be something the police could learn from it regarding Claire.

Time and time again their killer had been brought to their attention. Time and time again, he had been dismissed. It couldn't possibly be one of Theresa's close friends, they thought, all of whom had expressed their outrage at what was being done to her. But there he was, hidden in plain sight, always available, always willing to answer their questions.

Richard drained his glass. On the face of it, the case had been a success. He'd caught the killer, and brought him to justice, but he always regarded it as his greatest failure.

He stood up, suddenly terribly tired. He wasn't a serving officer anymore, but he was already deeply involved in this case, and he vowed that Claire would not have to live through the nightmare that Theresa Cardew had had to endure.

CHAPTER TWELVE

The following morning, Greenborough's police force hit the ground running. In the L-shaped CID room, DI Gill Mercer's team were gathered at one end, waiting for their daily orders. Gill herself was briefing the superintendent. At the other end, the low voices of Nikki's team could be heard discussing the cases, while they waited for Nikki and Joseph to furnish them with an action plan.

The cacophony of whirring printers and ringing phones, the buzz of voices filtered through to Nikki in her office, but she barely heard it. She was rereading Rory's report on the drugs used to kill Angela Sandford. Dr Bill French had been right when he said that they were nothing he'd ever prescribed. If it had been a suicide, how would a rather classy lady in an upmarket retirement village have obtained such dangerous illegal drugs? It was another factor confirming that this was a murder.

'Rory says they were synthetic,' said Nikki. 'Fentanyl, mixed with cocaine. He reckons it to be fifty to a hundred times more potent than morphine. Apparently, in an overdose the drug sends signals to the brain's respiratory centre to slow down breathing or stop it completely. The brain is deprived of oxygen, and the person goes into a coma or dies. Death can be very quick, apparently.'

'Fine, if you're already off your head,' muttered Joseph, 'but that poor woman was being forced to swallow those tablets, and she'd have known just what was happening to her. Heartless bastard!'

Nikki stood up, report in hand. 'Let's get this to Cat and Ben. They need to look very carefully at that poor woman's life story. What the hell did she do to warrant such a cruel revenge?'

Joseph shrugged. 'Probably nothing. Most likely she simply fell foul of a psycho.'

They went out into the CID room.

'Okay, guys! Listen up,' called out Nikki. 'We'll address the Sandford case first.'

They gathered around their whiteboard. Nikki recapped what they already knew, and added the conclusions of the forensic tests. Cat then stood up and reported on their interview with Angela Sandford's friend, Maggie Snow. She was running through the list of the people they wanted to speak to next when a voice rang out behind them.

'Sorry to interrupt.'

DI Gill Mercer was staring incredulously at Cat. 'Did I hear you say Claire Hereward?'

'Er, yes,' said Cat, looking puzzled. 'The counsellor. Apparently, our murdered woman had been seeing her following the sudden death of her son. She's one of the people we most want to talk to, as she can probably give us a great deal of information on her history.'

Gill shook her head. 'Would you believe it!' She sank down onto a vacant chair. 'Our two cases are connected, and in a significant way. Joanne Andrews, our hit and run victim, was employed by Claire Hereward, who is the target of a hate campaign.'

'Bloody hell!' exclaimed Ben. 'What on earth is going on here?'

'Gill, can we have a quick word in my office? We need to agree on how to proceed in light of this development.' Nikki turned to Joseph. 'Would you bring the others up to date on where we are with the Connaught case? I won't be long.'

Shaking her head, Nikki showed Gill to a chair. 'This job never ceases to amaze me.'

'You can say that again,' muttered Gill.

'First off, if you are agreeable, I'll get Cat Cullen and Ben Radley to give your team everything we have on the Sandford killing. It's not straightforward. For one thing, it might have been ruled a suicide if it hadn't been for her GP, who was also a close friend, plus the suspicions of two of our uniformed officers.'

'That in itself is worrying,' said Gill. 'It seems that one of Claire Hereward's former clients apparently committed suicide. Given what you've just told me, I shall have to get that verdict re-examined.'

Nikki grimaced. 'Oh dear.'

'Oh dear indeed,' said Gill, and then grinned at her. 'But get this! As we speak Claire Hereward, along with another potential victim, is holed up in the home of — you'll never guess who — none other than retired DS Richard Duckworth!'

'I don't believe it! Dickie Duckie? How on earth did he get involved?'

'Briefly, we now have an inkling as to why Joanne was killed, although it's not cut and dried yet,' Gill said. 'She started to get suspicious about what was going on with her boss. Richard, who had been seeing Claire following the death of his son, had written to her expressing his thanks for what she had done for him. Joanne decided to go and speak to him about her fears for Claire's safety and was killed the very same day.'

Nikki puffed out her cheeks. 'Blimey! Bit of a drastic way to ruin a business.'

'It goes far deeper than that, Nikki. Richard has told me about an old case of his that is an almost exact replica of this.

I'm going to get my sergeant to take a look back at it, and hopefully it will give us a better idea of what might be going on with Ms Hereward.'

'How about if you take Cat and Ben for today,' Nikki said after a moment's thought. 'They can get everything together for you. Angela Sandford's death is quite clearly related to your investigation in some way. I would have suggested combining the two investigations, but with us about to be swamped by a media tsunami over the death of our celebrity, all our resources are going to be concentrated on getting that one out of the way as soon as possible.'

'I quite understand,' said Gill, getting to her feet.

'But anything you need regarding Sandford, just ask. Joseph and I attended the crime scene and were both bothered by it. We can give you our first-hand impressions if you need them, plus we had a long interview with the GP, so don't hesitate to use us.'

'I appreciate that, Nikki,' Gill said. 'Now I'd better go and break this news to my flock. The dear little lambs won't have expected this one!'

* * *

After her conversation with Lionel the previous day, Eve awoke feeling much more positive. She had come to the realisation that only by seeing him in person could she get things into perspective.

Thus invigorated, she rose early, made two mugs of tea, and took them to Wendy's bedroom, where she sat on the end of the bed.

Wendy hauled herself up onto her pillows and blinked. 'Well, I must say, you look considerably more like the Eve I know and love.'

Eve smiled a little sheepishly. 'Sorry, old thing. I had a wobble there for a while, but I'm back on track this morning.'

'Glad to hear it. I'm not used to seeing you so down. It was a bit of a shock.' Wendy smiled at her. 'But totally understandable. I keep thinking about how . . . how *vibrant* Justin was.'

Eve nodded slowly. 'All that life — stolen. Which leads me to what you said last night. I've been thinking about it, and I've changed my mind about not getting involved. That would be denying Justin the benefit of our considerable experience, and we can't do that, can we? He asked for our help, and I think we should give it to him.'

Wendy beamed at her. 'Thank heavens for that! You really are back to normal. And I'm sure Lionel will want us on board.'

'Of course he will,' said Eve. 'He knows our record. Plus we have the advantage of knowing the family while being sufficiently detached to see things clearly. Once the shock wears off, we'll be as sharp as ever.'

Wendy raised her mug. 'For Justin.'

'For Justin,' echoed Eve. 'And for justice.'

* * *

Nikki explained to her team what she and Gill had decided regarding the Sandford case. She then reported the new development to Cam.

'Ah, Nikki,' he said as soon as he saw her. 'I was just about to give you a call. I'm afraid the press has got hold of the news of Justin Connaught's death. Until now they've been dining out on that poor kid in the hit and run, but the tide has turned and they're heading our way in waves. I'm giving a statement at midday — don't worry I'll be leaving you out of it this time.' He grinned. 'And not because of your aversion to press briefings. I just think it's prudent, given your tenuous connection to Justin and his family.'

'Well, I can't say I'm sorry to hear that. You know me and the press.'

'Only too well! Anyway, I'm going to give one of my famous speeches — you know the ones, where I talk a lot but actually say nothing. The word "murder" will not pass my lips.' He grimaced. 'Although it's going to be patently obvious in no time at all. I'm sorry, Nikki, but this is going to be a big one, which makes your job very difficult. I'll do all I can, but you can see where this is going, can't you?'

'I certainly can,' she said grimly. 'But at least I'll be back up to a full complement. Now, I have a piece of news for you.'

Nikki explained about the two cases having dovetailed. 'Cat and Ben are with Gill's team now, but as soon as they've transmitted what we have to date, we can go full throttle into Justin's murder.'

Cam smiled. 'Music to my ears. Now I can tell the press that Justin's death will be receiving the full attention of one of the most experienced teams in the county — and mean it!'

'In which case, we'd better get ourselves over to Jacobs Mere and try to save Lionel and Heather from a pack of hungry newshounds.' She grimaced. 'Although frankly I'd happily feed Heather to them and let them do their worst. I cannot take to that woman. I liked the father a lot, but the sister, well . . .'

'Oh dear.' Cam threw her a warning look. 'Promise me you won't . . . The old Nikki Galena isn't going to show her face again, is she? You do have previous for taking no prisoners where people you don't like are concerned.'

Nikki smiled sweetly. '*Moi?* Cam! How can you think such a thing?'

'And Nikki. Before you go . . . about you and Joseph. I'm going to ask you to do nothing for a while. Kaye and I had a long talk last night, and there might be a way forward, but I need to know more before I share it with you. Just hang on, okay? And try not to worry.'

Nikki thought about the letter in her desk drawer. She had replied, asking for time to consider, but that top job wouldn't remain open for ever. She studied Cam's expression, and saw something like hope in it. 'Okay, we'll go along with you, Cam, but we're both pretty anxious not to let this ride much longer.'

'Don't worry. It's just a matter of making sure we're on the right track. We won't keep you on tenterhooks any longer than absolutely necessary, I promise.'

Nikki left the super's office with a head full of questions. Right now, however, she needed to be at Jacobs Mere. She could tell Joseph what Cam had so mysteriously said on the way.

* * *

'You have a lovely house, Richard,' said Claire. 'You have no idea how grateful I am for what you are doing. It's a major upheaval having two strangers move into your home.'

They were having a late breakfast, still trying to get their heads around what had happened.

'If it weren't for the present situation, I'd say it's a pleasure. It's rather nice not to be wandering around this old house alone,' Richard admitted. 'It was a happy, lively place when the family were all here. It was my grandparents' home originally, and I often came here as a boy. My parents lived just outside Nottingham, and even after my brother and sister moved away, we always came back here for a family Christmas, and then again in the summer holidays.' He looked around, as if he were hearing the laughter of children. 'Oh yes, those were good times.'

'So, how come you're living here now, Richard?' asked Lizzie.

'Well, it's a bit of a melodrama.' He gave her a rueful grin. 'It so happens I'm last in the line, even though I'm only sixty-five. I inherited the house around four years ago, and as I'd had enough of Nottingham, here I am.'

'You're the last? You mean the rest of your family . . .' Claire looked shocked. 'You never told me that in our sessions!'

'It didn't seem relevant,' Richard said. 'I only needed help to come to terms with my son's death — and you did that very well, dear lady.' Richard pointed through the French windows

113

to the garden. 'With the added bonus that my garden has never looked so good.'

'Even so,' said Claire. 'I should have been aware of such a serious loss.'

'Honestly, there was no need. After all, losing your parents happens to most people at some point. You don't need counselling to deal with it. My brother Adrian was born with a serious heart defect, it was a miracle that he lived to almost forty. We wanted to celebrated his life, not mourn his death. My sister, Bethany, well, again it was an illness. She never married, she was one of those fiercely independent, outdoorsy women determined that nothing in life will get the better of them. Unfortunately a virus, caught while travelling abroad, proved her wrong. From an Amazon she became a pitiful shell. Frankly, her death was a blessed relief to both of us. Neither Adrian nor Beth had children, and you know what happened to my boy . . . so here I am, the sole survivor.' He cleared his throat. 'More toast anyone?'

Back from the kitchen with another round of toast, Richard said, 'Don't worry, we won't be living on toast. I've ordered a delivery from the supermarket.'

'Well, I hope you'll let us pay for it,' Claire said. 'I feel bad, imposing on your kindness like this. Apart from not being fair on you, it's as if we're giving the upper hand to whoever is orchestrating this horrible campaign. And we can't remain in hiding forever.'

Richard placed a second mug of tea in front of her. 'Think of it as a strategic move. We've prevented them taking any further steps — I mean, who knows what might have happened last night if we hadn't joined forces? The DI will be here shortly to talk to you, so let's see what she has to say and we'll take it from there, okay?'

'Have you had any thoughts about who might be behind this?' Lizzie asked.

Claire shook her head. 'I've lain awake most of the night asking myself that very question, and I still haven't a clue. I can't think of a single thing I might have done that might have caused someone to hate me so much. My God! Joanne is dead because of me, and I haven't the faintest idea why!'

'She's not dead because of you, Claire,' said Richard firmly. 'She's dead because someone is unhinged or evil enough to commit murder.' He sat down. 'When the DI gets here, make sure to tell her everything you can remember about your past relationships; your friends, family, and anyone else of significance. Can you recall anything odd, unusual, or worrying that happened to you or the people around you? Any arguments? Fallings out between you and someone close to you? If it's nothing in your past, well, then we'll have to look to your career, and the people you've dealt with in your professional life.' He still didn't believe it had anything to do with her clients, but he couldn't rule it out. Deep down, he had a feeling that Claire was holding something back, but whether it was intentional, or something she had genuinely forgotten, he couldn't say.

The doorbell rang, making them all jump.

'Phew! We are edgy.' Richard attempted a laugh. 'I expect that'll be our DI.' He checked the security monitor. 'Yes, it's her. Now don't be anxious, Claire. DI Mercer wants to help. It'll mean a lot of personal questions, but she's on your side.'

He opened the door to Gill Mercer, hoping she would feel as he did, that it was something in Claire's past that that had fuelled this deadly campaign of vengeance.

CHAPTER THIRTEEN

En route to Jacobs Mere, a call from Rory Wilkinson prevented Nikki from telling Joseph what Cam had said. She put the phone on loudspeaker.

'I've been slaving my fingers to the bone for you, dear heart, but I now have something more than a mere hypothesis to offer. Justin was killed by someone using a Browning L9A1 Hi-Power pistol. The lovely Joseph will tell you that these were used by all three of the armed services until they were replaced with the 9mm calibre Glock17 Gen 4.'

Nikki frowned. An ex-military handgun would be easy to obtain if you knew where to look and who to ask. Unless, of course, the shooter was a former member of the armed forces.

'He was shot from a distance of four metres, and the trajectory of the bullet as it entered the body shows that the person firing the weapon was standing in the doorway.' There was a rustle of paper; Rory was reading from his notes. 'On examination, we confirmed my exceedingly accurate prediction that the bullet struck the right axillary artery. Our friend Justin then went into haemorrhagic shock and died soon thereafter. What we do not know, and unless you catch the killer and ask him, might forever remain a mystery, is why Justin had his arm raised in the air.'

Nikki couldn't begin to think why that should be. 'And it's still your belief that it was not a professional hit, Rory?'

'Absolutely. I think whoever used that gun just pointed it at Justin and pulled the trigger. He, or she, didn't seem to be aiming at a specific target, meaning the head or the heart. They were firing at random. Oh, and you'll be ecstatic to know that my dear Spike heartily endorses my assessment of what took place. As you will recall, he has made ballistics his speciality and is fast becoming the go-to person where shootings are concerned. He went out to Jacobs Mere last night and confirmed my findings, as well as assisting in the post-mortem — he examined the wound itself with particular care.' Rory sighed. 'I'm afraid we have something of a job on our hands given the fact that this took place just after an obviously rather jolly party. We are contacting everyone who was quaffing copious quantities of Bollinger that night, and taking their fingerprints and a DNA sample. We need to eliminate all the bona fide guests, leaving only those traces left by our killer. Such fun!'

'Mmm, and your guests were a police sergeant, his wife and two retired MOD operatives, so good luck with that,' said Nikki. 'And thank you for confirming which make of gun was used. Now we know what we are looking for.'

'Indeed you do. Oh, and finally, we can confirm that Justin let his killer in. There was no sign of a forced entry, none of the locks had been tampered with, and it was Justin's prints on the inside of the front door, along with those of the cleaning lady. Nothing was found on the back door either, so they must have been careful in closing the door when they left.'

Nikki thanked him and ended the call, left to puzzle over who Justin could have let in that night, and why someone apparently unaccustomed to using a gun had shot and killed him.

'Okay, Joseph, you're the one with most experience of firearms, what kind of person might have fired that fatal shot?'

Joseph sucked in air through his teeth. 'Certainly no one who'd ever served in the military, despite it being a service pistol. Maybe someone who'd never used a gun on another human being before? Maybe it was just intended to be a threat, but they accidentally pulled the trigger. Or someone who was frightened.' He shook his head. 'Sorry, Nikki, too many maybes.'

'Okay, so let's try another tack. Why did Justin have his arm raised?'

'Simple. Surrender. That would also explain the shotgun. You know, "Put that gun down and raise your arms."'

Somehow that didn't seem right. Nikki frowned in concentration. 'What? In a dining room just after a party? When you've already let this person in, and it's most likely someone you know? No, Joseph, that doesn't make sense.'

'Well, none of it makes sense, does it?' said Joseph. 'A well-loved and popular young man, new to the area, who, apart from a touch of sibling rivalry, doesn't have an enemy in the world, is shot dead in his new home. What's anyone to make of that?'

'And it was certainly not a bungled robbery as nothing was taken. His father confirmed that.' Nikki heaved a long sigh. 'If only he'd had those security cameras fitted a few days earlier.'

They drove on in silence for a while, then Nikki said, 'Before Rory rang, I was just about to tell you what Cam said to me when I went up to see him.' She told him of Cam's request that they wait for a while before taking a decision.

'Bit cryptic, isn't it?' said Joseph. 'I mean, as far as I can see, there are only two choices: we stay as we are, until something happens and our situation comes to light, or one of us leaves the team.'

'You're right,' said Nikki. 'But you didn't see Cam's face as he was telling me. He and Kaye have clearly hit on a third option, but he refused to say what it was. I agreed that we'd give him a bit longer, but he knows we can't keep putting it off; we've reached crunch time.' Gently, she squeezed his leg. 'Come on, my love, we've battled on this far, it won't hurt us to wait a few more days. And we do have a murder to solve.

118

Who knows, it could be our last case together, so let's make it a good one.'

After a few moments' silence, Joseph gave a resigned sigh. 'All right. We'll give him as long as he needs. And if we don't crack on and find Justin's killer, either your mother will never speak to us again, or, worse, she and Wendy will take up the case!'

'Oh Lord! Heaven forbid! Can't you drive any faster, Joseph?'

* * *

Joseph had always been fascinated by instances of sibling rivalry, wondering how it was that two people brought up in exactly the same way could turn out to be such polar opposites. He just wished he could have met Justin rather than the sister. He had watched several episodes of the television show, and thought the archaeologist came over as a genuinely nice man. He obviously was in real life, too, as everyone who had met him, including Tamsin, and Nikki's mum, had said how much they liked him.

Now he was watching Heather throw a quite spectacular tantrum and wondering if it was worthwhile reasoning with her, or whether to just give her good slap. Glancing at Nikki, he was pretty sure which option she would choose. So, to head off any carnage, he waded in and took up the mantle of peacemaker once again.

'Mrs Blake, I'm so very sorry, but I'm afraid that given your brother's celebrity status, his death was bound to come to the attention of the media. Believe me, we've done our best to hold off the onslaught as long as possible, but it was inevitable that they would turn up at some point. There will be an official statement issued today, after which, hopefully, we can field most of their questions. And please be assured that as things stand, the public knows only that we are dealing with a sudden death.'

119

Joseph kept his voice low, his tone reasonable. Jesus, this woman was childish.

'These ghouls need to learn to respect people's privacy! We are trying to mourn the tragic death of my dear brother here, while that pack of wolves is baying at our door! It's intolerable! I won't stand for it!' Heather all but stamped her foot.

It took a good ten minutes and most of Joseph's patience, but he finally won her over. Somewhat mollified, she retreated to the kitchen.

'Don't say a word,' he whispered to Nikki. 'I'm having exactly the same thoughts as you.'

'I very much doubt that's possible,' growled Nikki. 'My thoughts are positively murderous. Did you hear that bit about "our" door? This is no more her bloody door than it is mine!'

'Not the most pleasant of women, to put it mildly,' said Joseph. 'And where on earth is Lionel when we need him?'

'One of the uniforms said he'd gone down to Tamsin's cottage to collect Bernie. He went not long before the press arrived.' Nikki grinned. 'Leaving our gobby Madame Diva to fend them off on her own until we arrived.'

'Nice timing on his part. Now, how about we do our best to send the media packing? If they know there's to be a statement at the station in a couple of hours' time, they might decamp for a while.'

'It's worth a try. Okay, come on, Joseph, let's issue a statement of our own. We'll ask them to respect the family's privacy at this sad time. Then we'll see how far our guys have got with the evidence collecting. Oh, and would you ring Tamsin and ask her to send Lionel back? I think he's hidden from the newshounds long enough, and we need to talk to him.'

Joseph made the call. 'He's on his way. And Tamsin is keeping Bernie until we have finished at Jacobs Mere House.' He chuckled. 'She's worried that this place will awaken too many traumatic memories in the poor fellow, and as she's still got a few days off work, Bernie is to stay with Skipper.'

He grinned. 'I rather think Lionel had little say in the matter. You know what Tam is like when she gets the bit between her teeth over an animal.'

'Good for her, although I can't help worrying about what will happen to Bernie in the long run.'

'He's in the best place for now,' Joseph said, 'and if he has my girl fighting his corner, he'll be all right. Now, let's go and fend off the press.'

Half an hour later things had quietened down considerably, and only a token few die-hards remained camped outside the house. Lionel had returned, but Heather hadn't shown her face, much to Nikki and Joseph's relief. Now they were back in the drawing room nursing much-needed cups of tea.

'The SOCOs are all but finished in the dining room, Lionel,' said Nikki. 'DNA samples and fingerprints have already been collected from the dinner guests, so now forensics will embark on the painstaking task of eliminating them before, so hopefully, only those of the killer remain.'

'Tamsin told me that she went to the station early this morning to get her prints taken and a DNA swab done,' Lionel said. 'You have a lovely daughter, Sergeant Easter, and I'm so grateful for her kindness to Bernie.'

Joseph felt quite flushed with pride. 'She's a good kid, and where animals are concerned — well, you've seen that for yourself.'

'Lionel,' Nikki said, 'have you had any thoughts about whether you'll be staying on at the house? I'm asking because I'm afraid that until we get a lot more answers and the forensic evidence comes back, it will remain a crime scene for a while. You can stay here if you wish, as only the dining room is really of interest to us, and it'll have to remain sealed until further notice, but there'll still be quite a bit of coming and going, including having officers stationed at the gate checking everyone arriving or leaving.' Nikki smiled sadly at the man, who sat staring into his mug. 'I'm so sorry, Lionel, it's the last thing you need at a time like this. We don't want to get in your way, but we need to find out what happened, so our presence here is essential.'

Lionel looked up, shifted in his seat. 'I fully understand. It's just that it's all happened so suddenly I haven't been able to think about tomorrow, let alone the future of Jacobs Mere House. Right now, I need to make all the necessary arrangements — you know, notifying the relevant people of Justin's death and all that. I do realise that holding a funeral is out of the question for the time being, so at least I don't have to think about that yet. I think . . . I think I should move in here for a while. I live four hours' drive away, and I don't want to distance myself from my son — or you. I can be of help, I know I can. Justin and I spent a great deal of time together working on this house, so I met a lot of his friends and acquaintances. I think you need me on hand.'

'I'm happy to hear that, Lionel,' said Nikki, meaning it. 'We'll be most glad of your help.'

Joseph nodded. He liked Lionel and believed that as soon as the initial shock had worn off, his years of experience in the security service could be a major asset.

Suddenly galvanised, Lionel half rose from his seat. 'Eve and Wendy are coming here this afternoon, and as soon as they've gone, I'll head off home and sort out my affairs. Thank heavens I have a damn good team of staff working for me. I'll make sure my sister is okay and has everything she needs, gather up some clothes and then I'll be back for the duration.'

Joseph noticed Nikki start slightly at the mention of her mother, though she made no comment. Instead, she asked, 'And what about Heather?'

Lionel frowned. 'Mmm, we have a bit of a problem there. She insists she isn't up to driving back to Grantham and wants to stay on. I think the idea is that her husband and the children come down to join her.'

'I'm terribly sorry, sir,' Joseph said at once, 'but we couldn't possibly allow that. We can't have children in the house, certainly not at this stage in the investigation. We'd be happy to provide a police driver to take Mrs Blake back to Grantham. It's not that far, and it'll be no bother at all.'

Lionel accepted the offer gratefully. 'I did tell her that would be the case, but she seems pretty determined. Perhaps you'd be kind enough to tell her yourself, Sergeant Easter? It might sound better coming from you.'

'With pleasure, sir. As soon as we're through here, I'll have a quiet word with her.'

'Perhaps you could find time before you go to give us a few names,' Nikki said. 'You know, people who were close to your son. We must try and get a picture of what was going on in Justin's life in the days and months leading up to his death. It will give us something to be going on with until you return.'

'Of course. I'll go through the contacts on his laptop and get you as many names as I can.'

'I'm sorry, Lionel,' Nikki said. 'We've had to take his laptop for forensic examination. We'll get it back to you as soon as our tech guys are through with it.'

'Of course. I should have known,' murmured Lionel. 'My brain's still not functioning properly.'

'Just the names and their relation to Justin is fine,' Nikki said. 'We can find the details ourselves.'

'I'll make sure to do it before Eve arrives,' Lionel said.

'You can email it to me, you've got my card, haven't you?' said Nikki, and put down her mug. 'Now, we'd better go and see how far our people have got and organise the security arrangements. This is a big property. By the way, does it have a back entrance?'

'There is one, but it's kept chained up and padlocked. It's actually an electric gate, but since it's never used, it seemed safer to leave it that way. Justin was going to use it when he was filming the place for his TV series. He thought it would attract less attention than bringing his crew and equipment in and out through the front.' Lionel sighed. 'I guess there's no need to worry about that now.'

How sad, thought Joseph. And not just for Lionel. Countless children had enjoyed *Digging History*, and who knew how many of them had been inspired to take up archaeology as a career. A large part had been down to the personality of Justin and his evident enthusiasm for the field. One of the former participants had already been snapped up by an ad agency, and his shock of ginger hair and cheeky smile was often seen on TV.

Thinking of children reminded him of Heather, and her intention to bring her family to Jacobs Mere. 'I must go and talk to your daughter, sir. We can't have her family turning up just to be sent home again.'

'Indeed,' said Lionel. 'I did tell her. I even offered to drive her home myself, and get a taxi back, but she wouldn't hear of it. If you could explain the position, I'd be most grateful. I'm sure it will sound better coming from you. Heather can be rather headstrong, and her father's opinion doesn't always count for much. I must say, Sergeant, you are very lucky to have such an amenable daughter.'

If you only knew, thought Joseph, recalling the years he had spent in combat with Tamsin. Despite all the heartache, he had never given up trying, and now they could not have been closer. Somehow he doubted that Lionel and Heather would forge a similar rapprochement.

Joseph headed for the kitchen in search of Heather. He found her on the phone.

'. . . and I think the green bedroom for Jack, and probably the one with the lovely window seat for Hayley, it will be perfect for her collection of teddy bears.'

Hell, he thought, *she's not moving them in already, is she?* He knocked loudly and walked in. 'Sorry to interrupt, Mrs Blake, but I need a word.'

Heather turned and glared at him. 'I'll ring you back,' she said into the phone. 'Yes, Sergeant Easter, what is it?'

'We have been discussing with your father what's to happen about the house. He says you are too upset to drive yourself home, so we are arranging for a police driver to take you.' He smiled at her. 'Unfortunately, it will remain a crime scene for quite some time while we continue with our investigations, so we're going to have to ask you to leave fairly soon.'

If looks could kill, Joseph would have been flat out on the floor. 'I'm sorry,' she said, 'but that won't be possible. My family are preparing to come and stay with me for a while, to support me through this terrible time. I really don't see how their presence here will affect anything. You said yourself, Sergeant, that you were almost finished, and this is a big house.'

And one you can't wait to get your hands on, thought Joseph. *Bitch.* 'I'm sorry, Mrs Blake, but we have to follow very strict procedures in these cases, and I think we've been more than accommodating. I would be grateful if you would inform your husband immediately that he won't be coming and that you'll be home later today. Your father will let you know when we have released the house to him. In the meantime, I suggest you get your belongings together and I'll organise a car for you.'

Somehow, throughout the furious onslaught that followed, Joseph managed to keep his cool. He even managed a smile. When she threatened to report him to his superiors, he merely responded that it was those very same senior officers — they never called them superiors, by the way — who had instructed them to keep the house closed.

Evidently determined to have the last word, Heather said, 'All right, I'll drive myself. I don't need any escort of yours. And if I'm involved in an accident, you'll bear the responsibility.'

Telling her the offer still stood, Joseph retreated from the kitchen.

He found Nikki with the uniformed officer in charge of the site. 'How'd it go?'

'Don't ask,' he said, rolling his eyes. 'Do you know, when I walked in, she was actually in the middle of allocating rooms for her kids. And not for a day or two either, unless her daughter always carries a bagful of teddy bears with her everywhere she goes.'

'Don't tell me you were surprised, Joseph. That woman is one of the most obnoxious people I've ever had the misfortune to meet — outside of the custody suite, that is.' They smiled at each other. 'I wouldn't want to be in Lionel's shoes when the time comes to make a decision about the house.'

'Doesn't bear thinking about, poor sod. Though I'm beginning to get the impression that Daddy's beginning to see that Heather isn't quite the "Little Princess" he thought she was.'

Nikki agreed. 'You can only make so many excuses for someone's bad behaviour. I just hope he remembers his son's wishes about the house he loved so much. Grieving indeed. What crap! That woman doesn't have the first idea about grief.'

Nikki sounded bitter. Joseph thought she had every right to be. Nikki knew all about grief, and was perfectly justified in pointing out the absence of it in Heather Blake. He changed the subject. 'Do you want to hang on here until Eve and Wendy arrive?'

'Oh no, I'd just be in the way. I've an idea this meeting will be rather difficult for Eve. It'll certainly be an emotional one. We'll head off as soon as we can, Eve will tell us about it when she's ready.'

Joseph was mildly surprised that Nikki seemed not to have seen that this visit was about more than expressing their condolences. He knew Eve and Wendy of old, and it just wasn't in them to let a mystery like this go unaddressed. But Nikki appeared convinced, so maybe he was wrong. Maybe.

CHAPTER FOURTEEN

Back in her hotel room, Haydn paced from wall to wall. Their mark had disappeared, probably only a short time before their planned hit. Now they had to find her, or their client would not only go apeshit, they wouldn't get paid either. She stood to lose a whole lot of money over this, apart from the damage it would do to her reputation. Not once, in all her years with the organisation, had she failed to carry out a job to its conclusion. Apart from being a source of pride, it meant more money, and she liked that a lot.

Back and forth she went, like an animal in a cage. She was under no illusions about the people she worked for. One cock-up, and she'd be history. Plus, she was beginning to hear whispers about a new set of operatives that the organisation had been grooming. If they were anything like the rumour suggested, anyone from the old guard who didn't have a flawless success rate could kiss their lucrative career goodbye.

They had to find where the mark had gone to ground and finish the job as fast as possible. Neville could no more afford to lose his cut than she could, so he'd agree to anything she said. She rang him on his burner. 'Okay, here's what I reckon has happened, and how we should proceed. Make a note of the address I'm about to give you and meet me there in twenty minutes.'

* * *

Like Richard, Gill Mercer had the feeling that Claire Hereward was holding something back. It just didn't seem right that this attractive, smart and caring person should have so few real friends. She had reeled off a list of people she knew — acquaintances, colleagues and some of her clients — but she seemed not to have a personal life. Gill tried to dig deeper.

'Have you ever been married, Claire? Or had a serious relationship that didn't end well?'

Claire looked uncomfortable. 'I've never married, but I did have one long-term relationship, and yes, we did part in the end, but it was never acrimonious. We just realised that we didn't want the same things. Danny thought I was taking on too much — you know, becoming too wrapped up in other people's problems. He was fairly demanding. Anyway, we had a happy few years, but eventually we decided to go our own ways rather than finish up fighting each other.'

'And where is Danny now? Is he local?' Gill made a note of the name.

'No, he moved to Newark after we split up. His job had an opening there, so he decided to make a completely fresh start.'

'Do you ever hear from him?' asked Gill.

'Only a birthday and a Christmas card. Our relationship didn't end on a sour note, Detective Inspector, but we've both moved on since then.'

Gill wondered about that. There was a chance that even if Claire had moved on, Danny possibly hadn't. So she asked Claire for his full name and contact details. 'Any other relationships? Not necessarily long-term ones, but were there any that left you feeling upset, or anxious in any way?'

It was only the slightest hesitation, but Gill picked it up. 'Look, I know this is unpleasant, Claire, and frankly I'd hate to have to reveal stuff like this to a stranger, but Joanne is dead, and your friends here could well be prime targets for whoever killed her. If there is anyone who you think might wish you harm, you must tell us.'

Again, that slight pause. 'I've had a few boyfriends, of course, but they've all been very casual, nothing serious, and since I started my consultancy, I haven't had the time or the inclination for romance. There is no one in my life now, Detective Inspector, and there hasn't been for some time.'

She didn't answer my question. She's lying, I know she is. But why?

Gill badly wished her sergeant, Ryan Compton, had been with her. They had decided that she should go alone, dressed casually. Two possibly rather obvious detectives could well draw attention to Richard's house, whereas no one would remark on a single woman caller turning up on the doorstep.

She decided to change course. 'I believe Angela Sandford was one of your clients. Is that right?'

Claire looked puzzled. 'Angie? Yes, she still is, although nowadays she only comes to me for a six-monthly review. She's done so well, and she's an amazingly strong woman. I have great admiration for her.'

Gill drew in a breath. 'I'm very sorry to tell you this, Claire, but a few nights ago, Angela was found dead in her home.'

Claire's hand flew to her mouth. 'Oh God! Please don't tell me it had anything to do with me! Not again.'

'It's too early to say. It's a suspicious death, but you do have a connection, so we'll have to bear that in mind during our investigations.'

Claire swallowed. 'How did she die?'

'It appeared to be an overdose, and if it hadn't been for the fact that her GP was on call to confirm the death and noticed some anomalies, it might well have been put down to suicide.'

'Her GP? Would that be Bill French?' asked Claire shakily.

'That's right.'

Claire sighed. 'Oh dear. That poor man. He was very fond of Angie, I believe. She told me about him during our last review.'

Gill regarded Claire intently. 'I'm so sorry to have to bring you this news, but can you now see why we are so anxious to delve into your past and find whoever is masterminding this campaign against you? We recognise that it's difficult for you, and we have no wish to cause you further distress, but we must find this person before anyone else dies, and that includes you.' Poor Claire, thought Gill. The woman who had been such an inspirational life coach now looked totally defeated. 'I'm going to have to ask you for the keys to your consulting room, and access to all your records, including your clients' names and addresses. I am aware of the issue of confidentiality, but we must have those names in order to interview them and, most of all, so we can be certain of their safety.' Gill waited. 'I can get a warrant, but speed is of the essence here, so . . . ?'

With an effort, Claire gathered herself. She said flatly, 'I'll give you the keys and my password for the office computer. All the contact details are on that, although not their personal histories. I can't give you those without their consent, but if you have their names and addresses, I assume that's what you want?'

'That's fine. If we need to find out more, we'll speak to them directly.' Gill prepared to leave. 'Look, Claire, I do need the names of those other boyfriends. People aren't always what they seem. One of them might have been more serious about you than you realised.'

Claire gave her three names, but no addresses. 'Sorry, they were a while ago, and I've wiped them off my contacts. I can't tell you any more about them. I haven't seen them around, although the first two were local, and the third lived somewhere over Saltern-le-Fen way, I think. As I said, they were just casual affairs — a few drinks, a meal or two, and I did go to the theatre a couple of times with one of them, but I never went to their homes.'

Claire looked exhausted. Gill thanked her and stood up to go. 'I appreciate everything you've told me. Oh, and I should tell you that my superintendent has put in a request to have you moved to a safe house. If all goes well, you'll be going there later today.'

'Oh no! Can't I stay here? I'm sure I'm safe here with Richard and Lizzie.' Her voice sank to a whisper. 'Please, don't move me away.'

Gill bit on the inside of her cheek. Part of her wanted to give in and let her stay. Richard's house was a fortress, but there was no police presence. 'I'll have to see. I promise I'll ring you after I've talked to the super.'

As Richard escorted her to the door, she whispered, 'I need to talk to you in private.'

'I was going to say the same thing, ma'am. Come along to my study. I'll ask Lizzie if she'd go and chat with Claire, take her a cuppa. She's probably feeling a bit wrung-out by now.'

More than you know, thought Gill, following Richard into his study.

He went off to speak to Lizzie, while Gill settled herself in one of the old leather armchairs. As soon as he was back, Gill told him what was on her mind. 'She's hiding something, Richard.'

'I know,' he said. 'I sensed it last night.'

'Then can you help us? She trusts you, more than anyone right now, certainly more than the entire Fenland Constabulary. She is refusing to go to a safe house and says she wants to stay here. I'm not sure how the super will take that, but, if she insists, how would you feel about it? It's a big ask.'

Richard didn't hesitate. 'Of course, ma'am. To be honest, I think it's best if she does stay here. As you say, she might open up to me. Otherwise, I can see her retreating into herself, and that's not good.'

Gill thanked him. 'So, while I'm trying to sort this with the super, do your best to find out what or who she's so reticent about. It might seem irrelevant to her, but you might pick up on a cause for concern.'

'I'm glad we're thinking along the same lines,' Richard said. 'What worries me is that it's something so traumatic that she's buried the memory. She's really upset about Joanne, and the fact that someone might be killing people to get at her is quite understandably making her feel overwhelmed with guilt. The last thing I want to do is push her over the edge.'

Gill regarded him shrewdly. 'I don't think you would do that, Richard. You were too good a copper not to read the signs. I have absolute faith in you, so just do what you can.' She glanced at her watch. 'I need to get back, but before I go . . .' She told him about Angela Sandford and her connection to Claire.

He groaned. 'As if she doesn't have enough to worry about!'

'I know, and I feel for her, but she's at the heart of all this, which means we'll have to take her whole life apart if necessary.' Gill stood up. 'I'll ring you later and make some arrangements for your, er, incarceration. Thank you for everything, Richard. You've got my card, so keep in touch, and if the slightest thing bothers you, or you make any kind of breakthrough, let me know.'

Gill left the house with a long list of names that would have to be painstakingly checked. It was something, she supposed, but she couldn't help feeling that the most important name was not on that list.

CHAPTER FIFTEEN

Eve and Wendy arrived at Jacobs Mere House at exactly two p.m.

'Oh dear,' Wendy murmured as she parked the car. 'This feels very different to the last time we were here.'

Eve nodded. Their last visit had been a joyous occasion. This time it felt unreal. She made her way up to the door as if in a dream, yet there was something else, too — a wish to see justice served. She pictured Justin's earnest face as he asked them for their help. And she was determined that he should get it.

A young PC stood at the door and asked them to follow him. 'This way, please, and please take care not to touch anything. Mr Connaught is in the drawing room.'

Much to her relief, meeting Lionel again wasn't as difficult as she had feared. Instead, they were able to laugh at what the process of aging had done to each of them.

After the hugs, and the words of condolence, the three of them sat down, and Eve was able to get a proper look at Lionel. Perhaps unsurprisingly, he had retained his striking good looks. 'Your daughter has been a tower of strength, Eve,' he began. 'I had no idea you even had a daughter.'

'I'm very proud of my Nikki,' said Eve, ignoring the raised eyebrow and inquisitive expression. 'She's a damned good detective, and I'm so pleased she's been given charge of this inquiry.'

'So am I. She is obviously highly competent, yet she is so sympathetic as well. Although I was sad to hear the reason for her understanding.' Lionel looked up at Eve. 'She told me that she, too, had lost a child.'

'Yes, sadly. I never got to meet my granddaughter,' Eve said wistfully. 'Life can be cruel sometimes, but we can't let it get the better of us.'

'I was hoping you'd say something like that. You see, there's a reason why I asked you here today.' Eve started to speak, but he raised a hand. 'Now, please don't think I doubt the abilities of your Nikki and her colleagues, but we three, well, we're not your average citizens, are we?'

'Certainly not,' said Wendy.

'Go on,' Eve said, already knowing what he was about to say.

'What I'm suggesting is that we conduct a parallel investigation to the official police one.' He sat back and regarded the two of them expectantly.

'It'll have to be covert,' said Eve hastily, thinking of Nikki. 'And only on the understanding that anything we uncover is handed straight to the police.'

'Absolutely, Eve. We have to use the correct channels. If we don't, the perpetrator could well slip out of our hands. We'll be helping the police every step of the way — only we'll be using, shall I say, more "unofficial" means that may not be available to the police.'

'Before we start, there's a couple of things you should know,' said Wendy. 'Never underestimate Nikki Galena. She is her mother's daughter in every sense of the term. Second, well, this is not so simple — let's just say that this won't be the first time that Eve and I have been involved in a police investigation and have found ourselves in a rather dangerous situation, so—'

'What Wendy is trying to say is that my daughter has banned me from becoming involved in anything risky or dangerous. She's concerned about me, and I wouldn't want to cause her any anxiety on my behalf. That said, we do want to help you, Lionel. We were both fond of Justin, and we can't just sit back and do nothing.'

'I understand,' Lionel said. 'In that case, I think that anything we do discover will be passed on by me, and your names will be left out of it. How does that sound?'

'I doubt it will fool Nikki,' replied Wendy dryly, 'but it will help.'

Knowing him as she did, Eve was sure Lionel would be discretion itself. Like her and Wendy, he was a past master of deception. They had to be back then, or lives could have been lost.

'That's agreed then,' said Wendy. 'So, tell us of your plans — for yourself and the house. Oh, and Heather, of course. Where is she, by the way?'

'Gone home. In a bit of a huff, I'm afraid.' Lionel looked both miserable and angry.

Eve glanced at him sharply. Had she detected a change of heart regarding his daughter? 'Oh? Why was that?'

'Without informing the police, she went ahead and arranged for her family to come here and join her. When your Nikki's sergeant told her that wouldn't be possible because the house was a crime scene, and children weren't allowed, Heather turned on me. She said that if I could have visitors, she didn't see why her family should be kept away. I'm afraid I lost my temper at that point, said I was sick of her always trying to get her own way. I've never, ever spoken to her like that. I've always believed she's a good soul at heart, and that people misunderstand her because she's so forthright. But I've seen a different side to her over the last few days. She's been terribly rude to the police officers, who were just doing their job. It was unacceptable.' Lionel's eyes were moist. 'It's made the loss of Justin even harder to bear, and for the first time in my life, I'm glad she's not here.'

The three of them were silent for a moment following this outburst. Eve could almost hear Wendy's silent hurrah.

'What about you?' asked Wendy. 'Are you going to stay on for a while?'

He'd be going home that afternoon, Lionel told them, to sort out his affairs. He would be returning the following day.

'As soon as you're back, we'll get to work in earnest,' said Eve. 'We'll need your input to try and build a picture of Justin's life in the last few months. Somewhere along the line, he crossed someone, he must have. And it was so bad that whoever that was saw fit to take his life.' She smiled at him gently. 'It won't be easy on you, I know, but we'll find him.'

'Or her,' added Wendy. 'We can't rule out a woman.'

'So, how do we play this?' Lionel asked.

'While you're away, Wendy and I will decide on a plan of action. You concentrate on getting home safely, and getting your things in order. By the time you're back, Wendy and I will have compiled a list of questions for you, after which we can get down to work.' Eve gave a little shrug. 'Um, I hate to say this, but the sooner you hit the road, the sooner we can get to work.'

Lionel nodded. 'Good. That sounds like a plan. I am so pleased that you two are here to help. Justin was over the moon at meeting you again, and that you lived nearby.' He shook his head sadly. 'I still can't believe this has happened. It's like some terrible nightmare, and I keep hoping I'll wake up.'

Eve felt for him. She remembered how cool and calculating he had been, how sharp. To be suddenly confronted like this with the death of your son didn't bear thinking about. It was hardly surprising that he was not his former self.

'We understand how you feel, we really do. But right now, we must be strong for your boy. You go home — just take care driving. Wendy and I will draw up a tentative plan, and then we'll all do what we did best. Okay?'

Lionel gathered himself. A look of determination replaced the sorrow on his face. 'I'm sorry. It just creeps up on me every now and again . . . There'll be time for tears later. But I'm not leaving until you tell me how you two come to be living way out here, and what you've been up to these past years.'

Twenty minutes later, Eve and Wendy were walking back to their car.

'Well, what a bombshell! I never thought I'd hear Lionel criticise his little princess so harshly,' said Wendy with a grin. 'It was music to my ears!'

Eve laughed. 'She must have been *really* nasty to upset her adoring Daddy. I'd love to have seen her face when he told her what he thought of her.'

'She's probably parking up her broomstick as we speak, or heating up her cauldron. Hubble bubble . . .' Wendy giggled.

'I can't wait to ask Joseph just what he said to her when he found she was actually arranging to bring her kids here. Honestly! What could she have been thinking?'

'Most likely she was thinking of how she can get her claws into Jacobs Mere House.'

Eve raised an eyebrow. 'Then I'm not sure that upsetting Daddy was her finest move.'

Wendy patted her leg and started the engine. 'I thought you handled your reunion with Lionel really well, Eve. I'm proud of you.'

Eve had to admit that she felt quite proud of herself. She was a different person now, and Lionel probably was too. Surely, they could be with each other as friends and comrades? 'I guess the situation with Justin kind of took precedence, everything else was, well, beside the point.'

'And henceforward, we'll be too busy to give old passions a chance to rekindle.' Wendy glanced at Eve. 'While we're here, shall we call in on Tamsin? Didn't she say she's off work for a day or so?'

'Yes, let's,' said Eve. 'I'd like to see how that that poor dog is getting on. I could hardly sleep last night for worrying about him.'

'I'm sorry to say it, but Bernie doesn't seem to be too high on Lionel's list of priorities,' Wendy said. 'Not that we should blame him, his whole world is collapsing around him.'

'At least Bernie's safe from Heather, which is a huge relief,' said Eve.

They found Tamsin in the overgrown garden, playing frisbee with Skipper, while Bernie sat quietly at her feet. Eve felt a pang of sadness. He should have been sitting at Justin's feet.

'Eve! Wendy! Come on in. Want some tea?' Tamsin cried.

'We'd love some,' said Eve, casting her eyes over the rampant growth. 'And don't think we've forgotten our promise to help out in the garden, Tam. Just as soon as things calm down, we'll be here with the strimmer and our rubber gloves.'

'That's the last thing you should be worrying about right now,' Tamsin said. 'Let's go into the kitchen, shall we, and I'll put the kettle on.'

Almost as soon as she sat down, Eve felt a gentle pressure on her leg and looked down to see Bernie's giant paw. She ruffled the fur around his neck, and he laid his head on her lap. 'How's he doing?' she asked Tamsin.

'He's been very quiet, but he did eat something this morning, which is a good sign. I'm worried about what's going to happen to him in the future. I can keep him for a few more days, but if Lionel can't take him, well, I guess he'll just have to be rehomed. And that might be difficult. Dogs of his breed are affectionate, intelligent, and very loyal, but they don't suit everyone. Apart from their size, they hate being left alone, are generally suspicious of new people, and need plenty of grooming. Worse than that, their life expectancy is only six to eight years, and as Bernie is already four . . .' She handed round the tea. 'I'd keep him like a shot, he gets on so well with Skip, but what with Niall's shifts and my two jobs, it wouldn't be fair on him. Skipper sometimes goes with me when I'm doing the rounds in the woodland, but I can hardly take Bernie as well. He needs someone with a big garden. Ideally, a retired person, or who works from home.'

Looking down at the big dog leaning against her, Eve began to wonder . . . What would Wendy say if . . . Monks Lantern had a very large garden, they even had the land next door, which they had turned into a tranquil woodland, where people from the surrounding area could wander and have some peace. They were retired — sort of. They had discussed getting a rescue dog several times but had decided that at their age, they wouldn't be able to cope with a young dog. Now here was Bernie, a large dog with only a few more years to live, who needed space, and who badly needed love. Maybe this was a conversation to be had later, over a couple of glasses of wine, not here and now.

'If Lionel has difficulty rehoming him, what with everything that has happened, Niall and I will do it for him,' said Tamsin. 'I won't let Bernie go to just anyone, that's for sure.'

'What's the betting that when it hits the media, he'll be inundated with offers for the poor dog,' said Wendy. 'What a status symbol! I can hear it now: "Meet Bernie, he was Justin Connaught's dog. You know, the famous TV celebrity who was murdered."' Wendy looked fierce. 'I just hope Lionel won't fall for some sob story.'

Tamsin smiled sweetly. 'Over my dead body. Don't worry about that, Wendy, I'll kidnap him first.'

Half an hour or so later, Eve and Wendy got up to leave. As they were about to get into their car, Tamsin said, 'Correct me if I'm wrong, but am I right in thinking that you two might be considering an investigation of your own into Justin's murder?'

They both looked at her wide eyed, as if to say, "What, us?" 'Oh, no,' Eve said. 'We couldn't possibly . . .'

'Oh, come on! When have you ever been able to turn your backs on a mystery? And didn't Justin tell you that something was bothering him? Even I'm eaten up with curiosity about that.' She smiled at them. 'All I'm saying is, if you need a bit of help from someone who's on the spot as it were, you must ask, okay? Totally between us, of course, Niall doesn't have to know.'

Eve and Wendy burst out laughing. 'Tamsin Farrow! You are incorrigible,' Eve said. 'But if we happen to find ourselves with time on our hands, and thought we might . . .'

'Which is hardly likely to happen,' added Wendy.

'Exactly, but . . . well, we'd be very grateful for your help. Thank you, Tamsin.'

CHAPTER SIXTEEN

DI Gill Mercer and DS Ryan Compton arrived at the Art and Crafts Centre and showed their warrant cards to a surprised-looking Mac.

'Blimey! That was quick. I only rang you lot a couple of minutes ago. Come on, then, I'll take you up to Miss Hereward's room.' With a growing feeling of dread, Gill followed Mac up the stairs.

Mac flung open the door to the consulting room, and she and Ryan surveyed Claire's formerly immaculate domain. It hadn't been completely wrecked, but the drawers of a filing cabinet were open, the contents strewn on the floor. Loose cables occupied the desktop where a PC had once sat. There were gaps in a row of notebooks and box files on a shelf, those remaining were lying on their sides.

'The computer from the shop is gone too,' said Mac. 'Although nothing else has been taken as far as I can see. Now that is odd — some of those crystals are worth a few quid.' He looked at Gill apologetically. 'We thought they were from the police, you see. The woman flashed an ID card at my mate who was on the reception desk but it was so quick he didn't have a chance to get a proper look at it. She said it was to do with the death of our lovely Joanne, bless her heart, so he didn't query it. It was only when I saw them leaving in a real rush, like, that I smelled a rat.'

'There were two of them, you say?' asked Gill.

'A woman and a man. Both were in black bomber jackets, black trousers, black boots, and they had those lanyard things round their necks.'

'Is there CCTV here?' Gill asked.

'Just one camera over the front door, because it's both entrance and exit. The monitor's in the back office. If we go back downstairs, I'll show you.' Mac turned, ready to go back downstairs.

'Thank you, Mr Mackenzie. If you could just wait a second while I ring this in.' She turned to Ryan and murmured, 'Someone really did not want us to see those records, did they?'

'Dead right,' he said, 'which makes me think it's to do with one of her clients, and not something from her past.'

Gill was forced to agree, even though she still had reservations. She pulled out her phone. 'You go down and take a look at that CCTV, while I get uniform and a SOCO out here. Hang on, I've just had a thought. Mr Mackenzie? How did they get into the consulting room? Surely it was locked?'

Now Mac looked really shame-faced. 'I'm sorry but my mate used the master key to let them in. He thought they were the police, you see. As a matter of fact, that's what made me think something was wrong. I mean, if they really were from the police, they'd have got Ms Hereward's keys from her, wouldn't they? Or she'd have come with them.'

'You're right. They would. Just like this.' Gill took Claire's keys from her pocket, held them up and shook them.

Mac sighed. 'Sorry. Though you can't blame him really. He was just taken in.'

'I'm sure they were very convincing.' Indeed, Gill knew all too well how clever such crooks could be. 'We'll need to get a description from him, and anything else he can recall about them. Now, if you wouldn't mind showing my sergeant that video footage?'

Gill called the station, and making sure both consulting room and shop were securely locked, joined Ryan in the poky back office.

'They knew exactly where that camera was,' Ryan said. 'They kept their faces averted or down. They'd either checked out the place beforehand, or sent an accomplice. Plus,' he made a face, 'the camera is total crap. I reckon it was last used on Noah's ark.'

As he said, the footage was of little use. Even so, she told Ryan to get it to the tech department. 'If you can, ask Spooky if she would deal with it herself. If there's anything of the slightest use on that footage, she'll find it.'

Sarah Dukes, aka Spooky — the head of the IT unit at Greenborough — was the best there was, but Gill suspected the fuzzy images might well defeat even her legendary skills.

'We'll just hang on for uniform to arrive, and then get back to base,' she told Ryan. 'But first I need to contact Claire Hereward. I want to know if she owns a laptop that might have her client list on it, and if so, where it is.' She groaned. 'Bugger! We might well find that her home has been turned over too.'

'God, yes,' said Ryan. 'Do you have her address? If so, we could go straight there. This only just happened, so, you never know, we could get there before them.'

'She lives in Lime Grove, it's only five minutes from here.' Gill turned to Mac. 'Can you please make sure no one goes near that consulting room, or the shop. Uniform will be here shortly, and they'll take it from there.'

'Will the whole building have to be shut down?' asked Mac anxiously. 'Only there's a lot of small businesses here that rely on this place for their livelihood.'

'No, that would cause too much disruption. We want to keep it low key. And whatever you do, don't let anyone into Miss Hereward's unit.' Halfway to the door, Gill, called over her shoulder, 'And tell the people in the other units that we'll be wanting to talk to anyone who might have seen those phoney police officers.'

While Ryan drove, Gill rang Richard Duckworth. 'Listen, does Claire have a laptop?'

'Yes, she brought it with her,' said Richard.

'Keep it safe, Richard. Her rooms have been ransacked and her computers taken, plus half of her records from the filing cabinet. We're on our way to check her home, I'll let you know what we find.' She rang off just as Ryan swept into the driveway.

The house, called Silvermere, bore no evidence of a break-in. Gill called the station and asked for a car to be sent to keep an eye on it for the rest of the day, only to be told there was no one available.

'Sodding budgets,' she muttered. 'Those people could well be involved in Joanne's murder — they might even be the perpetrators — and we can't get a crew to watch a location where they might just show up.'

As they drove away from Lime Grove, her mobile rang.

'Richard here, ma'am. I'm sorry to tell you this, but Claire's laptop has been hacked. It's pretty well annihilated. It did have a client list on it, *and* all of her patients' notes and histories, but the lot has been wiped out.'

Swearing under her breath, Gill said, 'Don't touch it, Richard. I'll collect it later and get it to IT. There's just a chance that our top techie may be able to retrieve something.' Unlikely, but it was worth a try.

It really did seem as if someone wanted to make very certain that they never got hold of any information about Claire's clients, so why did she still feel that it was personal?

'Surely she backed up everything?' said Ryan, carefully negotiating a roundabout.

'Did you hear that, Richard?' Gill said. 'Did Claire back up her files somewhere?'

'I asked her that,' said Richard, 'but she used cloud *storage*, not cloud backup. She also admits that she doesn't always select each file. The older files will be there, but not the more recent ones. She said she's had so much on her mind she forgot to do it.'

'Understandable, I guess,' Gill said. 'Now, can you get her to write down the contact number for every client that's on her mobile phone? At least we can ring them and ask for their details.'

'She's doing that as we speak, ma'am,' Richard said. 'It was the first thing I thought of when we realised what had happened to the laptop. She's calling out the numbers and Lizzie is writing them down to speed things up.'

'Ma'am'. Gill smiled. Old habits die hard, and Richard would always be a police officer at heart. 'Thank you, Richard. I'm very glad Claire has got you watching her back.'

She ended the call. 'Right, Ryan. The minute we get back, I want you to get Steve and Annie to drag up everything they possibly can on Claire Hereward's life. Why does a woman who spends every waking hour helping other people suddenly become a target for death threats? Was she always that way? Or did something traumatic happen in her life that made her change course? Oh, and tell them to use Richard. He's with her, on hand, and she trusts him. What else? Ah yes. I want you to find out all you can about that patient of Claire's who committed suicide. We have to know that there is absolutely no chance that he was, er, "assisted". I'll pick up the link with Angela Sandford, who we know damn well *was* assisted. Okay?'

This case was one bloody great knot that she would have to unravel, strand by strand. And who knew what might lie at the end of that rope.

* * *

Nikki stirred sugar into the coffee Joseph had just brought for them. They were in her office, drawing up their action plan for the coming day.

'We're back to a full complement now that Cat and Ben have offloaded Angela Sandford's death onto Gill. Poor Gill, she's already got a swine of an investigation into the events surrounding that grief counsellor. Apart from needing to keep the Hereward woman safe, there's the hit and run killing, and the suspicious death of at least one of her clients. That's a lot to take on.'

'And *we* have the death of a much-loved celebrity, something I wouldn't wish on any detective,' said Joseph grimly. 'It'll hit the nationals tomorrow, and when the TV news gets hold of it, the whole world will want to know what we're doing and how far we've got.'

'Indeed they will,' sighed Nikki. 'So we'd better move fast and get some answers before the media starts baying for blood.' She pulled a notepad towards her and picked up a pen. 'For once, we know exactly where, when and how our victim was killed, so everything hinges on the *why*.' She wrote the three letters across the top of the pad and underlined it. 'We should concentrate our efforts on the people surrounding Justin, and anything that happened while he was here in the Fens.'

'Which would give us a time frame of around twelve months in total, although he's only actually lived here for two, maybe three months. Is that right?' Joseph asked.

'That's right. It *could* be something from his past, but somehow I don't think so. My intuition is showing me someone so angry or desperate that they took a lethal weapon with them to visit Justin while he was alone.' Nikki bit her lip. 'Which doesn't fit well with an old grudge.'

Joseph looked thoughtful. 'I'm not sure we should dismiss it entirely, though. Some things do fester over time before coming to a head. That said, I think you're right about it being something recent.'

'So, we start with the present, and look at his friends, family, and people and situations connected with his work,' Nikki said.

'And his father will be pivotal,' added Joseph.

'He thinks he'll be back by late tomorrow afternoon,' said Nikki. 'In the meantime we'll split the team up and make a start on those people we do know about. I suggest we get Cat and Ben to contact the television company that produced his programmes. That will be a minefield, as so many people are

146

involved, but he probably only had dealings with a few while they were actually filming, mainly the crew. Cat can try to whittle it down to those closest to Justin, and find out if there were any problems, arguments, or other causes for concern.'

'And why not let Vonnie talk to the lady who cleans Jacobs Mere House?' suggested Joseph. 'It's a big old place, and she must spend a lot of time there. As soon as she's over the shock of finding him dead, she could be a great source of information about comings and goings. Vonnie is probably of a similar age, and she knows how to be tactful.'

'Good idea.' Nikki wrote that down. 'That leaves us with the family, and the unenviable task of questioning that poison dwarf of a sister.' She grimaced. 'Has to be done, I suppose. Once Lionel's back he can provide us with a list of tradesmen, and the builders they used for the work on the house. There might be a grievance there, I suppose.'

'And while we wait for him, we can be getting a lot of that information from his laptop, Nikki. Especially if he kept a record of the work done on the property.'

'Spooky has that in hand already,' said Nikki. 'I had a text from her earlier saying she'd prioritise it.' She stretched. 'Well, I guess there's not much more we can do tonight. Have you anything to add, or can we go home?'

'No. Best we get some food and rest, tomorrow could be bedlam.'

Nikki smiled hopefully at him. 'Takeaway?'

'No way! No junk food for you tonight, Nikki Galena. We'll probably be living on crap for the next week.' He grinned at her. 'And there's no need to look so crestfallen, because I just rang Mario's. He's expecting us in twenty minutes. You can have your pick of the whole menu, how's that sound?'

* * *

Haydn ticked off another item from her checklist. It wasn't often that she needed to resort to a Plan C, but needs must, and the thought of a large amount of money filtering into her bank account was a strong incentive to forge ahead and get the job done.

It hadn't taken too long to work out where their mark had gone; that ascertained, she devised a new strategy, to which Neville immediately concurred. Despite her original doubts about him, Neville was showing remarkable single-mindedness and an ability to get straight to the crux of an issue. When things failed to go to plan, he didn't whine or panic. He listened, added a few suggestions of his own, and they moved on.

Haydn found herself a tiny backstreet café in which to eat her evening meal. She tended to avoid the bigger restaurants, where a woman dining alone might stand out. Over the years, she had cultivated a talent for making herself inconspicuous. Neither over-friendly nor stand-offish, she was easily overlooked, even her age was hard to determine. This ability to blend into the background had allowed her to pull off some very tricky contracts in her time.

As she ate, she went over their day's work in her mind. It had gone very smoothly, all things considered, and Neville had revealed an impressive aptitude for car theft. She smiled to herself. He knew exactly which car to take, always selecting one of the more common brands less likely to be missed. He either returned it before its absence was noticed, leaving it either in plain sight or else so well-hidden that it could take weeks to find. She doubted the one they had used today would ever be found. Yes, Neville had his talents too.

They needed to make their next move as soon as they dared, while not being over-hasty. Another day was really neither here nor there, as long as it went to plan. They had one chance to pull this off, so they had to make it flawless. Then it would be over — at last.

CHAPTER SEVENTEEN

The following morning, as Joseph had predicted, he arrived for work to find a horde of journalists and photographers outside the entrance to the station.

'And so it begins,' he muttered, though he couldn't repress a smile at the thought of Nikki's language when she drove up in her turn.

He drove around the side of the building and down to the staff car park, only to find a large contingency of them there, too. He opened his window a crack to flash his pass at the automatic gates, and was at once bombarded with shouted questions. Nikki was going to love this!

He fought his way into the CID room, and went off to get two strong coffees. Nikki, he was sure, would be gasping for one.

Minutes later, she flung into the room like a hurricane-force wind. Luckily, there were few people around at that early hour to hear the torrent of abuse she hurled at the crowd of journalists outside the windows.

Joseph gave her a few minutes to calm down and then handed her one of the coffees. 'Sorry, I forgot to bring the Valium.'

She took the proffered mug with a wry smile. 'I just wish they would realise how it hinders our work. Even getting in and out of the station is a nightmare, which is *not* what you need when you have two major investigations on the go.'

'It'll never change. Not while the public clamours to know all the ins and outs of the duck's backside,' grunted Joseph.

They drank their coffees while they went through the overnight reports. Nothing in them pertained to their case, so they went out into the main CID room. The whole team were now at their desks, so Nikki called them together for a briefing, and gave them their instructions for the day.

Joseph glanced over at DI Gill Mercer and her team, all gathered around their whiteboard at the far end of the room. They appeared to be immersed in a deeper and far more lengthy discussion than theirs had been, and he pitied Gill. She really had drawn the short straw. Their own investigation was a straightforward murder, albeit a high-profile one, whereas Gill's was multifaceted, and bloody confusing at that. A deliberate hit and run. A woman and her business under threat, and the murder of one of that same woman's clients — Angela Sandford. He recalled the weird sensation he had had, standing beside the dead woman's bed. Something was terribly wrong, and it wasn't just what the doctor had said.

A nudge in his ribs brought him back to the present. 'Hello . . . When you return to the real world, maybe you'd like to join me in my office?' Nikki was staring at him, her expression half impatient and half amused.

'Sorry. Miles away there.' He followed her into her office where she flopped down in her chair.

'I've seen that look before, Joseph. Something bothering you?'

He shrugged. 'I don't know, and as it's now Gill's case, I shouldn't even be thinking about it. It's just that I was remembering Angie Sandford, and how we found her.'

Nikki regarded him thoughtfully. 'Mmm. Funny you should say that, it's been on my mind too. I keep wondering if we missed something.' She shook her head as if to clear it. 'But right now, we need to keep our focus on Justin Connaught.'

She was right, of course. 'So, where do we start?'

'Until his father returns later today, I suggest we get on the computer and dig up everything we can find on him. And for once, we'll use the media. Gossip, interviews, editorials, press articles, anything at all about his life in the months leading up to his death.' Nikki looked down at her notepad. 'Cat and Ben have got the work aspect covered, Vonnie is already heading over to talk to Justin's cleaner, so we'll concentrate on the man himself.' She looked up from her notes. 'But first, I'm going downstairs to have a word with Spooky, to see if she's dug up any nuggets from that laptop. You start on the press reports and the social media. Keep a sharp eye open for any conflict or dispute that he was involved in.' She grunted. 'Although I can't see Justin crossing swords with anyone.'

'No, from what I've read about him he seems more the peacemaker type,' Joseph said. 'Your mother obviously thought so, her description of him was positively glowing. Mind you, I don't think he was a walkover either. I remember Tamsin telling me he once got himself arrested in a dispute over the siting of an archaeological dig. It was too close to a temple or something like that. So I suppose there's always the possibility his death could have been connected to his actual work. Anyway, I'll see what I can dredge up.'

Back in his tiny office, Joseph switched on his computer and groaned as the results flooded in. Row upon row of commendations, obituaries full of praise for the well-loved TV personality. He took a deep breath and opened the first post.

* * *

With every hour that passed, Richard grew more certain that Claire was holding something important back from him — and the police. He was also feeling a mounting respect for Lizzie, who was proving to be a tower of strength. So, when

Claire went off to take a shower, he took the opportunity to have a quiet word with her.

'Do you think Claire might confide in you, Lizzie? She may well be more open with a woman, rather than some old codger like me.'

Lizzie laughed. 'Richard! You're hardly "some old codger". She trusts you completely, probably more than me, but I can give it a try if you like. Do you have any idea what she's holding back?'

'I'd guess it has something to do with a man. Someone she's being protective of, or who she's too frightened of to tell anyone about.'

'Hmm,' said Lizzie. 'Which one do you think is the more likely?'

'I'd say the second. Fear is always the most effective motivator.' Richard had often seen it at work in the past. Nothing sealed lips quite like a threat to a child or a loved one. 'I'll make myself scarce for a while this morning and leave you with Claire. I do have some bills to pay and that sort of thing. Have a go, anyway. Do your best, and we'll talk again later.'

That arranged, Richard called DI Mercer. 'Just an update, ma'am, no problems. Though I'm getting increasingly concerned that Claire is holding something back. Anyway, she and Lizzie have finished that list of clients from her phone, so I'll email it to you now.'

'Thank you, Richard. That's a good start. Now, I don't know how you'll feel about this, but I've drawn up a list of questions that I'd like you to put to Claire, and some of them are rather personal. I'd do it myself, but I shouldn't be seen coming to your house too often, in case it's being watched.'

'No problem, I'm used to asking difficult questions. I've asked Lizzie to help — you know, woman to woman. We can't get away from the fact that I'm a detective, albeit a retired one. And Lizzie is calm and easy to talk to.'

'Excellent,' Gill said. 'And don't be surprised if you hear from my DCs — they're Steve Gilbert and Annie Porter by the way. I've tasked them with finding out as much as they can about her early life, and I've told them to ask you if they have any questions they want to put to Claire directly. Is that all right with you?'

'Well, I'm not exactly going anywhere! No, that's fine. Tell them to ring whenever they like.'

'Great. I'll email you the questions for Claire. And thanks again for what you're doing.'

Call ended, Richard sat for a while, going over the situation in his mind. He was beginning to feel seriously uneasy. The threat to Claire was real. Whoever was after her had brazenly entered her workplace and seized her files and computers. What would they do next? His house was safer than most, and the police were keeping a regular watch from his neighbour's place across the road. There wasn't much more that could be done. However, experience told him that these people weren't about to give up. They were either being driven by a deep-seated desire for revenge, or someone was paying them a lot of money.

For the first time, Richard was afraid he had made a terrible mistake in bringing Claire and Lizzie to his house. Had he, with the best of intentions, gathered all the intended victims into one place? What could be more convenient for a killer?

* * *

Spooky had been out when Nikki went downstairs, but had left a message to say she'd be back in around half an hour, so Nikki had returned to her office to wait for her.

There was a soft knock at her door, followed by the smiling face of Julia Tennant, the force psychologist.

'Do you have a few moments, Nikki?' she asked.

'Come right in, Julia, and have a seat. I was just going to get someone to fetch me a coffee — do you fancy one?'

'Thank you. White, please, no sugar.'

Drinks ordered, Nikki smiled at her visitor. 'I haven't seen you for a while. How are things in the world of psychology? Mixed-up and confused as ever?'

Julia laughed. 'Too right!'

'A bit like us at the moment,' said Nikki. 'Especially the confusing bit.'

'Then I hate to add to your confusion, but there's something I'd like to discuss with you.'

Nikki's first thought was that it concerned Joseph.

'Well,' Julia began, 'for some time now I've been seeing a young man privately. I can't go into his medical history for reasons you will understand, just to tell you that he's deeply troubled following a childhood trauma.'

Phew. Not Joseph then.

Julia waited while Zena, the office manager, brought in the drinks, and then continued. 'From hours of confused rambling, a picture is beginning to emerge. I am convinced that the root cause of his trouble is an old memory that's struggling to come to the surface.'

'A bad one, I guess,' Nikki said.

'He believes he witnessed a murder, and I think he did.'

'Was this the childhood trauma you mentioned?' Nikki asked.

'No. That concerned an accident in which his much-loved father died. It has nothing to do with what's just come to light.' Julia regarded Nikki over the rim of her cup. 'I've been up all night trying to decide whether I should tell you at once, or wait. I can't break patient confidentiality, but he has expressed the wish for the proper authorities to investigate; he wants to know if there is any substance to this memory. He has given me permission to let you have his name and address, but, please, Nikki, do not contact him directly, only through me.' Her eyes met Nikki's. 'I'm telling you this now because he is a relative of Justin Connaught's.'

'Oh shit.'

'Indeed,' said Julia with a sigh. 'But don't start thinking he witnessed Justin's murder. This didn't happen recently, although I'm not sure when exactly the memory dates from. According to him, it could be two years ago, something like that. I've not tried to pin him down as to details. They're only emerging very slowly, and, I might add, painfully. The memories take the form of a series of vivid snapshots, and there have been three of these episodes so far. And I must say I'm finding them extremely disturbing, even for me, and that's saying something!'

Julia had years of experience, so to hear her say she was disturbed had to signify something truly horrific. Julia must have seen her expression, for she smiled. 'Yes, even a seasoned old bird like me can still be shaken on occasion.'

'We never become completely battle-hardened, do we?' Nikki said. 'Man's inhumanity to man still shocks us every now and again.'

'My dilemma,' continued Julia, 'is two-fold. First, I have no wish to muddy the waters where your present investigation is concerned, just because there is a family link to my client. It might be something completely unconnected.'

'Bit of a coincidence, though,' muttered Nikki.

'I know,' Julia said, 'but sometimes coincidences do happen. On the other hand, it could be a total red herring, but I had to mention it. The other dilemma is that it's very important that we don't undo the good that has come from all my months of therapy with this young man. He has made remarkable progress, which I'm certain has allowed this memory to start trickling back. He himself believes that if he can only confront it, he might have a chance at a better life in the future. And I wholeheartedly concur.'

Nikki stared into her mug thoughtfully. 'Maybe the best way to start would be to make a few discreet enquiries, and verify whether there really was another suspicious death in the Connaught family. Then, depending upon what we discover, we could take it from there. What do you think?'

'Excellent,' Juia said. 'My thoughts precisely. We can speak again if there is any truth to these terrible images my client is seeing.' She took a folded sheet of paper from her shoulder-bag. 'This is all I have to go on so far, but I'll update you if anything of importance comes up.' She got to her feet. 'Thank you for the drink, and your understanding. I do hope this doesn't turn out to be a waste of your precious time.'

'No, Julia, I'm glad you came to me about it. I'll ring you soon and tell you what we find — or don't.'

Alone in her office, Nikki read through Julia's notes. They certainly were sparse. Julia's client had described the victim as a woman, around twenty-five years old, with long, straight ash-blonde hair. She was dressed casually in denim jeans and a dark-coloured sweatshirt with a logo on the front. The woman was running away from something or someone in pursuit of her. He had pictured her looking over her shoulder, her mouth open in a silent scream of terror. The next time the memory surfaced, a dark, indistinct figure had materialised behind her and was covering her entirely with some sort of black material. The last memory was the sight of her body, lying in long grass, her neck at a strange angle.

Nikki didn't know what to make of it. Was it merely a fantasy, a product of a disturbed mind? Or was it a real event? Julia believed it to be the latter, and although she had no idea why, Nikki thought she was probably right.

The name at the top of the sheet was Paul Fletcher, the address a village about eight miles outside Greenborough.

She stood up. Joseph must see this.

* * *

Joseph read the note, then read it again. 'Strong stuff! And Julia is experienced enough to determine whether or not it's a real memory, so we can't dismiss it as a delusion, can we?'

'She's certain it's something that really happened, which is why she brought it to me, knowing about the murder of Justin. Not that it's necessarily connected. In fact I can't see that Justin's death is anything but an isolated incident, but—'

'I know,' said Joseph. 'There's always a "but".'

'Would you mind doing a bit of off-the-record investigating for me?' Nikki asked. 'Just to see if there's anything about a death approximately two years ago, where the victim was a woman of around twenty-five or so with long, very light blonde hair? She was possibly found on overgrown, untended ground.'

'And with a broken neck,' added Joseph darkly.

'The only thing that might help is that it must be somewhere nearby. Apparently, this Paul never travels far from home. He's not actually agoraphobic, but he's extremely nervous about going beyond Leedyke Village. If this murder really did take place, it must have happened near there.'

Joseph frowned. 'Then, surely, we'd know about it? Even if it's not our patch, it's close enough, and we'd have seen the reports.'

'Not necessarily,' Nikki said. 'These are only isolated flashes, images he remembers seeing, and not the full story. What if whoever killed this woman removed her from the kill site? What if the next image he comes up with is a body being loaded into a car boot? Or thrown into a river?'

'I guess so,' Joseph said. 'Or maybe it was never found, and we'll be looking at a missing person. Come to think of it, she might never even have been reported missing!' He gave her a doubtful look. 'Nikki, this could be a minefield. Can we afford to go off on a tangent like this when we're in the early stages of a high-profile murder case?'

'Normally I'd say not, but Julia has a point. Suppose there does turn out to be some sort of connection? I mean, that's why she brought it to me in the first place.' She shrugged. 'Come on, Joseph. Just a swift, superficial search. The team are already working on Justin, and we can afford to spend a bit of time on it before Lionel returns and we'll be fully occupied.'

'All right,' Joseph conceded, and rolled his eyes. 'Is it me, or has Greenborough become the epicentre of every single weird death in the entire Fens?'

She grinned. 'Don't. Please.'

'I'll get on with that, then, and in the meantime, I've managed to dredge up a few interesting facts about Justin, which indicate a somewhat different side to his persona — *if* they are true.' He passed over a handful of printed sheets. 'As you'd expect, the internet is awash with articles about Justin, and the overall opinion of him is very favourable. These snippets stand out because they're so different — either malicious gossip, or outright lies, or they might provide a glimpse of another Justin. See what you think.'

Nikki left, printouts in hand.

Joseph cleared his screen of searches, and stood up. This called for caffeine. He found Gill Mercer at the vending machine.

'Someone else needing a shot of something to get them through their bloody awful cases, I see.'

Joseph laughed. 'You'll need a bucket of the stuff to help you with yours. You've inherited a real monster, haven't you?'

'Tell me about it. Have you ever wanted to just sneak out of the back door and start running?'

'Many times,' he said. 'But then you think of the victims and their loved ones, and you take off your running shoes and buckle down once more.'

'Yeah. What else can you do? Right now, I have three innocent people to protect from a faceless killer, and not a clue how to go about it. I thought I had it nailed, but now I'm not so sure that I made the right decision.' She lowered her voice. 'And if forensic evidence arrives to confirm that another of Claire Hereward's clients was murdered and hadn't taken his own life as was believed, Cam Walker is considering bringing in the serious crime unit from HQ. It's that bad.'

'And unfortunately we're in no position to assist you, Gill.' He pushed coins into the slot.

'Not while you have a case that so interests the press that you practically need the riot squad to help you get to the front door.' She sighed. 'We could both do with twice the manpower. And talking of manpower, we'd better get back to work. I just hope this coffee does the trick.'

Back in his tiny lair, Joseph took a swig of coffee and typed in the name Paul Fletcher. He might as well find out who this young man was before he embarked on the more difficult task of searching for an unnamed murder victim.

It turned out that Paul Fletcher was indeed related to Justin, on his mother's side of the family. She had been Elizabeth Anne Fletcher before marrying Lionel, and Paul was her nephew. Further along the trail, he discovered that at the age of seven, Paul had witnessed his father fall to his death from a high ladder. This account was taken from a newspaper article that simply recorded the unfortunate death of Albert Fletcher of Leedyke Village, who had fallen from the roof of his house while repairing a gutter, and that the incident had been witnessed by his young son.

And from Julia's account, Paul was still suffering the effects of that early trauma all these years later. So, what was this other 'incident' that Paul believed he had seen?

An hour and a half later, Joseph was about to embark on a second trip to the coffee machine when a search result popped up that caught his eye. He read it through, then, coffee forgotten, printed it off and hastened to Nikki's office.

'Read this, and tell me what you think.'

She ran her eyes over it and let out a low whistle. 'Joseph! I think you've found what we're looking for!'

'And it only took one coffee. That has to be a first. However, we shouldn't get ahead of ourselves, it could be totally unrelated.' He didn't believe that for a second, but he'd had false leads in the past. They needed far more than that one old report to go on.

Nikki looked up at him. 'See what else you can find on that, Joseph, and if it all tallies, we'll decide how, or if, we move forward on it.'

Fifteen minutes later, he was back in her office, handing her his latest findings. 'You have to see this, Nikki! In a nutshell, two years ago, Patsy Shearer, a community nurse aged twenty-seven, had been in the area covering for a colleague who was off sick.

She had visited — wait for it — Mr Aaron Fletcher of Jacobs Mere House, and went missing on her way home. The case was handled by Saltern-le-Fen CID, as she lived in that area. Two days later, her credit card was used to purchase a coach ticket to Durham, online. On further enquiry, her partner admitted that they hadn't been getting on of late, and she had been threatening to leave him. The credit card was subsequently used several times to buy clothes in the Durham area, and then her employers received a letter, supposedly from Patsy, saying she was sorry to have left without explanation, but she had to get away from her live-in partner. After that, the case was put on hold, even though she had never been seen in person.' Joseph stared at Nikki. 'I really don't like the sound of this, do you?'

'No, I bloody don't!'

'I was thinking of ringing Saltern-le-Fen,' he said. 'Should I?'

'Go for it! If I was you, I'd try to get hold of DS Marie Evans, or whatever she calls herself now she's married. I'm willing to bet she handled it, so she should remember. Ask her if anything was a bit "off" about this woman and her disappearance.'

Joseph was soon listening to the soft Welsh lilt of Marie Evans's voice, which wasn't so soft when he told her the reason for his call. 'For heaven's sake, Joseph, please don't tell me the Shearer case is rearing its ugly head again!'

'I'm honestly not sure, Marie,' he said. 'But could you tell me something about it, if you have the time? We were wondering if anything didn't seem right about the way she ran off so suddenly.'

'*Nothing* about that bloody case seemed right! I have nightmares about it rising up from the archives to haunt us.' She paused. 'Look, if it helps, I've got a couple of hours before I'm due to conduct an interview. Shall I come over to Greenborough, and maybe we could talk over a coffee? If I leave now, I can be with you in twenty minutes or so.'

'That would be perfect, thank you. But be warned, you'll have to run the gauntlet — the station is under siege at present.'

'Justin Connaught?'

'Justin Connaught.'

'Not to worry, a few paparazzi are nothing to Tiger.'

'Um, Tiger?'

'My motorcycle, Sergeant Easter! Tiger has a very loud growl, and people tend to jump out of my way.' With a laugh, she was gone.

DS Marie Evans was a legend among the Fenland Constabulary. She had a backstory that would make you cry, but had recently married again, and he was looking forward to seeing her.

He went to tell Nikki to expect a visitor from Saltern-le-Fen. She was as pleased as he was.

'So, she recognised Patsy Shearer's name straightaway?' Nikki asked.

'Oh yes, and I get the feeling it was not an open and shut case.'

'I thought as much,' replied Nikki dourly.

'Mind if I shoot round to the Café des Amis and get some real coffee and a bag of Danish pastries? I mean, it's not every day we get a visitor, is it?'

'Considering Saltern's station vending machine is probably as rubbish as ours, I think that will be very welcome, Joseph. *If* you can make it through the sea of hacks!' She grinned broadly. 'Mine's a cinnamon whirl.'

CHAPTER EIGHTEEN

DS Ryan Compton stared at the report in front of him. Gill was with the super, but considering its implications, this really couldn't wait. He decided to take it upstairs.

Ryan took the stairs two at a time. For such a large man, he was remarkably light on his feet, thanks to hours at the gym. Stuffing down pizza while binge-watching a boxset wasn't on Ryan's agenda.

He hesitated in the doorway. 'Um, sorry to interrupt, sir, but I have this forensic report that DI Mercer . . .'

The superintendent smiled at him. 'Come on in, lad, and take a seat.'

Handing the report to Gill, Ryan did as he was told, and both waited while she read through it.

'Oh,' she murmured, looking up at the super. 'Listen to this: "Results of an autopsy conducted on seventy-nine-year-old Mr Keith Draper of Greenborough in Lincolnshire definitively confirms that said Mr Draper killed himself while the balance of his mind was disturbed . . ."'

'Ah, another of Claire Hereward's clients, and on this occasion,' Cam gave a sigh of relief, 'not another murder connected to your unfortunate counsellor.'

'Apparently, Mr Draper had recently been diagnosed with dementia, something he hadn't shared with his relatives.' She shook her head. 'Poor man; he knew what was in store for him. We'll talk to his nearest and dearest, of course, but it looks like they just lashed out at Claire in ignorance of his diagnosis.'

'That takes a bit of the pressure off you, Gill, so we'll hold off on bringing in any outside help — if you think you can cope?' Cam looked at her enquiringly.

She glanced in Ryan's direction, and he gave her a reassuring nod. Neither he nor Gill wanted the SCU taking over if they could help it. It would have felt like a failure.

'We've got this, sir,' said Gill. 'But rest assured, I'll let you know at once if it gets too much for us. What counts is that we get a result.'

'That's good. Now, anything else bothering you before I let you get back to work?' Cam asked.

'Well, there was one thing, sir. Claire is adamant that she wants to stay put, but I'm wondering if I should insist that she, and possibly the other two, be transferred to a safe house. Richard is doing a brilliant job, and is being a great help, but they aren't a hundred per cent secure. We have no presence in the house, and if something were to go wrong, we'll be to blame. And I hate to imagine what the public will make of it.'

To Ryan's relief, the superintendent responded immediately. 'Then we'll move them all out today. Leave it with me, I'll make all the arrangements.' He looked at Gill. 'What about Richard? Will he be more use to us on the inside, or the outside — if you see what I mean. Should we house the women in a distant location, and have Richard somewhere closer to us?'

'Claire trusts Richard, and he and Lizzie are working on her to get her to open up. I'd rather keep them together, sir.'

'Then so be it,' said Cam. 'I'll contact you when we're ready to roll. I have a suitable place in mind — it's a little way out of the county. I just need to organise the logistics. You can prepare Richard, but I suggest you say nothing to Claire.'

'Thank you, sir. I'll be much happier knowing they are out of the way. After all, if young Joanne was being watched when she visited Richard, they'll know exactly where he lives.' Gill stood up to go. 'It'll be one less thing to worry about.'

She and Ryan went back downstairs.

'I was dead sure that suicide would turn out to be another suspicious death,' said Ryan. 'It'll be a relief to Claire. At least she can stop beating herself up over that particular demise.'

'I'll give her a call,' said Gill, 'and let Richard know that they're about to be shipped out. I'm rather hoping he might have managed to drag a few more secrets out of that lady. If only she would open up! Richard feels exactly the same as we do — she's holding back, and in doing so she's not only hindering our investigation, she's also putting lives in danger.'

'Yeah,' Ryan said, 'her own most of all, but also the lives of the two people who're trying to help her. She's either a hard-nosed cow who doesn't give a toss for anyone else, or she's scared to death. And I know which one I'd choose.'

'Me too,' said Gill grimly.

* * *

While Joseph was out getting their coffee and pastries, Nikki had a look through the extracts that showed Justin in a more negative light. After a while she realised it wasn't that he was proud or aggressive, he merely didn't suffer fools gladly and he obviously hated injustice. In the altercations they cited, he was either standing up for someone who'd been wronged, or he was calling out an unfair situation. The only report that did show him behaving badly involved an affair he was supposed to have had with a married woman. A photograph that accompanied this article showed an enraged Justin taking a swing at a reporter.

Almost as soon as Joseph returned, having been held up in a queue at the coffee shop, there was a sharp rap on the door, and DS Marie Evans staggered in. 'Well! You said you had the press here, but that was something else.'

Marie was an imposing figure in her motorcycle leathers, until you saw the gentle eyes and ready smile. Nikki had always been slightly envious of her height and glossy, dark brown hair. She and her boss, DI Rowan Jackman, made a team much like her and Joseph. Like them, they managed to weather the storm of a changing police force, and hang onto their principles.

Marie told them about her recent marriage to a CID detective sergeant from Fenchester division, then they got down to business. 'It was good of you to come over,' Joseph said. 'We don't even know if your old case is directly connected to our present investigation, but when those warning bells start ringing, you can't ignore them.'

Marie wiped crumbs from her lips. 'Oh, I'm with you there, believe me. So, how can I help?'

'You said that nothing seemed right about the case,' said Nikki. 'Can you run us through the basics?'

'Patsy Shearer was reported missing by her partner, Sean, at around midnight; he said she hadn't returned home from work. At first, he hadn't been particularly worried, as she often worked late. That bothered me from the start, especially when I checked her rota and found she'd started at seven that morning. Surely, she would have rung her partner if she was going to be that late? However, he glossed over it, and said she often forgot to let him know. It made me wonder about their relationship.'

'And they lived locally?' asked Nikki.

'Yes, on the outskirts of Saltern town. A small house in a long lane leading out to the fen. Just the two of them, no children, and no pets. I found it a bit stark, not a homely place at all.' She took a swig of her coffee. 'Mmm. This is good. Anyway, we made enquiries, and she wasn't vulnerable or at high risk — she had no issues with alcohol and no mental health problems. Yet it didn't have a good feel to it somehow. Even when her credit card started being used, and several people had apparently been contacted by her, all swearing that it was Patsy herself, I never really bought it.'

Marie undid a brown envelope that she had brought with her, and took out a photo. 'This was — or maybe still is — Patsy Shearer.'

Nikki looked at it, and passed it to Joseph. His eyes widened. Neither spoke for a moment or two. The woman in the photo had long blonde hair, tied back in a ponytail, and wore a striped shirt, blue jeans and trainers.

Still silent, Nikki handed Marie the sheet of paper in which Julia had described the woman in her patient's memory flashes.

'Oh shit,' whispered Marie.

Nikki nodded, shaken. She hadn't expected to see that very same woman.

Joseph cleared his throat. 'One thing bothers me. If she was a nurse, why wasn't she in uniform? Community nurses have uniforms too.'

'Ah. I think I know how that could have happened,' said Marie. 'She had finished her shift and was about to go home when she had a call from a colleague who was feeling unwell. Old Mr Fletcher was the last one on her list, and she asked Patsy if she could just call in and check on him. Her partner, Sean, said she often changed into her own clothes as soon as her shift ended, so he described her uniform, *and* what she was wearing when she left home that morning. As her car has never been seen since she first disappeared, we can't prove that she changed out of her uniform, but it seems probable.'

Joseph narrowed his eyes. 'Would you be able to access your old case notes and find out exactly what she was wearing on the day she disappeared? Just so we're certain.'

'Of course. I'll do it the minute I'm back in the office.' Marie rubbed her temples. 'If she is dead, well . . . I never felt happy about any of it, especially as none of us ever actually saw that young woman. But we were pulled off the case and though it was never closed, nothing further was done about it.'

'What did the partner say when he knew there would be no further action taken?' asked Nikki.

Marie gave a dry laugh. 'Relieved, I think. He went to great lengths to tell me how bad their relationship had become, and how he always thought she'd up and leave him one day. I didn't like him, and I didn't believe a word he said. I mean, would Patsy really leave every single thing she owned, do a spot of overtime and, along with her car, just vanish into thin air? The whole thing stank, from beginning to end.'

Nikki was beginning to understand why. 'And the fact that the car was never traced didn't concern anyone? And the relatives and friends all accepted this fairy story without setting eyes on her?'

'Hook, line and sinker, Nikki. Her friends all confirmed that she and Sean were not exactly a happy couple. They did express surprise that she hadn't told any of them that she planned to take off, but they weren't unduly bothered. They assumed matters with Sean had come to a head, and she had simply had enough.'

'Did you ever go to Jacobs Mere House?' asked Joseph.

'Oh yes. The old guy was in no fit state to tell us much, although he confirmed that Patsy had indeed arrived. She made sure he was comfortable, made him a hot drink and gave him his medication. He died a few days later. I often wondered what happened to that old place. It was vast, and he lived there all alone. It gave me quite a shock when I saw your report on Justin Connaught's death and realised I'd been there.'

'For all we know, that house could be the site of two murders,' said Nikki. 'Old Fletcher seems to have been the last person, other than her killer and Julia's young man, to have seen Patsy alive. The attack could well have happened close by.'

'Well, it looks like your young patient really did see Patsy, and it's not just some wild imagining.' Marie glanced at her watch. 'I need to be heading off fairly soon, but if it helps, I'll send you a link to the whole case file, plus Sean's description of her clothing.'

'I'd appreciate that,' replied Nikki.

Marie smiled at them. 'And it goes without saying that any help I can give you, just shout. As I said, I wasn't happy about it from day one, and I'll be glad if Patsy gets the justice she deserves.'

* * *

'Richard! I'm really worried. Something seems to have happened to Claire.'

Richard looked up from his laptop. 'What's the matter with her?'

'I don't know,' Lizzie said. 'One minute we were talking, and the next she seemed to . . . She looked horrified, shocked, as if she'd heard some terrible piece of news. She ran out of the room saying she wanted to be alone.'

'What were you talking about, Lizzie? Something that triggered a bad memory?' he asked.

'Not at all. She was telling me about the positive care regime that therapists employ in order to maintain their composure and keep their emotions in check. I had read somewhere that therapists run the risk of burning out and wondered how she coped with all the pain and suffering she had to take on.' Lizzie spread her hands. 'One minute she was describing the practices she used, and the next she went silent. She sort of stared off into the distance, like she had been totally pole-axed. I have no idea what could have made her react like that, it was really strange.'

Richard closed his laptop and got to his feet. 'Where is she now?'

'In her room. I did knock, but she said she wanted to be alone for a while.' Lizzie looked bewildered. 'It just happened so fast.'

Richard went up the stairs and stopped at Claire's bedroom door. Inside, he could hear her weeping. Unsure how to deal with this, he went back down to where Lizzie was waiting anxiously. 'She's crying her heart out in there, Lizzie.'

He sat down on the bottom stair, thinking. Had whatever they were talking about brought back something from her past? 'Where were you when this happened?'

'In the lounge,' Lizzie said. 'She was watching TV, and I decided it might be a good opportunity for that woman-to-woman talk. She turned the sound off, and we started to chat about her work. I thought I might be able to steer it onto her personal life, but I never got around to it.'

About to respond, Richard received a call from Gill. Immediately, she asked him if he was alone.

'I'm with Lizzie, ma'am.'

'But not Claire?'

'She's in her room,' he said, puzzled.

'Richard, we're moving you out. There's a safe house ready for you. You and Lizzie get some things together, but the bare minimum, okay? Everything you require will be provided for you. Bring essentials only. No mobiles, no laptops. Do not tell Claire, as I have a feeling she might object if she's given time to think about it.'

'Has something happened, ma'am?'

'Not yet, but I want to make sure nothing does. I'll ring you the moment the transport is in place. As soon as that happens, get your things and take them to the vehicles. You'll go separately, taking different routes, but you will be housed together again, under close protection, somewhere a long way from here.'

'I understand,' said Richard. 'There's just one problem. Claire has had some kind of episode, almost like a breakdown. Something has upset her terribly, and I'm not sure how she'll respond to being hurried away in the state she's in.'

Gill sighed. 'Ah, just great! Look, I'll come over a few minutes before the escorts arrive. Between us, we'll try to make her see sense. She isn't safe at your place, and neither are you. Are you okay with this, Richard?'

In fact, it was a relief. With time, the responsibility of watching Claire and Lizzie was becoming increasingly burdensome, and he was glad to see it taken out of his hands.

'I'll be with you in less than thirty minutes. Make sure you're ready.' And Gill ended the call.

*　*　*

'Hello, Wendy. Just to say I'm an hour away from Jacobs Mere — if I don't fall asleep at the wheel. It's been a bit of a whirlwind.'

Wendy decided that Lionel was probably running on empty. 'And I bet you haven't even thought about eating.'

'My sister made me some sandwiches.'

'But you haven't actually eaten them, have you?' *Listen to me*, Wendy thought, *I sound just like a schoolmarm.*

'I just want to get back, Wendy.'

'In one piece would be good. Now listen, Lionel. At the nearest McDonald's or Starbucks or wherever, pull in, buy the strongest coffee they do, and eat those sandwiches. Another ten minutes isn't going to make a difference, is it?'

There was a brief pause, and then he laughed. 'Right as ever, Wendy Avery. It isn't.'

'One more thing, Lionel. Instead of going back to Jacobs Mere, come straight here to us. We're easy to find, I'll give you the directions. We'll have a hot meal ready, and you can relax and tell us how you got on. Then you can either go on to Jacobs Mere, or crash out in the guest room, and we'll get the ball rolling tomorrow.'

'Oh no, I can't possibly impose on you like that . . . though it does sound rather tempting.'

'Bollocks!' Wendy exclaimed. 'You won't be imposing at all. Get yourself here. You obviously need feeding, then we can take it from there. All right?'

'All right. So, what about those directions?'

Wendy told him. 'Mind you get that coffee first, now.'

'Yes, ma'am!'

CHAPTER NINETEEN

At four o'clock, Nikki was about to give her team an update when she saw Gill Mercer and Ryan hurrying out.

'Problem?' Nikki asked as they ran past.

'We're moving Claire and the others to a safe house,' Gill called back over her shoulder.

'Well, good luck.' Nikki turned back to resume her briefing, but before she could speak, she received a message on her phone. Marie Evans had sent the description of what Patsy was wearing on the day she disappeared. Blue denim jeans, a pale green shirt, and a dark green sweatshirt with a logo for a children's charity on it. She stared at the words on her screen. That clinched it. Paul Fletcher wasn't delusional, he really was getting his memory back.

She dragged herself back to the present. 'Okay, what have we got since this morning? You first, Vonnie.'

Yvonne Collins stood up. 'The cleaning lady, Mary Langrick, had nothing but praise for Justin, ma'am. According to her, he was the best employer she'd ever had. Finding him dead like that was a terrible shock.'

'Is she from around here?' asked Nikki. 'I couldn't get much out of her, as she was still in a state of shock.'

'She lives in the next village, a couple of miles away.' Vonnie smiled. 'She's well up on all the Fens gossip, believe you me. Apart from being a very nice woman, she's also observant. She said Justin and her chatted quite a bit, they even had coffee together. Among other things, he wanted to know all about the history of the area.'

'Did you glean anything from these "other things", Vonnie?' Nikki asked.

'I certainly did. First, she got the feeling he had some kind of romance going on, although this person had never been at the house while she was there. She said she guessed this from some of the calls he made; they weren't business calls, because he spoke softly and smiled a lot. He took a lot of these calls in his study with the door closed.'

Nikki frowned. 'Is she sure? We were led to believe that there was no one in his life, and hadn't been for a while.'

'I know,' said Vonnie, 'but Mary was pretty certain about what she heard. She did add that she thought it might be someone from his past, because he seemed to know this other person very well. Oh, and she once found a lipstick that had rolled under a chair — in Justin's bedroom.'

'Hmm. Well, there was that allegation that he was having an affair with a married woman, and didn't his father mention a relationship that didn't work out? Joseph, would you check that out, please?' Nikki turned back to Yvonne. 'Anything else Mary told you?'

Vonnie looked down at her notebook. 'Well, most importantly, there was some dispute going on to do with his work. There were some heated discussions about whether to continue with some project that this other person wanted to pull the plug on. There were also more personal arguments, but Mary didn't know what these were about. Apparently, he said things like, "How many times do I have to tell you? Please leave me out of it."' Yvonne looked up from her notes. 'So, all wasn't as rosy as we were led to believe, although Mary did say it had nothing to do with the house. Justin was absolutely delighted with it.'

172

Nikki turned to Cat and Ben. 'Did you find anything to indicate a disagreement over a work issue when you spoke to his colleagues?'

Cat shook her head. 'No, boss. We spoke to most of the people he worked with, and they were gutted about his death.'

'There was one bloke, though,' added Ben. 'Nothing specific, he just didn't seem as cut up over Justin's death as everyone else. No, more than that, he just didn't give the impression that he cared one way or the other about it. I only really noticed him because his reaction was so different from the others'.'

'Oh, and one of his research assistants said she thought that something was bothering him in the days running up to his death.' Cat glanced down at her notes. 'A Mrs Sheena Coates. She said there was one day in particular when he seemed particularly distracted and anxious about something, which wasn't like him. She even asked him if he was okay, but he said he was fine.'

'We do have a couple more to chase up,' added Ben, 'so we'll be going back tomorrow morning to see them.' He glanced at Cat. 'Beneath the shock and distress at Justin's death, we both sensed an undercurrent. Nothing major, but we feel there is more to dig up, excuse the pun.'

'In that case, get back out there as soon as you can, and try and get to the bottom of it. Something got this universally loved man killed, and I want to know what.' She perched herself on the edge of a desk. 'Now, something else has come up, and it's very disconcerting, even though it probably has nothing to do with Justin Connaught's death.' She told them of the missing Patsy Shearer, a disturbed young man's visions of her dead body, Marie Evans's visit and their suspicions that she might have met her death somewhere close to Jacobs Mere House.

Cat whistled. 'Bloody hell! I remember that case! A friend of mine was based at Saltern-le-Fen at the time, and she said it was dead iffy. She always reckoned that girl'd turn up dead at some point.'

'And we can't afford to ignore it,' said Joseph. 'We are hoping it's not a wild goose chase — we have enough on at present — but it does need a closer look.'

'As soon as we finish here, I'm going to have a word with Julia Tennant,' said Nikki. 'I'd like her to talk to her client, and hopefully get him to agree to speak to us directly. Julia was most insistent that he's suffered enough and shouldn't be further distressed, but the thing is, this young man is a relative of Justin's, and he could well have witnessed a murder.' She stopped and drew a breath. 'Anything else, anyone?'

Vonnie raised her hand. 'One last thing about the cleaning lady. She did say that Justin was very pleased with the work done on the house, and there were no quarrels with any of the builders and the like. However, he was definitely unhappy with one of the gardeners. She has no idea who he was, or what was the problem, but it ended up with Justin firing him.'

'Let's hope Lionel can give us his name, then,' said Nikki. 'He should be back tonight, so hopefully we'll meet with him tomorrow morning.' She stretched. 'Now, as soon as you've cleared any paperwork, go straight off home and get some sleep. Once Lionel's back, we'll be going full throttle. With the media hammering on our doors, we can't afford to miss a trick. Let's pull out all the stops, guys, and get a good, fast result.'

* * *

Soon, everyone had gone home, leaving Joseph and Nikki in her office. Nikki called Julia, who offered to call in to discuss how to proceed with Paul Fletcher.

As they waited for her to turn up, Joseph's thoughts returned to their own dilemma. Another day had passed without a word from Cam. Joseph was unwilling to just let it ride, he could see them drifting back into the same old ways, and he couldn't let that happen. This time they had to make a decision. A decision that would affect the rest of their lives.

Nikki's ringtone interrupted his reverie.

'Morgan. How nice to hear from you!' Nikki threw him an apprehensive look, and said, 'No, you can talk, Morgan, it's only Joseph and me here right now.' She put her phone on loudspeaker.

'It's about that offer of a post with us,' Morgan said. 'Just a heads-up, really. I know you've still got a few days' grace before you have to make a decision, but I thought you should know that there's now a couple of heavyweight applicants in the running. You still have the edge by a country mile — I've seen to that, don't worry. Nevertheless, the sooner you give them an answer, the better.'

Nikki's face fell. Pressure was mounting, and if what Cam proposed turned out not to suit them, this offer would be their one chance at a new life.

For once, Nikki remained cool. 'Thanks for that, Morgan. I appreciate the heads-up, and I promise you'll get our answer in a day or so. There's just one or two things to iron out this end.'

'No problem. And although I'd give my eye teeth to have you working here with us, I appreciate that things are never as straightforward as they might appear from the outside.'

Nikki proceeded to tell her about the odd case Gill Mercer was working.

'We are on standby for that one, Nik,' Morgan said, 'so if things get worse, we'll be camping out in your serious investigations room again.'

'If it gets any more complicated, we'll be bloody glad to see you,' said Nikki. 'What with the station under siege from the media over Justin Connaught, it's bedlam here!'

Conversation ended, Nikki hung up. 'We'll give Cam one more day, and then we go back to him. We won't let it slide, I promise.'

He gave her a grateful smile. How he loved this woman.

A tap on the door, and, with all the panache of a seasoned actress about to receive an award, Julia Tennant sailed in. 'I hope I'm not holding you up.'

'We are just grateful you could come,' said Nikki, pointing to a chair. 'We have something to tell you, and it's best we discuss it face to face.'

'You've found that Paul's "visions" are real memories.'

It wasn't a question.

'We have. A young woman did go missing. I've just received a text from someone who was working the case. It's a description of what the girl was wearing, and it tallies perfectly with what Paul told you he saw.'

Julia looked relieved. 'This is going to be massive for Paul. He was beginning to think he was truly mad.'

Joseph recalled a time in the past when he doubted his own sanity. Anything was better than that, even witnessing a murder.

'Julia, there's something I have to ask you,' Nikki said. 'In your opinion, is there any chance that Paul Fletcher could have committed that murder? Maybe he blacked it out, or he knows exactly what he's done, and is trying to put the blame on someone else?'

Julia sat back. 'I understand what you're saying. In fact, it was one of the first things I thought of when these memories started coming up. I know I'm not a copper, but I do know that people with damaged minds can be consummate deceivers. However, having spent a good deal of time with Paul in recent months, I am certain he is no killer. I'd stake my reputation on it.'

'That's got that out of the way, then,' said Nikki. 'So, can we meet him? With you, obviously.'

'I've already put it to him, and he says that as long as he doesn't have to come into the police station, he's willing to talk to you. I suggest you come over to Mill Corner in Cartoft, where I'm sharing Professor Sam Page's consulting room. It's where I usually see Paul, and he'll feel more comfortable in familiar surroundings.'

'Mill Corner . . . Hey! Isn't that DI Jackman's home?' asked Nikki.

'Yes, he lives in the main house. Sam is in the old mill, and he has a consulting room on the premises. As he's now retired, he asked if I'd like to use it for my private clients. And it means Sam is on hand to advise me on my more tricky cases.'

Joseph recalled that Julia and Sam had formerly been married. How nice that they could be together as they grew older. Julia always spoke fondly of Sam, and Joseph would have loved to have known their story.

'How about tomorrow morning at around ten thirty, if you can make it?' Julia said. 'Paul's at his best in the mornings.'

'That's fine, Julia. We'll be there,' Nikki said.

'I was just wondering,' Joseph added, 'if you think Paul might be amenable to hypnosis. We've had cases in the past where it has succeeded in bringing hidden memories to the surface. What do you think?'

'It can work, I grant you, but I'm not so sure about Paul. I don't think he'd be a good subject. Plus, he would have to be willing to put himself into the hands of a stranger.' Julia shook her head. 'If you knew how long it's taken for me to win his confidence . . .'

'Then forget I asked,' said Joseph. 'You know best, and we don't want to do him any harm.'

'And we'll be very careful how we speak to him,' Nikki added. 'We won't put any pressure on him. This young man is now a key witness to a probable murder. It's something we need to keep to ourselves, both for his sake, and for the investigation.'

Before Julia could answer there was a loud rap on the door, and a young uniformed constable hurried in.

'The duty sergeant asked me to call you, DI Galena. There's a man downstairs who's asking for you and DS Easter. He's very agitated, ma'am. We've got him into an interview room, but he insists he won't talk to anyone but you.'

'Did you get his name, Constable?' Nikki asked.

'He won't say, ma'am. He just keeps asking for you. He's in a right state.'

'Shall I go, Nikki?' offered Joseph. 'See if he'll talk to me?'

Nikki shook her head. 'No, if he's that upset, we'll go together.'

'I can come, too, if you like,' Julia said. 'It might be a mental health issue.'

Nikki stood up. 'Thank you, Julia, that'd be a great help.'

They hurried down the stairs after the constable.

'He's in Interview Room Three, ma'am. I hope you manage to calm him down.'

'I'll wait outside and watch on the video monitor link,' said Julia. 'Just say if you need me.'

Nikki and Joseph went inside.

'Dr French!'

Seeing him, it was all Joseph could do not to gasp.

The doctor looked wild-eyed and haggard, and Joseph was glad of Julia's offer of help.

'Whatever's the matter, Bill?' asked Nikki gently.

'I'm sorry! I'm sorry! It was never meant to happen, I swear! I thought I could do it, I really did! But I can't!' The words came tumbling out.

'Sorry for what, Bill? What couldn't you do? Why don't you just take a breath and start at the beginning. We're listening, Bill, we're not going anywhere, so just take your time.'

Even Nikki's unprecedently calm tone did nothing to soothe the doctor. He sat with his head in his hands, rocking backwards and forwards, muttering over and over that he was sorry.

Nikki glanced at Joseph helplessly. 'You try. He might respond better to you.'

'Bill,' Joseph said firmly. 'Calm down. Is this about Angie? Has someone threatened you too?'

Bill French gave a hollow laugh, and burst into tears. For once, Joseph had no idea what to do. He was just about to suggest calling Julia when the doctor started to speak.

'I'm so sorry. It's just . . . You see, once it was over and I realised what had happened, I thought I could walk away

178

from it. I mean, everything fell into place. None of it was planned, but it all came together far better than I could ever have dreamed.' The words came out between sobs and gasps. 'It should have been perfect. But . . . in the end I couldn't go through with it. Oh, I loved her so much!'

What he was saying didn't make sense, but Joseph felt dread creep slowly through his veins. He swallowed. 'Suppose you tell us what happened.'

The doctor seemed to deflate. He sat for a moment or two, staring down at the scuffed surface of the table, and finally began to speak.

'I killed her. Me. No one else.' He closed his eyes as if he were in pain. 'It was rage. It just overcame me, I've never felt such fury in my life. I asked her to marry me — and she laughed. She *laughed* at me.' He began to shake.

'We need help in here,' whispered Nikki.

Joseph stood up. 'I'll get Julia, and ask someone to find the FMO.'

A moment later, Julia came in and immediately began talking to him in a calm, reassuring voice. It took a while, but gradually he began to respond, and under her guidance, the whole painful story emerged.

It took thirty minutes, and when it was done, Joseph felt wrung-out. He had liked this man, felt for him in his loss, when all the time it had been Bill who had killed her.

Nikki dealt with the formalities, and as soon as the FMO arrived, they left Bill French with him and the custody sergeant and returned to her office.

They sat with three strong coffees that Joseph had collected on the way, and discussed what they had just heard.

Nikki shook her head. 'I still can't believe it. He was the last person anyone would have suspected.'

'Too right,' said Joseph. 'It was he who alerted us to the possibility that it might not be a suicide. He helped us, for heaven's sake, pointing out about those drugs, and about her inability to swallow pills. He was so clever he'd have got away with it if he hadn't broken down.'

Nikki nodded. 'I wonder why he caved like that when he was to all intents and purposes in the clear.'

'Possibly he's not a bad man, and the guilt was too much for him to handle,' Julia said. 'He's more or less given himself a life sentence.'

They fell silent. Then Joseph said, 'I've just remembered Gill. We'd better let her know that Angie Sandford's death had nothing to do with Claire Hereward.'

'She should be back soon, after she's made sure that everyone is safely out of Richard Duckworth's house. I'll tell her then.' Nikki bit on her bottom lip. 'It's odd, isn't it? From what Gill said, the other suicide who'd been on Claire's list had had nothing to do with her either.'

Joseph saw at once where Nikki's thoughts were taking her. 'That means Gill's case is reduced to some disgruntled email messages, one threat, and the death of Joanne Andrews.'

'Which leads us to the question of whether Joanne's hit and run had anything at all to do with Claire. Or was it because of something completely unrelated?' Nikki said.

Perhaps it was. After all, Gill had told them Jo had suffered a horrific trauma in her teens, one so bad it had made every newspaper in the country and beyond. Maybe it was a terrible coincidence that it had occurred at the same time as Claire was being threatened. It was a scary thought.

'I hate to leave you with such a conundrum, but I really have to go.' Julia stood up. 'But first I'll call downstairs and see if the FMO has managed to sort out some support for your repentant murderer. Are we still okay for tomorrow's meeting in Cartoft?'

'Absolutely,' said Nikki. 'We'll be there. It's up to Gill Mercer and her team to sort out the problem of Claire Hereward. Our priority is Justin Connaught.'

Julia paused at the door. 'And, dare I say it, the disappearance of Patsy Shearer. See you tomorrow, folks.'

Behind her, Joseph saw Gill Mercer arriving. 'Shall we go and break the news?'

'No time like the present. Come on, Joseph, let's offload this latest little bombshell, and get the hell out of here fast, before anything else happens!'

Joseph held the door open for her.

* * *

Haydn and Neville made their way along a field path that connected two small Greenborough villages. It was often used by dog walkers and as a short cut, so their presence wouldn't be remarked upon. Before they set off, and unbeknown to Neville, Haydn rang Terence. It had been quite some time since she had felt so unsure of herself, and she wanted to ask her old partner's opinion. Terence immediately told her to get out. 'While you still can. Things are changing in the organisation, new blood is coming in. If you bail out, so will I. I'm almost fit enough for active duty again, and I have a lot of good contacts. We'll easily find something to do. Ditch that loser Neville, and we'll go independent.'

Haydn surprised herself by saying, 'Neville's not such a dead weight as he appears. He's got skills that could be very useful to us. If we move on, I think he'd be an asset.'

'Well, all right. If you say so,' Terence said. 'I trust your judgement. Just let me know as soon as you make a decision, and if you do decide to go through with your assignment, be very, very careful.'

Now, she and Neville were trudging, hands in pockets, along the muddy track.

'God, I hate this place,' muttered Haydn.

'Yeah, me too,' grunted Neville, gazing bitterly over a massive field of cauliflowers. 'This is one job I wish I'd turned down.'

She heartily agreed, though she kept it to herself. 'Look. We have a decision to make, and we need to be in complete agreement about it. Whatever we decide, we must stick to it, no sudden changes of mind, and no recriminations.'

He shrugged. "Course.'

'The bottom line is, do we finish the job, or do we cut and run?' She kicked at a tussock of grass. 'Going on with it is risky, as we keep having to change the plan. Nothing to do with us, but there's now a massive police presence in the area. If we do proceed, there is no guarantee we'll be successful, especially as it has to be finished by tomorrow night.'

Neville stared at the path ahead, saying nothing.

'If we do abandon the job,' she said dispassionately, 'even though we've done most of what they asked, we won't get paid, and the organisation will never use us again. We'll be out on a limb; pariahs.'

'So, as far as I can see, if we continue with it and it works, we'll be rolling in it, and our bosses will be happy. If we fail, we'll either finish up in a high security prison or we'll be on the run — from both the law *and* our own people.' Neville swore. 'And if we jack it in, it means no money and no more work from this lot. But we could disappear and start again, have our freedom and a life.'

'That's about it,' Haydn said. 'Well, I never said it would be an easy decision, did I?'

They walked on in silence.

CHAPTER TWENTY

Nikki and Joseph caught up with Gill and Ryan at their end of the CID room, close to a whiteboard littered with photographs and hastily scribbled notes.

Gill listened to their story in growing amazement. 'Not the doctor! You're kidding me. But he was distraught over her death.'

'Oh, he was distraught all right! Distraught that he'd killed her.' Nikki threw up her hands. 'It's certainly a first for us. Criminals never come over all repentant, unless they've been caught.'

'Now I've got over the shock, there's something about it that bothers me,' said Joseph.

Nikki raised an eyebrow. 'Oh? Like what?'

'Well, if it was a crime of passion, as he said, how come he had those tablets? They were street drugs, not anything a doctor would prescribe.'

Nikki smiled at Gill. 'Now there's a nice little riddle for the doctor to answer when you interview him.'

'I'll certainly bear it in mind,' said Gill. 'Thank you, Joseph, I wouldn't have thought of that myself.'

'My pleasure, and I'm dying to hear what he says.' Looking slightly embarrassed, he said, 'You know, if there is a justifiable reason for him having those drugs and it wasn't pre-meditated, I can't help feeling kind of sorry for him. I mean, what he did to Angie was unforgivable and cruel, but I think he really did love her, and if she'd said yes to him, he would probably have been the happiest man in the world. Now he's passed up the chance of getting away with the perfect murder.'

'And landed me with another sodding headache,' muttered Gill. 'My team, with the aid of Lizzie and Richard, have been digging into the threatening mail she was getting. Lizzie gave them a name to start with, and it proved rather interesting.'

'It is all for real, I suppose?' asked Nikki, wondering if it was some small grudge that had got out of hand.

'Oh, it's real all right, but not as vindictive as it first appeared,' said Ryan. 'We've contacted the person whose name Lizzie gave us — what was it now — Andrea Johnson — and she explained why she was so upset with Claire. We'll be chasing it up tomorrow, but it sounds like sour grapes over a bequest made to Claire in one of her client's wills.'

'Ah, good old greed. The root of all evil,' said Joseph. 'Although in cases of murder, there's lust, hate and jealousy too.'

'Well, we're finding semi-valid reasons for just about all of those angry emails, with the exception of that note — you know, that really threatening one, that said she'd pay with her life for something she'd done. We can find nothing at all about that. It certainly has no connection to the emails.' Ryan frowned. 'And that worries me a lot.'

'Understandable,' said Nikki. 'A death threat is very different to a disgruntled relative whinging about their nearest and dearest's last wishes.'

Gill waved a hand at the cluttered whiteboard. 'First thing tomorrow, we are going to have to strip this whole thing down and start again from the beginning. At least Claire and her friends are now out of harm's way, though Claire seems to have had some kind of meltdown.' She rubbed her temple. 'The officers who drove her to the safe house said she never said a word the whole way, and it was a fair old drive. We have no idea what that is all about.'

'Maybe the shock has finally hit home — you know, Joanne Andrews being killed, and Claire believing it was because of her.' Nikki yawned. 'If I were you, I'd forget all about it tonight, have a good sleep and start afresh in the morning. You've had one hell of a day.'

'I couldn't agree more,' said Ryan. He glanced anxiously at Gill. 'You look all in.'

Joseph stood up, 'I think that goes for all of us. You guys have just lost one part of your investigation, and we've gained another, in the form of the missing Patsy Shearer. We could all do with some sleep, or we won't keep up with these ever-changing crimes.'

'Too right,' said Nikki, suddenly realising how tired she was. 'My brain aches!'

* * *

Lionel sat in his car for a few moments, looking up at the old chapel. Monks Lantern. So, this was where Eve lived. It was certainly a world away from the life she'd led in the past. Maybe she'd needed to retreat to a pastoral setting after the battlefields and war zones.

Exhausted, he closed his eyes for a moment, then shook himself. If he wasn't careful they'd come out and find him asleep in his car. He pictured Eve's face the last time he'd seen her. How beautiful she had been. He knew even then that there would never be another woman for him. She was still beautiful now, and it hurt him to look at her.

He undid his seatbelt and threw open the car door. Enough of all that! His son was dead, and right now he needed Eve, not as a lover, but as a fellow professional, someone who would join him in the search for his son's killer. Eve and Wendy had been remarkable operatives in their day, and he needed their help.

The door opened just as he put his hand out to ring the bell, and a smiling Wendy ushered him inside.

'You must have had a nightmare of a drive. We are both so glad you made it here safely. Come on through to the kitchen. Dinner is almost ready.'

He followed her in. Glancing about him, he was impressed by what they had done with the old building. It made him think of his and Justin's plans for Jacobs Mere House. He had called it a happy time, but it had meant a great deal more to him than that.

Eve was waiting for him at the kitchen table, and he took a seat beside her. 'I hope you like chicken chasseur,' Wendy said. 'It's an Eve and Wendy version, not exactly traditional, but it's better than the one we used to get in the canteen.'

'You look all in,' Eve said. 'Did you manage to get everything done that you needed to?'

'As far as I was able,' he said. 'Fortunately, I have a very reliable staff, and the business is running smoothly at present. They have my number in case of a crisis, but they can get on quite well without me. So, barring emergencies, I'm here for the duration — or at least until we . . . until we know what happened to my Justin, and that whoever was responsible is caught and locked up.'

Eve nodded understandingly. 'We've decided that you will stay here tonight, and go back to Jacobs Mere tomorrow. These fen lanes can be treacherous if you aren't familiar with them, especially in the dark. So that's that. No arguments.'

Secretly relieved that he wouldn't have to drive any further, he took the glass of wine she offered him and thanked them.

The supper was delicious. He hadn't realised just how hungry he was. Afterwards, they took their coffee through to the lounge, and he began to unwind. After a night's sleep, he would be better able to tackle what would come next.

'We've been very busy in your absence, Lionel,' said Eve with a glance at Wendy. 'We've established contact with people we think will be useful to us, one in particular. We won't go into it all tonight as you're tired, but as soon as you've seen my daughter tomorrow, we'll meet and decide on a plan of action. We can tell you then what we've done so far.' She sipped her coffee. 'Do you remember our friends, Lou and Rene?'

He laughed. 'As if I could forget them! Are they both well? Don't tell me they are living here too?'

'Oh, they're fine, believe me,' said Wendy. 'And, yes, they're not far away, so we meet up now and then.'

'In fact, we spoke with them yesterday,' said Eve, 'and we've enlisted their help. They're going to do some research for us. There are some aspects of the case that might be better approached from a more detached perspective. Rene has much better computer skills than we do, and you might remember that both she and Lou can be very handy when it comes to gathering intelligence.'

Each of the women in that group had had a particular expertise, and he was pleased that these two would be on board. He yawned. He was finding it hard to fight off a creeping drowsiness that threatened to overtake him.

Eve smiled at him. 'No more talking tonight. Get your things from your car, and we'll show you to your room. It's very quiet here, and I'm sure you'll sleep well. Have a good night's rest, and we'll go into action tomorrow.'

Having retrieved what he needed from the car, he went up to the bedroom they'd assigned for him. On the bedside table next to a carafe of water, he saw a small snifter of brandy in a crystal glass, and smiled.

Lionel undressed, climbed into bed and sat back against the pillows sipping the fine cognac. Convinced his mind would be too full of thoughts to allow him to sleep, he put down the glass and at once fell into a deep and dreamless slumber.

* * *

Richard Duckworth, on the other hand, lay awake most of the night. The safe house was comfortable enough but he missed the familiar surroundings of home. He recalled the people he had escorted to places like this, and the vacant and frightened expressions on their faces. Now he knew how they felt — helpless, no longer in control of what happened to them. And he was terribly anxious about Claire. He still had no idea what had made her retreat into herself, but could only guess it was a sudden access of guilt over young Joanne's death. Shock is often delayed, and it can hit at any time without warning.

He turned over in the unfamiliar bed. Above all else was the fear that he was letting Gill Mercer down. She was relying on him to find out about Claire's past life, and right now Claire was being more unforthcoming than ever. Somehow, he and Lizzie had to find a way to break through her refusal to speak, but how? She wasn't a hardened criminal, a fraudster, or even a frightened witness. If she had been any of those things, Richard would have known how to deal with her. Instead, he was faced with a frightened woman, under threat and vulnerable.

Richard was no stranger to this situation, having spent over eighteen months as a witness protection officer. He understood the ins and outs of a safe house, and the restrictions involved, and was well-placed to advise the women on dealing with the stresses of isolation, the long days that could easily become unbearable. They had no idea how long they might remain here, it could be days, weeks, or months, depending on how the case progressed. Much of the responsibility for that lay with Claire. Unless she gave the police the information they needed, they wouldn't make headway. But how to get through to her?

Giving in to insomnia, Richard got up and went down to the kitchen. Passing the lounge door, he heard someone say, 'Don't worry, mate. The first night is always the worst. Can I get you a drink or something?'

Richard smiled a little sheepishly, 'I was intending to raid the fridge, but a hot drink might be good.'

Colin Jones, the man tasked with keeping watch over them, was tall and lanky, with hair that badly needed cutting and a friendly smile.

'So, what'll it be? Tea? Or there's coffee, hot chocolate, erm, Ovaltine?'

'Just tea, please, milk, one sugar.' Richard opened the fridge. 'Blimey, this is a lot better stocked than mine.' He took out some cheese, a tub of butter and milk for the tea.

'Can't have you starving, can we?' Colin said as he filled the kettle. 'And boredom always gives you the munchies.'

'It does, doesn't it?' said Richard. 'I've been in a safe house before.'

'Really? It's not something people usually do more than once.' He laughed. 'Yeah, I know you're a retired detective, but not many coppers have much to do with witness protection.'

'I did nearly two years in it, which was more than enough. So then I went back into CID.'

'Now you need protection yourself.' Colin grinned, 'Bit of a turnaround!'

Richard spread butter on his bread and grimaced. 'It certainly wasn't in my retirement plan.'

While they chatted, Richard told Colin about the problem with Claire. 'She's had some sort of episode, and she's shut down on us. We need her to tell us what the hell is going on, but she's totally clammed up.'

'So I heard,' Colin said. 'I was told to pay particular attention to her. I got the case summary before I was sent here. Nasty business, that young woman getting mowed down. Anyway, the last update I got says there's been a few changes to the present situation.'

'As in?'

'One of the murders they thought was connected to the case has been discounted. It seems to have been a one-off killing, a crime of passion or something. They have the perpetrator in custody already.'

This news provided Richard with a glimmer of hope. Hearing that she had one less death on her conscience might just lift her out of the depression into which she seemed to have sunk. 'DI Mercer gave me a burner. I'm only supposed to use it in an emergency but I might just have a word with her about what you just told me. It could be of help to Claire.'

'I know about the phone, Richard,' said Colin. 'I know everything about this set-up, otherwise I wouldn't be able to protect you all.'

Of course he did. As a former witness protection officer, Richard was well aware of what was involved. He also knew that it was Colin's job, not just to protect them physically, but to care for their mental well-being. Not everyone responded well to isolation.

Richard finished his sandwich and thanked Colin for the hot drink. 'I suppose I'd better try and grab what sleep I can. Tomorrow, I've got the job of counselling the counsellor!'

'Well, good luck with that.' Colin clapped him on the shoulder. 'And don't forget, I'm here if you need me.'

Richard climbed the stairs to his room, grateful that he wasn't entirely on his own.

CHAPTER TWENTY-ONE

Joseph got up early, leaving Nikki asleep. He pulled on some joggers, a sweatshirt and trainers, and slipped silently from the house.

Shivering in the chilly early morning air, he set off at a run along the narrow fen lane. For once, the east wind wasn't blasting in across from the North Sea, and the sun was emerging above the horizon. It was not a stunning fireball of a sunrise, like some he had seen here in this water-world, but a soft and muted affair that seemed more like one of Eve's pastel paintings than a real-world dawn. He paused in his tracks and turned his face to the slowly unfolding light. Such moments of peace were all too rare in his life.

He ran on, the marsh coming awake around him. The song of birds, delighted to have survived another night, echoed across the dykes to the accompaniment of water trickling into the ditches. Far off in the distance the chugging of a boat could be heard setting out to sea.

Joseph had come a long way to reach this place. Once a war-damaged soldier, he had travelled the world in search of some way to ease his troubled mind, until, finally, achieving serenity. He returned home a changed man, and joined the police. Now he sensed a fresh sea-change approaching from beyond the horizon. It would take all his courage to confront it, but Joseph was ready.

There was no sound now but the rhythmic pounding of his feet. He could do this.

* * *

Nikki woke up alone, saw Joseph's nightclothes flung over a chair, and smiled. He would be out on Cloud Fen, running the lanes to get his head together ready for the new day. She'd get her own head together over a large mug of tea in the warmth of the kitchen.

Sitting at the old pine table, Nikki pondered the killing of Justin Connaught. Nothing about it was straightforward. Still there was no apparent motive, no shadowy figure lurking in the background and arousing their suspicions. Apart from a spoiled and rather stupid sister, obviously a changeling, swapped at birth by an evil witch, Justin had had no enemies. The outpourings of the hundreds of people expressing their sorrow at his sudden death were testament to that. Even her own mother had nothing but praise for him. Wait a minute. What had Eve said? That Justin had been anxious about something, and he wanted Eve and Wendy's advice. Then, after asking them to come and see him the following day, he had been murdered. Were the two things connected? How?

Her thoughts having arrived at this dead end, Nikki took herself off for a shower. She emerged having arrived at a decision. From now on, they would concentrate all their efforts on the days leading up to Justin's death. Whatever it was, the thing that had caused it had come to a head a short time before he was killed. She needed a step-by-step account of every single movement of Justin's, the people he spoke to and the places he went, for the week leading up to that fateful night.

That settled, Nikki heard Joseph coming in from his run. Perfect timing. And now . . . breakfast.

* * *

Long before nine o'clock the CID room was buzzing. Nikki was about to hand out the tasks for the day when she received a message on her phone. Lionel Connaught was back, Eve wrote. He had stayed overnight at Monks Lantern and was now on his way to Jacobs Mere. Nikki decided that she and Joseph would go straight there from Mill Corner, where they were to meet Paul Fletcher, their young visionary. She confirmed it with Lionel and continued with the briefing.

Soon, she and Joseph were on their way to Cartoft. Nikki had never been to DI Jackman's home and was curious to see how he'd managed to make a home out of a windmill.

It turned out to be beautiful. Jackman didn't actually live in the mill itself, but in the mill house, which was just across the courtyard. Sam Page occupied the mill, and had his consulting room there.

They parked next to Julia's car, and guessed that the old Ford Fiesta must belong to Paul.

'They've done a great job on the mill conversion, haven't they?' said Joseph, looking up. 'They've lowered it to three floors and finished it off in keeping with the old building. Didn't Laura Archer have her consulting room here when she was alive?'

Nikki nodded. Remembering their former force psychologist always made her sad. Laura had been such a beautiful woman, and she and DI Jackman had been very much in love. Nikki wondered how he had coped following her sudden death. 'It must feel strange to him having Sam and Julia here. I heard he had the dilapidated old mill renovated especially for Laura.'

'I heard that too,' said Joseph. 'But Sam was Laura's mentor and dearest friend, so I guess they've been able to support each other. And you can't not like Julia. I'm not sure how old she is, but she is the epitome of a strong and highly intelligent older woman, and she has charisma by the bucketful!'

They approached the entrance to the old mill, both wondering what Paul Fletcher would be like.

Later, when she thought about this first meeting, one word always came to her mind — haunted.

Paul Fletcher rose from the sofa where he had been seated. He was painfully thin, very pale, as if he never saw the sun, with wispy hair that fell to his shoulders. He might have been an impoverished artist, starving in a garret, or an undernourished student. What most stood out were his eyes, which were of a startling deep blue colour. Despite his smile of greeting, there was an anguish in his expression that he seemed unable to hide.

'Paul was here early,' said Julia, directing them to a second sofa. 'He woke up this morning having had considerably more of his memory return. He wrote it down in case it dissipated again, but remarkably, we think his capacity to remember is slowly seeping back.' She gave Paul an encouraging smile. 'I should also say that these good people here believe that what you saw was real, so there's no need to doubt yourself. You really are on the road to recovery.'

Nikki smiled at him. 'We are here to listen, nothing more. And we'll take anything you have to tell us very seriously indeed.'

Paul said he welcomed their involvement and was glad of the opportunity to speak about what he had seen. Yet despite his words, the troubled look in his eyes remained.

'Can you tell us what you remembered this morning, Paul?' asked Joseph gently. 'Julia has told us about your original flashes of memory. Is there anything new?'

Paul stammered, 'I ... I ... It wasn't like before. It wasn't a flash, not a visual image. It ... it was just like ... sort of like waking up and remembering a dream you'd just had.' He glanced at Julia. 'I can't think of a way to put it.'

'Suppose you start at the beginning,' prompted Julia kindly.

Paul closed his eyes and took a deep breath. 'Okay. Well, I was walking down a wide path, between two long rows of trees and bushes. There was a grass verge on either side. There were birds singing, I heard the call of a red kite way up on the thermals, and I kind of followed it off the path and wandered into a wilder area. There, I saw a green woodpecker, so I stopped and got my field glasses out. It's my hobby, you see, birdwatching.' He looked down. 'It's something I can do by myself. Back then, I couldn't handle being with other people.'

'You've come a very long way since those days,' Julia said gently. 'Go on.'

'So, anyway, I hunkered down to watch the bird, but suddenly it flew off with a loud call of alarm. I stayed where I was, wondering what had startled it, then I heard the sound of running feet.' Paul stopped suddenly, breathing faster.

'It's all right, Paul. Just relax, take your time. You're quite safe,' Julia said, smiling at him, 'nothing can hurt you here. Nikki and Joseph would like you to help them discover what happened, that's all.'

Paul swallowed. 'I saw a woman run into the clearing where the woodpecker had been. She looked, well, terrified. She kept looking over her shoulder, and veering from side to side. I wanted to help, but I couldn't move. I was frozen to the spot.' He looked down, as if ashamed of his cowardice.

'You have nothing to reproach yourself with, Paul,' Joseph said. 'In fact, you did the right thing. Who knows, if you had shown yourself, the same thing could have happened to you. We're glad you're here safe and sound and can tell her story, so that poor woman can have some peace.'

How good Joseph was at understanding damaged people, Nikki thought. People sensed the genuineness of his response. Joseph had been in dark places too.

'I didn't see what finally happened,' Paul continued. 'I saw someone throw something dark over the woman, and

195

then I buried my head in my hands and shut my eyes. I knew something terrible was happening, and I couldn't bear to see. There was a scuffle, and then everything went quiet.' Paul drew in a shaky breath. 'I don't know how long I stayed there like that, but the next thing I remember, I was standing over her, looking down. She was lying all twisted, with her head at this strange angle.' His voice caught. 'Then I saw my father again. Oh God, it was him lying there at my feet! He was all twisted too. Twisted and broken! Broken and dead!'

Julia moved closer to him. 'Take some deep breaths, Paul. You've done brilliantly. Now you can relax again.' She glanced up from the sobbing young man at Nikki and Joseph. Her client wasn't going to be able to give them much more. 'I'm going to suggest we take a breather, and I'll make us all a cup of tea.'

While Julia busied herself with the tea things, Nikki looked around the big room. Occupying the whole of the ground floor, it was designed so as to incorporate consultation area, office and kitchen in a single space. At the far end she saw a curved flight of stairs, and a small lift that obviously led up to Sam Page's living quarters. Nikki wondered if Laura herself had had a hand in the layout. It certainly seemed to have been devised with a psychologist in mind. Nikki noted the lighting, which could be changed to suit the mood. The whole atmosphere was one of tranquillity and calm.

She glanced at Paul and saw that the peaceful surroundings were having their effect on him too. Suddenly, he looked directly at her and said, 'Name. What was her name? Do you know who she was?'

There was no reason to keep it from him, so Nikki said, 'We believe her name was Patsy Shearer. Thanks to your very clear description of what she was wearing we found a report of a young woman dressed in exactly those clothes who went missing around the time you recall seeing her.'

'But you haven't found her?'

She shook her head. 'Not yet.'

Paul lapsed into silence. It was something of a relief when Julia returned with a tray of tea.

After a while, Joseph said, 'Are you ready to tell us any more, Paul, or is it too painful for you?'

'There's not much more to tell, really.' Looking miserable, he said, 'Because I ran away. I left her and ran.' He swallowed. 'What I do remember is that the further I ran, the more the memory of it faded. So I ran harder, and by the time I got home I couldn't remember a thing. It was like it never happened.'

'Paul suffered dissociative amnesia,' Julia explained. 'The trauma was too much for his mind to accept, and the amnesia was most likely triggered by reliving his father's tragic accident. It's not unusual, and takes different forms. Paul blocked out that one specific traumatic event, but still had full cognisance of everything else — he was aware of his surroundings, and still recognised friends and family. He retained his identity while blocking out that one terrible hour.'

'Until now,' murmured Paul.

Julia smiled at him warmly. 'And that's because you're so much stronger, and able to cope with the memory. Once you can look at the whole episode clearly, without flinching, you will move on, I promise.'

Nikki had no idea what state this young man had been in when he first went to Julia, but guessed he had been a total mess. Julia seemed honestly pleased with the progress he'd made, and used words like 'strong' and 'coping', whereas to Nikki he seemed merely pathetic.

Perhaps Paul had read her expression, for his voice was suddenly stronger. 'I'm so sorry. I don't know what you must think of me, but I didn't expect this to be so difficult. Worst of all is that I ran away and left her. And since I can't go back and change it, I will have to learn to live with my . . . cowardice.'

Nikki could see him sinking into a state of self-recrimination, and they'd never get anywhere. 'Paul, do you remember where you were when this happened?'

To her surprise, he said that he did. 'It came back to me this morning. It was my favourite place for birdwatching, because it was in the grounds of a place that belonged to some old relative of mine, so it was private. It's called Jacobs Mere House.'

CHAPTER TWENTY-TWO

Later that morning, Gill was given the go-ahead to interview Dr Bill French. She took Ryan with her. Would they find a grief-stricken, repentant man, or a consummate actor who had almost pulled off the perfect killing?

Closing the door behind them, they approached the table, where the doctor sat, shoulders slumped, staring dully at the wall. He looked up at them with a flicker of what looked like irritation.

'I thought I would be speaking to DI Galena.'

'I'm sorry, sir, but DI Galena is no longer in charge of this case.' Gill switched on the recorder. 'This interview is being recorded and may be given in evidence . . .' She ended with the date and time, and introduced herself, Ryan following suit.

The solicitor sitting with him was known for being exceptionally sharp; she wouldn't be giving her an easy ride.

For his part, Bill French looked anything but sharp. After his initial flash of annoyance he returned to staring at the wall, answering all her questions without meeting her gaze. It took all Gill's considerable expertise to wring any answers out of him at all. Speaking in a flat tone that was devoid of all expression, he confirmed what he'd said to Nikki, that Ms Sandford had led him to believe that his offer of marriage would be accepted.

When she rejected his offer, he felt he'd been made use of, he said. 'I was overwhelmed by rage. That's why I killed her.'

He spoke the words as if he were reading from a page, almost as if he were drugged, although he had been given nothing but a very mild sedative the night before.

After an hour of questions, all answered in the same lifeless tone, the solicitor — who appeared as puzzled by his responses as they were — asked for a break. Gill suspended the interview.

She organised for drinks to be taken to French and his brief, and she and Ryan took their own drinks into a vacant room.

'Talk about hard going,' she said. 'What the dickens do you make of that?'

Ryan shook his head. 'Like interviewing the living dead, wasn't it? He killed her all right, he said so himself, but was he putting on an act? I've seen people in shock behave in all kinds of ways, but that seemed a bit, well, over the top to me. Frankly, I don't buy it.'

'Nor me, but just to cover our backs, I think I'll call in Julia Tennant, if she's here today. I want a psychological evaluation of that man.' She swirled her coffee around in the beaker. 'But before I do that, there's one more question I'd like to put to him. Remember the one Joseph Easter posed? If it was as he said, a crime of passion, how come he had all those dangerous street drugs in his possession?'

'Oh yeah, I'd forgotten about that,' said Ryan. 'How's he going to answer that one? Hang on, boss, are you thinking that something else is going on there?'

'It's nothing concrete, Ryan, but all the way through that interview I had a niggling sense that we were being played. And now I think I might know why.' Gill looked at Ryan thoughtfully. 'I could be way off beam and he did indeed kill the woman he loved out of hurt and anger, but it's my belief that he planned this death, and his apparent meltdown is a ruse to get himself committed to a high secure hospital rather than a Cat A prison.'

A slow smile crept across Ryan's face. 'No wonder it seemed over the top. I think you're right!'

'But keep an open mind, Ryan. I could be wrong. Nonetheless, the moment we're back in the office, I want you to take that man's life apart. Go back to all the people Cat and Ben spoke to, and get me a complete run-down down on him, because I bet you'll find something in there that stinks.' She glanced at her watch. 'I reckon he's had a long enough break now. Let's go grill our doctor on his collection of street drugs.'

Back in the interview room, Bill French's lengthy explanation of how he came to have those drugs was unconvincing, to say the least. According to him, he had been given the tablets to dispose of by a patient whose son had been experimenting with drugs. The man had taken them off his son, and didn't know what to do with them, so had handed them over to the family doctor, Bill French. Bill, who had been hurrying off to see another patient had pushed the bag into his gilet pocket and forgotten about them.

'If it is a lie, it's not a very clever one,' said Ryan, pulling on his jacket. 'I'll check it out now, and then I'll start that background check.'

'Thanks, Ryan. I'll leave that in your capable hands and get back to Claire Hereward. I need to know if she's come out of that "episode" yet. We'll tie up again in a couple of hours.'

Ryan clicked his heels, and with a smart salute, headed for the door.

* * *

After an hour on the phone, Ryan's head was spinning. He had spoken to four people and had learned a lot about Angie and her star-crossed lover.

Unexpectedly, Bill's patient confirmed that he had handed over a small plastic bag of street drugs that he had taken from his son. The only variation was in the date he'd given them to French, who had given the impression that he'd only just received them when he killed Angie, whereas the concerned parent said he had given them to the doctor the day before. Did that point to French having held onto the cocaine-laced Fentanyl for a specific purpose? Ryan thought it highly unlikely that anyone, especially a doctor, would walk around with a pocket full of lethal drugs, no matter how much they had on their mind. The trouble was they would never be able to prove it.

Something a lot more provable, though, came from a rather more reliable source, namely the Rev Judy Cornwell. She had been on the list of contacts provided by Cat and Ben, and had turned out to be most helpful. She knew Angie Sandford well, having spoken with her often and at length, over a period of several months, and told Ryan that in the weeks leading up to her death, she had been very concerned about her state of mind. She said Angie was extremely distressed about Dr French. According to Angie, what had always been an easy and companionable friendship with Bill had now become a burden, and she was coming to resent his constant attentions. Angie had been an independent woman, who enjoyed her own company, and Bill wanted more than she was prepared to give. Angie had adored her husband, and losing him had been a terrible blow. No one could replace him in her affections and she had no need of another partner. Bill had been a good friend, but she feared he was becoming almost obsessed with her. 'I advised her to make it absolutely clear to him that although she valued his friendship, that was as far as it went.' The Reverend sighed. 'I just pray that my advice didn't set off a chain of events that culminated in her death.'

Ryan assured her that Bill French had been deluded about Angie for some considerable time, and could have snapped at any point.

After speaking to the Reverend, he went to see two of the other people on Cat's list, both of whom confirmed that Angie had never intended Bill to accompany her on her walking trip to the Bulgarian forests. It was true that she had agreed to go to the Lakes with him, but only to explain that he must expect no more from her than friendship.

Ryan flexed his broad shoulders and was about to get up when his phone rang.

The caller was Maggie Snow, Angie's closest friend. 'I do hope I'm not speaking out of turn, Detective Sergeant, but something has been worrying me, and I thought you should know about it.'

'Please, do go on,' Ryan said, reaching for his notepad.

'It's to do with Angie's financial situation. You may not be aware of it but she was a very rich woman. Her husband, an astute and successful businessman, had invested wisely. After his death, with the help of a clever financial advisor, Angie sold off the businesses at a considerable profit, and her assets just grew and grew. As I said, few people knew just how wealthy she was — you have to have a certain amount of money to live at St Nicholas Court but it's not exactly ostentatious. After her son died, she chose to live simply, using her money to fund various charities. Nevertheless, at the time of her death she was an extremely wealthy lady.'

The click and the whirr were almost audible as the cogs turned in Ryan's brain. 'Did Dr French know about this, Maggie?' he asked, although he already knew the answer.

'Oh yes, Detective. He was one of the "few" people I mentioned.'

'Well, thank you very much, Maggie. You did the right thing in telling me about this.' *And how*, thought Ryan, ending the call. The DI needed to hear this. Her suspicions were fast becoming reality, and their poor remorseful killer was turning into something much more sinister.

* * *

Eve and Wendy decided to call in on Tamsin on their way to Jacobs Mere House, and check how Bernie was doing.

Eve had been wondering how to broach the subject of the dog with Wendy. Perhaps she would think taking on a dog would curb their activities too much. Suppose they wanted to go off somewhere on the spur of the moment, what would they do with Bernie? With that in mind, Eve had rung Tamsin that morning while Wendy was out in the garden. Tamsin assured her that if they did decide to give him a home, she would be pleased to have him for a few days' holiday with his pal Skipper. Besides, hadn't Bernie always accompanied Justin in his travels around the country filming digs for his show? So, that was one less hurdle to get over, but it was still a big undertaking and they needed to be in complete agreement about it.

Now the two of them were putting away their laptops. 'Not a bad few hours' work, was it?' Eve said.

Wendy nodded with a satisfied smile. 'We still know how to organise a strategy, don't we? As soon as Lionel comes up with a few more names and contact details, we'll be well on our way.'

'And I've just had a very informative text from Lou,' Eve said, 'regarding Justin's history. I'll print it off and you can read it. She says she and Rene are still working their way through the finer details of Justin's past, plus all the info we supplied about what happened to him. However, she says, what they've already uncovered is pretty conclusive. They are now awaiting further instruction.' Eve glanced at her friend. 'Um, Wendy. Can I ask you something?'

'Oh yes? It's not about a certain orphaned Bernese Mountain dog by any chance, is it?'

Wendy roared with laughter at the look on Eve's face.

'For heaven's sake, Eve! Don't you think I know you well enough by now? You've been fretting over that dog's future ever since he went to Tamsin's.'

'Well, er, yes . . .'

Wendy smiled happily at her. 'Of course we should have him! I'd have said something before, but I wanted us to avoid a knee-jerk reaction to the situation.'

Eve felt as if a weight had lifted from her. 'I know we've discussed getting a rescue dog before and always put off making a decision, but this feels right to me, doesn't it you? Bernie needs a stable environment and a lot of love, and we have both the space and the time to give him.'

'In abundance,' Wendy said. 'We'll tell Tamsin and get her seal of approval, then we can tell Lionel what his precious daughter can do with her dog pound.'

'I could hug you, Wendy Avery!'

'Anytime, you old fool! So, how about a cuppa before we head off to Jacobs Mere? We have an investigation to get underway.'

CHAPTER TWENTY-THREE

Now it was empty, Justin's grand old house seemed somehow forlorn. Forensics had packed up and gone, leaving just a couple of officers to monitor visitors and turn away journalists and any members of the public curious to see where the celebrity had lived. The life had gone out of it as if the house, too, was in mourning for its departed owner.

Nikki gazed up at the blank windows. It seemed inconceivable that he could have been happy living alone in this vast echoing place. She supposed he had spent most of his time on the refurbishment. How tragic that he was never granted the time to enjoy the fruits of his labours.

'Lost in thought?' Joseph asked. He locked the car and came round to stand beside her.

'Can a house be bereaved?'

Her question took him by surprise. This wasn't the sort of comment hard-nosed Nikki Galena usually came out with. He looked up at the elegant facade. 'It does look rather sorrowful, doesn't it? I guess that without its human and animal occupants it's nothing but a heap of bricks and stone. It's living beings that make it a home, and infuse it with energy and spirit.'

Nikki nodded. Joseph always managed to put into words what to her were vague impressions beyond her understanding. Suddenly, she turned to face him. 'Whatever happens to us, Joseph — I mean, in the future — we'll stay at Cloud Cottage Farm, won't we? I wouldn't want to live somewhere that contained nothing of my past.'

He squeezed her arm. 'Why spoil something so perfect?'

Relieved, she blinked back a tear.

'And before you burst out crying, Detective Inspector, we need to get inside before Lionel Connaught wonders what's happened to us.'

Nikki giggled. 'Well, I must say that was a first. I've never got emotional over a pile of bricks and mortar before.'

'I promise I won't tell anyone, scout's honour.'

The front door opened, and Lionel, looking haggard but determined, welcomed them in.

'All the rooms are open now,' he informed them, leading the way into the lounge, 'apart from the dining room, of course. That will remain closed until the forensic department give me the all-clear.'

From somewhere in the house, the sound of a vacuum cleaner could be heard.

'Justin's cleaner, Mrs Langrick, has kindly offered to stay on with me,' Lionel said, 'until I decide what to do with the house. She was adamant that she wasn't going to stop coming twice a week as usual. It seems these fen women are more resilient than I gave them credit for.'

Nikki proceeded to give him an overview of what they had discovered in his absence. In return, Lionel handed over a list of names that he had garnered that morning, consisting mainly of people who had been involved in the renovation work, along with a few of Justin's colleagues from the TV show.

Among the latter, Nikki noticed some names that Cat and Ben had mentioned. 'To your knowledge, did Justin ever fall out with any of the gardeners, or maybe one of the landscape designers? I got the impression he might have let one of them go.'

Lionel's brow furrowed. 'I couldn't really say, to be honest. You see, after we got the house up and running I spent more time back at home, and left the garden to him. I do seem to recall him being a bit upset about something.' He looked at his copy of the list of names. 'Ah, here we are. This man might be able to help. Len Fordham. He's a local chap, nice fellow, runs a company that does garden services. He was in charge of clearing some of the areas ready for landscaping.'

'Got him,' Nikki said, looking at her own list. 'I'll give him a bell as soon as we are through here.' She looked up at Lionel. 'Now we need to know everything you can tell us about Justin's former girlfriends — in fact, anyone close to him, especially the woman he split up with recently.'

'That would be Victoria,' said Lionel. 'Victoria Williams, lovely girl. She's at the top of that list. It was a very amicable separation. Note, I said "was". I thought I should ring her and let her know what had happened — after all, they'd been quite close for a while. I couldn't get through to her, so I spoke to a mutual friend who knew them both well. He told me that not long after she and Justin parted, Victoria had a freak accident. Apparently, she was in her parents' kitchen and tripped over a dog's toy, hitting her head on the corner of a granite work surface. She sustained a concussion, and was admitted to hospital for observation. She died the following day.'

'And Justin had no more serious relationships after Victoria?' Nikki asked.

'None at all. I admit I was spending less and less time here by then, but I'm sure he would have told me if he'd been seeing someone new.'

'No one from the past who might have felt aggrieved after they split?' asked Joseph. 'I'm thinking of someone who liked being seen with a celebrity and felt they might have missed out.'

'Justin had few serious relationships that I knew of, Detectives. He was so passionate about his work and the show that he didn't devote a lot of time to socialising.' He looked away for a moment. 'The show. Oh dear, I hope someone takes those lovely youngsters aside and explains what happened properly, and they don't get to hear of it from the media. They all got on so well, there wasn't a prima donna among them. They loved my Justin, every single one of them. He was really good to them, too. They'll be terribly upset.'

'If it helps, Lionel, two of our detectives mentioned that when they went to talk to his colleagues, they were told it had been handled very sensitively, and the kids had been given a great deal of support.'

'Well, that's good to know,' Lionel said. 'I wish I could be of more help. Justin and I discussed all sorts of things while we were organising the work here, but affairs of the heart never really came up.'

Nikki wondered about that. Justin had been a very good-looking man, and a popular TV personality, so where were all the adoring women? Was he gay, and had been keeping it under wraps? She didn't think so. The slightest hint that he was anything but straight would have emerged in the social media, and it had never been mentioned. The image of a lipstick lying under a bedroom chair rose into her mind. Nikki resolved to have a quiet word with Mary Langrick, the cleaning lady, before they left. It was hard to believe that in the bonding between father and son as they worked side by side, there wouldn't have been some mention of women, some bit of banter regarding in Justin's love life. The things some of the male coppers joshed about together would curdle milk, though she supposed Lionel and Justin weren't exactly the type to tell bawdy jokes in the mess room.

It looked as if they were going to need to widen their field of enquiry. Lionel obviously knew next to nothing about his son's social life. Now for the big question.

'Lionel, we'd like to ask you about two things that happened here. They might have nothing at all to do with Justin's death, but even so, Jacobs Mere House connects them.'

She proceeded to tell him about Paul Fletcher and his returning memories of seeing a woman who they now believed to be Patsy Shearer attacked and killed in the grounds of the house.

Lionel looked as if a bomb had fallen on him. 'Little Paulie? You can't mean it!'

'We understand he's a relative on your wife's side of the family. Is that right?' asked Joseph.

'Yes indeed. A sad boy, badly damaged, his life ruined by a tragic accident.'

'We know about his father, Lionel, and we are aware of his mental health issues, but his psychologist is certain this event he witnessed is no flight of fancy.' Joseph regarded him steadily. 'And we have verified that his description of the woman he remembers seeing tallies exactly with that of a community nurse who went missing after visiting a client here at the house. She was never seen again.'

'My God! That's terrible! But what on earth was Paul doing here? As far as I know, Paul lived in a village called Leedyke, and I can't think why he would be in the grounds. I know little about him, other than what my wife told me about his father's accident and the boy having witnessed it. I'm afraid we weren't that close to her side of the family, and none of us had anything to do with old Aaron Fletcher.' Lionel rubbed at his temple. 'The fact is, Aaron was a nasty old man. My Beth, and the few remaining members of her family, would have nothing to do with him.'

'Forgive me for asking, Lionel, but your wife has passed away? Is that right?' Nikki asked.

'Years ago. Cancer. She died when Justin and Heather were children. If it hadn't been for my sister and her husband, who moved in with me, and a stream of wonderful helpers, I can't bear to think what would have happened. At the time my job was vital to the country's security, and as you can imagine, I was caught in a cleft stick.' Lionel shook his head.

'So, why didn't your wife's family inherit the house when the old man died?' Joseph asked.

'Because there was no one, other than Paul and his mother left. My Beth and her brother — Paul's father who fell from the roof — were the only remaining members of what was a very small family to begin with.' He stopped speaking for a moment. 'Aaron left a signed letter with his solicitor disowning his entire family, thereby preventing them from benefiting from his death. He also refused to make a will, so you can imagine the legal mess he left behind. As it was, Paul's mother wouldn't have touched this house with a bargepole, even if it had been left to her or her son. She and my Beth agreed wholeheartedly that Aaron Fletcher was poison.'

'Yet Paul came here regularly, even if no one knew about it, in order to watch birds.' Nikki found that rather odd, considering that his mother hated the owner so much.

Lionel shrugged. 'Sorry, that has come right out of left field, Nikki. I had no idea he came here.'

'Forgive me for asking, but given the extent of your wife's dislike of Aaron Fletcher, why did you and Justin buy it?' asked Nikki.

'Why not?' he said. 'Look around you. The moment we set eyes on it, we could see its potential. And Justin longed to find a retreat from the hectic world of television. And what's more, the grounds are possibly a site of valued historic interest. A Roman village, no less.' He spread his hands. 'Turn all this down because of some old family feud? I don't think so!'

'Point taken,' Nikki said, somewhat abashed.

'By the time we came to view it, my Beth was long gone, and so was her brother. Paul had his issues, and his mother wouldn't have cared if it had burned to the ground. We wrote to her, and she made it clear that she had no opposition to our acquiring the house; in fact, I think she saw it as a fitting parting gesture to Aaron. After all, he would have hated the fact that the house had gone to the family after all his efforts to prevent it.'

Nikki grinned. 'She probably sees it as a kind of karma. Anyway, we'd like to ask your permission to bring Paul Fletcher here, so that he can pinpoint the exact spot where he saw the attack take place. Is that okay with you?'

Lionel hesitated. 'Couldn't it wait until the investigation into my son's murder is further underway? There can be no connection to something that happened a few years ago, surely? I'd have thought his death was your priority.'

'And it is, believe me,' replied Nikki firmly. 'But we cannot say for certain that there isn't a link, no matter how tenuous. We can't ignore what occurred here. If there is the slightest connection between the two incidents and we miss it — well, we can't afford that happening.'

'I'm sorry. Of course you must do whatever you think correct. I suppose this has come as a bit of shock. I have no objection to your bringing him here. Just don't damage him further. Returning to a place where he saw another terrible thing happen could be too much for him.'

'He wants to come, Lionel,' said Joseph. 'And his counsellor will be with him. She'll know how to handle it. He's in a better place after working with her, and she has hopes that seeing this place will aid his recovery.'

Not one hundred per cent sure about that, Nikki nonetheless nodded reassuringly. 'He's in the best possible hands.'

'Then I suggest you arrange it for tomorrow. I've got some things to attend to this afternoon, but I'm free tomorrow.'

Nikki stood up. 'We'll leave you in peace now, Lionel. I'm sure you have a lot to do. Do you mind if we have a quick word with Mary Langrick on our way out? We'll contact you as soon as we've arranged a time with the psychologist and with Paul.'

'You'll find Mary in the kitchen,' said Lionel. 'And come whatever time suits you.'

* * *

They went to find Mary Langrick to ask her about Justin's phone conversations with a mystery woman. She winked at

Joseph. 'Oh, there was someone special all right, I just *know* it, Sergeant. It were just the same with my boy, Jamie, when 'e met 'is Lucy. 'E were 'ead over 'eels in love with 'er but didn't want us to see 'im all soppy-like.'

'And the lipstick you mentioned to the other officer?' asked Nikki.

'Well, the thing is, two weeks before I found it, I'd moved all the furniture, *and* pulled everything out from under the bed — I likes to be thorough and not let the dust build up. Anyway, there was no lipstick anywhere in that room. Following week, there it was.'

'But you never saw this woman?'

'Not while I was 'ere, Inspector, but I only did three hours a day, three days a week, so who's to say she didn't come when I weren't there?' She looked pensive. 'There's another thing. Your nice lady who talked to me before asked about that gardener Mr Justin sacked . . . well, I saw 'im yesterday. 'E was talking to one of those reporter people who've been hanging around the gates. I'd liked to have been a fly on the wall and 'eard what 'e was saying, and no mistake! If I'd 'eard 'im bad-mouthing that lovely Mr Justin, I'd 'ave lamped 'im one, good and proper!'

Picturing Mrs Langrick 'lamping' a burly gardener, Joseph couldn't restrain a smile. 'Thank you, Mrs Langrick, we'll certainly be talking to him. And I must say, it's very good of you to stay on, all things considered. Mr Connaught really appreciates it, he's told us so.'

Mary nodded stoically. 'Fact is, I feels sorry for that poor man, and he needs some help with this big old place. Not that I'll ever be able to set foot in that dining room again, and I couldn't be here alone, I'm afraid. I've made it quite clear to Mr Lionel that I'll not be here after dark.'

'Did you know Aaron Fletcher, the old man who lived here before?' asked Nikki.

'I only heard him talked about, and if that was anything to go on, I was glad I never met 'im. Unfriendly old bugger, so I was told. Mind you, they say he mellowed a bit at the end, especially when he got too sick to help himself and needed carers. He had that dementia, too, they reckon.'

Nikki raised her eyebrows.

'Did you ever hear about a young community nurse who visited him here once and then went missing?' asked Joseph.

'Oh yes,' replied Mary immediately. Joseph was surprised: very few people seemed to have known of Patsy Shearer's disappearance. 'My niece was one of his carers, and she had this nice detective lady come to interview her. They said that nurse turned up somewhere up north, she'd run away from the chap she was living with.'

So, the Fenland grapevine extended as far as Jacobs Mere. Joseph decided to leave it there, and he and Nikki turned to leave.

Just as they reached the door, Mary added, 'Don't think I'm being fanciful-like — I mean, not coming 'ere in the dark or alone, but folk round 'ere are a touch superstitious about this 'ouse and, well, it rubs off after a bit.'

'Superstitious? In what way?' Nikki asked.

'It's the gardens, Detective. There's acres of them, and they're wild, though not so much since Mr Justin started work on them. But parts of the land have always had a bit of a reputation, going back donkey's years.'

Joseph knew only too well how rumours of the supernatural attached themselves to places like the Fens. 'Like what? The Black Dog, or a boggart, maybe?'

'No, I don't think it's anything like that. It's more like things that was done here. Things that don't belong on God's earth. Evil things,' said Mary darkly. 'Lordy, listen to me goin' on. Most likely it's all a load of flam, but what with poor Mr Justin comin' to such a bad end, the old stories have flared up again.'

They left the house and got into the car in silence, both deep in thought. 'You know, Nikki,' Joseph said, 'once we've arranged Paul and Julia's visit here, I think I'll do a bit of ferreting into the history of Jacobs Mere House.'

214

'Good idea. I was thinking the same thing,' Nikki said. 'And I know the very person to help you. Remember that young local historian who was so helpful with Mum and Wendy when they were investigating dark secrets in Beech Lacey?'

'Oh, I know who you mean, that writer chap — er, Jacob Rush. I'll get his number from Eve and give him a call. Good thinking!'

'Talking about thinking, I'm guessing your thoughts are the same as mine. What better way to keep superstitious locals away than to start a rumour about unearthly goings-on.'

'Exactly, and why would you want to keep people away from that particular place?'

'Because something *is* going on, but it's not unearthly,' said Nikki. 'We've seen this before, haven't we? Out on Flaxton Mere.'

Joseph shuddered. *Not again, please.* 'It might well be nothing, just tales, and as Mary said, a death in a place like this always makes people bring up all the old stories about hauntings and the like.' He started the car and pulled out of the driveway. 'That said, I'll be ringing Jacob Rush just as soon as I get hold of his number.'

'Good. I'll see Cat and Ben to find out what, if anything, the TV people have told them. After that, I'll get hold of that landscape gardening company, and see if I can get a name for the guy Justin got rid of.' She patted Joseph's leg. 'Looks like we've got our work cut out for us, so put your foot down, driver!'

CHAPTER TWENTY-FOUR

Ryan handed Gill a printout. Gill scanned the columns of figures, her eyes growing wider and wider as she read.

'Angela Sandford was worth *how* much? Bloody hell! That's a fortune.'

'Yeah, a fortune that Dr French knew about.'

'Hmm, this is a tricky one, isn't it, Ryan?' she said. 'Our good doctor knew Angie had money, but it was she who told him. If this really is a crime of passion, the money is neither here nor there — you can still fall in love with a rich person. On the other hand, what a blindingly good motive for marrying her, and if she told him that wasn't going to happen, it's also a blindingly good motive for murdering her.'

'My money's on the latter,' said Ryan. 'And his performance in the interview room is exactly what you first thought, a ruse to get himself into a hospital rather than a high security prison.'

'So why give himself up in the first place? He didn't have to, he wasn't a suspect, he was home and dry.' Gill groaned. 'We need to talk to Julia Tennant. Bloody Dr French is doing my head in.'

'Good idea,' Ryan said, 'maybe she'll—'

As he was speaking, Gill received a call from Richard. 'Is everything okay there?'

'No, ma'am, far from it. Claire has disappeared from the safe house!' Richard sounded beside himself. 'Lizzie had been trying to reach out to her, and felt she was beginning to get somewhere. She had got Claire to promise to talk to both of us after lunch. Lizzie came to tell me, and we both waited for her to come down. When she didn't show, I went to her room, and found her gone. We checked the whole house from top to bottom and couldn't find her anywhere. Our protection officer has reported it in, but I wanted to tell you myself. I'm sorry, ma'am, I've let you down.'

'Cobblers, Richard!' said Gill. 'You should never have been caught up in all this in the first place. No way have you let me down, you've been nothing but a help. Now, shut up and listen. Have you checked the CCTV?'

'I was just coming to that, ma'am. Colin Jones checked it at once. He saw her climb out of a downstairs window at the back of the house and make off. There was no one else in sight, so it seems she left of her own free will.'

Gill felt guilty. She was pretty certain this wouldn't have happened if they'd been left at Richard's house. Claire had been moved to safety with the best of intentions, but she clearly had other ideas. Where could she have gone? 'I need to make the super aware of this, but I'll get back to you as soon as I can. Sit tight, and get Lizzie to tell you every single thing that Claire said to her before she did a runner. Your protection officer will have arranged to get people out there to look for her, but she could be miles away by now.' She thought for a moment. 'Did she take anything with her?'

'Nothing that Colin could see on the CCTV, and as we only brought a few clothes and toiletries, she really had nothing to take. No phone or handbag.'

'So, no way of getting a taxi, or phoning a friend to collect her. This doesn't seem right, does it?'

'Not right at all,' Richard said. 'But nothing makes sense where Claire is concerned. She's been acting strange ever since she clammed up back at my house.'

'Go over it all again with Lizzie, and I'll get back to you in half an hour or so.' Gill ended the call and stood up. Cam wasn't going to be pleased with this new development. Not pleased at all.

* * *

Julia Tennant was noting the time of the following day's visit to Jacobs Mere in her diary when the phone rang. 'Hello, Detective Sergeant Compton, how can I help you?'

Ryan told her of their discovery that Angela Sandford had been a very rich woman, and that Dr Bill French knew of it. 'We need to get your take on his behaviour, Professor Tennant. We are struggling to understand why he confessed when he wasn't a suspect and probably never would have been.'

'I've just been talking to him, as a matter of fact,' she said, 'and in layman's terms, he's a mess. I can't give you his history, since I am bound by my oath of confidentiality, but I've discovered a lot in my last two sessions with him. I can assure you that it was indeed a crime of passion, and not premeditated.' Julia pictured Bill's wild, empty eyes as he struggled to explain his feelings when Angie turned down his offer of marriage. Old hurts and rejections had bubbled to the surface, and with them a boiling anger that had overwhelmed him, transforming him, in the space of thirty minutes, from caring doctor to sadistic murderer. When he remembered the small packet of lethal drugs still in his jacket pocket, Angie's fate was sealed. 'What I can tell you is that his younger life was far from easy, and it took many years to turn an angry and bitter young man into a highly respected medical professional. But the years of his youth left their mark. He admitted to alerting the police to the fact that it was a murder rather than a suicide

218

with the aim of diverting suspicion from himself. Then he realised that he would have to perjure himself in court, and, worse, speak openly about his feelings for Angie. At that point, the horror of what he had done hit him like a runaway lorry, and he couldn't live with it. He really did love Angie, there is no doubt about it. He killed her on the very night he planned to put a ring on her finger. Yes, he knew she had money, but that meant nothing to him. He's comfortably off himself, and certainly had no need of cash. I believe you can forget that motive, Sergeant. Now the realisation has set in, he's eaten up with remorse at what he's done, and his mind is dangerously close to shutting down completely. I've recommended that he be taken to a secure psychiatric unit for assessment. It's also my belief that the only person to whom he represents a danger is himself.'

Julia thought Ryan Compton had sounded a little disappointed with her verdict, but there it was. She had no doubts about Bill French. She hadn't been able to tell the detective about the childhood Bill thought was long buried, the rages long overcome. The times when he had been laughed at, ridiculed, and mercilessly taunted. With the murder of Angela Sandford, all that was over. Dr French was as dead as the woman he had loved.

* * *

Judging from his appearance, one would think Jacob Rush spent his time in fashionable bars and nightclubs rather than the recesses of some dusty archive. He greeted Joseph warmly, and took him up to his big, airy apartment over a stable block attached to his parents' home. Besides his passion for local history, Jacob Rush was a successful novelist, with ten critically acclaimed thrillers under his belt. Having invited Joseph to take a seat, he asked after Eve and Wendy.

'They're fine, Jacob. As usual, we're struggling to keep them out of trouble.'

Jacob grinned broadly. 'Oh, don't ever stop them, Sergeant Easter. Those two are something else. I had a great time helping them with that investigation of theirs. Anyway, I understand you need some help with a local legend, or something like that?'

Joseph told him about the rumours concerning Jacobs Mere House and gardens, and Jacob laughed. 'You've come to the right person, Sergeant. In fact, I got my name from that place. There's an old windmill out there, which, along with hundreds of acres of farmland, once belonged to my grandfather. My mother always says that no matter where I go in the world, I'll be taking part of her home with me.'

'So, you know the place?'

'Of course. And, naturally, as soon as I heard the tales of what was supposed to have gone on there, I did some research for myself.'

Well, well. This could speed things up considerably, Joseph thought.

'Would you like a coffee? Then I'll tell you all I know.'

While he waited, Joseph looked at his surroundings. Jacob's home consisted of a single, lofty open plan room. Tall windows let in the daylight, which fell on the walls opposite, lined with bookshelves so high that Jacob used a library ladder to reach the top rows. At one end of the room was a desk with a PC, along with filing cabinets and a run of cupboards and drawers. Two long sofas faced each other in the centre of the room, between them a low coffee table crafted from restored reclaimed wood.

'What a place to work in,' he said admiringly, as Jacob set their mugs onto the table.

'I never thought I'd end up actually living here,' he said. 'It was meant to be a studio, somewhere quiet for me to work. I liked being here so much that after my first four books took off, I made it into a home. Luckily, I get on really well with my parents, so having them next door suits us all perfectly.' He picked up his mug. 'Now, if you're ready, I'll tell you something of the history of Jacobs Mere House.'

Joseph sat back on the comfortable sofa and listened.

'You really need to understand a little of the topography of that part of the Fens. That tiny hamlet has been there for centuries. It's one of those small islets you get that are formed out of land that was a little higher than the marsh. The original settlement dates back to pre-Roman times.'

Joseph nodded. 'I did hear that Justin Connaught believed there might be Roman remains in the grounds of the house, but I admit I'm not too clued-up about Roman Lincolnshire.'

'Well, the county was occupied by the Romans for over three centuries. Lincoln, known then as Lindum Colonia, became one of the most important Roman garrison towns. It was the second most northerly Roman outpost in England after York. You can still see markers in the Bailgate area of the city depicting the exact location of the forum's impressive colonnade, and the Newport Arch is the only Roman Arch still open to traffic.' He grimaced. 'Sorry, I get carried away sometimes, you didn't come here for a history lesson. Back to the goings-on at Jacobs Mere House.'

Joseph could see why Eve and Wendy liked this young man so much. He was quite clearly passionate about history, and his enthusiasm was infectious.

'Tell you what, I'll give you a brief history of the place, and if it helps, I can print off a more detailed account for you to take away and read at your leisure.'

'That's perfect,' said Joseph.

'Well, where do I start . . . Parts of the house go back to the seventeenth century, although it was added to and altered over the years. Previously, there had been an old Franciscan friary on that spot. Believe it or not, there are the remains of several monastic houses in Greenborough itself. Anyway, the friary was eventually abandoned, and fell into disrepair, which is when the rumours and old wives' tales began to circulate. You can imagine, can't you? People out after dark swearing they've seen hollow-eyed apparitions in monks' habits rising up out of the mist. Sounds carrying over the marsh, ghostly choristers.' He rolled his eyes and grinned. 'Great stuff. Perfect black and white B-movie footage.'

Joseph could imagine it. 'And that kind of thing gets woven into the history of a place, doesn't it? Passed down through the generations.'

'Exactly, and over the years the rumours solidified, and became fact.' He took a swallow of his coffee. 'After several generations in which nothing much was done with the place, the land was sold and a grand house began construction on the site of the friary. This should have put paid to the belief that it was a "devilish" place, as people put it, but it actually did the opposite. If anything could go wrong with the building work, it did. There were numerous accidents, two builders even lost their lives when a wall collapsed and crushed them. It finished up taking far too long to build. Workers had to be brought in from outside, as the locals refused to go near the place. In the end, the stress became too much for the man who had commissioned the building, and he killed himself.'

'Phew! I see now why people think the place is cursed,' said Joseph.

'And some!' agreed Jacob. 'But now we come to the interesting bit. The partially finished house stayed empty for decades, naturally adding fuel to the haunted house stories. Then it was bought for a ridiculously low price by a rich landowner from up county who had no time for local superstitions.' Jacob grinned. 'But he *was* greedy, and cunning; in fact, he was a particularly unpleasant man all round. He knew the place's reputation and used it to his advantage. He brought in a team of craftsmen from the north, and the house was finally completed in the mid seventeen hundreds. The new owner, whose name was Henry Hillsborough, was a follower of the infamous Hellfire Club.'

'Not Francis Dashwood, eleventh Baron le Despencer,' Joseph said, 'satanic rituals and devil worship?'

Jacob laughed. 'Oh no! The one Hillsborough was so enamoured of was the original Hellfire Club, founded by a young aristocrat called Philip Wharton. His club was even worse than what went on in London — they indulged in entire nights of drunkenness, gluttony, fornication and blasphemy.'

'Nice.'

'It must have been quite something, as Wharton died at the age of thirty-three. Drank himself to death, by all accounts. It was after that that your Dashwood formed his club at Medmenham Abbey in Buckinghamshire. Contrary to popular belief, he never called it the Hellfire Club but the *Knights of St Francis*, and it was a decidedly unholy order. Not quite satanism or devil worship, but they dressed in habits, called each other "Brother", and basically indulged in all the same things as Wharton did, including making a mockery of religious practices, especially the monastic orders.' Jacob took another gulp of coffee. 'Knowing that his grand house was built over the remains of a Franciscan friary, Hillsborough really relished the title, *Knights of St Francis*. He thought it was a great joke.'

'And he followed in their footsteps? Copied their practices, I mean,' said Joseph.

'Without a doubt. And he made use of all the old superstitions, stirring them up so as to keep nosy parkers from venturing into his grounds.' Jacob drained his coffee. 'Talking of which, it was rumoured that he built a "temple" in the gardens, hollowing out a number of caverns beneath it, a little like Dashwood did in his estate at West Wycombe Park. He used it for nocturnal gatherings of a few chosen friends, who shared his unnatural appetites, and to which they brought prostitutes. Though I suppose if it ever existed, it's probably a ruin by now.'

Joseph shook his head. 'And I thought Jacobs Mere was such a peaceful place. For heaven's sake, my daughter and her husband live there. They'll *love* this story!'

Jacob laughed. 'Don't worry. After two generations of exceedingly bad behaviour, Henry and his equally depraved son were killed when their carriage overturned and threw them both into a river, thus bringing the Hillsborough line to an abrupt end. From then on, a series of more "acceptable" owners came and went until, finally, the Fletcher family bought it. Old man Fletcher was an unfriendly and ill-tempered man, he lived as a recluse and kept people off his grounds and so the stories of evil goings-on resurfaced.'

'Oh my!' said Joseph. 'That's some history to inherit! Yet Justin and his father loved that house and everything about it. How weird is that?'

'I understand he was an archaeologist, so maybe that explains it,' said Jacob. 'They are interested in artifacts, tangible things, not stories. They tend to be level-headed, pragmatic people. Justin probably saw nothing more than an exceptionally lovely house.' He sat back. 'Well, that's about it. I'm not sure if my ramblings have helped at all, but I will let you have my notes if you like. They're quite extensive, so it might be best if I email them to you rather than print them out.'

Joseph thanked him, gave Jacob his email address and stood up to go. 'You know, for some reason, I can't help thinking that all these rumours and superstitions are somehow linked to what happened, although I have no idea how or why.'

Jacob grinned. 'If I was you, I'd run it past Eve and Wendy. Knowing them, they'll find you an answer in no time.'

'They've been to that house twice already, we couldn't keep them out of it if we tried,' Joseph said with an answering grin.

'Excellent! Please pass on my very best wishes to them, and tell them I said it's time we caught up again.'

The whole way back to the station, Joseph couldn't shake the strange feeling that somewhere in the midst of all Jacob had told him was something crucial, but he couldn't for the life of him work out what that was.

* * *

'Well, apart from being the best news ever, I need to make quite sure you're aware of what you are taking on.'

Trying not to smile at Tamsin's serious face, Eve said, 'We've done our homework, Tam, I promise. We know Berners are a high-maintenance breed, but we have the perfect environment for Bernie at Monks Lantern.'

'And he'll have all the time in the world to readjust at his own speed.' She looked across to the big dog lying quietly in his bed. 'We're thinking of going by the three-three-three rule, you know, like you use with any rescue dog. What do you think?'

Tamsin broke into a smile. 'Okay, I'm convinced. You have been doing your homework. Three days to adjust to his new surroundings, three weeks bonding and training, and three months settling into his new home, building his confidence, and strengthening the bond you'll be creating.' She looked fondly at the dog. 'He's going to adapt, I know it. I believe he understands on some level, but he can't know what the future holds for him. He might test the boundaries, but don't be discouraged. Seeing him relax into his new life will be one of the most rewarding experiences you'll ever have.' She grinned. 'Even for two old daredevils like you!'

'I'm sure Lionel won't object. Our only concern is that we have committed a few days to helping him get some information on his son and what was going on with him just before his murder,' Eve said.

'Well, as it happens I've got another three days before I return to the field. I might even be able to swing another day to do some admin work from home. Then he must go to you.'

'Perfect,' said Wendy. 'We've already done quite a bit of research, and for Bernie's sake, we'll set ourselves a deadline. Give us those three days to assist Lionel, and then we'll hand everything over to him or Nikki, and pull out.'

'And that's a promise,' added Eve.

Tamsin's eyes lit up. 'Talking of that, I've discovered something about Jacobs Mere House that no one may be aware of.'

Eve at forward. 'Oh?'

'People — two men, possibly more — gain access to the grounds on a pretty regular basis.'

'How do they do that with police on the gates and a securely locked back entrance?' asked Wendy.

'Because there's a third way in, and I have an idea that even Justin didn't know about it,' said Tamsin smugly.

'How the dickens did you discover that?' demanded Eve.

'Because of a buzzard's nest, and the local baker's old granny.'

Eve stared at her. 'Um, excuse me? Even my brilliant mind can't get a handle on that one.'

'Have you time for a cuppa before you go to meet Lionel?' Tamsin asked.

'We have, and it would be very welcome after that little bombshell,' exclaimed Wendy.

As she made the tea, Tamsin explained. 'You know I work with farmers to promote agricultural biodiversity. Well, I'm now doing a few odd days with the Woodlands Trust as well, just updating them on local issues along with sightings of various species of flora and fauna, especially migrant birds.' She placed mugs of tea in front of them. 'One of my regular spotters is Charlie Lambert, the local baker. He has a small family bakery next to the pub, and he's an avid birder. I saw him yesterday, and just in passing, he mentioned that it had been quite something to see buzzards nesting at Jacobs Mere House for the third year running. He said he was looking forward to seeing whether they continued to do so, they love the mature trees there. He went on to say he'd identified the actual nesting area.' Tamsin frowned. 'Knowing the size of the grounds, the high wall, and the trees surrounding the perimeter, I asked him how he'd managed that. He told me his gran had shown him a way into the property, back when he was a little kid. They knew they were trespassing, but they also knew it was haunted, and it was too tempting to resist having a look.'

Eve saw immediately just how important this information was. If this means of access was known to the locals, it could have been known to Justin's killer too.

'So, I asked him if he'd show me,' said Tamsin. 'You'd never find it on your own, it's so well-hidden. It's an old wooden gate in the wall, completely obscured by a thick clump of shrubs and trees. It's the same on the inside too. It's not visible from the house or the gardens, and you'd have to do an inch-by-inch search of the perimeter to find it. Charlie says the local birdwatchers have been using it for years.'

'And what about these other men you mentioned?' asked Eve.

'Well, Charlie thought they were probably birdwatchers too. The thing is, until Justin arrived, the estate had been virtually untouched, left to grow wild over decades. There are birds there that you just don't get to see normally. It's home to all kinds of wildlife — badgers, foxes, deer, muntjacs, water voles . . . Charlie said it's no wonder people get in there to have a look.'

Eve was very keen to have a look herself. One glance at Wendy's expression told her she was just as eager.

'Not only that, but there are some ruined buildings in the gardens. Charlie says there's one like an old folly — looks a bit like a temple, he reckons — that owls nest in. He's seen all sorts — Tawny owls, Barn owls, Long-eared owls and Little owls.' Tamsin's face lit up with enthusiasm. 'He said his father even spotted a Eurasian eagle owl there once, and you don't see many of them.'

'So, he thinks these other men are on the lookout for rare birds. They could be stealing eggs — I'm told there is money to be made from that nasty little crime,' said Wendy thoughtfully. 'I wonder.'

'Possibly, he's not certain. He's seen them several times recently. It puzzled him because local birders tend to share their sightings with each other, and everyone knows everyone else, but he didn't know either of those men.' Tamsin frowned. 'And that makes me wonder if they're there for a very different reason.'

'You're not alone there,' murmured Eve. 'By the way, did the men see Charlie?'

'No, he kept well out of sight. For one thing, he didn't want the police knowing he was getting inside the estate.'

'So, what could they have been up to?' Eve was already considering spending a night by that secret door. 'Thank you for telling us, Tamsin. Do you think you could show us where it is exactly? Then we really should get down to the house, or Lionel will think we've forgotten him.'

'Sure. I'll just settle Bernie and Skipper with a treat, then we can walk over. It's only ten minutes or so from here.'

Soon they were standing in front of the hidden gateway. It was clear from the flattened grass leading up to it that it was used regularly, but did the footprints belong only to bird-watchers? Eve didn't think so, not for one minute. There were goings-on here that Lionel knew nothing about, but maybe Justin *had* known, and this was what he had wanted to talk to them about. It was tenuous, but possible, and Eve had a suspicion that this secret entrance was the gateway to something rather sinister.

'Come on, Eve, we'd better get going,' Wendy was saying.

'Oh, yes, of course.' Eve pulled herself back to the present. 'And thank you again for showing us this, Tam. You're an asset to the team, and we owe you one!' She regarded Tamsin narrowly. 'But no sneaking out after dark to get a glimpse of these unknown men, understand? We have no idea what the hell is going on here, but a pound to a penny, it's not good. Your Niall would never forgive us if he found you coming down here on your own.'

'What? Me?' Tamsin said, all innocence.

'Yes, you,' said Wendy. 'We just might, as I'm sure you've guessed, but we have experience of that kind of sleuthing. And we don't want to get on the wrong side of your law-abiding husband. We have no idea what we're dealing with here, and your safety must come first. If someone saw fit to kill a lovely man like Justin, they'd have no qualms about killing an equally lovely young woman, especially if they thought she was nosing around where she wasn't wanted.'

'Put like that, I'll probably stay at home with the doors locked, trembling in my socks.' Tamsin laughed. 'But promise you'll let me know what you find out. All right?'

Eve hugged her affectionately. 'We will. Now we really must get on. We have three days to solve a murder before we introduce a very sad boy to his new home.'

* * *

The single police car at the gate took their names and car registration number and waved them inside. As Wendy pulled away, Eve's phone rang.

'Jacob Rush! This is a surprise. How are you?'

'I'm ridiculously well. I have a new book coming out next week, and I've just heard that you two are once again delving into another murder. You are quite incorrigible!'

With a laugh, Eve put her phone on loudspeaker. 'Who told you that?'

'A very nice detective sergeant by the name of Easter.'

'Joseph? Oh my! He didn't warn you off talking to us, did he?' she asked, wondering if Nikki was ring-fencing them.

'No, he didn't. In fact, he all but admitted that it would be a lost cause to try and hobble you and Wendy when you had the bit between your teeth.' Jacob laughed. 'But listen. I'm not sure how involved you are, but if you are doing what I think, then I can be of help to you. I know a lot about Jacobs Mere House, and I've sent all the notes I've compiled to the sergeant. Since you are probably looking at the case from a different angle, I thought you might like the same information.'

'Too right we would!' Eve said.

'Then I'll email it to you. Knowing you two, you could most likely find it for yourselves, but I'll be saving you a whole lot of time.'

'Well, Jacob, thank you. You've just earned yourself one of Wendy's special chilli con carne dinners.'

'I was hoping you'd say that.'

'Sorry, Jacob, but I've got to go, we have an appointment. I'll ring you tonight after we've had a look at your email. Is that all right?' asked Eve.

'I'll be all yours. Speak later. Oh, and take care. Murder is not to be taken lightly.'

'We never do. That's why we are still here and not dead and buried decades ago!' Eve said.

'Even so, do look after yourselves.'

Smiling, Eve ended the call. Another helpful ally. Things were looking up.

CHAPTER TWENTY-FIVE

Nikki's call to the landscape gardener hadn't been particularly informative. Len Fordham had only taken the man on a short-term cash-in-hand basis after two of his usual men were off sick. He hadn't worked out, so he'd let him go. It sounded to Nikki as if Len was disappointed with the man, whom he only knew as Dennis, because he had upset a good well-paying client. He knew nothing about this Dennis, who although he had a local accent, wasn't from Jacobs Mere. When Nikki asked if he had any idea what the dispute with Justin had been about, he said he was sorry but he'd only heard about it second-hand and couldn't say.

'I'd have let him go anyway, Detective Inspector. Apart from upsetting a valued customer, my seven-year-old grandson knows more about gardening than that bloke. I wouldn't have taken him on, but I didn't want to let Mr Connaught down. Besides, it was a big project, and a very lucrative one at that.'

Nikki asked him if any of his workforce might either know what the argument had been about, or could tell her the man's name and where they could find him. 'He was seen talking to reporters outside Justin Connaught's home in the last couple of days, Mr Fordham, and we'd like to speak to him urgently.'

'I'll have a word with my men and get back to you,' he promised.

Nikki rang off, almost certain that she would hear no more from Len Fordham. The whole episode had lost him the biggest contract his company had ever been awarded, and, understandably, he wanted nothing more to do with it.

'Boss?'

She looked up to see Cat and Ben standing in her doorway. 'Come in, you two. Anything tasty from the TV company?'

Cat sighed. 'We hit a brick wall, boss. No quarrels, nothing other than the usual minor differences that arise between professionals working together.'

'It appears that Justin was exactly as everyone says — a bloody nice bloke, with no side to him, passionate about archaeology and keen to pass on that love of it to others, especially the young.' Ben shrugged. 'Even that thing with the married woman turned out to be a crock of shit.'

'Yeah,' grumbled Cat. 'A female colleague dismissed by the TV company, who decided to get back at them by slinging some mud at their precious star. She had nothing personally against Justin, she simply wanted to make the series out to be a sham and the presenter a sleazy womaniser.'

'Why was she taken off the series in the first place?' Nikki asked.

'Again, nothing to do with Justin,' Ben said. 'She wasn't a team player, and tried to get ahead by bad-mouthing her colleagues. In other words, she's another red herring.'

'Ben's right,' added Cat. 'And it's been the same with every other issue we thought might be a bit suspect. We've now spoken to everyone we missed on our last visit, and also crossed off that guy who didn't seem upset by the news of Justin's death. Apparently, he's got a loved one with a terminal illness.'

'The only remaining thing is what his research assistant, Sheena Coates, told us. Remember she said Justin had seemed unusually anxious about something? We spoke to her again, and she swears she was right. It was so unlike Justin that it stuck in her mind,' Ben said.

'She also said it came on very suddenly,' added Cat, 'from one day to the next. We've pinned it down to about three days before his death.'

'That explains why his father wouldn't have been aware of it,' Nikki said, 'if something was indeed troubling him.'

'And it also ties in with what Eve and Wendy said, that he wanted their opinion on something that was bothering him,' said Cat. 'I reckon that whatever it was it had nothing to do with his past, but was something that happened just a few days before he died.'

Nikki agreed. 'And since the last woman he was known to be involved with is dead, too, I guess that avenue is closed to us — even though that lipstick under his bed does rather haunt me.'

Ben laughed. 'Sorry, boss, but even if people regarded him as a saint, he wasn't a monk. If he didn't occasionally succumb to a pretty face, I'd be worried there was something wrong with him.'

Cat rolled her eyes. 'Typical bloke. But he does have a point, doesn't he, boss? I'm sure there's any number of women who wouldn't say no to a night with Justin Connaught. A rich, handsome television celebrity? They'd be jumping at the chance.'

'Point taken,' said Nikki, though she still wondered. What if this particular one-night stand had involved a woman with a jealous partner? They couldn't just dismiss that lipstick. 'Okay, so anyway, as soon as Joseph gets back from seeing the historian, I suggest we all pitch in and concentrate on the last three days of Justin Connaught's life. I want an hour by hour, blow-by-blow, account of every movement, every place he went, and everyone he interacted with during that time. Somewhere in there is the reason for his death.'

* * *

As Joseph entered the CID room, Gill Mercer was walking towards him, her face set in a grim expression. He held the door open for her. 'Dare I ask?'

Gill puffed out her cheeks. 'Well . . . How would you feel if the woman you have taken great pains to conceal buggers off out of a window of the safe house you've arranged for her?'

Joseph winced. 'Ouch! I'd feel much like you look. Any hint as to why? I'd have thought she'd be well pleased to be somewhere out of harm's way.'

'We have no idea what's going on in her head, Joseph. She has no money, no phone, and is out of the county, so what is her plan? I'm buggered if I know!'

'Maybe she doesn't have one,' said Joseph softly. 'Incarceration, even when it's for your own good, doesn't suit everyone. Maybe the whole situation, especially Joanne's death, just got too much for her.'

'And I'm scared shitless for her.' Gill heaved a sigh. 'I should never have moved her out of Richard's house, but we really believed it to be for the best. Now it's backfired, big-style.'

Joseph felt for her. Gill would feel responsible for Claire's safety, even though it wasn't her fault that Claire had chosen to disregard the help she had been given.

'Their protection officer is climbing the walls. Poor guy, he'll be for the high-jump, even though he couldn't have prevented it,' said Gill. 'He'd been paying particular attention to her too. It seems she spent most of her time alone, refusing to talk even to Richard, and she'd been so close to him until we shipped them out. Richard says she had some kind of episode, as if something she recalled had suddenly scared her half to death. Neither he nor Lizzie can fathom it out.'

Before she could say more, her mobile rang. Joseph was about to walk away, but she caught hold of his arm. 'It's Richard.'

Joseph listened to what Richard was saying. 'We've found a note, ma'am! Claire left one in her room. She's planning on killing herself! I'm desperate to go and look for her, but Colin

234

won't allow it. She can't have gone far, surely. I know I can be of help.'

'Steady, Richard, just calm down. I know this is a shock, but Colin is right. You are going nowhere. It's far too dangerous. Can you tell me what the note says?'

Richard took a deep breath. 'Sorry, ma'am, I understand. It's just so . . . so awful. I've got the note here, I'll give it to Colin to bag for evidence. She says she's sorry for all the trouble she's brought on everyone and goes on to say, *There is no longer any point in going on. I would have ended it here and now, but you, my dear friends Richard and Lizzie, have been through enough without having to find my dead body. So it's best I leave. My greatest hope is that whoever wants me dead will find me and then leave you both alone. It's me they are after, and they only murdered my lovely Joanne to get at me, so if I'm out of the equation there will be no point in them hurting you. Please apologise to the protection officer, as he has done his duty in exemplary fashion. He couldn't be expected to know that the danger came from within, and that I was going to leave of my own accord. Thank you for trying to protect me, but enough is enough. It ends here. Claire Hereward.*'

Gill thanked him, and told him to look after Lizzie, as it must have been a terrible shock for her too. 'Stick it out, Richard. We have to assume the threat to you is still active until we know otherwise. There are officers combing the area around the safe house, and we have alerted all forces to keep a lookout for sightings of Claire. We can't do more than that. We can only hope that she sees sense when she's been out there a while. Meantime, I'd still like you and Lizzie to try to work out what might have been said to cause that memory to resurface. I think it's vital. That memory is what gave rise to her sudden withdrawal, and most probably her decision to take her own life. Can you do that?'

Richard assured her that he would do his best and, apologising for his lapse in professionalism, ended the call.

'Once a copper always a copper,' said Joseph. 'Even down to the "ma'am".'

'Poor sod, he didn't deserve this to happen. Some retirement!' Gill said.

'There's nothing you could have done to protect Claire from herself, Gill. You couldn't control what went on in her mind.'

'You can imagine what the press will do with it, though, can't you?' Gill said. 'I can see the headlines now.'

Sadly, so could Joseph. 'Let's hope they don't get wind of it. They're dining out on Justin Connaught at present, so maybe they won't be quite so interested in your runaway victim — especially if the super manages to keep it under wraps.'

'I'm on my way to see him now, Joseph. Cam isn't exactly Harry Potter, but he's got some amazing powers when it comes to throwing a cloak of invisibility over things we don't want the media getting their hands on. Wish me luck!'

Joseph went directly to his office, opened his emails, and true to the young historian's word, found several files from Jacob Rush. He skimmed through them, and then went to find Zena, the office manager, and asked her to print off five copies of each. They would take a bit of reading, so each member of the team would need their own copy if they were to go through them thoroughly.

Fifteen minutes later, Zena handed him five neat plastic folders. As she did so, he heard Nikki calling for a campfire. Well, at least he had something to share with them, and he was going to be very interested to see if they felt as he did — that something from the past had emerged, and that something had led to murder.

* * *

Almost automatically, Eve, Wendy and Lionel slipped back into military mode. They found themselves discussing the case like a group of wartime generals, and the gleaming, newly designed kitchen acquired the air of a strategic operations room.

They presented facts, put forward hypotheses and considered options. Clinical and efficient. Detached. It was the only way they could deal with an event that had touched them all personally. Lionel was obviously the most affected — after all, he had lost his precious son. But Eve and Wendy, too, had been shaken by the death of a young man they had known as a boy, and both cared about.

Finally, Eve summed up. 'So, I take it that using all the information provided by our researchers, Lou and Rene, we are in agreement that Justin was involved in no nefarious dealings, had no contact with anyone of dubious character, was universally liked and highly respected in the field of archaeology.'

'Therefore,' added Wendy, 'we may conclude that his death is related to something that happened after he moved into Jacobs Mere House.'

'And most probably after my return to the Lake District, when I had less direct contact with him.' Lionel sat back and looked at his two companions. 'That narrows the time frame considerably, doesn't it?'

Both women murmured in agreement. 'Especially considering his last words to us, in which he mentioned that something was bothering him. We also know that the police are looking at past events that occurred in the grounds of this very estate. We know this from a contact of ours who was approached by Joseph this morning. He is a local historian with considerable knowledge of Jacobs Fen, and this house in particular.'

Wendy smiled. 'And, luckily, he is sending us the same information that he has given to the police. We should have it by the time we get back to Beech Lacey.'

'We'll send it to you immediately we receive it, Lionel,' said Eve. 'You might find an event or possibly a story there that Justin expressed an interest in, even in passing.'

'I'm beginning to wish I'd paid more attention to Justin's plans for the grounds.' Lionel shook his head. 'I must confess I'm more of a bricks and mortar man myself, and took little interest in the gardens and the surrounding estate. To be honest, I've barely set foot out there.'

'Then maybe now's the time to rectify that,' suggested Wendy, 'since so much happened here in the past, not to mention what's still going on, probably as we speak.'

'Like people using a third entrance to gain access to parts of your land,' concluded Eve.

'What?' Lionel looked aghast. 'Trespassers! Here?'

'I'm afraid so. How about a walk, Lionel? We'll show you the Secret Gate.'

'One thing before we go,' said Wendy. 'Did Justin draw up any plans for the layout of his new garden?'

Lionel frowned. 'Yes, I remember now. He told me that next time I came down he'd show me what he had in mind. He was always a great one for blueprints, produced them all the time for his archaeological digs. He used ground penetrating radar surveys for those. Maybe we should check his study? I know the police took his laptop, but he liked to put things down on paper. I'm fairly sure he had one of those big folio cases that artists use. He used it to carry his diagrams of digs, but he might well have done the same for the garden designs.'

'Let's look for that now, shall we?' suggested Eve. 'And the landscape designers he used must have had one.'

'Yes, indeed. Len Fordham was his name. He had a local company that undertook quite big projects,' said Lionel. 'Your daughter was going to contact him today.'

'Why don't you ring him?' Eve said. 'He should be able to tell you exactly what Justin commissioned him to do, especially if you make it sound as if you might be considering going ahead with your son's plans for the place. Big job, big money. I think he'll suddenly be very forthcoming. What say you?'

'Smart move. I've got his number, I'll do it right away,' Lionel said.

'And we'll go and look for that portfolio carry case — that is if you don't mind us going into Justin's study?' Wendy looked a little sad. 'We know where it is. He was very proud of it when he showed us around the house.'

'By all means. Go wherever you like,' said Lionel. 'You are streets ahead of me already. I'll ring the landscaping company and see how convincing I can be.'

They met back in the kitchen twenty minutes later. Wendy produced a large black carrying case. 'You were right, Lionel. It's full of plans, sketches and diagrams, all of different areas of the Jacobs Mere grounds.'

'And Eve was right, too,' said Lionel. 'Mr Fordham went into great detail about the project, and is emailing me all Justin's instructions for it. What's more, he mentioned some parts of the garden that Justin wanted left alone. Apparently, he left strict instructions that no one was to touch them, and had even intended to cordon them off. He believed these areas to be possible sites of archaeological interest. Fordham asked me if I wished them to remain untouched.'

'Is that the Roman village he spoke of?' Eve asked.

'Must be,' Lionel said. 'Justin was very excited about the possibility of a discovery on his own land. He had an idea for footage that would be incorporated into his TV programme.'

'He told us about that, he said he wanted to make it in sepia, so it looked like old archive material. He didn't want to bring the whole crew out here but would shoot it himself, with perhaps a couple of trusted camera operators — and Bernie, of course.' With a lump in her throat, Eve recalled Justin's almost boyish enthusiasm. 'And talking of Bernie . . .'

She and Wendy told him about their wish to adopt Bernie — with his permission, of course. For a moment Lionel seemed close to tears, and then he beamed at them.

'Thank God for that! I've been so worried about Bernie, and what would happen to him. I'd have taken him like a shot, but my sister's allergy is a serious one. I'm the same way with horses, it hits me like an asthma attack, and I struggle to breathe. It was a standing joke in our family, given that we deal in equestrian equipment and animal feeds. Of two siblings, one is allergic to dogs and the other to horses. You couldn't make it up!'

'Well, we've been thinking about adopting a rescue dog for a while now,' said Wendy. 'It's true we hadn't thought of one quite the size of Bernie, but we have the space and can give him a good home. And to be honest, we'd like to do it for Justin. He loved that dog, and so will we.'

'I have no doubt about that. Naturally, I will cover the vet's bills and anything else you need for him.'

'Oh no you won't,' said Eve. 'We can afford his care, otherwise we wouldn't have suggested it. If we take him, he is our responsibility.'

'Then let me at least supply you with his food. I was doing it for my son, ever since he first got Bernie. After all, it's what we do. We produce top quality organic dog food — and believe me, that lad can eat!'

Eve held up her hands in surrender. 'Okay, we'll agree on that one, but the rest is down to us, no arguments. Now, let's take a walk in your garden, then when we get back, you will put the kettle on and we'll have a look at Justin's plans. Agreed?'

'Yes, ma'am!' chorused Wendy and Lionel.

'Oh dear, I'm being bossy again, aren't I?'

'Just a tad, Eve dear, but that's nothing new,' said Wendy.

* * *

Richard and Lizzie were kept up to date with the search for Claire by a crestfallen Colin Jones. Poor Colin. Richard felt terribly sorry for him. There really was nothing he could have done, but he obviously saw it as a failure on his part. In truth, it would have been far worse for Colin if Claire had taken her own life while she was still in the house.

There was no news. The search had been extended, but there were still no sightings of her. She had most likely gone to ground somewhere, possibly waiting for nightfall to slip away undetected. Now that he had recovered from the initial shock and got his head together, Richard decided that this simply didn't make sense. He said as much to Lizzie and Colin.

'I feel the same way too,' said Lizzie. 'Although nothing makes sense right now. I keep wondering what could have made her suddenly go from talking perfectly normally to looking like the end of the world was upon us. I just wish you'd been there, Richard. I mean, we weren't discussing anything in particular, just the various techniques therapists use to protect themselves from the effects of all the distressing cases they have to deal with. Then, for no apparent reason, her face went blank and she didn't utter a single other word. It was really unnerving.'

'It sounds to me like it was connected to one of those upsetting cases you mentioned,' said Colin. 'I wonder if she suddenly recalled someone she couldn't help and she felt guilty about it.'

'That's what we think too,' said Richard. 'But without her here to tell us, how can we know? The only thing I can suggest is that DI Mercer gets Claire's client list going back a few years and tries to pick out one that failed. Other than that, we're stumped.'

No one said anything for a moment or two, then Richard cleared his throat. 'But about this idea of theirs that she's lying low and waiting for night to make her escape? I mean, why, if she wants to die. "It ends here" is what she said. She is miles from home, with no money or credit cards, and no way to purchase any drugs, so if she's that determined to kill herself, why not just find a busy road, wait for a lorry, and that's that. Game over.'

He saw Lizzie wince. 'I'm sorry. That was thoughtless of me. But you see where I'm heading, don't you? We came here in cars with blacked-out windows, ones you can't see out through. We had no idea where we were going, and still don't know where we are. In the state she was in, Claire wouldn't know at all. But whichever direction she took, she'd arrive at a main road eventually. Or a river, or a lake, or a railway line. So why is there no sighting of her? It doesn't equate.'

Colin went to make tea. It was something to pass the time. When he returned, he said, 'Okay, I'm going to play devil's advocate here. It would be extremely unusual, but it's not beyond the realm of possibility that one of your cars was tailed. What if someone was waiting for her? She gets out, walks out of range of the security cameras and they pick her up. Just how well do you both know Claire Hereward?'

Lizzie and Richard looked at each other. Neither answered immediately. Then Lizzie said, 'Apart from our therapy sessions, very little. She knows everything about me from those, but I know nothing about her. Nothing at all.'

'Same here,' Richard said. 'I owe her my life after she helped out of a very dark place, but, well, therapists don't confide in their clients, do they? They listen. Because of what she did for me I would call her a friend, but like Lizzie, I don't even really know what kind of person she is. I don't even know where she lived.'

Colin regarded them thoughtfully. 'So, you have no actual proof that anything she told you was correct?'

Richard shook his head slowly. 'None at all.'

'I think you're right, then. It doesn't equate. In fact, it stinks. I think we should talk to DI Mercer, don't you?'

CHAPTER TWENTY-SIX

Campfire over, Joseph and the team immediately got on their phones and called everyone who had had anything to do with Justin Connaught during the three days leading up to his death. Nikki was in her office, reading through the information provided by their historian. Joseph had told her it contained something important, but all Nikki could see was a group of rich letches promulgating a load of old wives' tales in order to cover up their sleazy activities. So much for the high moral standing of the landowners of Olde England. It was an eye-opener all right, but was it really linked to the shooting of Justin Connaught?

Nikki sat in the relative quiet of her office and jotted down the basic facts of what had happened:

A universally loved man gets shot in his own home. No apparent motive.

His sister expresses considerable interest in acquiring the house, but has made no move to take it further.

A seriously disturbed young man professes to have seen a woman murdered in the grounds of that same house. DS

*Marie Evans confirms that a community nurse bearing the
same description went missing after calling at the house. Her
name was, or is, Patsy Shearer. She is rumoured to have run
away to Durham, but no one has actually seen her.*

*The murdered man, Justin, fires a garden labourer following
a disagreement, the nature of which is unknown. Other than
a couple of heated phone calls overheard by his cleaner, this
appears to be the only occasion on which Justin was seen to
display anger. Of the calls, one was about work, and one, in
which the words 'leave me out of it' indicated a more personal
matter. What that something was they had no idea.*

*The night before his death, he confides in Eve and Wendy
that something is troubling him, and arranges to see them the
following day. His research assistant, Sheena Coates, confirms
that something is troubling him.*

Nikki stood up and began to pace her office. 'Okay,' she
muttered under her breath, 'let's take things a step further.
Fact: Over the years, the house has acquired a reputation
for evil-doings. Fact: there may be Roman remains, even an
entire settlement, beneath the grounds. Fact: Justin was an
archaeologist and planned to excavate parts of the estate.' She
stopped for a moment, then resumed her slow pacing. 'Okay,
Detective Galena. Suppose you receive confirmation that the
argument with the gardener concerned the excavation work
on the grounds. What does that tell you? It tells me that someone did not want Justin digging up certain areas of his property, because it might expose the body of a young community
nurse called Patsy Shearer.'

She looked up to see Joseph standing in the doorway. He
was smiling.

'I think we just came to the same conclusion, Nikki.'

'Someone stopped Justin before he could start digging
up the gardens.'

Joseph came in and closed the door behind him. 'And they have been resuscitating the old rumours of malevolent spirits to deter trespassers.'

Nikki sat down heavily. 'Shit! That bloody estate is vast. We can hardly move in and start digging our way through acres of ground. But I'm certain this is why Justin was murdered.'

'It answers so many questions, doesn't it?' said Joseph. 'Like why such a genuinely good person should be killed. No one hated him, he had no dark secrets, he was simply about to unearth a murdered woman, and had to be stopped. Permanently.' He looked up at Nikki as if the thought had just crossed his mind. 'It could even explain the fact that the shooter was no pro. If he had been Patsy's killer, he didn't use a gun on her. Maybe he'd never used a gun before in his life, but it was the easiest way he could think of to put an end to a big guy like Justin.'

They sat in silence for a few minutes, thinking. 'I suggest we go over Marie's reports about those reported sightings of Patsy Shearer in the Durham area and then contact Durham Constabulary, possibly even Northumbria Police. If she had ever worked in that area, they'd be able to find a record of it. I want absolute confirmation that after leaving Jacobs Mere House that day, she was never seen again.'

'Let's get Marie on it, too,' Joseph said. 'She offered to help, maybe she could contact those relatives of Patsy's who said they'd heard from her. If she had been alive, someone must have met her. It's hard to suddenly cut all ties with loved ones and friends. If we find that someone did see her in person, we'll know we're on the wrong track. Though I don't for a minute believe that's the case.'

'Neither do I,' Nikki said. 'Okay, I'll contact Durham, you get hold of Marie.'

'And Justin must have drafted plans for his proposed dig at the estate. Finding those would considerably reduce the area we'd have to search.' Joseph stood up. 'I'll get on to Marie immediately, then call Lionel Connaught.'

'Excellent! And the others can be looking into the last three days of Justin's life. We'll tackle as much as we can before six, and tomorrow morning we'll all meet up and see what we've got. Okay?'

Joseph gave her a thumbs-up.

As the door closed behind him, Nikki could hardly contain her relief. They'd made a massive step forward, and tomorrow Paul Fletcher would show them the site of Patsy's murder. Smiling, she picked up the phone and asked to be connected to Durham Constabulary.

* * *

While Nikki had been pacing her office, another woman paced her living room floor. 'Dammit, I want that house!'

'And so do I,' returned her husband. 'But there are a few things to consider.'

'What things? There's nothing to consider, Reginald, other than how we get hold of it.'

'Have you even thought about what the upkeep would cost? Your brother made a lot of money, he could afford it. We aren't exactly TV stars, Heather. The way you spend money, even your inheritance isn't going to last you much longer.' Reginald did his best to keep his tone reasonable. Her single-mindedness and determination had been the attributes he had most admired in his wife. Now he wasn't so sure.

'Come on, Reginald. If we can get Father to give it to us, it won't cost a penny. And this,' she swept a hand around the room, 'may not be a palace, but it is a nice four-bed detached property — double garage, designer kitchen, nice location . . . It'll fetch, what? £550,000? Maybe even six. That's half a million to keep us going until we sell off some of the land and start to rake it in. I mean, that estate is huge. We fence off what we want to keep and get a property developer in to value the rest. So what's your problem? And another thing. If you got yourself moving on that promotion you keep missing

246

out on, we wouldn't have to worry about our income until the land sells, would we?'

He hated her when she kept going on at him like this. He said icily, 'If you really want that house so badly, you'll have to curb that temper of yours, won't you, and go and sweet-talk your father into giving it to you. And that's going to be difficult, after what happened when the two of you last met. I think you may have cooked your goose where Daddy is concerned, dearest; he's never been angry with his precious little daughter before. If you don't eat some humble pie for once in your life, you'll never get to live in Jacobs Mere House.'

For once, she didn't answer back, but her stony silence spoke volumes. He'd hit a nerve, and it felt good. Could she really go to Daddy with her tail between her legs? As far as Reginald was concerned, the jury was out on that one.

* * *

Eve, Wendy and Lionel ambled through the overgrown grounds, Eve and Wendy amazed at the sheer extent of them.

'You can imagine what these gardens were like back in the day, can't you?' said Wendy, gazing up at a towering blue cedar.

'And I fully understand why Justin wanted to restore them to their former glory,' said Eve. 'I hadn't realised they were quite so vast. I'll be very interested to see where he thought his Roman village might lie.'

From their earlier observations from the other side of the wall, it didn't take long to locate the hidden gate. Lionel eyed it in horror. 'I shall have to get it locked immediately. I can't have people wandering in whenever they feel like it.'

'Could you hold fire on that for a day or so, Lionel?' Eve said. 'I'd rather like to come back after dark and see exactly who does come here, and what for.'

'Eve's right, Lionel,' said Wendy. 'We do need to see what they are up to. It might have a bearing on Justin's murder.'

'Of course,' Lionel said. 'I wasn't thinking.'

They strolled on through the gardens, pausing here and there to admire some plant or tree, or an overgrown piece of stonework, coming to a halt in front of three fenced paddocks.

Lionel shook his head. 'I can't believe I never took the trouble to look at the grounds properly. I didn't realise quite how magnificent they are.'

They took a different route back, which led them to a clearing. Eve stopped in her tracks. 'What on earth is that?'

In front of them stood a stone building, a kind of folly, that resembled some oriental place of worship.

'That must be the Temple,' said Lionel. 'I remember how enthusiastic Justin had been about it, and how he intended to delve deeper into its history.'

'Well, you'll shortly have the whole thing, chapter and verse, courtesy of our historian friend.' Eve went up to the entrance. The door was locked, but someone had been inside, possibly very recently. 'I'm assuming Justin went in here at some point?'

'I suppose he must have done, but he didn't mention it, so it was most likely after I returned home,' Lionel said.

'Is there a key to this door?' she asked.

'There is a key cabinet in the boot room where all the exterior keys are kept. Justin put tags on them, so we should be able to tell which one it is.'

Eve tried the door, but it didn't budge. 'It's an old Chubb mortice lock, shouldn't be hard to spot amongst the others. I reckon that as soon as we've gone over the plans for the garden, we should come back here and take a look inside.'

Wendy agreed at once, but Lionel didn't seem terribly keen. Maybe all the talk of Justin's ideas for a future that he would never see was getting too much for him. He was only human, after all, and a bereaved father to boot. 'Don't worry, Lionel,' said Eve, 'you don't have to come. We'll take a look and let you know what we find. We'll also decide when would be the best time to come back and watch the gate. Now, I feel a sudden need for a cup of tea. Shall we go back to the house?'

Lionel's relief was evident, and in virtual silence they wound their way back beneath overhanging trees and over unkempt lawns until they were once more at the house.

As soon as they were inside, Eve went to find the boot room key cupboard, returning with a leather key fob bearing a label with the word 'Temple', with a long, old-fashioned key dangling from it.

Lionel made tea while Eve and Wendy laid out Justin's blueprint for the garden on the kitchen table. Now they had seen it for themselves, they could visualise what he had had in mind for the garden and parts of the grounds beyond.

Lionel set down their mugs and said he'd go and see whether Len Fordham had sent the instructions for the landscaping.

'He's struggling, isn't he?' murmured Wendy after he had left the room.

'He is, but it's hardly surprising. He's trying to keep a stiff upper lip, but you can see he's suddenly realising that he'll never do all the things he had hoped to be doing with his son. He can't ask him what he meant by something, or what he had planned for something else. And he can't tell him how proud he was of him.' Eve felt terribly sad for their old friend. 'That's why we need to fathom out what the hell happened to Justin, so that he can finally grieve properly.'

They turned their attention back to the drawings.

'He had incredible imagination, didn't he?' said Wendy. 'If these plans had been brought to fruition, the estate would have been spectacular. I can't help wondering what will happen to it now.'

'I dread to think,' said Eve. 'A project like this would take an enormous amount of money, far more than most people could afford. Certainly Lionel is in no fit state to make any decisions about it yet, and luckily, he's aware of that. If he acted rashly, I could see this lovely house and garden go to rack and ruin.'

For a while they pored over the plans, setting Justin's ideas in places they now recognised.

'It looks like he was intending to keep the Temple, and plant a Japanese Zen garden with water features around it. What a peaceful place it would have been—'

Eve was happily envisioning a tranquil garden with the trickle of water in the background when she heard Wendy gasp.

'Oh, I say! Look at these!' She had taken a large envelope from the carry case and removed from it a handful of papers and photographs. 'Eve! Justin was on the brink of going ahead with the dig. Look, there's a memo, he'd even sent up a drone to take aerial photographs, and here's the results of a geophysical survey he had done.' She looked at Eve. 'He *knew* there was an archaeological site right here!' She pointed to the fenced paddocks where they had stopped on their tour of the grounds. Superimposed on top of each were layers at increasing depth, in different colours. A hidden past, right beneath the grassy meadow where horses now grazed.

On the final sheet of paper a diagram showed rectangular sections filled in with diagonal lines connected by long narrow channels.

'He'd mapped the ground out ready to begin excavation,' murmured Eve. 'He was about to go ahead.'

'Until someone stopped him,' breathed Wendy.

They were staring at each other when Lionel strode into the kitchen.

'I've got the printouts from Fordham. They planned to tackle the work in three separate stages. They had already started to clear the first area ready for landscaping and replanting. They would then move on to the Temple section and clear it in preparation for some kind of, er . . .'

'Japanese garden,' finished Eve. 'You were right, Justin produced very detailed sketches and diagrams. His ideas for the place were truly inspirational — the way he incorporated existing parts of the landscape into the finished garden.'

Wendy sighed. 'It would have been a real testament to him.'

'I had no idea he was so passionate about it,' Lionel said. 'I knew what he wanted for the house, of course, but now I'm beginning to think that getting it straight was just a prelude to the more exciting part — the gardens and the hunt for a Roman village.'

Eve agreed. The plans showed zeal and commitment on a grand scale. She picked up one of the sheets of paper. On it were written the seven guiding principles of a Zen garden, followed by a string of Japanese characters and their meanings: Austerity, Simplicity, Naturalness, Asymmetry, Mystery or Subtlety, Magical or Unconventional, and Stillness. Then came a list of plants including bamboos, azaleas, and Japanese acers, along with a selection of different ferns and mosses. A meditative pathway was to wind between carefully placed rocks and stones, the element of water represented in pools

. . .

Eve blinked, and stopped reading. Now this beautiful dream would never come to fruition. She looked up at Lionel. 'Is it okay if Wendy and I go back and check out the Temple? And if so, do you have any flashlights?'

'No problem at all, I'll get you a couple of torches.' Lionel went out, returning with two big hand-held torches. 'Before you go, there's something that I meant to tell you earlier. Your daughter and her sergeant told me that Paul Fletcher, a nephew of mine, has been receiving counselling, in the course of which a suppressed memory has come to the surface.'

'Oh? Is it connected to Justin in some way?' Eve asked.

'They have no idea, but they need to follow it up, just in case it's relevant.' Lionel shrugged. 'I can't see it myself, but anyway, he's coming here tomorrow with your Nikki and her sergeant.'

'Here? What is this memory, Lionel?' Eve asked, puzzled.

'He believes that while he was birdwatching in these grounds, he witnessed a woman being attacked and killed.'

'And does my daughter believe this story? Forgive me, but it sounds a bit off the wall,' Eve said.

'It does, doesn't it?' Lionel said. 'It's perfectly true that little Paulie, as my wife and I used to call him, has struggled with mental health issues following a childhood trauma. Well, apparently a woman matching Paulie's description, a community nurse, went missing after having visited old Fletcher at this house. According to Nikki, his psychologist is convinced that it is a memory of a real event that was so traumatic for him that he blanked it out.'

'Bloody hell!' said Wendy. 'And we haven't even started reading our historian's tales of the nefarious goings-on here.'

'And is there really a chance that it could be connected in some way?' Eve said. 'Anyway, I'm glad you told us, Lionel. And please let us know the outcome of your nephew's visit.'

'Of course.'

Five minutes later, Eve and Wendy were on their way back to the Temple.

'Call me a suspicious old bird,' said Eve, 'but what if a woman really was killed here, and buried in the grounds, and along comes an enthusiastic archaeologist who wants to dig up the gardens—'

'And said archaeologist is murdered before he gets the chance.' Wendy raised her eyebrows. 'I'd say we have our motive for Justin's murder.'

'Ah, but there's a hitch. Why bury your body in an open paddock when you've got an overgrown garden a few steps away? And secondly, if you did, for some unknown reason, bury it in one of the paddocks, Justin's geological survey would have shown it up. After all, they do use GPR to locate human remains. The notes detail buried foundations, wall footings, and possibly a hearth. There's no mention of a body.'

'Meaning it was buried in the garden itself. It doesn't negate the motive. The killer could have been afraid that Justin might dig further into the garden itself, especially if he had discovered a Roman village. I mean, such a village could extend for miles.'

Still pondering this new development, they at last reached the Temple.

'Now, Wendy. Before we go in, take a look at the door and the surrounding ground and tell me what you think.'

'Used by more than one person, I'd say, and regularly. The ground is well-trodden, coming from that direction.' Wendy indicated a wooded area that extended to the perimeter of the estate. 'Roughly where the secret gate is, wouldn't you say?'

'Exactly. So I wonder what on earth we're going to find inside.'

'Well, I can tell you it's not going to be a birdwatcher's reunion for a start. Okay, you've got the key, let's find out.'

* * *

Shortly after Eve and Wendy had left, Lionel received a call from Heather. He toyed with the idea of letting it ring out, but decided she would probably only ring back, so he answered.

'Daddy? Oh, Daddy! I've been such an idiot, haven't I?'

'I can't deny that, Heather. And you were bloody rude to the people who were trying to help us.'

'I'm *so* sorry, really I am. I suppose it was the shock of losing our Justin, but I just felt so angry at everyone.'

'What do you want, Heather?' he said wearily.

'You're still cross with me, aren't you, Daddy? Don't be cross, please.'

'Heather, I'm tired, and yes, I was angry at you. Your behaviour certainly didn't help at such a terrible time.'

'Listen, Daddy darling. Reggie has offered to take some time off work, so we can drive over to Jacobs Mere and help you. There must be *so* much to do, and Reggie is a whizz at organising that sort of thing. I mean, the police must have gone by now, and the children will be no bother—'

'Let me stop you right there, Heather,' he said evenly. 'As a matter of fact, the police *are* still here.' It wasn't really a lie — after all, there was still a crew at the gates. 'And tomorrow the detectives are coming back. There have been, er,

253

developments, so I'm afraid the place is still off limits until further notice.'

'But we're family! Surely—'

'I'm sorry, but they did explain the situation to you. You will be notified when it'll be possible to visit. If you try and come before then, you'll just have a wasted journey.'

There was a lengthy silence. 'In that case, please do let me know when we can come. We are both worried about you having to shoulder everything by yourself. And Daddy? I really am sorry.'

'I hope so, darling, I hope so.' Lionel ended the call. He suddenly felt very old and tired. He also felt very alone. It wasn't his daughter's company he missed, it was his son's.

CHAPTER TWENTY-SEVEN

Haydn received a call from Terence, who didn't sound pleased. 'I don't know what the hell is going on with you, Haydn, but your job is taking far too long and it's been noticed. They're wondering why there's police crawling all over the area where you're supposed to be operating. From what I've heard, the clock is ticking. You need to either wrap the job up fast, or take that other option we talked about. Look, Haydn. Think about it seriously. We know we work well together, and if Neville is as solid as you say, well, it might be a good thing to have a man on the team.' The line broke up briefly, then Anna Terence said, 'Remember those new young operatives I told you about? Well, they're the real deal. I reckon the organisation is about to undergo a major shake-up, and they'll be bringing in new blood. I'm unfit for full duties, while you and Neville are under scrutiny, which means they're not likely to be handing out any fat redundancy packages. Ring me back within the hour with your decision.' She fell silent, Haydn heard her breathing. 'And if it helps you make up your mind, I've some interesting work lined up — all private contracts, no oversight. And Haydn? One other thing. Be *very* careful if you choose to complete this assignment. I know you've never walked away from an unfinished job before, and neither have I, but on this occasion . . . Look, I've already got a place organised for us to move into, and it can also accommodate your Neville. Have a think and talk to him. Your choice. A new life? Or a life spent looking over your shoulder?'

The line went dead. Frowning, Haydn pushed her phone back into her pocket. It galled her to walk away from a job, but in her business, too much pride could get you killed.

Haydn straightened up. This wasn't just her decision. Neville was part of this assignment, and the clock was ticking for him, too. She had to talk to him.

Neville answered from the car, where he was still watching their target's last known location.

'Neville. We need to speak. Collect me now.'

'With you in five.'

In exactly five minutes, the car drew up below her vantage point, and she went down, her binoculars still around her neck.

'This place is getting far too dangerous. It's teeming with coppers.'

It was the first time Neville had sounded anxious.

She got into the car. 'I've had a warning, and an offer. It's crunch time, Neville.' She told him what Terence had proposed.

It didn't take him long to give her his answer. 'I've no ties. No family and no close friends. If you're up for it, I'd go with a new start. I'd like to be able to breathe again.'

'Is the tank full?'

'We've enough fuel to cross two counties before we need to stop.'

'In which case, I'll make that call. Then you and I need to discuss how we disengage from the organisation. We have bank accounts to close, for one thing. We'll need to move our funds around, because they mustn't know where we are. We'll need to disappear without a trace. You understand?'

'I can do all that in minutes, Haydn. I've already made arrangements in case of emergencies. I trust no one, you see.' He gave her a rare smile. 'Except possibly you?'

'You can trust me all right, Neville — unless you give me reason to think otherwise.' She smiled back, somewhat cautiously. 'Now, let me make that call. We need to know where we are going before we disappear. Just one thing. None of this was our doing. It was a series of unforeseen events that made pursuing the contract untenable. Right?'

'Correct.'

'But it will never happen again. From now on we answer only to ourselves. And we don't make mistakes. Ever.'

'No mistakes,' he said.

Haydn rang Terence. 'Please make the necessary arrangements and give me the coordinates. Present contract abandoned as impractical to pursue, given the current situation in the area. We are coming home, Terence. If you'd tell us where that is?'

With a chuckle, Anna Terence gave her the name of their destination.

'What? There?' Haydn exclaimed. 'Is that wise?'

'Oh very. Think about it. They'll expect us to cut and run, won't they, as far as we can get, maybe even out of the country. The last thing they'll expect us to do is move into the area we absconded from. No, we'll be right here in the misty Fens. I think you'll like my choice of accommodation. No near neighbours. Right off the beaten track — perfect! New beginnings, Haydn. New beginnings.'

* * *

'Okay, everyone' called out Nikki. 'Time to call it a day. Get off home, and we'll reconvene at eight thirty tomorrow morning.' There followed the sound of computers being shut down, and chairs scraping the floor.

To calls of 'See you tomorrow, boss' the detectives gathered their things and headed for the door. Soon, only Joseph was left.

'Joseph? You okay if I do another half hour here? I'm waiting for Northumbria to call back, and I've yet to get hold of Lionel Connaught.'

'Sure. I've got some stuff from Marie Evans that I haven't had time to go over. I've just had a thought — have you heard from your mother today?'

'No. Maybe I should give her a bell and see how she and Wendy are bearing up. They were very fond of Justin, and you could see it hit them hard. I'll try Lionel first, then get on to my mother.'

Back in her office, she tried Lionel again.

'Yes,' he said curtly. Somewhat taken aback, Nikki gave him her name.

'Oh I'm sorry, Detective Galena, I thought you were my daughter. The fact is, I've just been on the phone to her. She was pleading to be allowed to come back to Jacobs Mere — which I refused, by the way — and I thought I was about to face Round Two.'

Nikki chuckled. 'You have my sympathies. How did you manage to put her off?'

'I'll admit to a slight deviation from the truth, but I've managed to dissuade her for the time being. So, do you have news for me? Any developments since we last spoke?'

'Actually, I need your help, Lionel. It's vital we learn all we can about where Justin was planning to carry out his excavations for that Roman village. We found very little on his laptop, so we were wondering if he made any drafts on paper?'

Lionel didn't reply immediately. 'I'm sure he would have done. He always produced diagrams and maps for the television programme. I'd better go through his study and see if I can locate any plans he drew up for here.'

'I'm sorry to have to ask, Lionel. I know it will be painful for you, but it is rather important.'

'I'll see what I can find. Hopefully, I'll have something to show you when you bring Paulie Fletcher here tomorrow morning.'

Nikki thanked him, confirmed the time they'd be coming and rang off. Something niggled at her about that conversation, but before she had time to think about it, Northumbria Police were on the line.

As she had suspected, their Northern colleagues had found no indication that Patsy Shearer had ever actually been in Durham, or anywhere else in Northumbria. Their words confirmed her supposition that Patsy Shearer was resting, though maybe not in peace, somewhere in the grounds of Jacobs Mere House.

She glanced at the clock — just time for a quick call to her mother, then it really was time to shut up shop for the night.

When Eve answered, Nikki could hardly hear her, the reception was terrible. 'Where on earth are you, Mum?' asked Nikki, wincing at the loud crackling of static in her ear. Her mother's voice came and went, and in the end Nikki gave up.

She yawned, rubbed her eyes and switched off her computer. She'd ring her mother from home. She was well aware that the Fens did have poor coverage, but really, that was off the scale.

Picturing a large glass of white wine, Nikki pulled on her jacket and shut the office door. 'Ready when you are!'

Joseph waved his car keys at her. 'First one home pours the wine.'

The two of them clattered down the stairs like kids on their way out of school. How good it was to have the old Joseph back, but for how long? If Cam didn't come back to them soon, what then? Would Joseph be overcome with anxiety again, and would they then make a wrong decision?

Nikki told herself to get a grip and concentrate on solving Justin's murder. Only then would they be free to make a decision about their future.

* * *

Eve pushed her phone back in her pocket. 'That was my daughter. Now she's going to be asking herself where the dickens we are.'

259

'Good question,' said Wendy. 'What is this place?'

Eve gazed around her. Built like a crypt, the interior of the Temple was the size of a generous triple garage. At one end, forming an altar of sorts, a plain stone slab rested on two stone plinths. On the wall behind it, a discoloured rectangle showed where a painting, or perhaps a religious mural, had once hung. The stone slab bore the unmistakable traces of candlewax, along with some other rather disconcerting dark stains, which could either be blood or red wine.

The interior was dim. The light coming from the open doors threw tall shadows, giving it a sinister feel. They switched on their torches, and shone the beams across a series of small alcoves, each closed off by an iron grille. Some had a stone ledge at the back, others were empty. Several had heavy metal rings set into the walls, which Eve pictured chains hanging from, swinging ominously. Quickly, she swung her torch beam around to the centre of the Temple, where it lit up three wooden benches arranged in a square, as for a meeting or an act of worship.

'So this place wasn't just a folly,' Wendy said in a hushed voice. 'It had a purpose, although I dread to think what that purpose would have been.'

'And where does this lead, do you suppose?' said Eve, gently lifting the corner of a faded, musty-smelling tapestry hanging to one side of the altar.

They stared at the heavy wooden door for a moment or two, and then Eve lifted the catch. To her surprise, it swung open.

Neither of them was prepared for what they saw.

'Oh my!' Wendy shook her head and stared at Eve. 'No wonder Justin paid so much attention to this Temple!'

'It's just a shame Lionel wasn't interested,' said Eve. 'Just think what he missed.'

The floor sloped steeply down, away from them, and in the light from their torches, they could just make out a passageway with what looked like the entrances to caves leading off it on either side.

Without another word, they stepped forward and descended into the dark.

The first cave turned out to be a tunnel, which they followed, careful to take note of their route so they wouldn't get lost. It opened out into a vast cavern.

'Man-made,' noted Eve. 'But what for?'

Wendy stopped. 'Wait a minute! I've seen something like this before, years ago. I know. It was Chislehurst Caves in Kent. I did a tour of the place when I was young. It was just like this, only much bigger. Initially, it was intended for chalk used in the burning of lime, and brick-making for building London. It went on to be used as a munitions store, and an air-raid shelter for thousands of people during World War Two. Finally, it became a venue for concerts and functions, along with guided tours like the one I went on. Funnily enough, one thing the guide told us stuck in my mind, which was that Romans, Druids and Saxons all occupied the surrounding area at different times. No wonder Justin was delighted to find this on his own doorstep.'

'And some bastard stole, not just his life, but his dreams of one of the most exciting finds of his archaeological career,' Eve said angrily. 'If I ever got hold of—'

'Eve, have you noticed that odd smell down here?' Wendy said.

Only when Wendy pointed it out did she detect it. 'Not cannabis?'

'Let's have a look at the other tunnels,' Wendy said. 'It's not very noticeable in here, so maybe it's coming from one of them.'

In the third cavern, which was considerably larger, they found a massive wooden table with chairs around it, and, much to their surprise, several old couches — worn and stained, but not damp. The caves were all remarkably dry, but since neither of them knew much about caving, this could be perfectly natural. They also saw any number of lamps — some old oil lamps and candle lamps, along with new battery-powered lanterns. Here, the smell of pot was considerably stronger.

'Oh dear,' said Eve. 'It seems that wacky-baccy is the least of our concerns. Look.' She pointed to the table, and the white dust gathered in different spots on the surface. 'Correct me if I'm wrong, but I think we've just found why there's so much traffic in and out of that secret gate, and it has nothing to do with the migratory habits of the spotted flycatcher.'

Next to the table was a large wooden chest. Wendy went up to it and opened the lid. 'I think I've just found what is known as "paraphernalia". Look. A whole lot of small plastic bags, and a weighing machine. You're right, Eve, this was no haven for birdwatchers. I don't think they'd be very welcome in here. Well, I don't know about you, but I've seen enough.'

They retraced their steps and went outside, both glad to breathe the fresh early evening air. Eve locked the temple door, and they hurried back towards the house.

'I think,' said Eve after a while, 'that — with Lionel's blessing — I should call Nikki and tell her rather more than that I'm doing okay, don't you?'

'Absolutely,' said Wendy. 'We agreed at the start that we'd pass on to the police anything serious that we find. And I reckon discovering a place where drugs are being bagged up counts as pretty serious.'

When they told Lionel what had been going on right under his nose, he was incandescent. Of course they must tell Nikki, he said when he had calmed down sufficiently.

'Ah, that's better,' said Nikki brightly. 'I was beginning to think you'd gone off to darkest Africa. The signal when I called earlier was truly awful.'

'Er, darkest, yes. Africa, no.' Eve told her that they had made a disturbing discovery whilst checking out a temple-like folly in the grounds. 'Do you think you and Joseph can come here now, rather than me trying to describe it over the phone? You really should see this for yourselves.'

She ended the call and turned to her two companions. 'They're on their way.'

'Then they ought to see all this as well,' said Lionel, indicating the project diagrams spread out on the table. 'Nikki rang while you were out, asking if Justin had drawn up any plans for his proposed dig for the Roman village. I stonewalled a bit, in case you wanted to keep them back, but I guess we shouldn't withhold information, should we?'

'Not this time, Lionel. We're not in competition with the police. They need all the help we can offer. The only thing I *am* going to withhold is Tamsin's name. Her husband might be annoyed if he knew she was helping us in secret. We'll just refer to her as a local snout who told us about men using that hidden gate.'

Lionel grinned. 'Snout? Do they really call them that these days? It sounds like something from *Dixon of Dock Green*.'

'Oh yes,' Eve said. 'Yvonne Collins — who works with Nikki — uses it all the time.'

'Well, if you say so,' Lionel said. 'But do you think that poor young woman might really be buried here, in our grounds? And that's why my boy was killed?'

'It's possible,' said Wendy. 'But what we've just seen in the Temple provides another possible motive for murder, doesn't it?'

'Wendy's right,' said Eve. 'We have no idea if the people that come here are small-time distributors bagging up coke or whatever it is for the locals, or big-time drug dealers.' She frowned. 'And, frankly, from what we saw in that chest, I think it's the latter, and it could well be Class A drug trafficking, not just small quantities of cocaine for personal use.'

'Then I'm glad Nikki and Joseph are on their way,' said Lionel.

Eve wasn't quite so enthusiastic at the prospect, knowing full well what Nikki would have to say about her mother being, once again, in the thick of dark goings-on. Still, if it helped catch Justin's killer, she'd just take the flak with a smile.

CHAPTER TWENTY-EIGHT

Nikki stared at the two freshly poured glasses of wine, and sighed. 'I swear I'm going to have my mother locked up in a high tower, ideally in the middle of the high seas. Not only have I been dreaming of that glass of delicious Chablis for the past hour, but I also find she's up to her sodding elbows in a dangerous crime — again! It's . . . it's *unbelievable!*'

Joseph burst out laughing. 'Oh, Nikki. Talk about "like mother, like daughter". Eve wouldn't be five minutes in that tower before you were unlocking the door to let her out.'

'I'm not so sure about that. Only *she* could go wandering around a sodding temple and unearth . . . what did she call it? *Something very disturbing*? I give up!'

'Come on, then. Let's go and see what Granny Super Sleuth has discovered this time. Knowing her, it's bound to be worth the drive. Take a good slurp of your wine, Nikki Galena, and I'll drive. Then, when we get home, you can finish the bottle if you want.'

'Can I have that in writing, please?' He handed her the glass, and she took a long drink. 'Heaven!'

Lionel met them at the door. Every time she saw him, Nikki thought, he seemed to have aged another ten years.

Tonight, he looked exhausted, almost at the end of his tether. So, she cancelled her planned tirade, grateful that her mother and Wendy were around to give him their support.

They went into the kitchen, where her eyes at once fell on the plans on the table. So that was the reason for Lionel's slight hesitation when she'd asked about them. She should have guessed that her mother and her friends would be one step ahead of her. She glanced at Joseph, who was trying to conceal an amused smile. For a moment, she wondered if the Fenland Constabulary might set up a special division for inquisitive, military retirees with a knack for solving cases faster than a crack team of experienced detectives. Then she saw the three serious faces and decided against mentioning it.

'Where do we start?' she asked.

'In the gardens,' said Eve, 'before it gets too dark. We have torches, but it's best done in the light. You'll understand why when you see it.'

'Well, lead on, then,' said Nikki.

'I have more torches,' said Lionel. 'I think I'll wait here, if you don't mind, and we can discuss this,' he pointed to the plans, 'when you get back.'

With uncharacteristic tact, Nikki said, 'Excellent, and thanks for finding that for us so quickly, Lionel. It could be very important.'

Carrying the torches Lionel had provided, they followed Eve and Wendy out into the gardens, where the two women told them their story.

'Someone told us that there was a third entrance into the estate,' said Eve, striding ahead. 'They said birdwatchers used it to sneak in and photograph the birds that have begun to flourish in the garden wilderness.'

'However,' continued Wendy, 'one birder noticed a couple of regular visitors that he didn't recognise, and since the local bird lovers are a quite close-knit bunch, he was a bit suspicious of them.'

'Yeah,' Joseph said. 'That's why Paul Fletcher used to come here. He was watching the birds.'

'And that might well be the case,' said Eve, 'but they aren't the only ones using this third gate. And when we, purely by chance, happened to come upon what we believed to be a folly, we discovered exactly what kind of person these "other" visitors were.'

'*By chance*, Mother? *Happened?* Does anything just happen to you two?' said Nikki.

'Point taken, dear, but when we get back to the house you'll see for yourself that Justin planned to plant a peaceful Japanese garden in front of this folly, and we wondered what was inside. That's all.'

Eve was clearly telling the truth, but Nikki suspected that a lot was being glossed over. Well, it'd most likely come out later. 'So, what did you find?'

'A damn sight more than we expected,' said Wendy. 'To begin with we seemed to be in a kind of chapel, but then . . . Well, you'll see.'

It wasn't like either Eve or Wendy to be so reticent, but what they had discovered had obviously shaken them. Nikki was starting to feel uneasy.

They emerged into the clearing, where stood a building like a chapel, but with an Oriental feel to it. Whatever it was intended for, it certainly wasn't beautiful.

'The Temple,' said Eve.

'Temple to what, I wonder?' said Joseph.

Eve produced a key and unlocked the door. In the light that poured through, they saw a bare room containing nothing but an altar and some pews. Nothing too shocking about that, although Nikki wasn't happy about some rather weird cell-like alcoves closed off with iron grilles. She'd seen something like that in a castle museum once. The alcoves had held waxwork figures of chained prisoners undergoing torture.

'Now it starts to get interesting,' said Wendy, holding aside a tapestry, behind which was a big old wooden door. She swung the door open.

'Bloody hell!' exclaimed Joseph. 'Are those caves down there?'

'Man-made,' said Eve. 'There are tunnels leading off, with several caverns at the end of them. We looked at three, but there might well be more.' She shone her torch beam down the steep slope. 'Come on. We'll show you what we found.'

'How come they managed to dig out caves? And why are they so dry?' asked Nikki. 'It's the Fens! Silty soil? Flooding?'

'Well,' Joseph said, 'you see, Jacobs Fen is one of those little islands of higher ground, you know, like Wisbech, Ely, and that one DI Jackman found out at Roman Creek. What was it called — Windrush?'

Nikki shivered. She remembered Windrush all right, and what her colleagues had found there. She pushed the memory away. Whatever Eve was about to show them couldn't possibly be as bad as that.

Eve hurried ahead. 'We'll go straight to the third cave.'

The first thing Nikki noticed was the smell. Kids probably got in somehow, to smoke dope and chill out. Then she saw the white powder residue on the big table and peered into the big wooden chest. Nope. Definitely not kids.

'I wonder how long this has been going on?' she said. 'Well, Joseph, with a little careful planning, we could bag a nice little drugs ring, couldn't we?'

'We could, and not necessarily so little either,' he said.

'Do you think you've seen enough?' Eve said, sounding rather edgy.

'Yes, let's go,' said Wendy. 'We have no idea when your drug dealers come here, and we don't want them to catch us sniffing around.'

Nikki cast her torch beam across the big cavern, took one last look around and followed the others out. They were right. Who knew when the dealers might turn up.

As Eve locked up again, Joseph looked up at the building's facade. 'I think I know why this was built. According to your friend Jacob Rush, a previous owner of the house was a follower of the Hellfire Clubs. I think he built it to hold his nefarious activities in.'

'We didn't know that,' said Wendy, 'but it would explain a lot.'

Nikki smiled to herself. No doubt her mother and Wendy would be contacting their friend Rush in the very near future.

Back in the house, they gathered round the kitchen table and examined Justin's plans. It was clear that he expected to find extensive Roman remains within the boundaries of his estate, which, if he'd turned out to be right, would be a find of huge national importance. Then there were the man-made caves they had just seen beneath the Temple. Aside from being a convenient place for drug dealers to stash their haul, they, too, were of historical interest. Imagine, a chapter of the Hellfire Club at Jacobs Mere House! Lionel was sitting on a veritable treasure chest of historical wonders.

'So, it seems to us,' Eve said, 'that we have two valid motives for the murder of Justin. Either someone didn't want him digging up the grounds because they had concealed a body there. Or a very different kind of criminal wanted to stop him finding out about their drug-dealing activities while he was landscaping the garden.'

'So they murdered my innocent boy,' said Lionel bitterly. 'And the irony of it is, he couldn't have known much at all. He had been perfectly happy until just hours before his death, when he admitted to Eve and Wendy that something was bothering him. If only he had spoken about it there and then. If he had, he'd probably still be alive today.'

No one knew what to say. For a while they sat in silence, reflecting on what they had just heard. Eventually, Nikki said, 'We agree with what you said about motive, Eve. From a police point of view, both scenarios represented a serious threat to Justin: the drug dealers, and the person who knew that Patsy Shearer lay buried in the grounds.'

'And we are gathering more and more evidence that Patsy was never in Durham,' said Joseph. 'It appears that someone laid a trail to divert both the police and any of her friends or family who might be looking for her. The last sighting of Patsy was right here, when she visited old man Fletcher.'

'And Justin had no idea of the danger he was in.' Lionel swallowed. 'While I walked away and left him! Why the hell didn't I take more interest in his plans for the garden? Who knows, if I'd stayed, I might have picked up something he'd missed. He was so full of his Roman remains that he had eyes for nothing else. I'll never forgive myself for that.'

Nikki understood his rage and frustration. She'd been there herself when her daughter had died. She too had suffered under the burden of a guilt that was not hers to bear. She leaned across the table and squeezed his arm. 'You mustn't blame yourself, Lionel. You said yourself that he was happy. How could you possibly know what lay in wait for him?'

She knew that mere words couldn't possibly assuage the pain he felt, but she wanted him to know that he wasn't alone in his suffering. 'Whoever is to blame, we'll find him, and he'll pay for what he's done. And that means we have work to do. Can we take some of Justin's drawings, especially the one with the different levels superimposed on top of one another? We'll get them copied at the station and send them back to you straightaway.'

'Of course. Take whatever you need,' Lionel said, his voice stronger now. 'So, about these drug dealers, or whoever they are. What are you proposing to do, may I ask?'

'We'll need to think it through carefully,' said Nikki. 'As things stand, they are unaware that we know of their exist-ence, but before we do anything, we need to determine who, exactly, we'll be bringing in — a handful of small-time dealers, or a killer. We can't afford to jump the gun and miss finding our murderer for the sake of a few pushers. So, Joseph, we need to do some quick research into the local drug situation. According to what I've heard, DI Anders over at Fenfleet is up to her neck in drug-related crimes, so she'll know all there is to know about it. Then, Lionel, with your permission, we'll watch, wait, and raid those caves, hopefully while there's a full complement of dealers inside. I'm afraid it will mean that you'll have us in your grounds for a while.'

'But don't worry, Lionel, they won't disturb you. The surveillance team are like wraiths, believe me.' Joseph eyed Eve and Wendy. 'We'll have to ask you to keep well clear of the third gate, as well as the area around the Temple and the caves. I know it's not in your nature to back off from an investigation, but we can't let our trespassers know that we're on to them.'

'No way would we jeopardise your operation,' Eve said. 'You have our word on that.'

'Absolutely,' added Wendy. 'It's far too important.'

For once, Nikki believed them. 'You guys have done brilliantly in finding those caves, *and* their contents. If nothing else, you've certainly put an end to a local drug-dealing ring. We really appreciate it.'

Eve grinned at her. 'My! That's a first.'

'Don't push your luck, Mother! You have previous, remember? Now, we need to get home and decide on a plan of action. We'll update you when we come back tomorrow to meet Paul Fletcher and his therapist. I'm thinking that if one of the drug dealers is watching they won't be alarmed to see a group of people just taking a walk in the grounds.'

'You're right,' said Lionel. 'But there must be something we can do to help with your investigation. Thanks to our former profession, we have certain contacts who could well be of use.'

Nikki smiled. 'Am I right in thinking those contacts include Lou and Rene? Not to mention a couple of others with more clout than the Pentagon.'

'Needs must,' said Wendy.

'Well, there is one thing you could do, Lionel,' Nikki said. 'We're very keen to trace a man called Dennis — Len Fordham employed him on a casual basis. He's the gardener

Justin fired, and has been seen hanging around the gates talking to the press. Find him, and the reason why Justin argued with him, and you'll get a whole lot of Brownie points, and, who knows, I might even stop hounding my mother!'

Lionel looked considerably brighter at having something positive to do. 'Leave that to us, Inspector. We're on the case.'

CHAPTER TWENTY-NINE

Gill Mercer knew perfectly well that she should have gone home hours ago, but with Claire Hereward still missing without trace, walking out felt like abandoning her. Was she dead? Had she really meant what she'd said in that note? Twice, Richard had called to tell her that he and the others had all come to the conclusion that there was something decidedly odd about the way Claire had absconded. The second time he called, he told her of Colin Jones's suggestion that someone might have known where she was and had picked her up.

Gill mulled this over. It was possible, she supposed, but unlikely. The drivers assigned to the job were shit-hot, trained to the highest level. Anyone attempting to tail them would have had to be very clever indeed. Failing that, the only other way someone would know where she'd been taken was if Claire told them herself, and to do that she would need access to a mobile phone, and her phone had been taken from her before she left Richard's. Unless . . . Could she have concealed one? Or did she use one of the only two phones in the safe house — Colin Jones's, or Richard's? Again unlikely. Both men were professionals, and wouldn't have left them lying about, they'd have made sure of that. One thing was certain,

Claire had not wanted to go to a safe house, and that was a puzzle in itself.

Gill massaged her temples. She had a ferocious headache, and paracetamol hadn't touched it. Perhaps she should go home. There seemed little point in sitting here going over the same speculations again and again. She suspected that the real reason why she couldn't bear to leave was that she was waiting for a call to tell her a body had been found, and she could perfectly well take that call at home.

Reluctantly, Gill shut down her computer and pulled her jacket off the back of her chair. Unless there was a development overnight, tomorrow morning she and Ryan were going to have to take a deep breath, plunge back into Claire Hereward's life, and rip it apart. There was something neither they nor anyone else knew about that woman, and they would damn well find it!

She slammed her office door behind her, drawing a line under a miserable day. It didn't help, she succeeded only in making her head throb even more.

* * *

Going home to Monks Lantern felt to Eve like returning to the real world from an alternative dark and very sordid one. Neither she nor Wendy were strangers to the evil humanity was capable of, but there was something both contemptible and depressing about the world of drugs and the people who dealt them. *Wasted*, she thought. Young lives ruined, health and vitality gone, along with relationships and rewarding careers. No wonder people under the influence of such substances were referred to as being 'wasted'.

She saw Wendy eyeing her shrewdly. 'Got to you, has it, our voyage into the underworld?'

'I do believe it has, my friend, although coming home is restoring my equilibrium a treat.'

'Well, I reckon we've earned ourselves a drink, don't you?' said Wendy, casting about for her slippers.

'A large one! I'll pour.'

'Have we actually eaten since breakfast?' Wendy asked. 'I can't quite remember; today has been a bit of a blur.'

'We had an early lunch, remember? We had that sandwich, just before we went to Tamsin's. Why don't I throw an omelette together, and you do some French fries in the air fryer? Not exactly a feast, but it'll fill a gap. And then, over a large glass of wine, we can go over our lovely young friend's email and take a look at the history of Lionel's mysterious estate.'

'I'm not sure if I'm strong enough for any more creepy tales, but I'll be interested to see what Jacob says about that man who so admired the Hellfire Clubs.' Wendy headed for the kitchen. 'Anyway, first things first. I'm starving. Pour that wine, Eve, and let's eat.'

An hour later they were seated in the lounge, sipping wine, and reading through Jacob Rush's copious notes. After a while, Eve said, 'Shall I ring him? Or will you?'

'You go for it. I'm still up to my ears in debauchery.'

With a chuckle, Eve reached for her phone.

Jacob Rush sounded delighted to hear from them. 'There's more where that came from. I've been going over my notes from when I was a teenager. Jacobs Mere has always fascinated me, especially as it's where I got my name. It's always felt kind of personal.'

'Well, we've got some news for you about that house,' said Eve. 'Wendy and I have been down and seen your Hellfire Caves for ourselves, and when all the furore has died down, I'm certain Lionel Connaught won't mind if we take you there too.'

Jacob whistled. 'So they *do* exist! It's not just legend, and they're still there, after all this time. Eve! This is mega.'

'We thought you'd be pleased — although you won't like the next bit. We can't say too much at present, but the area will be off limits for a while. A few unsavoury characters have been using it for illicit purposes. Nevertheless, once that's sorted, you'll get to see your precious caves.'

Jacob spent the next ten minutes subjecting her to a grilling. He wanted to know their exact location, their layout, their possible usage, and her overall impression of them. In the end, Eve had to call a halt. 'Whoa! My head is spinning. Don't worry, Jacob, you'll see them for yourself before too long, just not yet. You see, when we realised what they were being used for, we had to call the police.'

'Okay, okay, I understand. But you have no idea how exciting this is.'

Eve smiled. He sounded like an overgrown schoolboy. 'What I'd like us to do is, as soon as the police have finished, we'll take you to meet Lionel, and then we'll investigate the place thoroughly. With your knowledge of its history, and Justin's drawings, we should be able to come up with a comprehensive overview of exactly what Lionel is sitting on. How does that sound?'

'I'd sell my soul for a chance to do that,' said Jacob.

Eve laughed. 'You've been doing too much research into the Hellfire Clubs, Jacob. There's no need for anything quite that drastic. I'm pretty sure Lionel will be delighted. Wendy and I have all sorts of questions about those caves and that creepy Temple. I'll contact you the minute the all-clear is sounded. And a big thank you for all the amazing material you sent. You really are an invaluable source of information. Take care, and speak soon.'

Eve ended the call and drained her glass. 'All that enthusiasm! I'm quite exhausted.'

'I heard him,' said Wendy. 'And I'm looking forward to learning more of what went on beneath the grounds of Jacobs Mere House. Jacob's amassed such a lot already. It's all quite fascinating, but it won't help us find Justin's killer, will it?'

'No, but finding that groundsman will,' Eve said. 'Who knows, it might give Nikki a lead to the drug ring. I'm certain there's a connection between that man and what we found in the Temple. I bet they argued because he tried to prevent Justin from making a garden there.' Eve was delighted that for once, they'd be working with Nikki and not keeping their activities from her. 'I'm sure we'll get his full name for her before my daughter's bum even touches her office chair. Well, make that lunchtime, but they *will* trace him, that's a given.'

'Knowing Lou and Rene, there's not a shred of doubt,' said Wendy. 'And we'll get a gold star from the Fenland Constabulary. Makes a nice change, doesn't it?'

'I'm getting to like it,' said Eve, 'but I'm not expecting it to last. We do have a habit of going "off-piste", don't we?'

'True, so enjoy it while it lasts.' Wendy gathered up the printouts. 'I'm off for a shower before bed. The smell of that cavern is still clinging to me.'

'It stank of corruption, didn't it? I'll be having one too, after which I shall lie in my bed smelling of roses and ylang-ylang, and turn my thoughts to our new adoptee. Well, that's the plan anyway . . .'

* * *

Nikki and Joseph went for a late evening walk down to Knot Cottage, which had been Joseph's home before he moved in with Nikki. It was a calm evening, with only a slight breeze blowing in from the Wash, and they both felt in need of fresh air. Hand in hand, they followed the lane, deliberately avoiding the subject of work.

'It's funny,' said Joseph, 'but I just can't bring myself to sell it.' He gazed fondly at the old marsh cottage. 'I know it's a waste, leaving it sitting there unoccupied. Even though I know that I'll never return to live there, I still love the old place.'

'And I know how I'd feel if someone else was occupying it. Imagine seeing smoke rising from the chimney, and knowing it had nothing to do with us. This part of the fen is ours. It's part of our history, isn't it?'

Joseph opened the gate and they went into the small garden. His post was still delivered to the cottage, and until they knew which direction their lives would take, it would continue to be that way. 'I suppose we'll have to make a decision about it at some point,' he said. 'Meanwhile, we're still in limbo, waiting for what Cam has to say.'

Nikki nodded. Their lives were on hold. At work, they had scarcely a free moment, but at home on Cloud Fen, they remained in a state of suspended animation.

As Joseph unlocked the front door and gathered up his mail, he said, 'Try as I might, I still cannot think what Cam can possibly be contemplating. Surely, we really only have two options, and we've known what those are for ages. One of us moves to a different team, or we stay as we are and continue to live a lie.'

'I can only assume that he's trying to pull a few strings in the higher echelons,' said Nikki. 'But as we know, things rarely stay the same these days; new directives and new personnel could easily put paid to anything he might put in place.' She wandered around the little cottage, checking that all was as it should be. 'I'm hanging onto one thing — his expression when he asked us to give him a little more time. It was . . . hard to read, sort of excited somehow. He and Kaye obviously believe they can help us, but how? To be honest, I can't even think about it, otherwise it'll drive me nuts.'

'It's not easy to do, though, is it?' said Joseph. 'Every time you take your mind off work, it just rolls back in. Anyway, everything's okay here. Shall we head off home?'

They locked up and started back up the lane.

'Hey! Look at that!' Joseph pointed to the tiny spike of a flower nestling amid the grass beside the path. 'It's an early marsh orchid, but it's stockier than usual, and there's that lovely reddish colour. It's certainly not a common variety. I'll need to look it up when we get home.'

Nikki squeezed his hand. 'I love the way you notice little things like that. I'd have walked straight past it.'

'If we don't pay attention to these small things, they'll be gone before we know it. So much of what surrounds us is starting to disappear, we need to appreciate what we have — and try to save it while we can.'

'You sound just like your daughter.'

Joseph laughed. 'I think even she's come to realise that we are more alike than she knew. And you, Nikki Galena. You're not quite the "material girl" you once were, you're a lot more aware of nature's beauty these days.'

It was true. She had been "material", and bloody hard with it. Joseph had opened her eyes to so much. 'I'm glad of it, Joseph. Even I didn't like the woman I'd become. Heaven knows what would have happened to me if you hadn't turned up.'

'We were lucky to meet when we did,' he said. 'I wasn't in the best place, either. For one thing, I believed I'd lost my only daughter. I have you to thank for bringing her back into my life.'

She laughed. 'Well, I'm pleased I got something right.'

Joseph grinned at her. 'Oh, I can think of a few other things you got right.'

She cuffed him on the arm. 'Joseph! You know very well I wasn't talking about that sort of thing.'

'But I was, and I think it's something we might take further . . .'

'Joseph!'

'Ouch! Watch it, or I'll have you up for assaulting a police officer.'

'Oh yeah? You just try.'

As the evening drew in, they strolled on, hand in hand, chatting happily. For once, the word "murder" never arose.

* * *

Without a sound, the old gate opened, a figure slipped through and was swallowed up in the darkness. Despite the brambles and overgrowth that encroached the path, over which it would be easy to trip and fall, the figure carried no torch. Fortunately, the sky was almost clear with just the occasional cloud obscuring the moon, which was almost full. Nevertheless, it would

278

pay to be cautious. What had to be done had to be done tonight. The dark outline of the Temple appeared, etched against the sky, and taking a key from their pocket, the figure ran to the door.

CHAPTER THIRTY

The morning meeting was about to end when Nikki received a call from her mother.

'Dennis Larimer,' said her mother without preamble. 'Has a rented flat in Foxholes Court, Greenborough. Calls himself a gardener but is basically an odd-job man. Most of his work is off the books after he was sacked from that big plant nursery on the Fenchester Road, A&K Nurserymen Ltd. They were cagey about the exact reason for letting him go, and we didn't pursue it, as we thought it was something you could follow up if you considered it relevant. As far as we know, he is currently unemployed.'

Nikki shook her head. 'We should give you guys a job! Thanks, Mum. That's much appreciated.'

Nikki ended the call and glanced at the clock. Nine thirty, and they needed to be at Jacobs Mere House in half an hour to meet with Paul Fletcher and Julia Tennant. She looked across the room at Cat. 'Slight change of plan. We've got a name for that man Justin argued with and then chucked off the property. I'd like you and Ben to get out there and find him. His name is Dennis Larimer.' She gave them the address.

'No problem, boss, we'll find him.'

She and Ben gathered up their things and hurried out. That sorted, she glanced at Joseph. 'Ready when you are. I'd like to get there before Julia, if possible, so I can see how Lionel is bearing up.'

'I'm all set,' he said.

'Hold the fort, Vonnie. Ring us if anything interesting turns up, won't you?'

With a smile, Yvonne looked up from her computer. 'Sure, boss. I've got a pile of stuff to sort out here.'

They hurried downstairs and were just heading for the doors when the desk sergeant called after her.

'Sorry, ma'am, but there's someone here needs to speak to you urgently.'

'Not now, Jonesy. We've got an appointment.'

'Er, sorry, ma'am, but I think you might want to see this lady. She says her name is Patsy Shearer.'

'What!'

Joseph took her arm. 'You go on to Jacobs Mere, Nikki. I'll stay and talk to this woman. It might well turn out to be a crock of shit, in which case I'll join you shortly.'

'And if it isn't?'

'I'll be on the phone at the speed of light, don't you worry.'

She hesitated, undecided for a moment. 'All right, but do keep in touch. This is a bit out of the blue, isn't it?'

'I'll say,,' Joseph said, running his hand through his hair. 'Anyway, I'll go and see what she has to say.'

Nikki continued on to the car park. Would anything in this damned case *ever* make sense?

* * *

Joseph went into the interview room, where the woman was waiting for him at the table. She had brown hair, cropped very short, and was wearing a white shirt under a navy blue blazer. She looked nothing like the picture Marie had given them — although . . . He looked at her more closely.

'I know what you're thinking,' she said. 'But I really am Patsy Shearer.'

Joseph introduced himself, saying he was sorry but the detective inspector was out on an appointment. He took a seat facing her. 'So, if you are who you say you are, what do you have to tell me?'

She appeared to struggle for a moment, and then she began to speak: 'I ran away from an abusive relationship, fearing for my life — or my sanity, or both, I don't know. I didn't plan to do it that particular day, but it had been on my mind for quite a while. So, anyway, I finished work for the day, and all at once I had this terrible attack of panic. I was absolutely terrified at the thought of setting foot inside that house again — I mean, home. I had nothing with me except my handbag, with my purse, my driving licence, and a few personal bits in it, but I just couldn't go back to get anything else.'

'Do you mind if I stop you there, and ask you a few questions?' Joseph needed to know the exact sequence of events, and why she was now sitting in Greenborough police station. 'I understand you were a community nurse in Greenborough. And on the day you disappeared, you had taken on a last call on behalf of a friend who was sick. You attended an elderly man named Aaron Fletcher at Jacobs Mere. Is that right?'

'I was supposed to, Sergeant, but I never actually went.'

Joseph stared at her. 'But the old man swore you arrived at the house. He said you made him comfortable for the night. How do you explain that?'

'I can't, because I never went anywhere near Jacobs Fen. I felt bad about not seeing the poor old man, though I had heard he suffered with dementia and was a bit of a handful. I did mean to go, but as soon as I got in the car I just had this overwhelming need to get away.' She bit her lip. 'It sounds ridiculous, I know, but that's how it was. I can't tell you how scared I was.'

Watching her, listening to what she said, though he was certainly none the wiser, Joseph had a strong feeling that this woman was telling the truth. It was possible that in the confusion of his dementia, Aaron Fletcher had mixed up the days, thinking she had visited when in fact she hadn't. 'You've changed your appearance, haven't you? Can you describe what you looked like back then, on the day you went away?'

She nodded. 'I had long blonde hair. I usually wore it in a ponytail or in a bun when I was working. When I wasn't in uniform I dressed casually, I was never one to dress up much. I think I had on jeans, trainers, and a sweatshirt.' She bit her lip. 'I knew I had to do something with my hair if I wanted to disappear, so I had it cut short and dyed brown. I hoped that if Sean did come looking for me, he wouldn't look twice at anyone with short, darker hair.' She gave a brief laugh. 'As it was, I didn't even recognise myself. I'm sorry. I never dreamed the police would get involved. I mean, hundreds of people go missing for one reason or another, don't they?'

'If you really are Daisy, I think you should know that you are still classed as a missing person, since no one has established your whereabouts or seen you in person.' Joseph regarded the slight woman sitting opposite him. 'Would you like a coffee, or a cup of tea? Because I have an awful lot of questions for you, and it could take some time.'

'I'd love one, please, Sergeant. Tea with milk, no sugar.'

Joseph went outside and asked a constable to organise them some tea.

'Would you mind if I recorded this?' he asked when he came back in. 'It would make life a lot easier for me when I come to type it up later.'

She smiled. 'It's all right with me. Go ahead, do whatever you have to. I came here to help. A friend of mine who lives in Durham contacted me and told me that people — well, you — were making enquiries about me. She even said you suspected that I'd been murdered. I never meant to cause any bother for anyone, so I decided to come to Greenborough and sort things out. Sean is long gone now, married to some other poor soul. They've moved to the West Country, or so I'm told. So, here I am.'

283

Their drinks arrived, Joseph started the recording, and they went back to the day she chose to disappear. As she spoke, a picture began to emerge. There were still questions, things he needed to have clarified, such as what happened to her car, which hadn't been seen since.

'An old boyfriend let me leave it in his barn, Sergeant. It's still there. I'll give you his number and he'll confirm it. His name is Tom Avery, and he's always been a good friend. When I took off, I went straight to him and asked if I could leave my car at his farm. He has a lot of clapped-out farm machinery and tractors. He lent me a runaround of his sister's that she left with him when she went to live abroad.'

'If you had the use of a car, why did you purchase a coach ticket to Durham?' asked Joseph.

'It's a long way to Durham, and I didn't feel up to driving that far, so I took the coach.' She made a face. 'I was a bit of a wreck, in no fit state to do anything very much. I stayed with a friend of mine and her mum in Durham for a couple of weeks, bought some clothes and things, and got my head together. Then I rang my friends back here and told them I was okay and was going to make a new start up North.' She sipped her tea. 'I wasn't intending to, it was just to cover my tracks in case word of my whereabouts got back to Sean. I wrote to my employers and apologised for leaving without giving them notice. Then I came back, collected the car I'd borrowed from Tom, and settled in a different part of the Fens. I've been here in Lincolnshire all along.'

'But how have you survived?' Joseph asked. 'There has been no employment record for you since you left.'

'I am a private carer for an elderly lady with health and mobility problems. I live in, and I'm on call twenty-four hours a day. She's actually my great-aunt, she looked after me when I was small, after my father died and my mother wasn't coping. She pays me in cash, not very much, but as my board and lodging is covered, I only need a bit of spending money. You won't find an official record, Sergeant, because there isn't one.'

Joseph took note of the names, addresses, and phone numbers she gave him. Already, he knew what they would say, that this woman really was Patsy Shearer.

'And there's these, too.' She took some documents from her handbag. 'Somehow I must always have known that I'd run away one day, because I kept my driver's licence, my birth certificate, and a few other personal papers in my bag.' She pushed them across to Joseph. 'You can check them out, they really are mine.' When she smiled, Joseph had an inkling of the attractive, fun-loving girl Patsy Shearer must once have been, and possibly still was. 'Here. Look.' She leaned forward and parted her hair. 'Blonde roots. I've been thinking of going back to my own colour now there's no threat anymore.'

Joseph smiled back. 'Okay, you've convinced me.'

'Can I ask you something?' she said.

'Of course.'

'Why did you think I was dead? I was shocked to hear that Durham Constabulary were looking for me, and I didn't understand why.'

Tough one to answer, thought Joseph. He couldn't really tell her that a young and disturbed man had a clear recollection of being present at her murder. 'Well, we received a report of a woman matching your description visiting the house you say you never went to — Jacobs Mere — and subsequently disappearing without trace. And as you were still recorded as missing, we didn't know what else to think.'

She didn't look totally convinced, but asked what would happen next.

'If you leave me your contact details, I'll have to verify what you've told me, and then I'll be in touch. And thank you for coming in, we do appreciate it.' Getting to his feet, he added, 'And I'm very glad to see you're alive, Miss Shearer.'

Her expression brightened. 'Then you believe me? Really?'

He smiled. 'Like I said, I'll have to verify what you've told me, but on a purely personal level, yes, I do.'

* * *

285

Down a badly breaking line, Joseph gave Nikki the news of Patsy Shearer's resurrection.

'Bloody hell, Joseph! Now what? If you believe this woman really is Patsy Shearer, where does that leave Paul? You really should be here, Joseph. I'm telling you, the kid is not making this up. I've seen fear enough times to know he's not putting it on. He really did see what he says he did. So, either one of us is mistaken, or . . .'

'Has he pointed out the exact spot yet?' asked Joseph.

'We were just heading there when you rang.'

'Okay, then hang up and call me back when you've finished,' said Joseph. 'By that time I'll have spoken to her great-aunt and her former boyfriend.'

She rang off and hurried over to where Paul, Julia, and Lionel were waiting for her. Lionel was chatting to 'young Paulie', asking him how he was doing and what he was up to. He seemed to be genuinely concerned about his welfare.

Seeing her approach, Julia raised an enquiring eyebrow. As the others went on ahead, Nikki took her aside and whispered, 'We'll talk later.'

Paul led the way, looking about him. He stopped and pointed. 'Here is where I saw a volery of long-tailed tits.'

'A what?' queried Nikki.

'It's another term for a flock of birds, referring especially to wagtails or long-tailed tits, although some people use it for doves or pigeons. I saw those, and then I walked on down here.' He pointed to a line of trees just ahead. 'I heard the red kite up on the thermals, and a bit later I saw the woodpecker. Then . . .'

Paul walked ever more slowly, rubbing his hands together as if he were cold. He seemed to have forgotten the presence of the others.

'Are you sure this isn't too much for Paulie?' Lionel asked Julia.

She gave him a reassuring smile. 'He's going to be fine. He needs to do this, Mr Connaught. Only then can he move forward. It was his choice, you know. No one forced him to come here.'

Nikki recalled Joseph's words: *Patsy is alive, Nikki. Paul never saw her being killed.*

Meanwhile, Paul was moving forward again, dragging his feet, as if resisting some invisible force.

'That's where I hid to watch the green woodpecker.' He pointed to a clump of trees and shrubs bordering a clearing just off the path they were following.

Nikki thought back to his original description, it was identical to what she was looking at now. But he had often been here to watch birds, so he would know the layout of the grounds. However, there'd be time for questions later. Now there was nothing for it but to hear what he had to say, get the site of the possible attack fixed in her mind and photographed, and then get Paul Fletcher out of here before he disintegrated.

He continued, speaking in a monotone. 'She came from that direction. Running, she was. Scared — no, terrified. Looking back over her shoulder.' He gasped. 'Oh God! I can see her!'

Julia moved forward to stand at his side. 'It's all right, Paul, it's just your memory coming back to the surface, and because of where you are, it's much more vivid. Just go with it, all right? Breathe, like we practised, that's it. And remember, it can't hurt you. Once it's all out there, it won't haunt you any longer.'

Nikki was far from sure about that. She watched him, waiting for what would happen next.

The breathing exercises seemed to work, and he continued along the path. 'That's where she fell. Right there.' Sounding calmer now, he pointed to a grassy area just off the path. Suddenly he stood stock still. 'Oh. I made a mistake, it must have been the light, the sunlight. I can see it now, so clearly. Her hair, it wasn't blonde at all, it was golden! A deep, rich, burnished gold.'

Amid the welter of thoughts flooding her head, one question stood out. If the woman he saw being killed wasn't Patsy Shearer, who the hell was she?

At that moment, the air was rent by a blood-curdling scream that gradually resolved into a low animal-like groan.

Nikki ran towards Paul, who had sunk to his knees, but Julia and Lionel were already kneeling beside him.

'That's enough!' said Lionel, looking at Julia. He put his arm around Paul's shoulders. 'Come on, son, let's get you back to the house.'

But Paul shrugged him off. 'No! You don't understand! It's all back, all of it! I have to tell you, I must tell you what happened!'

They watched, mesmerised, as he got to his feet.

'After I saw her lying there, dead, just like my father, I ran away — or so I thought. But I know now, I didn't. I stayed. The man who attacked her ran back towards the house, so I remained where I was, hiding, and waited to see if he came back.' He swallowed. 'He did, and another man was with him, and they were each carrying spades. They lifted her up and,' he pointed down a narrow, barely discernible track that led off the clearing, 'carried her down there. They dug a hole and . . . just threw her in!'

Nikki became aware that she was holding her breath. If this turned out to be true, they would have evidence at last. Tentatively, she asked, 'Do you think you could show us where that was, Paul?'

Without a word, he picked his way slowly along the track, the three of them following.

Nikki realised that they were heading away from the wooded area and were approaching a long stretch of post and rail fencing. She took a gulp of air. The paddocks! The very place where Justin had been planning to excavate.

'There.' Paul indicated a grassy area beneath a row of alders growing a little way back from the fence.

Nikki moved ahead. At the spot Paul had pointed out, there was a rectangular area where the grass and weeds were thicker and lusher. She knew at once that this was a grave.

'Oh my God! He's right.' Lionel looked quite pale. 'I've seen this before, when we were searching for the unmarked graves of dead servicemen and women. Areas like that even show up on aerial photographs.'

Nikki straightened up. 'I need to call this in, and I'm sorry, Lionel, but your home will once again be overrun by police and forensics people.' She turned to Paul. Julia was speaking softly to him, words of comfort and praise for his bravery. Nikki smiled at him. 'Thank you. I can't begin to imagine what it cost you, but I am so grateful for what you've done.'

'And you've earned yourself a brandy, my boy,' added Lionel. 'In fact, I think we all have. Shall we go back to the house, and leave DI Galena to do her job?'

She may have been imagining it, but Nikki thought Paul seemed to stride away purposefully. And wasn't that the hint of a smile on his face?

Maybe Julia had been right all along, and he had needed to do this in order to leave the past behind and move forward. Nikki could only wish him well.

Nikki was now in the horns of a dilemma. Obviously, the grave of a murdered woman would need to be investigated as soon as possible. But here was the problem: if they brought in the forensics team and its accompanying circus of police officers and detectives, their drug dealers would disappear like fen mist on a sunny day. Taking out a drug-dealing operation was a big thing. It could save lives, and result in some wicked people being banged up for years.

Nikki needed to speak to both Joseph and Cameron Walker before she made the call. She reasoned that the unfortunate woman had been dead for a long time now, and a few more days would hardly make much difference, but that wasn't quite true, was it? Someone was praying desperately for the return of a daughter, a sister, a wife, or a dear friend. She remembered the awful case of a mother who had never given up on her missing son. When they finally went to break the news of his death to her, they found they had arrived too late. She had taken an overdose three days before their visit.

Lionel had fallen behind the others, and was walking at her side. 'How does that saying go? Between the devil and the deep blue sea. I'd be in the same quandary if I were in charge.'

Nikki chuckled. 'Got it in one. But I'm going to kick this one upstairs. At least my super is a sensible man, and he doesn't toady to the top brass. He'll do what he believes is right for the greater good, and I'll be happy to go along with it, no matter what he decides.'

'That's good to hear. Just let me know, won't you?'

'I'll ring him as soon as we're back in the house.' Nikki had a good idea that Cam would go along with her. They would mount a drugs bust, and as soon as that was taken care of, get forensics in to investigate the grave site.

As they neared the house, Lionel said, 'I've been thinking. For my wife's sake, and for the lad himself, I intend to see if I can help young Paul Fletcher. He and his mother have suffered enough, and they aren't exactly rolling in it, are they?'

'That sounds good. Help them in what way?' asked Nikki.

'I'm not sure yet, but I have the germ of an idea in my head. I'll give it some thought, and in the meantime, I'll keep in touch with them, and also monitor Paulie's health. This has been terribly stressful for him. I hope it's been cathartic, but when the reality hits him, it could be one hell of a shock to the system.'

'True, but from the way he looks right now, I think that having faced his demons, he can start to live a proper life.'

'Let's hope so. Now, would you care for a small restorative brandy, or are you going to tell me you're on duty?'

'Unfortunately,' said Nikki. 'More's the pity — I could kill for a drink right now.'

'Another time, then.' Lionel unlocked the front door. 'When this is over, I'd like you and Joseph to come over one evening, perhaps with Eve and Wendy? Hopefully by then I'll have decided what to do with Jacobs Mere House, and I'd value your opinions.'

Saying she'd be delighted, Nikki went to make her calls.

'Use the lounge. I'll take Paul and Julia into the kitchen and organise the drinks. I don't know about them, but I badly need one!'

* * *

Joseph put down the receiver. As Patsy had said, her car was safely hidden away in a barn on Tom Avery's farm. Tom had even been kind enough to take a video of it, making sure the registration number was clearly visible. Joseph had already run a name check on the car Patsy had borrowed, and found it to be registered to Lindsey Avery, so there was no doubt about that part of her story. In fact, there was no doubt about any of it. She *was* Patsy Shearer. Her great-aunt had been most forthcoming: 'On God's own bible, that is my beloved Patsy, and I'm glad I was able to help her get away from that beastly man she was living with. She's an angel, and she deserves much better than him.'

'So there it is,' he said to himself. 'Never attacked and never killed. I wonder what Marie Evans will say when I tell her?'

Nikki called. He listened in growing amazement to what she had to say. 'Look, while you're on the phone to Cam, I'll jump in the car and come over to Jacobs Mere. I'm finished with my calls, and I'd really like to take a look at that grave site. Is that okay with you?'

It was, so he went to find Vonnie. 'Do you mind keeping an eye on things here for a bit longer?' he asked her.

'Sure, Sarge. Where are you off to in such a hurry?' she said.

'Back to Jacobs Mere. Looks like we do have a body, but it's not the one we thought.' He smiled at her confused expression. 'I'll fill you in when I get back.'

'You'd better, Sarge! My head is spinning. Is it me, or is the whole world out to confuse us?'

'Oh, it's not you, Vonnie, believe me!'

291

CHAPTER THIRTY-ONE

Time lay heavily on Richard's hands. To give himself something to do, he decided to tackle the weeds in the small enclosed patio. He had been at it for about half an hour when Lizzie came out of the house carrying a couple of drinks in tall glasses.

She set them down on the garden table. 'Colin says there are no new developments, so I'm wondering if they might let us go home soon. I mean, if Claire's not around, we're not in any danger, are we?'

'No, we're not,' said Richard, accepting a cold lemonade. 'Perhaps if they're not ready to throw us out into the big, bad world just yet, they might at least let us go back to my house. We'd have a bit more comfort there, and we wouldn't feel so isolated.'

'I'd love that,' said Lizzie wistfully. 'You have a lovely home, Richard, and if you don't mind me sharing it for a little longer, it would be so much better than being here. I'm grateful for the protection, and Colin is a lovely man, but, oh dear, what a life!'

'It's no fun, is it, Lizzie?' Richard took a sip of his drink. 'One thing about being here, though, is that it's given me time to have a bit of a rethink about my life, and the way it's going. When things get back to normal — whatever that is — I'm considering making some changes.'

Lizzie laughed. 'Funny you should say that, I've been thinking the exact same thing. This business with Claire has shaken me to the core. I've decided that for however long I've got left, I'm going to live my life more simply, spend my time doing what really matters. I'll sell my big house and move into a cottage in the countryside, get myself a dog, and maybe a cat, and go for long walks. I'm going to enjoy spending time with friends, eat whatever I want, drink wine if I feel like it, read books, and travel to places I've always wanted to see before I'm too old — oh, and I'm going to be kinder to people. How does that sound?'

Richard laughed. 'Like the perfect life! I hadn't got quite that far yet, but I like the idea of simplifying one's life.' They fell into a companionable silence, sipping their lemonade and enjoying the feel of the sun on their faces. 'This business with Claire,' Richard said after a while, 'especially not knowing whether she's dead or alive, has hit me hard too. I've come to the conclusion that someone twisted and dark was drawn to her for some reason, and they went after her relentlessly. Someone wanted to destroy her, and in order to do that, they were prepared to take the life of an innocent young woman, Joanne, just to get at Claire. That is hate on a grand scale, isn't it?'

Lizzie nodded. 'Or love.'

Richard frowned. Love, or hate? Which was the stronger? It was one of the eternal questions, to which an answer might never be found.

'Love,' Richard said. 'I hadn't thought of it, but it is possible, isn't it? We know nothing about that side of Claire's life.'

'Only that she's single and doesn't live with anyone,' said Lizzie. 'But she was so kind and compassionate, and I thought rather beautiful, too. So what caused someone to want to destroy her?'

'Maybe it was a jealous wife. Or someone's former lover.' Richard shrugged. 'Those are the main reasons for someone wanting to take revenge.'

'Or a jilted admirer? Someone obsessed with her. After all, love can easily turn to hate, and the stronger the love, the more powerful the hate, especially if the would-be lover is rejected.'

Richard placed his glass back on the table. 'I'm sure the police will have looked at every one of Claire's past relationships. They'll have interviewed former boyfriends, girlfriends, and anyone else she might have had an affair with, and they are very good at spotting liars and deceivers.'

'I'm not so sure, Richard, we women are pretty good at keeping secrets. I reckon it'll all come down to love.'

After Lizzie had gone back inside, Richard finished weeding the patio and continued on into the small garden. He found gardening therapeutic, it had seen him through some bad periods in his life. Right now, he was using it to focus his thoughts.

Lizzie's words continued to echo in his mind: *It will all come down to love.*

Tugging at a dandelion, he thought, if that was the case, what kind of love was it? Bad Love? Dangerous love? Forbidden love? Unrequited love?

After ten minutes, he decided that Lizzie was probably right, but as they knew so little of Claire's history, it wasn't a puzzle they could solve unaided. He straightened up and went to find some secateurs, and set to work pruning the old growth from an overhanging lilac bush. What really puzzled him was the sudden change in Claire that had occurred while they were still at his house. He wished he had seen it for himself. Lizzie had repeated practically word for word what had been said immediately before it happened. But Lizzie wasn't a detective and had no training or experience in picking up warning signs as he had. Indeed, if he had been there, he might have seen the episode from a very different angle.

Cutting the woody lilac stems into manageable lengths, Richard went over in his mind everything that Lizzie had told him. Then a thought struck him. What if that sudden change in Claire had had nothing to do with what they had been talking about? What if the shock, if that's what it was, wasn't a memory, but some outside occurrence? He squeezed his eyes shut and again went through everything as Lizzie had described it. His eyes flew open. Of course!

He dropped the pruners and ran into the house. He found Lizzie in the lounge, chatting to Colin. Both looked up at him in surprise.

'It's all right, I haven't chopped my finger off or anything. Lizzie, listen! Go back to when you were talking to Claire just before she suddenly clammed up. You said she'd been watching the television and she turned the sound down to talk to you. Is that right?'

'Yes, that's right,' Lizzie said, looking puzzled.

'Do you remember what was on?' he asked.

Lizzie screwed up her face in concentration. 'Just adverts. Yes, that's right. I remember because there was that irritating one about some household cleaner turning a filthy bathroom into a palace in a couple of squeezes. You know the one I mean.'

'Damn,' muttered Richard, still thinking hard. 'But she never actually turned the TV off, did she, just the sound? So did you happen to notice what came on after the ads?'

'Oh dear,' Lizzie said. 'I was concentrating on her, not the telly.'

'Don't worry,' said Richard. 'If we know the time, we can check in the TV listings. You see, I've just realised that what happened had nothing to do with your conversation. It was something she saw on that television that stirred up a bad memory. It could even have been a drama that had a storyline similar to hers.'

'It can happen,' said Colin. 'My sister can't watch anything that deals with children being stolen or abused. She switches to another channel at once.'

'That's right,' said Richard. 'Even a single image of something too close to home can trigger a panic attack.'

'So she wasn't staring into space after all,' said Lizzie. 'That's right! Thinking about it, she *was* looking in the direction of the TV set when it happened.'

So, he was right. Now all they had to do was work out exactly what time the episode occurred. He was going through the events of that day when a gasp made him stop.

'It was a news flash!' Lizzie sat bolt upright. 'Yes! When that terrible look came over her face, I must have glanced towards the TV, because I saw the news presenter, but I didn't catch what it was about since I was focusing on Claire. It must have been an update on poor young Joanne.'

Richard wasn't so sure. 'Colin, can you use your phone to find out what that report was about?'

'Date and approximate time?' asked Colin, his phone already in his hand.

Richard told him, as far as he could remember and waited anxiously while Colin searched.

'Got the day,' Colin muttered, thumbs working madly. 'Now I need to know what news was breaking . . . Ah, this would be it.' He read from his screen: *'Archaeologist Justin Connaught, the well-known presenter of the popular television series,* Digging History, *has been discovered dead at his home in Jacobs Mere. Currently, there is no word as to the manner of his death, although it is believed to be suspicious. We will bring you more on this tragedy as soon as the police have issued an official statement.'*

No one spoke. They didn't have to. All were thinking the same thing. If the death of that television celebrity had affected Claire so badly, possibly to the point of considering taking her own life, then she must have known him well. Very well. Was Lizzie right, and it really did all come down to love?

'I think we've just discovered Claire's secret, don't you?' said Lizzie, with a relieved smile.

Richard reached for his burner phone. 'I think I need to get hold of DI Mercer.'

* * *

Cat and Ben hurried into the CID room. 'Boss still out, is she?' Cat asked Vonnie.

'Yes, she went to Jacobs Mere House, and the sarge has gone to join her,' said Vonnie. 'Any luck with Dennis Larimer?'

'Dennis the bloody Menace has gone to ground,' said Cat. 'Hasn't been home for two days, although we've been told he's been seen around the town. It looks like he's keeping a low profile.'

'We've left word with his neighbours to contact us if he shows up,' added Ben. 'We've been told he's been extremely twitchy of late, but no one seems to know why. As far as we know, he's not been involved in anything particularly criminal.'

'Maybe he's just like that,' Cat said. 'The woman next door reckons he's one of those people who'll argue with the leaves on a tree if they rustle too loudly for his liking. He doesn't like authority in any shape or form, and struggles to hold down a job. Bit of a chancer, too. She said he might be passing on stolen goods, as he'd offered her a few "real bargains" on small electrical goods like hairdryers and that. Nothing particularly serious.'

'We are now wondering if the row with Justin just comes down to his dislike of taking orders.' Ben flopped into his chair. 'Disappointing.'

'Well, I reckon you can forget about our Dennis,' said Yvonne. 'Nikki is almost certain she's found a grave in the grounds of Jacobs Mere House.'

Cat let out a low whistle. 'So Paul Fletcher was right! Patsy Shearer was murdered there.'

'Not exactly,' said Yvonne. 'Yes, he did see a woman being killed, but as the sarge was with Patsy Shearer in one of our interview rooms an hour ago, it looks like he got that bit wrong.'

Ben and Cat stared at each other.

Vonnie laughed. 'You look as baffled as me. How about I get us all a coffee, and we'll try to make some vague sense out of all this?'

'I think it'll take more than just coffee,' said Ben. 'But, yes, please, Vonnie. A strong one for me.'

'And an extra sugar in mine, please,' said Cat sinking into her chair. 'I could do with the energy. What a mind-bender of a case!'

* * *

Gill Mercer threw down her pen and stared at her notepad, on which she had written two names, heavily underlined: Claire Hereward and Justin Connaught.

She rubbed at her temples. How likely was that? It was a fact that Claire had been holding back on something personal, almost certainly sentimental in nature. So, yes, it was perfectly likely.

And if it did turn out to be the case, what were the implications? For a start, it meant the fusion of two massive murder hunts. *God, what a logistical nightmare!* She wondered if she should talk to Nikki and Cam Walker right now, when it was still just a supposition. Though, as Richard had explained, Claire had been looking in the direction of a television that had been showing a newsflash announcing the death of Justin Connaught. At that exact moment, she appeared to have been overtaken by shock, and later, Richard had heard her sobbing in her room. There could be little doubt as to the cause of it.

Her mind made up, Gill marched into the CID room in search of Nikki.

She found Cat having a coffee with Ben and Yvonne. 'Your boss out, is she?'

'Yes, ma'am,' Cat said. 'She's at the Connaught place. They have had a big development out there, so I'm not sure when she'll be back.'

'Her too, eh? Well, I'd better phone her, then. I need to speak with her, fast.'

Cat raised an eyebrow. 'Be warned, the signal's not good out in the grounds.'

Thanking Cat, Gill hurried off to Cam Walker's office.

'Are you sure Richard's not jumping to conclusions?' Cam said. 'It's a helluva big jump to make.'

'It's the only thing that makes any sense, sir, and he has absolute faith in Lizzie's judgement. He said she recalled their conversation almost word for word. She even remembered seeing a banner across the bottom of the TV screen just as Claire went into shock, but in her anxiety about her friend, she didn't read it. Jones, their security officer, confirmed that the newsflash was broadcast at that precise moment, and was reporting the death of Justin Connaught. I can see no other plausible explanation for her behaviour.'

Cameron Walker was silent for a moment or two. Then he said, 'All right. Are you prepared to combine your two teams into a joint effort? I see no other way we can handle this new development.'

'Absolutely, sir. I was hoping you would say that. Nikki and I work well together, and so do our respective teams. There won't be any problems.'

'Good. In that case, let me tell you what they discovered at Jacobs Mere, and as soon as Nikki gets back, I suggest you both work out your *modus operandi*. Make sure to keep me informed every step of the way, and I'll give you all my support. You can see for yourself that the media is still sniffing around, though fortunately, they seem to have lost interest in the house. I'll have to call another press conference, and give them the usual guff about major developments as yet unconfirmed, and progress being made.' He grinned. 'I'm becoming quite a master of the art of obfuscation.'

Gill returned the smile. 'I'm glad to hear it. As for me, I'm wondering what the new development at the Connaught place could possibly be.'

CHAPTER THIRTY-TWO

'So, Cam said to go ahead with the hit on the drug dealers?' Joseph asked, gazing at the lush green rectangle which could be the gravesite of an unknown woman.

'We have two days — well, two nights to be precise — and if no one shows up, we're to assume they have abandoned their lair. Then we get forensics in to both check out the caves, and see what's underneath this patch of grass.'

'Oh, it's a grave all right, no doubt about it.' Joseph had often seen similar areas of luscious vegetation in war zones where those fallen in battle had been hastily interred.

'My gut instinct says "yes", but as always, we'll have to wait for hard evidence before we can move forward,' Nikki said.

'Have the surveillance guys received their orders yet?' Joseph asked.

'They're already here. Cam sorted that as soon as I spoke to him. They arrived while I was out with Paul and Julia. Not that we saw them, of course. They know their jobs. I have a direct link with them, so I'll know at once should any of the dealers show up.'

Nikki turned her gaze to the paddocks. 'Justin was planning to excavate just over there, so it does look as though someone was afraid he might uncover more than he bargained for.'

'Yeah,' Joseph said. 'It fits, doesn't it? I bet they were furious to learn that an archaeologist had bought the estate. Especially since this whole area could be the site of a Roman settlement.'

'Let's go back to the house, and I'll show you his maps and plans,' said Nikki. 'They are amazingly detailed. Oh, and guess where they come from — courtesy of my mother and her bestie!'

Joseph laughed. 'As if I didn't know.'

Just as they were approaching the house, Joseph grabbed Nikki's arm. 'See that car parked out front? It's that damned twisted sister, bloody Heather. I thought I'd managed to warn her off.'

'Daddy too. He was far from pleased with her. So what's she doing here when you've both told her to stay away?'

'What she's doing here is making sure she gets her hands on this house,' Joseph said between clenched teeth.

'Well, I hope she doesn't sweet-talk Lionel into letting her stay.'

'One thing's for sure,' Joseph said, 'we're going to be in for an Oscar-winning performance. Just you wait, there'll be tears by the bucketful.'

Nikki grinned. 'Tell you what, I'll let you have the pleasure of throwing her out a second time. There's no way on earth we're having her here when we are just on the verge of closing down a drugs ring.'

'And exhuming a dead body,' Joseph added. 'I'll be delighted to evict her on your behalf. Unless,' he said innocently, 'you'd rather have the pleasure yourself?'

'Best not,' said Nikki. 'You might find me getting physical, which is a bit out of order in a respected DI.' Joseph was about to reply when her phone rang with a call from Gill Mercer.

'Is it a bad moment, Nikki?'

'No, Gill, it's fine. What's the problem?' Nikki listened in growing amazement. 'Justin and Claire Hereward? An item?'

The image of a lipstick lying on the bedroom floor rose into her mind.

'. . . so, as soon as you get back, we need to work out a way to pool our resources. It looks like suddenly we're fighting the same war.'

'Of course,' Nikki said. 'I'll make sure the drugs operation is all in place and get straight back to the station. And there's something else here that I need to tell you about. Give me half an hour and I'll be with you.'

She pocketed her phone. 'Come on, Joseph, we need to talk to Lionel and Julia about that grave, then I have to let the surveillance team know I'm not going to be here, and then get back to the station. This is a turn-up for the books!'

'Just goes to show, doesn't it? Never disregard anything the cleaning lady tells you,' Joseph said. 'Mary insisted that Justin had someone special. Claire Hereward. Who'd have thought it? I imagine we're not sharing this one with Lionel just yet?'

'No, we need to be sure it really was the case before we tell anyone. So far, it's still supposition, but according to Gill, everything points in that direction.'

'I gather Claire's not been found yet?' asked Joseph. 'Oh, shit! I forgot about Heather. We need to get her off the premises as fast as we can.'

'You do. So you'd better get on with it, Sergeant.'

'You're so good to me,' he muttered.

Within fifteen minutes, Heather's car was speeding out through the gates. Joseph apologised to Lionel, saying a new piece of information had just come in that made it essential that no one other than Lionel himself and the police must be present on the premises.

With a shrug, Lionel said that if his daughter had had a wasted journey, she could blame no one but herself. To Nikki's relief, there was nothing but irritation at his daughter's temerity in his voice.

Nikki went to speak to Paul and Julia, who were still at the house.

'Paul, we can't thank you enough for coming out here. You are one courageous young man. Thanks to what you've told us we have to open a fresh investigation, but I promise we'll keep you updated on our findings, it's the least we can do.'

'I could never have done it without Julia's help and her belief in me,' said Paul.

'He's right,' Nikki said to Julia. 'You are one special lady.'

'Nonsense!' Julia said, looking slightly embarrassed. 'Paul did all the hard work.'

'And now, I'm afraid we'll have to throw you both out,' said Nikki. 'We have just received some very interesting information regarding Justin's case, and we need to talk to Lionel. But we'll be in touch very soon.'

'So will I,' added Lionel, resting his hand on Paul's shoulder. 'And if it's all right with you, I'd love to come and visit you and your mother.'

'She'd like that,' Paul said. 'I'll give you our number, and when things are less stressful for you, please do ring.'

'Thank you, Paul.'

'And I'm sorry I trespassed on the estate. It was just that it was somewhere I could go and find some peace when I was feeling really low. I never even told Mum. I knew how much she hated old Aaron, and she might not have understood.'

Lionel gave his shoulder a squeeze. 'Well, I'm glad you found a safe haven here, and I hope you'll feel that you can come back, whenever you like.'

Paul smiled at him. 'Maybe it's just me, but it feels as if a curse has been lifted. There's no darkness here anymore. I would very much like to come back when the police have finished their work here.'

Nikki watched him leave. Already, he looked very different to the person she had met at Mill Corner, his eyes especially no longer looked haunted.

'And I must go too, said Julia 'I expect you want to get on.'

Nikki went with her to her car. 'Can I have a quick word before you head off?'

Nikki told her that the grave Paul had shown them was not that of Patsy Shearer, but a different, unknown woman.

'My goodness!' Julia said. 'This is getting very complicated. But what about the clothes? I thought his description matched that of the missing woman perfectly, even if he did make a mistake about the hair colour.'

'I know,' said Nikki. 'We'll only find the truth when we investigate that grave, but we can't do that until another serious matter has been cleared up.' She glanced at her watch. 'Listen, Julia, I can't go into detail right now, I need to close this place down and get back to the station.'

Julia climbed into her car. 'I won't hold you up, then, but do ring me if I can help with anything. It looks like I might be around for the foreseeable — Professor Sam Page and I are talking about going into partnership. It's early days yet, but it would mean I'd be based at Cartoft, which isn't far from Greenborough.' She turned on the ignition. 'See you soon!'

Back in the house, Nikki and Joseph asked Lionel if he would keep a low profile until the drug dealers were apprehended, and the same went for her mother and Wendy.

This made Lionel laugh. 'You do need to keep them on a short leash, don't you? But I'm pretty sure that this time, at least, they won't be getting in the way. Finding that the Temple had been used for dealing drugs unnerved them, and they'll be only too glad to see you put a stop to it. They'll be no bother, I'm sure of it, and neither will I.'

'It's just a pity that it means we can't get forensics in immediately to check out that grave, but we'll use the time to gather further information regarding your son. Then, as soon as we slap the cuffs on those drug dealers, we'll be calling in the SOCOs and our pathologist, and we can ascertain whether there is any connection between that buried woman and Justin's murder.'

'I'm not sure if this is useful or not,' said Lionel, 'but I've suddenly remembered that Justin kept some of the equipment for his excavations in one of the garages. Among the items is a

GPR scanner, which I believe cost him over twenty thousand, so it's a good one. I had a look at it once, and it resembles a sort of lawnmower. It dawned on me that if you wanted to do a bit of informal investigating yourselves, before the official search begins, you might like to make use of it — if you can fathom out how the thing works.'

Joseph's eyes immediately lit up. 'Well, thank you, Lionel,' Nikki said. 'If our dealers don't show up tonight, we might well take you up on that. Now, we really must get away. And, please, try and keep to the house as much as possible, and if you need to go out in the car, make sure you inform the crew manning the gate of your destination, and a rough estimate of when you'll be back. And I know it's teaching your grandmother to suck eggs, but be sure to lock all your doors and windows, especially at night.'

Lionel smiled at her. 'Understood. I just hope you nail these damned dealers.'

'You and me both,' she said with feeling. 'But we won't let this drag on. We've given ourselves only a short window in which to catch them, mainly because we want to get on with our murder investigation. Justin comes first.'

* * *

The first meeting of the two combined teams was unusually subdued. The assembled detectives indulged in none of the usual banter, most of them listening with an air of slightly bewildered thoughtfulness. Prior to the briefing, Nikki and Gill had had a brief discussion in which they decided to share the position of Officer In Charge.

Nikki began the meeting by presenting a comprehensive overview of the Justin Connaught murder, followed by a summary of their most recent findings. Gill followed with details of the investigation into the death of Joanne Andrews and the threats made to Claire Hereward, ending with Richard Duckworth's suggestion that Claire's sudden change in demeanour was caused by shock at learning of Justin Connaught's death.

Following these presentations, they selected a number of key elements to focus on. It was decided that Joseph should work with Ryan, while Cat and Ben teamed up with Steve Gilbert and Annie Porter. The remaining officers would support whoever most needed their help.

'We were led to believe that at the time of his death, Justin wasn't involved in any relationship. However, we later learned that he may have been having a clandestine affair,' Nikki said.

'For our part, we have long suspected that Claire was withholding information about someone she was involved with,' added Gill. 'So, Richard's belief would make sense. What we don't know is why they seemed so determined to keep their relationship secret — if indeed they were in a relationship at all.'

'So, our first task is to obtain concrete proof that they really were connected in some way,' Nikki said. 'Cat, Ben, Steve and Annie, please make that your priority. We need to find when and where they met, and take it from there.'

Gill then assigned Ryan and Joseph the task of looking into Claire's and Justin's past relationships. 'I know we've done it already, but we need to go into them at far greater depth.'

'And all of you, try to find out why they needed to keep their relationship secret. What was the reason for not being open about it? Was it something from their pasts? After all, we're talking about murder here — Justin shot in cold blood and Claire threatened with death. Was it an ex-lover of one of them? Someone so eaten up with jealousy that they were prepared to kill Joanne Andrews when she started to show undue interest in Claire's affairs? Is it even the same person, or yet another twist in the tale? Whatever, there is a ruthless killer out there, and we must root them out.'

For another ten minutes, questions and suggestions were tossed about, until Gill and Nikki brought the meeting to a close.

'Finally,' Gill said, 'there have been no sightings of Claire Hereward since she climbed out of a window in that safe house, leaving what amounts to a suicide note.'

'And if Claire's dead, too, it's going to be hard to discover anything about their relationship,' said Ryan.

'In which case,' added Nikki, 'we had better get our arses into gear and find out what the dickens is going on.' She held up a hand. 'One final word. This case is not to be mentioned outside the station. The media are still camped outside the doors and they're desperate for something new to feed the public with, so keep schtum, okay?'

With a general murmur of assent, the detectives set about their assigned tasks. Gill followed Nikki into her office, where her desk phone was ringing.

'Spooky, hi! Have you got something for us?'

'Nothing spectacular, Nikki, but we've discovered that Justin Connaught made a lot of calls to a pay-as-you-go phone, occasionally during the day, but mainly in the evenings or at night. Oddly, there were no incoming calls. We've traced it to the Greenborough area, but that's as far as we can go, I'm afraid.'

Nikki thanked her. 'Hmm. Calls made to a burner phone. Our Justin had a secret all right, didn't he?'

'And Claire lived in the Greenborough area. It's still just another supposition, but they all add up. I wonder why he didn't receive any calls?' Gill said.

'No bloody idea,' muttered Nikki. She glanced at the wall clock. Half past two. 'Before we do anything else, I'd better tell you about another thing we've stumbled across at Jacobs Mere House. Have you got time now?'

'As long we can organise a strong coffee, and maybe something to eat,' Gill said.

Nikki smiled. 'A woman after my own heart. How about if I send out for sandwiches?'

'I have a better idea,' Gill said. 'The others won't be coming up with any results yet, so why don't we slip out to the

Café des Amis and treat ourselves to a proper coffee and a freshly made sandwich?'

'Excellent idea! I'll just make sure everyone is fed and watered, and then we'll be off. I think we've earned it, don't you?'

Over lunch, Nikki told Gill about the discovery in the Temple. 'We have no idea how long the dealers have been using those caves. Initially, we assumed it to be a small local gang, but Joseph's just told me he's had a call from DCI Anders at Fenfleet, who've been trying to track a large, well-organised group, who not only deal, but bring in the stuff from Europe. DCI Anders said they knew they were based in the area, but didn't know where.'

'Which means,' Gill said after a moment's thought, 'that they'd probably be willing to go to extraordinary lengths to keep their operations from being discovered.'

'Absolutely,' said Nikki, through a mouthful of tuna mayo sandwich. 'I've been thinking about those caves. At the time we thought it prudent to get out of there fast, in case any of them came back and found us. Now I'm wishing we'd taken the time to investigate them more thoroughly. The one we went into was certainly used for bagging up heroin, but we don't know what was in the others.'

'But you can't investigate further in case you jeopardise your own operation,' said Gill.

'Yeah,' said Nikki. 'We already know they are man-made, which makes me wonder if whoever built them also dug an escape route.'

'Good point.' Thoughtfully, Gill stirred her coffee. 'Still, if you've got the entire grounds covered, I doubt they'd get far. It sounds like that third gate is the only way out. My, what a mysterious place Jacobs Mere House is!'

'What with the grave as well, I'd say it's one of the most mysterious places I've ever carried out an investigation in,' Nikki said.

'I'll be interested to get out there myself, now the two cases have merged,' said Gill.

'Yes, you really should. Why not come with me? I'm expecting a call from the officer in charge of the surveillance team, so you could join me then. They are watching the whole area, not just the grounds. Which reminds me, I can't be away from the station for too long. It'd be just my luck to miss the big performance.'

Gill smiled. 'Count me in!'

'Okay, let's finish up here and get back to base. Our informant said they come and go at various hours of the day and night, and don't stick to a routine.' Nikki chose not to mention that the source of that little piece of vital information was her own mother. 'It was always assumed that the visitors were just birdwatchers. Now we know otherwise.'

Gill stood up. 'Well, that coffee has just hit the spot. And I'd hate to miss the final showdown when it happens.'

CHAPTER THIRTY-THREE

Since their services weren't required that afternoon, Eve and Wendy spent the time preparing for the arrival of Bernie. Lionel had told them to take whatever they needed from the house, and although they knew that the dog would be happier with familiar things around him, they nevertheless paid a visit to the nearest pet superstore and purchased an assortment of 'extras' for their new family member. Furniture was moved to accommodate a dog bed of gargantuan proportions. Wendy recalled seeing interviews with Justin, filmed in the house, in which Bernie could be seen reclining on a rather splendid three-seater couch, so they covered the sofas and armchairs with throws. The wooden floor of the hallway provided the biggest problem, because Bernie might slip. To obviate any accidents, they went off and bought several lengths of carpet runner.

'I hadn't expected it to entail so much disruption,' said Eve, moving an occasional table to accommodate a vast snuggle bed.

'Well, at least he won't be left alone,' Wendy said. 'He's a gregarious chap, has to be part of everything — we've seen that from Justin's TV show. He'll settle, I know it. Probably the best thing that could have happened was that thoughtful police officer allowing him to see Justin's body. Not many people know that animals understand about death. And, apart from being the best thing for Bernie, he probably did us a massive favour as well.' She straightened up and surveyed the results of their labours. 'I don't know about you, but I can't wait for this dreadful case to be over, so we can get back to normal again and enjoy our new boy. By the way, you are handling being around Lionel very well. How do feel about seeing him so often?'

Eve flopped down onto the freshly covered sofa. 'After all these years without seeing him, I find I look upon him simply as a friend who has lost a loved one. I still think he's a rather wonderful man, but the truth is, I no longer have any deep feelings for him. I'm happy to help him while he seeks justice for Justin, but afterwards . . . I can't see him being part of my life, other than as an old, distant friend. I hope he returns to the Lakes and finds some sort of peace . . .'

'And if he decides to stay here?' asked Wendy. 'Because, frankly, I think our Lionel still has hopes where you're concerned, old girl!'

'Then some firm lines will have to be drawn, won't they?' Eve stood up. 'Anyway, we'll face that hurdle if and when it arises. Now. Water bowls . . . I think we'll need mats under them, or the kitchen floor will be afloat.'

'You're right, Eve Anderson,' said Wendy with a wry smile. 'On both counts.'

* * *

Although he missed having Nikki around to bounce ideas off, Joseph soon got used to working with Ryan. He appreciated his sharp mind, and his willingness to consider Joseph's opinions. They decided on a plan of action, and since Joseph's office was too small to accommodate both of them, Ryan went back to his own work station to get on with his part of the inquiry.

While Ryan was busy revisiting some of Claire's past lovers, Joseph thought about how to approach the question of Justin's previous relationships. In his experience, people asked about their past affairs were never truthful. An acrimonious separation would be dismissed as nothing more than 'a big mistake'. Often the truth of what lay behind the split was never revealed. And when the individual concerned was dead, it was well-nigh impossible to uncover.

He scrolled through their previous findings until he got to Victoria Williams, the girl who had died in an accident at her home. Should he leave her out entirely? She certainly wouldn't be able to answer any questions.

He stared at her name on the screen. Then, for some reason, he decided to start with her. He reread the initial report, in which words like 'amicable' and 'happy' kept cropping up. So, why the need to dig deeper? The woman was as dead as Justin, and she certainly didn't shoot him.

He sighed. Well, he might as well get her out of the way so he could concentrate on the more feasible suspects. He picked up the phone and called Victoria's parents' home number. Victoria's father answered. 'Best you speak with me, Detective. Her mother will only get upset all over again.'

Joseph asked him if it would be convenient for him to visit so he could talk to him in person.

The father hesitated. 'Like I said, I really don't want my wife distressed any further. So if you can come immediately, she'll be out until six.'

After informing Ryan and leaving a message for Nikki, Joseph drove to the village where Victoria's parents lived.

He found the old ivy-clad house on the outskirts of the village. Adrian Williams, Victoria's father, opened the door and led him into a warm and homely lounge.

Indicating a high-backed armchair on one side of an open fireplace, Adrian settled himself into the one facing him.

'So, what can I tell you, Detective Sergeant?'

'We know that Justin and Victoria were together for almost eighteen months, and we've been told that they parted amicably. Could you tell me a little more about why they decided to call it a day? And also, what you thought about the relationship, and the way it ended,' Joseph said.

Adrian sat back and linked his fingers together across his chest. 'We all of us liked Justin. My wife, in particular, hoped they might get wed. She absolutely adored Justin, and she couldn't understand why they chose to end the relationship. She never quite forgave Victoria for it.' He sighed. 'I understood their reasons, especially after Justin had a private word with me, but sadly, Maggie never has been able to come to terms with it.'

'You say you understood their reasons for separating, sir? Can you explain?'

Another sigh. 'My Victoria was a lovely girl, and would have made a devoted wife, but she was a homebird, Detective. She got travelling out of her system during a gap year from university, and she wanted nothing more than a house and a family of her own. She had no interest in the world outside her home, and spent all her time in domestic pursuits — gardening, or cooking, that sort of thing. More than anything else, she wanted children. I don't know if you knew Justin Connaught, but if so, you'd be aware that he was a traveller, an explorer with a thirst for knowledge. He wouldn't have taken kindly to a life spent in some chocolate box country cottage with kiddies and a little woman in an apron.' He looked apologetic. 'I'm not running that kind of life down, many people would give their right arm for it, but Justin wasn't one of them. He loved her, but he was aware of what she wanted for her life, and he simply couldn't give it to her. Luckily, Victoria was sensible enough to realise that a husband who would likely be absent for half their life wasn't for her. So they parted.' He sighed. 'And now neither of them have a life at all, let alone the one they dreamed of.'

So that was that, thought Joseph. A sad story, but with nothing sinister behind it. He would finish up here and move on to the next name on his list.

'So, there were no other parties involved in the break-up?' he asked.

'None. They kept in touch for a while, but I advised Victoria that it would probably be better to cut her ties with Justin and move on. And that's what happened. Their calls dwindled and finally stopped.'

Adrian looked drained, so Joseph decided to bring the talk to a close. 'I appreciate what you've told me, sir. Oh, before I go, you mentioned that the whole family liked Justin. Who would that be exactly?'

'My wife, Maggie, my mother, Ginette — she lives here with us — my son, Leyton, and my two other daughters, Lisa and Bethany.'

'Quite a houseful,' said Joseph.

'We actually built an annexe for Leyton in the garden. It's a running joke in the family — granny in the annexe — but he loves it. He's a graphic designer, and works from home.' Adrian gave Joseph a weary smile. 'He admired Justin, but he'd always said the relationship wouldn't work out. He knew his sister well.'

'And Victoria's sisters? Did they like him, too?'

'They adored him! Heavens, their big sister was going out with someone famous *and* good-looking. Lisa and Beth were quite starstruck.' He gave a little laugh. 'Oddly enough, Bethany was most impressed with Victoria, who she said must have amazing willpower to let a man like Justin go in order to follow her own path in life.'

'And Lisa?'

'I'm afraid, like my wife, she couldn't come to terms with it.' He sighed again. 'All water under the bridge now, I suppose. When it comes down to it, it's all in God's hands.'

There was nothing else to say. Joseph thanked Adrian Williams for his time and took his leave.

All in God's hands. Joseph thought about himself and Nikki, waiting for some kind of resolution.

'Excuse me, Detective.'

Joseph started. A good-looking man of around twenty-five was standing by the car, looking in through the window.

'I'm Leyton Williams, and I'd like a word with you before you head off.' He looked behind him. 'Not here, though. A little further down the road there's a pub on the right-hand side called the White Rose. I'll meet you in the car park.'

Intrigued, Joseph drove to the pub. A few moments later, Leyton appeared. 'We can talk here or inside, whichever you prefer, though I wouldn't mind a beer . . .'

It was still early, and the bar was almost empty. Joseph got Leyton a pint, and a coffee for himself, and they sat down at a corner table.

Joseph eyed Leyton curiously. 'How come you didn't want to talk at the house?'

'First, in case Mother came home. Second, my father knows nothing of what I'm about to tell you.' He smiled faintly. 'And, thirdly, I really needed a beer.'

Joseph regarded the young man who'd just accosted him. He was well, but casually dressed. Joseph recalled his father saying he was a graphic designer, so he must be fairly bright. He appeared extremely jittery and anxious.

'I imagine,' he began, 'that Victoria's death has affected all of you badly—'

'You have no idea!' Leyton broke in. 'It's been pure hell. Not that we were exactly the perfect family before it happened.'

'I guess very few families are — perfect, I mean,' said Joseph.

'Look, I'm not sure I should even be saying this. I could have got it all wrong . . .' Suddenly, he burst out with, 'You'd do well to look to this family regarding what happened to Justin Connaught.'

Joseph stiffened. 'All I came to see your father for was to gather a few facts about Victoria and Justin's relationship. So, what you're saying is rather unexpected. Perhaps you'd like to explain what you mean.'

'This cannot come from me.' Leyton put his glass down hard, spilling a little of the beer. 'I'll give you a few facts for you to think about. If they make you suspicious, fine. Follow it up, but I never told you anything, okay?'

'All right, I'm listening,' said Joseph.

Leyton took a deep breath. 'Things you need to consider: Justin met my younger sister Lisa *before* he met Victoria. They worked together for a while. She fell head over heels in love with him, but she never let on. For his part, he never showed the slightest interest in her. One day, Victoria turned up to collect Lisa from work — Lisa's car was being serviced — and bang! Instant attraction.'

'How did Lisa take it?'

'She shrugged it off — at least she appeared to. In reality, she hated them both. That's just my opinion, of course, she never spoke about it to me, but I know my family. My mother is in a world of her own. Nothing bad ever happens, the sun always shines and bluebirds sing in trees made of candy floss. My grandmother believes she is the dowager duchess of the village, and we her devoted servants. Then there's my sisters. Both highly intelligent, but they haven't a scrap of common sense between them. They both need each other in different ways: without Lisa to make her go out and meet people, Bethany would be a recluse, leading a life entirely of the mind. Lisa is outwardly independent, and has a good job in the television industry, but struggles to express herself in writing. She's also like a sponge. She absorbs the opinions, mannerisms and knowledge of others, and comes out with them like they're her own. She uses Beth as a walking search engine, and she never forgets a thing she's been told.' He took a long drink of his beer and gave Joseph a faint smile. 'Listen to me. I sound like I despise them, and I don't. I love my family. Until Vic died we were always able to laugh at ourselves, but since then we've become, well, frankly, we're all messed-up.'

'You didn't mention your father,' Joseph said.

Leyton gave a little laugh. 'Dad is the most normal man I know. He's what keeps us all grounded. If anything happened to him, I swear everyone would spin off and float into space.'

'And you?' said Joseph.

'I like to think I resemble my father. At least I'm capable of supporting myself, I have my own opinions, and I'm fully aware that bad things do happen.'

'Then, as a grounded and sensible man, what makes you think your family has anything to do with Justin Connaught's death?'

Leyton said nothing.

When he still got no response, Joseph said, 'So, assuming I believe you, what is your reason for implicating the family you say you love in a crime as serious as murder?'

Leyton shrugged. 'Yes, I do love them, but there are limits. There are some things a human being just does not do. If I suspect someone of murder, I tell the authorities. Right is right, and wrong is wrong, family or not.'

By now, Joseph was totally bewildered. 'Let me get this right. You suspect that your sister Lisa was so enraged by Victoria and Justin's affair that she killed him *after* Victoria died. It doesn't make sense, Leyton.'

'Because you're looking at it one-dimensionally. You need to look at the train of events. What if she approached him, and he rejected her? What if there were other reasons?'

Joseph was about to answer when Leyton abruptly stood up. 'I have to get back before Mother gets home. We try to keep everything as normal as possible for her. Vic's death totally derailed her, and she needs order, routine. The last thing she needs is another missing child. Thank you for the beer.' He turned to go, paused, and whispered, 'Oh, one last thought for you. I'm not totally certain that Victoria's death *was* an accident. Bye.'

CHAPTER THIRTY-FOUR

The minute Joseph came into the CID room, Nikki knew something had happened. She was about to speak to him when Cat jumped up, waving a printout. 'We've found it, boss! The link between Justin and Claire!'

Nikki and Joseph hurried over.

'Ben and I have been downstairs with Spooky, who's been trying to recover the data from Claire's laptop. Most of it's been wiped, but she did manage to get her client list back — well, parts of it.'

'Justin Connaught was a client of hers, eighteen months ago,' added an excited Ben. 'We got on to his research assistant, Sheena Coates, who told us he'd been badly affected by the death of one of the crew members he'd worked with around two years back.'

'It was a freak accident, apparently, and Justin saw it happen. The guy died in front of him. She said he struggled to come to terms with it, he kept having nightmares. She knew he finished up seeking help, but she didn't know who from, or what kind of counselling it was, but later she said she thought she might know more.'

'So, we can absolutely tie them together?' Gill hurried over, having overheard them.

'For sure, ma'am,' said Ben, glancing at his watch. 'And we might learn more in about fifteen minutes.'

'We've always thought Sheena Coates knew more about Justin than she was letting on,' Cat said. 'So we pushed her a bit. Finally, she said she didn't want to talk where her colleagues might overhear, so she's offered to come here as soon as she finishes work.'

'Excellent!' said Nikki. 'Are you guys prepared to stay on this evening?' She glanced around the big office. Everyone was still here, working. It was well after clocking off time, but not a single person had gone home. 'If we throw in a pizza?'

'The pizza just clinched the deal,' said Ryan with a grin. 'Though we were all going to work on anyway.'

'Rats! I could have saved myself a hefty bill,' said Nikki. She glanced at Joseph and saw his expression. 'Want to run something by me first, before you tell the troops?'

'Too bloody right I do,' he muttered. They headed for her office.

'Okay, Joseph. Spill the beans. I haven't seen that look on your face for a long time.'

Joseph shook his head. 'I hardly know where to begin. I have no idea if I've just been handed the biggest crock of shit ever, or something extremely worrying.'

'Go on then, tell, and I'll give you my opinion.' She waited for a moment. 'You went to visit the family of the late Victoria Williams. And?'

He told her about meeting the father, Adrian Williams, and then his puzzling encounter with the son, Leyton.

No wonder he looked so confused. 'Well,' said Nikki slowly, 'I'm not sure if I can give you my opinion after all. Let me think. It sounds to me like he's probably unhinged — maybe by grief. But whether or not that's the case, I think we have no option but to take a close look at that family. A slightly unorthodox one.'

Joseph grinned. 'Unorthodox? Nikki Galena, what are you thinking?'

'We need to put the Williams family under the microscope, but I'm loath to do it openly. If there is a bad egg in the family nest, I'd like to deal with it fast, and with the least possible fuss.' She was thinking of the slow turning of the wheels of the law, and the newshounds still camped outside their foyer.

'I get the why,' said Joseph, 'but I'm not sure about the how.'

'This will probably come as a shock to you, Joseph, but I have in mind two of the most skilled intelligence gatherers known to man, who happen to be sitting in an old chapel in Beech Lacey . . .'

Joseph could only stare.

'Well, then? What do you think?' Nikki said.

'Apart from your mother possibly succumbing to a heart attack when you ask her for her help, I think it's a fantastic idea. Your best yet! But what do we tell the teams? This is a joint effort, isn't it?'

'We certainly can't exclude Gill and her team . . . I know, we'll say we've given the task to a specialist researcher whom we've used before, in order to keep it low key. How does that sound?'

Joseph stood up. 'You ring Monks Lantern, and I'll tell Gill and Ryan. I'm having trouble believing anything Leyton told me, but something about that family is making me very uneasy.'

'Do it before Cat and Ben get back from talking to Justin's research assistant, then we'll have a quick catch-up with everyone.' She threw him a wicked grin. 'Meanwhile, I'll call Mummy. Do you think I should message Wendy first, and ask her to pour her a large brandy?'

* * *

Joseph found Gill talking to Ryan and her two DCs, Steve and Annie, and explained what Leyton had told him. 'Nikki's farming out the background search to a couple of trusted experts in covert intelligence gathering. She wants it kept low key, since it could either be the biggest red herring ever, or an extremely serious development. Whatever, we don't want it getting passed around the nick, and we definitely don't want the media hearing about it.'

'Good move,' agreed Gill. 'I'd hate us to get egg on our faces at this stage in the game. Do *you* believe this guy, Joseph?'

'All I'm saying is that I wish I'd taken Ryan with me for a second opinion. Try as I might, I could *not* read that man.'

'From what you say, I think I'd have been about as useful as a chocolate poker,' said Ryan. 'But you're right, we can't disregard it.'

'We can't indeed,' said Gill. 'We'd be hung out to dry! Anyway, while the family is being investigated, perhaps we should find out exactly when Justin visited Claire for counselling, and compare it with his work schedules, and against the dates when he first purchased Jacobs Mere House and started work on it.'

'Then try to piece together Claire's movements from the date of that first appointment, to the day he died, and see where their paths cross.' Ryan frowned. 'Which won't be easy as all of her computer records were nuked, other than part of a client list.'

'We need to comb that house for any diaries, notebooks, letters and the like — oh, and we must ask Richard for a key to his house and retrieve her mobile phone. He said he locked their mobiles and credit cards in his safe before they left. That mobile could be a massive help, especially if she used the calendar.'

'There's a good chance she did,' said Joseph. 'Maybe we should get that first?'

Putting her phone on loudspeaker, Gill called Richard.

The first thing he asked was whether he and Lizzie would be allowed to return to his home in Greenborough. Joseph thought it was a reasonable request. Her eyebrows raised, Gill glanced at Ryan, who in turn looked at Joseph. Joseph gave a thumbs up.

'Okay, Richard, I'll go and speak to the super. As far as I'm concerned, you're no longer in danger now that Claire has gone. I'll need Cam's blessing, but I think he'll agree. I'll ring you back when I've seen him.'

As Joseph waited for Gill to come back from Cam's office, his thoughts returned to Leyton, and his remark about Victoria's death. Was it true that it hadn't been an accident? It was hard to believe. Could he believe anything that strange young man had said? According to him, the rest of the family were off the wall, so why shouldn't Leyton be too?

He wasn't even aware that Gill was back, until she said, 'All sorted. They can leave the safe house, as long as they both remain at Richard's place until Claire Hereward is found.'

'Dead or alive,' added Annie Porter.

Gill gave her a rueful look. 'We can only hope. Anyway, I'll ring Richard now and tell him. A car will pick them up in an hour. But just because they're out of the safe house, it doesn't mean we won't be keeping them under guard. We can't afford to play Russian roulette with their lives.'

Meanwhile, Cat and Ben had returned.

'We were right,' said Cat to the assembled officers, who had all gathered round to hear what they had to say. 'Sheena Coates had been withholding the information out of loyalty to Justin. We managed to persuade her that now he's dead, there's no longer any need for silence.'

'Sheena had been Justin's research assistant and confidant for almost the whole of his career. First as an archaeologist, and then as the presenter of *Digging History*,' Ben said.

'She remained with the TV company after Justin's death in order to help edit the footage that had been shot for what will be the final episode in the series. They want to air it as a tribute to him. Sheena was devastated by Justin's death, and needed time to assimilate it before deciding to speak to us.'

'Now she's eager to help us find his killer.' Ben smiled. 'And believe me, she knows a whole lot more about Justin than even his father does.'

'That's a surprise,' said Steve. 'I thought he was very close to his dad.'

'He was. But he never discussed his love life with him,' Cat said. 'In fact, he didn't talk about it with anyone. For one thing, Sheena said, he was anxious not to hurt anyone, and above all, to keep the woman he had fallen deeply in love with safe.'

'Safe from what?' asked Yvonne Collins.

'To start with, an old boyfriend. We'd actually tried to get in touch with him, but he had conveniently disappeared. I believe Claire did mention him to Gill, but she never gave her the full details, and chose not to tell her he was terribly jealous, and obsessed with her. He threatened to harm her new lover, and it scared her badly.' Cat glanced at Nikki. 'The main thing to know is that Justin and Claire became lovers soon after he started seeing her for counselling. And if we can come up with a firm timeline, I've a feeling we'll find that he was still seeing Victoria Williams when his affair with Claire began.'

'Which does give some credence to Leyton's suggestion that one of the Williams family was out for blood,' said Joseph, 'if they discovered that he was two-timing Victoria.'

'And is that where the bit about not wanting to hurt anyone comes in?' asked Nikki.

'According to Sheena, Justin and Victoria were already talking about breaking up, and it had nothing to do with Claire. He and Victoria wanted different things from life, and getting married would have been a terrible mistake. Justin continued to see Victoria for a while, but gradually, they drifted apart. Sheena said that Justin was anxious not to hurt Victoria, and wanted to make their separation as pain-free as possible.'

'Which is exactly what Victoria's father told me,' said Joseph. 'He said they were too different, and their marriage would have been a disaster.'

'I don't quite get it,' said Annie. 'Does that mean that the jealous boyfriend was responsible for all the bad things that started to happen to Claire? The death threat and the death of Jo Andrews?'

'No,' said Ben. 'He really did disappear. There are unsubstantiated rumours that he might have acted in a similar way towards a more recent ex, and was punished for it, quite harshly.'

'When the threats began, and her clients started cancelling their appointments and so on, Claire honestly had no idea who was behind it. In fact, I'd go so far as to say that if she's alive, she still doesn't.' Cat gave a shrug. 'And if she's dead, she'll never know.'

'One last thing Sheena told us,' added Ben. 'If you recall, both she and Eve told us that something had been bothering Justin in the days leading up to his death. She said he didn't tell her what it was exactly, but he had mentioned receiving a number of unpleasant phone calls, and she believed his anxiety stemmed from those.'

'Which ties in with one of the phone calls Mary the cleaner overheard,' said Vonnie.

Nikki broke the ensuing silence. 'Okay, that's given us a lot more to go on, and we know where to direct our enquiries. The moment we hear from the people looking into the Williams family, we can set about interviewing them. That okay with you, Gill?'

'Absolutely. The whole bloody lot of them.'

And about bloody time, Joseph thought.

* * *

Somewhat surprisingly, Eve took Nikki's request for help with perfect equanimity. There were no exclamations of disbelief, no humorous remarks; instead, she simply asked her daughter to give her all the relevant details and assured her that she and Wendy would get down to it at once.

As good as her word, Eve called Lionel to ask him about Victoria Williams. 'I assume you met her. I'd like your opinion, please, I mean as a professional.'

'Physically attractive, friendly, she came across as a genuinely honest and kind young woman. From all appearances, she was very fond indeed of my son, and tended to be a bit clingy. Having met her a couple of times, I soon realised that it would be a mistake for them to get married. Justin was, you might say, wedded to his career and I couldn't see him giving that up. It was a relief to me when they parted.'

'Did you ever meet her family?' asked Eve.

'No, I didn't. Though I admit to being curious about them. Some of the things Justin said, left me wondering how such a conventional, home-loving girl could have emerged from the chaos in which they appeared to live. Apparently, they all lived together — three generations under one roof — and relations between them were often what Justin described as "fractious". He was witness to a number of arguments, none of which involved Victoria, and which never seemed to result in any serious falling out.' He stopped. 'To be honest, I tended to switch off when he talked about the Williamses, especially when their relationship started to wane. So, I'm sorry, Eve, I can't be of much help much on that score. I assume I can't ask why the sudden interest in them?'

'I'll explain soon, Lionel.'

'Fair enough.'

Eve found Wendy measuring up the utility room for a second washing machine — one that would cope with Bernie's bedding and towels. They loved him, but didn't fancy muddy towels getting washed in the same machine as their underwear.

'We are needed,' she said, and hastened back into the lounge. Wendy put down her measuring tape and followed her.

Wendy pondered Nikki's request. 'Hmm. Tricky, but doable. We'll be using Rene and Lou, I assume?'

'Yes,' said Eve. 'We'll split the family up between us. Oh, and I was thinking we might contact an old friend of ours who's well placed to help in matters such as this. What say you?'

'If it's something that needs to be kept totally under the radar, I'd say it's essential.' Wendy tilted her head. 'Shall I do the honours?'

'You are closer to him than me, Wendy. Do it now, and I'll ring the others. Let's open some tightly closed doors and see what lies behind them.'

* * *

Nikki had barely ended the call to her mother when she received a call from the surveillance team at Jacobs Mere.

'DI Galena. I'm calling to report unusual activity in the Jacobs Mere area. Two vehicles, total of five occupants. One, a four by four, is registered to a company that DCI Anders has been watching for months, on suspicion of involvement in drugs trafficking. I suggest you make your way over without delay. I think this is what we've been waiting for.'

Nikki ran out of the office, calling for Joseph and Gill, and a few minutes later they were in an old Ford estate, one of the vehicles they used for travelling incognito. She had already agreed with the observation team OIC that she would drive past the gates, park in a small copse on the other side of the estate, return through the main gates on foot, and await instructions.

Joseph drove, while Inspector Barney Greenacre, who was heading up the uniformed team inside the estate, kept them informed of developments.

'Our observers on the road in have them eyeballed in two different locations. Both are now five minutes from Jacobs Mere House. The teams are standing by, one unit watching the third gate from inside the grounds, and another observing the Temple. No action will be taken until we've given them time to settle themselves inside the temple. Then we'll hit them.'

They flew across the flat countryside towards the old house, Nikki hoping they would be there in time to see their officers bringing out the drug dealers in handcuffs. Such a coup would be a major feather in Greenborough's cap, but for Nikki it was merely a means to an end. She needed this out of the way, and then they could commit all their efforts to finding Justin's killer, and the person who was likely responsible for destroying Claire Hereward's life.

Nikki's phone crackled. 'Car one, occupants two white males, now on foot towards the third gate. One has a camera around his neck, the other has binoculars. Birdwatchers, apparently.' Nikki smiled grimly. *I doubt that very much.*

Gill and Joseph were silent, Joseph concentrating on negotiating the dangerous fen lanes, while Gill appeared to be deep in thought. Nikki knew that look of old. They had been battered by a maelstrom of information in a very short space of time, and it was hard to make sense of it all.

Finally, Joseph eased the old car into the side of the lane at the edge of the copse. A couple of minutes and they would be inside the grounds, the first two men having already entered the Temple.

'With luck, we'll be into that clearing in time to see our uniforms escorting five cuffed suspects out of the caves,' Nikki said.

Showing their IDs to the crew manning the gate, they slipped inside. Nikki felt a shiver of anticipation. They had deployed a crack team to go into the caves, who had the element of surprise on their side. Barring some unforeseen occurrence, the operation should proceed like clockwork. Nikki crossed her fingers. She had seen enough perfectly planned hits go pear-shaped to know that no outcome was ever one hundred per cent assured.

She led the way through the overgrown shrubbery, keeping well into the tree line. There was always the chance that these guys had left a lookout on guard for unwanted visitors.

'The clearing is up ahead, and so far, it looks deserted.' Nikki was now listening to Barney through ear buds.

Suddenly, she stopped, and held up her hand. The three of them froze. Barney had just said that the three suspects from the second car had come in through the gate and were entering the clearing.

They crouched down and peered through the undergrowth. One man led the way, the other two following, all looking around warily. They were dressed for the countryside in cargo pants, boots, and many-pocketed gilets. Two of them had binoculars. For all the world they could have been ramblers out for a spot of birdwatching. Except that one of them had a heavy rucksack on his back, and another carried an old and slightly battered suitcase. Nikki wondered if they were delivering or collecting.

Soon, dark figures began to emerge from the shadows and flitted across the now empty clearing. They were too far away to be seen clearly, but Nikki knew their faces would be set, determined, the adrenalin pumping. She had provided a map of the layout, as far as they knew it from their one visit to the caves. Now, they could only wait.

The suspense was killing, but they had agreed to hold until off until a deal was underway. They needed to catch the traffickers red-handed, at the very moment drugs and money were changing hands.

With her heart hammering, Nikki saw the signal being given, and the officers began to converge on the Temple entrance, four disappearing inside. Another wave of officers moved forward, but then hesitated.

'Barney!' Nikki hissed. 'What's occurring?'

'We have a situation inside. They are reporting hearing shouts coming from one of the caves, I'm sending the whole squad in, Nikki. Our men are in there.'

'We're coming with you,' she said, getting to her feet.

'No! Wait outside until I give the all-clear. We have protective vests, you guys don't. This is an unexpected development. I need to deal with it as I see fit. No interference, Nikki, please.'

Reluctantly, she lowered herself onto her haunches.

The sound of shouting reached them, there seemed to be a fight going on. Suddenly, she heard, 'He's on his toes!'

'Come on!' she urged Gill and Joseph. 'Someone has slipped the net.'

They arrived at the Temple door just as one of the bogus birdwatchers burst out. Nikki stuck her foot out while Gill took him to the ground, all in one fluid movement.

Hauling the man to his feet, Joseph grinned back at them. 'I'm impressed. Very neat indeed.'

Moments later, the man, now handcuffed, was being led to one of the waiting vehicles.

They stood back as Barney reappeared from inside the Temple, followed by the four other men, now under escort.

'Successful?' asked Nikki, not liking the look on his face.

'In part, yes,' he said sombrely. 'We did what we came to do, and there's a fortune in hard drugs down there. Those guys won't see the light of day for a good few years.'

'But?' said Nikki. 'Come on, Barney, what's the problem?'

'I think you'd better come with me.' He turned and went back inside.

They followed him through the Temple, and under the tapestry arras, where he stopped at the old wooden door.

'You said you went into three caves, Nikki. Well, there's another smaller one. It seems one of the dealers stuck his head inside and wasn't prepared for what he saw. Bloke went ape, and I'm not surprised. They came to do a deal, not to find a woman's dead body.'

Nikki heard Gill sigh, and knew immediately what they would find in that small cave. The search for Claire Hereward was over.

CHAPTER THIRTY-FIVE

Gill identified the body as that of Claire Hereward, which Rory later confirmed. Her fingerprints were found on the lid of the chest containing the drug paraphernalia. She had found a pack of razor blades, probably used to cut the cocaine, with which she slit her wrists. Her death wasn't unexpected, but what was, was the place where she had chosen to end her life.

Nikki and Joseph stood in the entrance to the small cave, roughly the size of her lounge at Cloud Cottage Farm, and gazed around them in amazement.

Claire's final resting place was a rather splendid couch, in front of which stood an old wooden coffee table. There were bookcases, and a chest of drawers. There were oil lamps, at least four candle sconces and a couple of halogen torches. At one end of the room — it hardly felt like a cave — a curtain pole had been screwed into the stone wall, from which hung a pair of long rich brocade curtains. They were closed, giving the impression that there was a window behind them; a French window with a view over a delightful garden.

'I reckon this must have been their meeting place in the early days of their affair, when they were still seeing each other in secret.'

'Sure, but how did she get here from the safe house? It's miles away,' Nikki said.

Joseph scratched his head. 'I suppose she must have had either money or a phone she'd smuggled into the safe house.'

'So where are they now? She had nothing on her when her body was examined. It doesn't make sense, and I don't like it when things don't make sense.'

'She hitched a lift, then,' said Joseph. 'It's the only way she could have made that journey with no money on her.'

It was possible, she supposed, but Nikki wasn't convinced. Posters bearing Claire's likeness had been put up in shops, on trees, everywhere people might see them. There were head-line reports in the media, but not a single sighting had been reported. No, this case was far from being over.

They went back outside, into the late-evening air.

Joseph squeezed her arm gently. 'Cheer up. We've got the drug dealers banged up, caught with a stash of cocaine that's worth a bloody fortune on the streets. Now Lionel can lock that gate up for good, that case is closed. Plus, we now have twice the manpower, and a possible lead on the killer. Come on, Nikki, stop looking like a slapped arse!'

Nikki laughed. 'You sure know how to make a girl feel good about herself, Joseph Easter.' Suddenly, she felt very tired. 'Are we done here, do you think? I know Gill wants to get back so she can put things in motion regarding Claire. She wants to visit Richard, too, and give him the news of Claire's death in person. He and Lizzie are going to be pretty gutted, aren't they?'

'Yeah, you get close when you are forced to stay together for any length of time,' said Joseph. 'And Barney is well in control here. The SOCOs will be here for hours yet, and there are a couple of officers from the National Drugs Intelligence Unit arriving to oversee the collection and transportation of the drugs. We can make our getaway as soon as you like. Gill will take over as SIO after she's seen Richard. Steve and Annie are already on the way to hold the fort for CID, so let's find her and get back to base.'

'Hang on, we forgot Lionel,' Nikki said. 'We should tell him what's been going on, and that he can now lock that gate.'

'Good point. Let's do that now.'

Lionel seemed much more positive than the last time they'd seen him. He thanked them for letting him know and said how relieved he was that his garden would no longer be the centre of a drugs ring. Nikki had to tell him that a suicide had taken place in the caves, meaning that the mayhem in the Temple would continue for a few more days.

He took it remarkably well. Awful as it was, he said, at least it wasn't another murder — the house's dark history seemed to be leaching into the present.

They left him with a promise that they would return the following day to bring him fully up to date on the investigation into the killing of his son.

'Please don't think that all this business in the garden is taking precedence over Justin's murder,' Nikki said.

Lionel responded with a smile. 'I realise how complicated his case is, DI Galena. I'm sure it's in the very best hands, and I appreciate your efforts.'

Wearily, Nikki wondered if this case would ever be brought to a close, so they could all start living their lives again — Lionel needed closure, Richard and Lizzie needed to come out of hiding. Above all, she and Joseph needed to stop treading water and find out where their own lives were heading, hopefully before they were collecting their pensions!

* * *

Eve looked across at Wendy and raised her eyebrows. 'It's almost eleven o'clock, and I'm totally bug-eyed from staring at that screen.'

Wendy yawned. 'I say we let the girls know we're standing down for the night, and will be back on duty again at seven. We need some sleep, or we'll start missing things that could be important.'

'I'll ring Lou now,' said Eve, trying ease an aching back. 'Sitting for hours really buggers up the joints, doesn't it? Frankly, I'd rather be digging over the vegetable patch. Then I'll feel I've achieved something *and* earned the muscle pains!'

Wendy smiled. 'Well, I'd say we've achieved a lot. Between the four of us, and courtesy of our old MOD boss, we have compiled a bloody impressive Williams family history. Just a couple more hours on that one particularly problematical area, and I think Nikki is going to get one heck of a surprise.'

Eve wasn't going to deny that. 'After I've spoken to Lou, I'll message Nikki and tell her to expect something in time for her morning meeting. Even if we are still tying up loose ends, we can give her what we have. It's more than enough to start with.'

Wendy stood up. 'Want a hot drink?'

'I'd love a hot chocolate.'

Unlike Eve, Lou sounded wide awake. 'Nearly there, Eve. How goes it your end?'

'We've hit the wall, Lou. We're going to call it a day and go for it again at seven.'

'Okay, no problem. Rene and I might soldier on for a bit longer. We've found a rather unexpected skeleton in the cupboard, so going to bed and leaving it floating just isn't an option.' Lou laughed loudly. 'This is fun, I must say, just like the old days. Until you rang us, we were both afraid we would soon be doing jigsaws and playing bowls.'

Nothing wrong with bowls, Eve thought, apart from those awful white plimsolls. Having to wear those really did go against the grain. She said goodnight, and then sent a WhatsApp message to Nikki to tell her that things had gone well, and she'd be in touch tomorrow before nine.

As she lay in bed sipping her hot chocolate, she wondered what that skeleton could possibly be. The Williamses were far from being your average family, as their research so clearly showed, but a seriously dark secret?

Eve's last thought as she succumbed to sleep was to wonder which one of that odd family could be keeping a skeleton in their wardrobe. Given what they'd discovered, it could be any of them.

* * *

Neither Richard nor Lizzie felt like sleeping. By now, they had all but given up hope that Claire might be alive, but hearing definitively that she was dead had still come as a shock.

After Gill left, Richard poured them both a brandy, and they fell to reminiscing about Claire, and how kind she had been to both of them.

'I can well imagine that constantly listening to other people tell of their grief would take its toll,' Richard said. 'I suppose it could have a bearing on other areas of your life, too. It happens with coppers who work as victim support officers, or who have to deal with cases of rape or child abuse. It can all become too much.'

'Strange, isn't it?' Lizzie said. 'That's what my last proper conversation with Claire was about. She was telling me how you protect yourself from becoming drained by the emotions of the people you're trying to help.' She stared into her glass. 'I suppose there comes a time when you can't take any more . . .'

Aware that they were in danger of growing maudlin, Richard changed the subject. He asked Lizzie what she had done for a living before she retired. With a laugh, she said her husband had roped her in to help with his kitchen design business, but before that she had worked as a human resources officer for a large organisation. It was basically office work: typing, making calls and that sort of thing. In other words, boring, especially compared to Richard's job, which must have been full of excitement.

Richard dismissed the comment with a wave of his hand. 'Human resources. I would think you were very good at that, Lizzie. You have such a wonderful way with people. Actually,

I'm thinking even more seriously about taking a new direction. This business with Claire has been a real wake-up call for me.'

'I can understand that,' Lizzie said. 'It does feel like a watershed moment, doesn't it? A time to face one's choices in life, and make changes.'

They fell silent. Eventually, Richard said, 'At least we'll only be confined to barracks for a couple more days. There can't be any threat to us now. You'll finally be able to go home, Lizzie.'

She nodded slowly. 'I almost don't want to. I've really enjoyed your company, Richard, even if the circumstances have been so harrowing. And I am very grateful to you for allowing me into your life and your home for all this time. It sounds like an odd thing to say, but I've rarely felt so . . . well, alive. Yes, that's it. It's like I've come out of hibernation and found myself in a different world.' She smiled. 'I'm rambling. It must be the cognac. I'd better get off to bed before I say something really stupid!'

Richard sat on for a little longer. It had been a terrible time for them both, but he did understand what Lizzie had been trying to say. He felt the same way. One thing he did know was that having come out of hibernation, as she put it, he could not go back to his old life.

He would miss Lizzie. Still, she didn't necessarily have to disappear from his life, did she? Maybe she might feature in his new beginnings. Who knew?

CHAPTER THIRTY-SIX

Despite a late night, Nikki and Joseph were back in the office early. Gill had remained at the Temple overnight, so they were covering for her while she caught up on her sleep, although they both guessed she'd be back at her desk before long. Things were moving fast, and none of them wanted to miss out on a possible breakthrough.

Nikki looked up from her computer screen. 'I hope we're not making a mistake by focusing entirely on the Williams family. Aren't we putting all our eggs in one basket?'

Joseph shook his head. 'No. We need to get to grips with them first. If we find nothing amiss after all, we can rule them out once and for all, and move on.' He made a face. 'Though don't ask me where to. We might possibly have to change direction and concentrate on our mysterious grave. If there's a body there, it should be exhumed.'

'I was about to mention that,' Nikki said, rubbing her eyes. 'Once we have Eve's report, we'll get the team working on that. As soon as we've interviewed the drug dealers, I'll get authorisation for that area to be properly investigated.'

'Shame, I was looking forward to giving that GPR machine a go,' said Joseph.

'Knock, knock.' Eve stuck her head around the office door. 'I know it's early, but I thought I'd probably find you here. I hope you don't mind, but I've brought the results of our search myself, rather than jam up your email with scanned documents.'

'Mum! Come in, sit down.' Nikki caught sight of the thick folder tucked under Eve's arm. 'Good Lord! Is that all for us?'

'I'm sure some of it will be totally irrelevant, but we decided to include the wheat with the chaff, as it were.' Eve placed the folder on Nikki's desk. 'There is one further aspect that Lou and Rene are working on, so until they get in touch, I have no idea what it's about. They did say something about skeletons in cupboards, but apart from that, all they'll say is that it concerns a member of the family who doesn't live with the others in Rippingdale.'

While Joseph went to get coffee for them, Nikki told her mother that the drug dealers had finally been ousted from the caves.

'Oh, darling! That's such a relief, and it'll be a weight off Lionel's mind, too, I'm sure. I feel so sorry for him, he really didn't need all this on top of the death of his beloved boy. Life can be so unfair sometimes.'

'I know,' Nikki said. 'And to make matters worse, we found the body of Claire Hereward in a small cave that we'd all missed when we were there.' Nikki told her mother that Claire had committed suicide in the very place she and Justin used to meet in secret. 'Oh, and we still have to excavate the place where Paul Fletcher believes he saw men burying a dead young woman. I dread to think what we'll find if it turns out he's right. That reminds me, I mustn't forget to get on to the company we use for that sort of thing.'

'Well, I know there's a lot of red tape in the police force these days, but can't you just get a couple of Niall's PCs to do it now? Lionel knows about it, and I'm sure he won't object to someone digging in an area that you say is overgrown anyway,' Eve said.

Nikki sighed. 'Those were the days. The way things are now, I need official sanction, a budget review and a project proposal just to order a new stapler for the office! Trouble is, the only evidence we can present is a sort of vision that appeared to a rather unstable young man, and some particularly lush foliage.'

She glanced up at Joseph, who had just come in with their coffees.

'The frustrating thing is that right there in his garage, Lionel has this amazing gizmo that used to belong to Justin, something called ground penetrating radar equipment. I suppose Joseph and I could engage in a little extracurricular activity, but we're going to be run off our feet today, and we really don't have the time.'

Eve's eyes lit up. 'Well, if you were going to do it anyway . . . It just so happens that we're at a loose end while we wait for Lou and Rene to get back to us . . .'

Nikki opened her mouth to say they would do no such thing, but Joseph was already asking Eve if she thought they'd be able to work out how to use it.

'Joseph Easter!' Eve said indignantly. 'You seem to have forgotten that Wendy was an experienced aviator, better than most others half her age. A mere GPR is hardly going to present a challenge, is it?'

Nikki closed her mouth again.

Eve smiled benignly at Nikki. 'Now, why don't you forget about bringing in your expensive company and save the force a hefty bill. *Should* Wendy and I happen to call on Lionel later . . . it's a nice day, just right for a stroll around the gardens . . . I'll call you later, shall I?'

Despite her misgivings, Nikki heard herself say, 'I suppose what you do with your time is none of my business, is it? Just stay away from the Temple, and don't let any of the police or forensics people see you.'

'Luckily, the paddock, and that spot beneath the alders, is well away from the entrance to the caves,' added Joseph. 'Lionel knows exactly where it is, so good luck.'

Defeated, Nikki changed the subject. 'Thanks for the information, Eve, it's much appreciated. Did you come across anything particularly disturbing about the Williamses during your investigations?'

Eve became serious. 'Hard to say. They are far from being an average family, if there is such a thing. We've highlighted certain areas that could be cause for concern, but by the time we finished, neither of us could decide whether you have a nest of vipers, or a family so eccentric they should be featuring in a TV sitcom.'

'And which one's your money on?'

Eve looked pensive. 'Sixty–forty on the vipers. Although we're still waiting for Lou's skeleton in the cupboard.'

They finished their coffee, and then Eve got up to leave. 'You need to get on. We'll message you about the skeletons — if indeed there are any, and should Wendy and I discover anything other than tree roots beneath the alders, you'll be the first to know.'

After she'd gone, Joseph leafed through the reports with growing amazement. 'I'd hate to get on the wrong side of your mother and her friends. They've accessed personal information that even Spooky would struggle to get hold of! And they've done it in a matter of hours. It beggars belief!'

Nikki picked up a medical report concerning the wife, Margaret Williams, and whistled. 'I sometimes wonder what exactly Eve's role in the MOD was — she and her friends. It's clear they still have high security clearance even now, after they've retired. It shows how important they were, and how well regarded.'

'It's a pity they'll never be able to tell you. It's a part of their past that will go with them to their graves,' Joseph said.

'And for once, we are able to reap the benefits without threatening to nail them both to the floor.' Nikki chuckled. 'Perhaps I should have made use of their skills right from the beginning.'

Joseph grinned. 'Nah. And deprive me of the fun of seeing you nigh on implode every time they got involved in something?'

'That's enough now, Joseph Easter. Pull up a chair, and we'll go through what they've gathered. Then we'll be able to make up our minds about Leyton Williams, and whether he needs a stringent warning about wasting police time, or we're pulling the lot of them in for questioning.'

* * *

It took them two hours. Having skimmed through the documents, they decided to apportion parts of it to members of their two teams. Calls had to be made, questions posed and the answers recorded. At eleven o'clock, Nikki called them together in order to ascertain how far they'd got, and whether to proceed further. Joseph, meanwhile, kept seeing images of Eve's nest of vipers.

Having listened to everyone's input and opinions, Nikki could only come to the conclusion that the jury was still out as regards the Williams family.

'In short, it seems that Leyton may have been correct in asserting that one of them had been involved in the murder of Justin Connaught. Lisa, Leyton's sister, seems to be the most likely candidate. She is obviously intelligent, having received a master's degree, and has a good job in the television industry. She also responds very badly to any sort of criticism, real or implied. She is probably jealous. It must, however, be borne in mind that Leyton is both a teller of tales and a meddler in other people's affairs, and has been in bother on more than one occasion for causing trouble. That said, there's always some element of truth in what he says. He isn't a liar exactly, he just embellishes the truth.' She looked at Joseph for confirmation.

'I believed what he said, despite not being able to make him out,' Joseph said. 'Having read the reports, I wonder if he might have misinterpreted something he saw, or maybe twisted it so as to make a better story. For me, the most telling piece of information was the coroner's report on Victoria. She

340

died, apparently, after tripping on a dog toy and hitting her head on the corner of a granite work surface. She was alone in the house with Lisa when it happened.' His words caused some eyebrows to be raised, and a few murmurs. 'Although he didn't mention her by name, Leyton did hint at a sister eaten up by jealousy because Justin preferred her sister.'

'And if she did kill her sister, she could have been capable of killing Justin, too,' said Yvonne. 'It wouldn't be the first time that a jilted woman has taken revenge on the person who rejected her.'

'And the father was in the military years ago, so she might have had access to an old service weapon,' added Ben. 'And she's not likely to be a crack shot, hence the lucky strike that killed him.'

'Another thing that coroner's report mentions,' said Ryan, 'was that Leyton said he heard shouting as he approached the house. According to Lisa, it was her, calling for help. But was that really the case? Could he have heard them arguing?'

Nikki held up her hand. 'Okay, it appears that this needs investigating further. Joseph, you told me Leyton made you promise not to repeat what he'd told you. Is that right?'

'His precise words were, "It never came from me."'

'Then you'd better convince him otherwise, or we'll bring him in for questioning. Perhaps you could remind him of the consequences of withholding evidence. He could be a Walter Mitty character, embellishing a humdrum life, or he could be the only one in that family to have realised they had a killer among them.'

Nikki was right. They needed to discover the truth in what Leyton had implied. 'I'll get across to Rippingdale as soon as the meeting is over. He works from home, so he should be there.'

'Go now,' said Nikki. 'We're nearly through here. Perhaps you might ask him to come back with you so he can talk without anyone from his weird family overhearing.'

Joseph stood up. 'I'm not sure if he'll go with that, as he doesn't like to leave his flaky mother, but I'll see what he says.'

He made to leave, but turned back. 'What about Lisa? Should we bring her in?'

Nikki thought for a moment. 'Not yet. Let's speak to Leyton first. If you can get him to come back with you, I'll get Julia Tennant to sit in and give us her opinion of him.'

Joseph raced down the stairs and out into the car park, fuelled by the certainty that the answer to Justin's murder lay with the Williams family. He just wished he knew what that skeleton in the cupboard could be.

* * *

Having just received a call from Eve, Lionel decided to have a closer look at Justin's garage and what he had been keeping in there.

Contemplating the tools and survey equipment, he heard Justin enthusiastically describing an old technique he still used, called earth resistance survey, employed to detect buried masonry that possibly indicated the presence of ancient buildings. It seemed fitting that his son's GPR should be used to reveal buried remains, like them inanimate, but this time human.

He tentatively inspected the GPR scanner, hoping that Wendy would be able to work it out, because he certainly couldn't. At least he could tell that it was battery-operated, so he checked to see whether it was charged, which it was. That was something, he supposed. He'd seen that after Justin used it, he downloaded the data it had recorded. Daring to move the rugged all-terrain cart, he found it to be light and easily manoeuvred. Noting the touch-screen colour display, he muttered, 'All singing, all dancing, eh.'

Closing up the garage again, he wondered what to do with himself until Eve and Wendy arrived in the afternoon. Why not take another walk around the garden that Justin had loved so much?

He strolled through the grounds, seeing features he'd never noticed until today. For the first time his eyes were opened to the beauty of the estate, and he now understand why Justin had been so keen to restore it. He saw avenues of trees, shrubberies that could be magnificent if correctly thinned and pruned. Overgrown flower beds and formerly landscaped areas that had gradually fallen prey to rampant weeds.

He walked on, angry with himself for having shown so little interest. The anger was followed by a new emotion, the joy of discovery. Yes, Justin would have the garden he so wanted, and he, Lionel Connaught, would bring it about. The police, the sinister-looking SOCOs in their protective suits, would soon be gone, and then he would take a fresh look at his son's plans for his little piece of Fen paradise.

He strode back to the house, his head buzzing with ideas. His mind was made up. This is where he would stay, not the Lakes with its pet food and horse blankets. He'd fulfil a dream, not his, but Justin's. He would make of this place a fitting memorial to his only son.

* * *

Nikki was in her office with the door open when she saw Gill Mercer walk into the CID room. She looked much as one would expect someone to look who had grabbed three hours' sleep amid the stress and anxiety caused by more than one unsolved murder.

'How's it going?' Gill called out.

Nikki beckoned her into the office and gave her a run-down on the information their 'outside source' had provided on the Williams family.

Gill rolled her eyes. 'Bloody hell. That's a family and a half, isn't it? It's a wonder Victoria was so "normal".'

'Joseph is already talking to Leyton again. He rang me a few minutes ago to say Leyton had refused to come here, but was willing to give him a bit more information if Joseph would interview him at his home. I've no idea how it's go—'

343

Nikki was interrupted by her phone ringing. 'Okay, got that, and thank you. We'll speak later.'

Gill was getting to her feet, but Nikki stopped her. 'Don't go! You'll want to see this. I've just received a piece of disturbing news, they're sending me the details in an email.'

It didn't take long for Eve's message to come through. Nikki read it out:

'Enquiries into members of the extended family revealed that an aunt by the name of Miss Ruth Elizabeth Williams disappeared not long after Victoria's death. She had been godmother to Victoria, who was her favourite among the Williams children. Never married, and childless herself, she looked upon Victoria as her own daughter. See attached telephone interview with Mrs Celia Grey-Smythe, Ruth's closest friend, who provided in-depth background and history.'

Nikki downloaded the attachment for later and read on:

'Ruth, much loved by the children and trusted by the parents, had in her youth suffered from a neurosis that had multiple symptoms, mainly obsessive and intrusive negative thoughts and emotions. Note early medical history suggesting her problems might be related to anomalies in the striatum, a set of structures located at the subcortical level of the brain . . .'

Nikki grunted. 'Okay, skipping the jargon . . . ah, here we are: *Her abrupt disappearance was not reported as she had gone missing before. She once went abroad and was gone for over a year, leaving no forwarding address. This absence coincided with a gap year Victoria took in order to travel. It is believed that Ruth left the country at that particular juncture because she found Victoria's absence too painful to wait out at home.'*

For a few seconds Nikki skimmed through the rest until she came to a paragraph near the end.

'Hang on, Gill, this is what I was looking for: *We have traced Ruth to an address in one of the Greenborough villages. See below. She rents the property, under a different name, leaving her home in Sleaford empty, though the bills are paid regularly, and a gardener, paid monthly, comes in to mow the lawn. Neighbours believe she is travelling abroad. She is very well off, and was rumoured to own a second home in France, which is not, in fact, the case. Finally, she never uses her first name, Ruth, only her second, and the Williams children always referred to her as Auntie Lizzie.'*

'Lizzie?' Gill said. 'Please tell me that's a coincidence.'

'And the address of her rental house is Oak Lodge, The Green, Fenny Bridge Village, where she goes by the name of Mrs Lizzie Harper.'

'Lizzie Harper! I can't believe this!' Gill stopped suddenly, staring at Nikki. 'Oh my God, Nikki! If this is correct, Richard Duckworth could be locked in a house with a killer.'

CHAPTER THIRTY-SEVEN

From the outside, Leyton's 'log cabin' was an attractive, well-designed building, so Joseph was somewhat surprised when Leyton invited him in. The furnishings, which could well have originated in a car boot sale, were placed here and there at random, as if he'd only just moved in. The whole place had the temporary feel of a student flat rather than that of a professional with a good career.

Joseph was fifteen minutes into his interview when Nikki called. What she had to say threw him completely off-balance. For a moment he was tempted to call an end to the interview and get back to the station as fast as he could.

'Ask him about his Auntie Lizzie, Joseph, every little detail. It's vital!'

He hung up and turned back to Leyton. 'So, Leyton, your Auntie Lizzie. I'd like to know more about her.'

Leyton looked as if he'd been slapped. 'Auntie Lizzie? What do you want to know about her for? She has nothing to do with anything, and anyway, she's abroad.'

'No, Leyton, she isn't. Tell me about her.'

Leyton began to stutter. 'Leave Auntie Lizzie out of this. We love her. We all of us love our auntie, and she loves us. When I said look to this family, I did *not* mean her!'

Joseph continued to fix him with a penetrating glare.

Averting his eyes, Leyton said, 'I want you to leave now. I'm saying nothing more.'

'I'm staying right where I am, and you, Leyton Williams, are going to tell me everything you know about your aunt. If you refuse, I will arrest you for perverting the course of justice. If you are found guilty of withholding crucial evidence, thus damaging police investigations and wasting the court's time, we'll find you a nice little cell to live in, instead of your cosy cabin. Which means you'll be leaving your mother alone, and in consequence, she'll most probably lose what little hold she still has on reality. It's up to you.'

Cruel words, but Joseph didn't have the luxury of time. Nikki wanted answers, and he was going to make sure she got them.

So Leyton talked. He also gave him a photograph of his aunt, taken with him and his siblings when they were small.

Twenty minutes later, Joseph was flying back towards the police station, certain in the knowledge that their murderer was sitting in Greenborough, house guest of retired police officer Richard Duckworth, respected, highly commended, and all-round nice guy.

* * *

Relieved at finally being back at home, Richard began to relax. The restrictions that had been imposed on them having been lifted somewhat, he spent an hour or so on his computer, catching up on emails, while Lizzie prepared lunch. Finally, their enforced lockdown was coming to an end, and today was probably their last day in confinement.

He was halfway downstairs when he received a message on his phone. He read it and stood stock-still. He read it again. It had to be a mistake, surely? He remained there, poised, while the last line flashed at him like a beacon. *Get out! Fast!*

He heard her soft voice, addressing him from the kitchen. 'She knows, doesn't she? I could see it on your face.'

Unable to move, Richard felt oddly disconnected from what was happening. This was a dream from which the policeman in him refused to wake up.

'Come in, Richard, take a seat.'

The policeman stirred, just enough for him to know he must do exactly as she said. The policeman had seen the knife block just within reach of her hand.

He went in and sat down. She seemed just the same, only a little sad. 'Lizzie?'

'I'm so sorry, Richard. But I'm glad we were able to spend at least a short time at your home. I suppose we don't have very long now, which is a pity. There is so much I'd like to have told you, so much I'd like to explain.' Lizzie stood with her back against the kitchen counter, barely a foot from the knives. Her face wore its usual warm and friendly smile. 'My name is Ruth Elizabeth Williams, though I've always been known as Lizzie. It all began when the dearest thing in all my life was taken from me. No, not my husband. I never had a husband. It was my lovely Victoria who died, and the grief was more than I could bear.'

The smile had gone, to be replaced by a look of utter desolation.

'What have you done, Lizzie?' he asked, his voice hoarse.

'I had to make things right again, of course. But it's done now. It's cost me dearly, but I've managed. There was only one unexpected hitch in the whole operation, and that hitch was you.'

He stared at her, uncomprehending, while the policeman reminded him that hitches were generally troublesome things that had to be removed.

'We had so much in common, didn't we? It rather took me by surprise. Remember how we talked about starting life anew when all this was over, the dreams we had?'

'I remember the country cottage you wanted, the dog, the cat. Life choices, life changes, you said. All the things you wanted to do. You sounded as if you really meant what you said.' Richard heard himself speaking and realised that, perilous as his situation was, he really wanted to know the answer.

'I meant every word. But they were just dreams, weren't they? Surely you realised that? You said it sounded like the perfect life, and if Victoria hadn't died, we might have had that life, the two of us. But she did die.' Her eyes shone, misty with tears. 'She was the sunshine of my life. They say the brighter the sunshine, the deeper the shadows, and after she'd gone, all I had left were shadows.'

'What have you done?' he asked again.

'Oh, you'll learn soon enough from the police. Let's not waste the few minutes we have left together on all that. I'm sorry things couldn't have been different, because I think you are a very special man and I regret losing your company and your friendship. Other than that, I regret nothing.' She shifted her stance, and Richard couldn't help glancing at that knife block.

'What do you intend to do now?' he said, his throat tight.

She said nothing for two long, terrifying seconds. 'Me? Nothing. It's you who are going to act. You will ring DI Mercer and tell her I'm ready now. She doesn't have to storm your house. There will be no dramatic finale. It all ends here, in your comfortable kitchen.' She gave a faint smile, went to the table and sat down. 'Ring her, Richard, then go and unlock the front door.'

He did as she said, and then returned to sit across the table from her.

'Pity I didn't get lunch a little earlier,' said Lizzie. 'And now the tea will be stewed.' Their eyes met. 'I'm sorry, Richard, really I am.'

'So am I, Lizzie. So am I.'

* * *

Unaware that his son's killer was sitting quietly in a holding cell at Greenborough police station, Lionel Connaught

349

watched in awe as Wendy found the instructions to Justin's scanner on her phone. She read through them quickly and gave a satisfied smile. 'Piece of cake. Now, we need a strimmer to level off all that overgrowth. This thing works best on the flat. Luckily, there's no tree roots in the way.'

Twenty minutes later, Wendy was ready to go. 'Okay, it's working, and, yes, it's collecting data. Excellent. Here we go, it's showing disturbed soil, and . . . at a depth of approximately one metre, we have an unidentified object. I'm no expert, but I believe it's showing us a clandestine grave. Sorry, old friend, but it's time to call Nikki.'

* * *

It was approaching five o'clock in the afternoon when Nikki and Gill went to interview Lizzie Harper, whom they now knew to be Ruth Elizabeth Williams.

They found her sitting quietly with the duty solicitor, her back straight and a rather sad smile on her face.

They had agreed beforehand that Gill would take the lead, so, once the formalities were out of the way, she took a deep breath and began. 'Should I continue to address you as Lizzie?'

'Please do, DI Mercer. It's what everyone calls me.'

'Then, Lizzie, you have admitted to killing Justin Connaught, and conspiring to cause the death of Joanne Andrews and Claire Hereward. Is that correct?'

'Perfectly.'

'Could you tell us why? From the beginning, please.' Looking at her, it was hard not to see the friendly, helpful Lizzie, sent into a safe house for her own protection, and who had seemed so anxious about poor dead Jo, and her dear friend, Claire.

'Simple, my dear. I was righting a wrong.'

'By wrong, do you mean the accidental death of Victoria Williams?' Gill said.

Lizzie's flinch at the mention of the word 'death' was so slight as to be almost imperceptible. 'My Victoria would never have died if she had been where she should have been — with Justin. They were destined to be together, but something came between them.' She looked weary, suddenly old and tired. 'On the day of my beautiful girl's funeral, I stood at her graveside and I vowed to put things right. That's why.'

Gill glanced at Nikki, who looked just as baffled as she. Were they to believe that the quietly spoken lady sitting opposite them was raving bloody mad, or was she torn apart by grief? Were all her actions prompted by nothing more than a broken heart?

Nikki took over the questions. 'Did you move to the Greenborough area in order to be nearer Claire Hereward? And did you do it with the express purpose of killing her?'

'Yes, I did. I also wanted to be closer to Justin Connaught. Although at the time, I didn't intend to kill either of them.'

'Let me go back a bit,' said Nikki. 'You said Victoria and Justin belonged together, but according to his father, they decided to go their separate ways because they realised they wanted different things from life, not because Justin had met someone else. Everyone we spoke to agreed that it was an amicable separation. Justin wanted to travel, and Victoria wanted a home and children.'

'Oh, she did!' exclaimed Lizzie. 'And so did Justin. You had only to see his television programme. Was there ever a man more suited to be a father? The way he behaved towards those children, the rapport he had with them, it was truly heart-warming. And with my Victoria by his side . . .' A tear formed in her eye and rolled down her cheek. 'He did want that, I know he did. And he loved Victoria, he told me so on the night he died. But for Claire Hereward, they would have been the happiest couple in the world.'

Gill narrowed her eyes. 'A friend of Justin's has given us a sworn statement saying that he and Claire kept their relationship a closely guarded secret. Even his father didn't know about it. They never once met in public, so how did you know he was seeing Claire?'

'I'm a rich woman, DI Mercer. It wasn't difficult. I can afford to employ the best private detectives.'

As the questioning went on, Gill started to realise that once Lizzie had made up her mind that Justin and Victoria would have married if it hadn't been for Claire, there had been no stopping her. The fact that Victoria's death had come about as the result of an accident was neither here nor there. Her beloved child was dead, and someone had to pay.

After a while, they took a break. It was clear to both of them that Lizzie had gone on a carefully planned crusade to avenge Victoria's death. Claire and Justin were blameless, but Lizzie would never see it that way.

'She feels perfectly justified, and the fact that she'll spend the rest of her life in prison means nothing to her,' said Nikki. 'Do you know, I find that woman far more disturbing than some evil bastard who swears blind he's innocent, even though he's guilty as hell.'

Gill knew what she meant. Added to which she had to suffer the mortification of having been duped by the loyal friend of Claire and Richard, the oh-so-supportive and thoughtful Lizzie Harper.

After a further forty-five minutes of questioning, Lizzie's brief called for a halt to the proceedings. His client was tired, and needed to rest. Gill and Nikki agreed.

It had become clear that Lizzie had invented a past and a dead husband in order to get Claire Hereward to take her on as a client. The counselling had to all intents and purposes been a success, and Lizzie had terminated the sessions declaring herself to be extremely satisfied with the help Claire had rendered. She hadn't deceived Claire as to the depth of her grief, simply its object. As soon as she had found out all she needed to know about Claire, she did what she always did, and paid for services rendered. When Nikki asked how on earth she knew how to contact a hit man, Lizzie had responded with, 'It isn't *what* you know, but *who*.' Later, it transpired that she had spent a number of years working at HMP Lincoln, first in personnel, and then in rehabilitation. 'All it took was a phone call to someone I once helped, who told me who to contact.' However, she said, the arrangements hadn't gone to plan, forcing her to step in and finish the job herself. Not that it had made any difference in the end, and she had saved herself a lot of money. The contract hadn't been honoured, so they hadn't been paid, a fact they hadn't disputed. It had been Lizzie who sent the death threat, and Lizzie who orchestrated the complaints and cancellations.

The people she had contracted to carry out the hit had gone into Claire's home and re-arranged her belongings, and it had been they who terminated Joanne Andrews. Lizzie had ordered the hit on her because she learned that the girl was asking questions of Claire's former clients, and could well have discovered what Lizzie was up to. She was sorry, she said, about Jo's terrible family tragedy. If only she hadn't meddled, she could have gone on to live a happy and fulfilling life. Nevertheless, she had her mission to accomplish, and nothing could stand in her way. Her hired assassins were supposed to then kill Claire, and were on the point of doing so when the three of them were whisked away to the safe house. At that point, Lizzie knew she had no option but to finish the job herself. She had been wondering how to set about it when Claire saw the newsflash about Justin's death, and she was able to take advantage of it. In the days that followed, Claire said very little, but she did confide that she intended to kill herself. Lizzie gave her some money that she had smuggled into the safe house, so that she could get to Jacobs Mere and be close to the place where her lover had died.

When the session finally ended, Gill went to her office and tried to rest for an hour. Exhausted as she was, her mind kept racing, and all she managed was a brief doze. At eight o'clock, she received a message from the custody suite saying that Lizzie was ready to continue.

She and Nikki went back downstairs. They had thirty minutes to get Lizzie to admit to killing Justin before they were obliged to break for the night.

'Now, Lizzie,' Gill began. 'Tell us exactly what happened on the night you killed Justin Connaught.'

Lizzie closed her eyes for a moment, as if to summon the memory. 'I waited for the guests to leave, and then I knocked on the door. Justin answered. I was a bit taken aback when I saw the shotgun in his hand. He apologised, saying that he thought he'd seen an intruder and had taken the gun to frighten them off. He told me it wasn't even loaded. Such a delightful young man.'

Such a delightful young man. Gill had trouble keeping her composure. Like Nikki, she wished the person before her had been a nasty old scrote, she'd know where she was then.

'So I told him the intruder was probably me,' Lizzie said. 'I said I'd arrived earlier, but seeing he had guests, I waited till they'd gone. I said I wanted to talk to him about Victoria. That made him angry. He always was angry when I tried to get him to see reason where my darling girl was concerned. I'd tried phoning him on several occasions, but it made no difference. Anyway, we went into the dining room, where he offered me a glass of champagne, which I naturally declined. I kept hoping he would see sense. I might have let him live then. He said he would always love Victoria, and was sad when she died, but . . .' She looked up at Gill. 'But. He didn't say what I wanted. He refused to admit that he bitterly regretted not marrying my beautiful girl. That he'd spend the rest of his life reproaching himself for not having had children with her. He went on to say he'd had enough of me. Why wouldn't I leave him alone and stop persecuting him, he said. Those words sealed his fate. I went towards the door, as if I were about to leave, then turned and took the pistol I'd been carrying from my pocket. I told him it was a pity he hadn't taken his chance to be with her in this world, rather than the next. He flung up his arms, shouting, *"What do you want me to say? Victoria and I were through!*

Finished! She would have found someone else to love, like I have. Why must you keep harassing me like this? Just leave me alone, will you!" You can guess what came next. Yes, I shot him.'

Gill ended the interview, and watched as 'dear Aunt Lizzie' was escorted to the custody suite. Nikki put her arm around her shoulders. 'We both need a strong coffee. That, or a strong drink. I don't know about you, but, as for me, I don't know whether to laugh or cry.'

* * *

As midnight approached, Nikki, Joseph and Gill were seated in the half dark of the CID room. They were still reeling from the mounting tidal wave of events that had washed over them with the force of a cyclone.

They had decimated a drugs ring, a ring so big that DCI Anders of Fenfleet was in all probability still celebrating. They had all the main suspects downstairs in the custody suite, and an unexpected stroke of luck had answered Nikki's one remaining question. As the police team were going into the caves, they heard one of the gang members shouting, 'You've fucking well done it again, haven't you? Another woman dead! Well, you're not pinning that one on me, you bastard!' The man shouting had been one of the runners, and, suddenly coming upon Claire's body, he mistakenly assumed she'd been killed by a fellow gang member. Now, when thieves fall out, they do it in style, and he was currently singing his heart out. It transpired that an addict desperate for a fix had followed the gang into the caves, and had hidden there while they were moving some of the merchandise out. Having stolen a couple of bags, she was spotted as she ran off with her booty. One of the gang chased her and threw a coat over her, causing her to lose her footing. She stumbled, and he hit her hard, breaking her neck. When they saw she was dead, he and one of the others buried her. Unbeknown to them, a young birdwatcher had seen the whole thing unfold.

It had taken Paul Fletcher years to recover the memory of what he had seen that day, but now that poor woman's remains were about to be exhumed and delivered into the care of Professor Rory Wilkinson. Another ghost had been exorcised.

The three detectives sat in silence, staring into their mugs of coffee. Nikki was feeling as if she had just been through the spin cycle of a washing machine. Could it really be over?

'One thing that still bothers me is that row Justin had with the gardener, the one he sacked,' she said.

'Oh?' Gill said. 'I think I missed out on that one. Do tell.'

'I haven't quite got the whole story yet, but according to our chatty drug runner, it seems that the dealer paid Dennis Larimer to get into the house and steal the temple key for them. Larimer duly did so, and handed it over. The dealer got it copied, and gave it back to Dennis, who was supposed to return the original to the key box. We think that Justin caught him sneaking out of the house, and an argument ensued.'

Joseph drained his mug. 'I imagine a lot more loose ends will get tied up when we receive the forensic reports on the cave Justin and Claire used as a meeting place. And Spooky left a message saying that she has found notes Justin made in the margins of his designs for the Zen garden. I expect they'll fill in a few more gaps.'

'It's a bit of a creepy place to hold a lovers' tryst in, isn't it?' said Gill. 'I wouldn't like to have been Claire, creeping through that overgrown garden in the dead of night, and down that dark tunnel. It makes me shudder just to think of it.'

Joseph smiled at her. 'Ah, but that would depend on how much you loved the person you were going to meet, wouldn't it, and how much you wanted to be with them. Anyway, most likely Justin met her by the gate, and they went in together.' He grinned. 'Come to think of it, that cave had a rather romantic feel to it, in a Gothic sort of way.'

Nikki sniffed. 'It would have been a lot more romantic if it didn't have the dead body of Claire Hereward in it.'

'Just think,' said Joseph. 'She travelled ninety miles to get to their one special place.'

'Well, I still think it's creepy,' Gill said. 'Anyway, it's Lizzie that's really getting to me at present. I mean, the extent of her obsession with one of her god-children, and the lengths she was prepared to go to in retribution for a death that was purely accidental.'

'Obsessions are dangerous things,' Joseph said. 'Let's not forget she had mental health problems when she was younger, which must have got worse as she grew older. Nevertheless, I think she'll be seeing out the rest of her life in prison rather than a psychiatric hospital, because the murders were premeditated. She employed hired assassins, for heaven's sake! No, she'll do her time in a Cat A unless I'm very much mistaken.'

Nikki's thoughts drifted to her mother. Eve and Wendy, along with their friends, had been stars. No longer did she consider Eve to be a nuisance, a pain in the arse, she had been indispensable to the case, and Nikki was proud of her. Suddenly she wondered how Eve had managed to remain so detached, so 'professional'. She had been conducting her investigation alongside a man who had clearly been in love with her, and maybe still was. It couldn't have been easy for her. Nikki determined to go and visit her tomorrow and thank her for her help.

'Nikki, sorry to bring this up now, it's about Victoria's death. Lizzie believes it was an accident, but Leyton suspects that, in fact, she was killed by her sister Lisa. He swears the shouts he heard were not Lisa calling for help, but voices raised in anger. Should I press Leyton on this?'

'Oh, Joseph, not now,' Nikki said wearily. 'How about we sleep on it, yeah?'

'Yeah, and how about we all jump ship,' he said. 'My head's a shed.' He glanced at Gill, who looked bemused, and smiled. 'Which basically means I'm confused, stressed, and disorientated — among other things.'

They laughed. 'I'm all those things and more,' Nikki said. 'Nevertheless, I'll leave here tonight in the knowledge that we've got the custody suite filled to the brim with drug dealers and murderers, and as far as I'm concerned, that's a bloody good day's work. Well done, guys!'

EPILOGUE

It was two days after the arrest of Lizzie Harper, as they still thought of her. She had held nothing back. She admitted to engaging in malicious acts — including orchestrating the death of Joanne — with the intention of causing harm to Claire, and had furnished them with details of the criminal organisation she had used. To no one's surprise, the addresses and contact numbers she provided no longer existed, or never had. When the three of them were suddenly taken to the safe house, thus preventing the contract killers from completing their mission, Lizzie realised she would have to kill Claire herself. In the end, however, all she had had to do was listen sympathetically to the distraught woman and offer her money to finish the job on her own. Lizzie said she found it fitting.

She had remained unperturbed throughout, her belief that all her actions had been justified unshaken. The only thing she was reticent about was the time she had spent in the safe house with Richard Duckworth. Indeed, wherever possible she avoided mentioning Richard at all. From the few remarks she let fall, Nikki got the impression that she was genuinely fond of Richard, and was sorry that she had been obliged to deceive him.

Nikki stretched her aching back. It was only ten thirty, but they'd been working since seven that morning, and she was feeling an attack of the munchies coming on. Joseph was over at Rippingdale, or she would have suggested a trip to the Café des Amis. Ostensibly, he had gone to offer the family his support following the news about their favourite Auntie Lizzie. In reality, his aim was to sound them out, and if possible, have a further talk with Leyton. Nikki wondered how Lizzie would react if she learned that there was a possibility that Lisa had killed her precious Victoria. Would she wish her niece dead? Would it make her believe that all her actions had been in vain? Or would she persist in her belief that none of it would have happened if Justin had married Victoria in the first place.

'Penny for them.' She looked up to see Cam standing in her office doorway.

'The case, as you might expect. It certainly is thought-provoking, isn't it?'

'You can say that again. I went downstairs to take a look at our murderer, and found Julia Tennant with her.' He shook his head. 'They might for all the world have been discussing their favourite restaurants, or the best way to grow tomatoes. I've never seen anyone who looks less like a ruthless killer.' Cam took a seat opposite her. 'Where's Joseph?'

She told him of their supposition that Victoria's death might not have been accidental at all.

'God almighty!' Cam said. 'Will this never end?'

'Don't fret, Cam. It might well come to nothing,' she said. 'Even if they did have an argument and Lisa pushed her, it doesn't necessarily mean she wanted to kill her. Nevertheless, I think we'll be keeping Lisa Williams in our sights for the foreseeable future. Who knows, her name might crop up again.'

'If we never hear about any of the Williams family again, it can't be too soon for me,' Cam said. 'Anyway, why I'm here now is to ask you and Joseph to come up to my office as soon as he gets back. I'm in all day, but the sooner you can make it the better.'

'Oh! It's not about . . . ?' Nikki looked at him hopefully.

'Soon as you can, all right?' Cam gave her a wink. 'See you soon.'

So this was it. Make or break time. '*Come on, Joseph,*' she muttered, '*get your arse back here.*'

* * *

Eve and Wendy called in to see Lionel on their way to collect Bernie. As they drew up in front of the old house, they were surprised to see him out on the drive, talking to a stocky man in a wax jacket and heavy boots, who was scribbling on a rather snazzy-looking iPad.

Seeing them arrive, Lionel went over to their car. 'Eve! Wendy! Lovely to see you. Liam is just finishing off, so give me two minutes and I'll be with you.'

As far as Eve could tell, Liam appeared to be some kind of landscape designer. 'Is he thinking of staying, do you reckon?' she asked Wendy.

'Who knows?' returned Wendy. 'He could be getting the grounds in order in preparation for selling up. That's probably more likely. This place must have far too many bad memories for him, don't you think? Could you live in the house where your son had been murdered?'

Eve wasn't so sure. She'd seen a new air of determination in Lionel's gait as he strode across to greet them.

Liam and his iPad soon departed, and Lionel welcomed them in. 'I have a lot to tell you. For one thing, the police say they'll be gone by the weekend, and I'll have the place to myself.'

Yes, there it was, she had been right. The old Lionel was back. Eve smiled. 'And it looks as if you've been making plans.'

'I certainly have,' he said. 'And I'm anxious to run them past you two. I'd like your opinion of them.'

They followed him into the kitchen, and all three sat at the table.

'Did they tell you about the woman in the grave?' asked Wendy.

'Not much,' replied Lionel, 'Just that they've identified her, which is pretty amazing. When the drug dealers buried her, they didn't think to check her pockets, and the SOCOs found a folded prescription for methadone from a drug treatment service in her jeans. It survived being buried because it was in a plastic wallet.'

'Thank heavens!' said Eve. 'At least she won't be yet another Jane Doe. By the way, did they say what she was wearing?'

'Exactly what young Paulie described. Jeans and a sweatshirt with a logo on the front.' Lionel smiled broadly. 'I was against it, but he did the right thing in coming here, that psychologist was perfectly correct. He's a different person now it's all out.' He looked away for a moment. 'Which brings me to my plans for the future. To be honest, I should have retired years ago, but I was stubborn, and couldn't bring myself to give the reins of the business over to other, younger people. Justin wasn't interested, and as for Heather, well, no need to say how that would go. The team I have running the business are top notch, and the workforce are willing to work their socks off for me. When I was here with Justin, working on the house, they did perfectly well without me, and its high time I learned to let go.'

So she'd been right, Eve thought. Lionel was going to stay.

'Anyway, I can only say that I've had what you might call an epiphany. I spent some time walking around the grounds the other day, and for the first time I appreciated what my son wanted for this place. And, damn it, I'm going to do it! I'm going to make Jacobs Mere House into something very special, and I'll be doing it for him. It will serve as a memorial to a man who had the capacity to appreciate both the past *and* the future.' He grinned at their amazed expressions. 'I know. Something of a change in outlook, isn't it? Well, I'm not going to see my son's dream given over to a housing estate, or blocks of hideous flats. What's more, I've come across some correspondence from Justin relating to his idea that there might be Roman remains where the paddocks are. He brought a couple of other archaeologists in for a second opinion, and they confirmed his belief that there really is a Roman villa there. He would never forgive me if I let someone put up a bunch of "desirable" properties on top of it. So, I'm giving my permission for an excavation, to begin early next year.'

'Well done you!' said Wendy excitedly. 'Oh, Justin would be so happy!'

'I hope so,' said Lionel. 'What do you think, Eve?'

'If I were in your position, I'd do just as you're doing,' she said, and meant it. 'And you'll live here?'

'I will. I've already tackled my sister, who says she'll be delighted to come and be with me. She says she's heard Justin and I discussing the place so often that she feels like she knows it already. I'm telling you, I've moved mountains in the last couple of days. I've discussed with my solicitors the possibility of making my employees shareholders in the business. They will be paid substantially more to compensate them for the additional responsibilities. I'm not relinquishing my hold entirely, so I will still have money coming in. In any case, the house won't suffer, as there is quite enough family money in the coffers.'

Eve felt so carried along by his enthusiasm that she almost forgot her reservations about having Lionel so close again. Almost.

'You mentioned an idea you had for Paul Fletcher,' said Wendy.

'Ah yes, little Paulie. That was my next idea. He's an intelligent lad, whose main interest is the natural world.'

'Ah, yes, the birdwatching,' said Wendy.

'Exactly. Well, the chap you saw earlier, Liam, is from up in my neck of the woods. His company specialises in the landscaping of estates and stately homes. I've shown him Justin's diagrams, and he thinks they are perfectly doable. However, Justin noted the need for an environmental impact assessment before undertaking any work. I plan to enlist Tamsin Farrow, along with an apprentice — Paulie — to undertake the assessment.' He beamed. 'And when that is complete, I will need someone to oversee the smooth running of the estate — a kind of estate manager — and I reckon Paulie would be perfect for the job. I've even suggested that he and his mother might like to live here. It's much too big for just my sister and myself. There is ample room in the house for them to live independently, or else there's the annexe, which was originally intended to house a live-in housekeeper and gardener. I am aware that his mother hated old Aaron Fletcher so much that she wanted nothing to do with the place, but Paul thinks she might come around when she realises his malign presence no longer haunts it.'

'You've thought of everything, haven't you?' said Wendy.

'Oh, I'm full of ideas. The question is, ladies, am I doing the right thing?'

Wendy nodded enthusiastically. 'I'll say! What a venture.'

Eve stared at her old friend thoughtfully. 'Wendy said you've thought of everything, but you seem to have forgotten something.'

Lionel and Wendy looked at her, puzzled.

'Heather.'

'Ah,' said Wendy. 'Yes, Heather.'

Lionel smiled. 'What would you say if I told you the veil has lifted, albeit decades too late?'

'About bloody time!' exclaimed Wendy.

'So, she and her family won't be taking up residence in the west wing, then?' asked Eve with a wicked grin.

'Not even the caves!' said Lionel. Then he frowned. 'Talking of the caves, they're the only thing I can't make up my mind what to do about. They've never been used for anything but evil purposes, so I'm tempted to fill them in.'

'If you do, could our historian friend come and see them first?' asked Eve. 'He knows all there is to know about the history of Jacobs Mere; in fact, he was named after it. His first name is Jacob.'

'Bring him along! I'd love to talk to him. He might even help me decide what to do with them. But, Eve, you haven't answered my question yet. Am I doing the right thing?'

There was no way she could dampen his enthusiasm. 'Yes, you are, Lionel, and as Wendy said, Justin would be so happy. But we have to be off, I'm afraid. We're on our way to Tamsin's to collect the newest resident of Monks Lantern. Your Justin's Bernie is about to inspect his new home.'

'Thank you, Eve, I love you for what you are doing for Bernie,' said Lionel. 'Both of you,' he added quickly, but his eyes remained on Eve.

* * *

As Joseph walked back into the station, he saw Gill Mercer with a tall, older man.

'Joseph! Come and meet Richard Duckworth. Now you're here, do you think you could take him to Interview Room Two and keep him company for a few minutes? I need to go upstairs and pick up some information for him.'

Joseph shook his hand, and escorted him to the interview room. Inviting him to take a seat, Joseph said, 'You've really been through the mill in the last week, Richard. How are you coping?'

Richard shook his head. 'To be honest, I have no idea. Lizzie was . . .'

In the confusion and bewilderment of his expression, Joseph saw something similar to the way he had felt after the Pelham case. 'Things aren't always black and white, are they?'

'Neither are people,' said Richard ruefully.

Suddenly Joseph found himself telling Richard about his last conversation with Pelham, a convicted murderer.

It had been about love, of all things, and it had affected him so badly that he had needed to seek help. 'I know it's early days, Richard, but as a retired police officer, you are eligible to consult with the force psychologist. Her name is Julia Tennant, and she helped me a lot. If you find yourself struggling, don't bottle it up. Pay her a visit.' He smiled. 'It can't do any harm, can it?'

'You could be right, Joseph. I'll see how it goes, and if I can't make sense of it myself, I might just do that.' He stared down at the table. 'I thought I'd seen it all. I was in the force for enough years, and I encountered my fair share of evil, but this . . .'

Joseph's heart went out to him. 'Richard, if it helps, Gill, Nikki, Ryan and I have all spoken with Lizzie in some depth. One thing we are sure about is that she is not some psychopath. She is capable of genuine emotion; she's just been derailed by a grief so profound it took away her reason.' He reached across the table and gripped Richard's arm. 'I think the person you spent all that time with was the real Lizzie.'

Richard looked up at him. 'I hope so, Joseph, or I'll never be able to trust my own judgement again. I should have seen what was happening right from the start. I'd even dealt with a similar case in the past — I mentioned it to Gill Mercer — the Cardew investigation. I said we could learn something from it, but in the end it was me who should have learned. I remember telling Gill we needed to look for our killer in the helpful one, the caring one, the one who was always there with a kind word.' He shook his head. 'On the very night before she was arrested, I had a long talk with Lizzie. I said it took hate on a grand scale to enable someone to carry out this kind of crime. She disagreed. She said it would all come down to love, not hate. And she was right. It did.'

Joseph nodded. 'Yes, she was. Strange how often it does come down to love in the end.'

Gill bustled into the room. 'I'm glad you two have finally met. Joseph's been dying to meet you, Richard.'

Richard smiled. 'And I'm pleased we met, too.' He glanced at Joseph. 'Thank you. I appreciate you telling me what you did. Maybe we could keep in touch?'

'That would be good,' Joseph said. 'Take care.'

* * *

Nikki waited in an agony of suspense. It seemed Joseph would never arrive, but finally she saw him come into the CID room. 'Joseph! Super wants to see us! Now!'

Joseph looked exasperated. 'Give me a minute, Nikki. I've just spent a crappy few hours with the Addams Family, and then—'

'Sergeant. I said, Cam. Wants. To. See. Us. Get it?'

'Ah, right. Then what are we waiting for? Come on!'

Two minutes later, they were in Cam's office, both perched on the edge of their chairs.

'I'm sorry this has taken so long, my friends. But we're here now, and you are going to have to listen to a little speech that I've prepared, so are you sitting comfortably?'

Far from comfortable, Nikki gritted her teeth and nodded.

Cam looked directly at her. 'Well, Nikki Galena, you've finally made it. From angry maverick DI with her job hanging by a thread to one of the most respected officers in the Fenland Constabulary.' He looked down at the fat personnel file in front of him on his desk. 'Reading this, I've noticed that throughout your career, your superintendents have always gone out on a limb to keep hold of you. They evidently saw something in you that others didn't. Superintendent Rick Bainbridge even put his own job on the line to prevent you being thrown to the wolves. Then there's Greg Woodhall. He might have given you a bit of a hard time on occasion, but when things got sticky, he backed you to the hilt. So, as your current superintendent, it gives me great pleasure to add to their efforts and do something for you that could positively affect your future.' He cleared his throat. 'My lovely Kaye has spent a great deal of time discussing your situation with various officers of different ranks, along with others who have found themselves in a similar quandary. She found there is no hard and fast rule dictating that married couples of a certain rank must not work together, rather it has merely become police force practice. Armed with this knowledge, she suggested I put in a special request to a number of higher-ranking officers, all of whom hold you and your success rate in high regard, in order to ascertain whether they might see a way forward for you.'

Nikki shot a quick glance at Joseph, who was listening on tenterhooks.

'So, here's what they say. It only landed on my desk early this morning:

'*Superintendent Walker. With regard to your request. If the officers concerned are to marry, their position will be made considerably easier if they are both of the same rank. In our opinion, having a DI married to a DS would be quite untenable. However, if DS Joseph Easter were to be promoted to Inspector, thereby working different cases to DI Galena, while both remaining at CID Greenborough, we would find this to be acceptable. The case will be reviewed again in six months' time to assess the outcome in terms of their professional success rate.*'

Cam beamed at them. 'Now it's down to me to monitor how things are going and report back up the ladder.' He looked at Nikki. 'You've met the new Chief Constable, haven't you? He's quite a bit younger, and forward thinking, and he's very impressed with the way you've been handling things here. As long as you're happy about Joseph's promotion, I can't really see much changing. If it works out for you both, *and* for the force, and there are no complaints or problems, then neither of you needs to move away. So, what do you think?'

'And we really will continue to work together?' asked Nikki.

'Yes, Nikki. What it comes down to is that as long as the work gets done, the top brass are willing to turn a blind eye. You'll be working as you always have, and your team can remain the same.' He grinned. 'As long as you don't object to working with another DI?'

'As if! Joseph should have been promoted years ago!'

'And you, Joseph?' Cam said.

'If Nikki's happy with it, I've certainly got no objections. It's fantastic news!'

'Then, with my blessing, and that of the Chief Constable, you are free to marry. As I said, DI Nikki Galena, you've come a long way. A very long way. Congratulations to you both!'

THE END

NOTE TO THE READER . . .

Nikki and Joseph married on 7 June 2024 in the registry office in the municipal buildings in Greenborough. It was a quiet ceremony, witnessed by Eve Anderson, and Tamsin and Niall Farrow. However, the party later in the day was anything but quiet! When they realised the extent of their friends list, they gave up on the intimate, low-key affair that they had talked about, and booked the banqueting suite at the White Hart Hotel.

Their honeymoon was a three-day break in a small hotel in the heart of the Yorkshire Moors.

It rained every day, and they didn't give a damn!

The letter that had been locked in Nikki's office drawer was answered, and the offer politely refused. She thanked them profusely but said that she would be staying at Greenborough with her team.

She and Joseph agreed that whilst at work, Nikki should remain as DI Nikki Galena, but at home, and the moment she walked through the door of Cloud Cottage Farm, she was Mrs Joseph Easter . . . at last.

THE JOFFE BOOKS STORY

We began in 2014 when Jasper agreed to publish his mum's much-rejected romance novel and it became a bestseller.

Since then we've grown into the largest independent publisher in the UK. We're extremely proud to publish some of the very best writers in the world, including Joy Ellis, Faith Martin, Caro Ramsay, Helen Forrester, Simon Brett and Robert Goddard. Everyone at Joffe Books loves reading and we never forget that it all begins with the magic of an author telling a story.

We are proud to publish talented first-time authors, as well as established writers whose books we love introducing to a new generation of readers.

We won Trade Publisher of the Year at the Independent Publishing Awards in 2023. We have been shortlisted for Independent Publisher of the Year at the British Book Awards for the last four years, and were shortlisted for the Diversity and Inclusivity Award at the 2022 Independent Publishing Awards. In 2023 we were shortlisted for Publisher of the Year at the RNA Industry Awards.

We built this company with your help, and we love to hear from you, so please email us about absolutely anything bookish at feedback@joffebooks.com

If you want to receive free books every Friday and hear about all our new releases, join our mailing list: www.joffebooks.com/contact

And when you tell your friends about us, just remember: it's pronounced Joffe as in coffee or toffee!

Printed in the USA
CPSIA information can be obtained
at www.ICGtesting.com
CBHW011102011124
16792CB00014B/262